Testing the Edge

Book Three
Into the Light

From adolescent to adult through twenty years in the United States Marine Corps, the most efficient system on the planet for challenging the body, the mind and most particularly, the soul.

By Colin Ruthven

Cover Photo Courtesy of Robert Beavis, Colonel, USMC, Retired

Back Photo by Fran Doggerel
Memphis, Tennessee

Copyright©2021 Colin Ruthven

All rights reserved

Author's note

This is a memoir. It contains adult language, so hide it from your children. The book is based upon actual events that I have charged with fictional license when I got bored with the story. Please do not feel left out if you do not find your name. I have protected your complicity with a very creative alias. I should have given myself an alias. The names of those who have aided me through this endless adolescence, some who have saved my life, appear unadulterated. The innocent remain unnamed and untouched. I am sure they have had quite enough of me.

I dedicate this book to my wife, Alice Goodman Ruthven, without whose encouragement, support, and editing skills this book would not have been written.

I want to thank Russ Tilton and Danny Burke for their thorough reads through early edits. They encouraged me to continue when I thought the work was a pure indulgence and something I should keep to myself. I am enormously grateful to Colonel Leonard Fuchs, USMC Retired, for his technical help and laser attention to detail.

https://colinruthvenauthor.com/

Table of Contents

1. The Turning Point 1
2. Return to El Toro 17
3. Learning to fly 29
4. The Sutter County 41
5. Iwakuni 59
6. Da Nang 77
7. Ubon 95
8. Millington 111
9. Choices 131
10. Sheldon 151
11. Orders 171
12. Vietnam 187
13. Winding Down 205
14. Cherry Point 221
15. Blue Axe 235
16. Retirement 253

1

The Turning Point

"Yeah?" A dull, disinterested voice answered after six rings, "Tell me about it," it said. I was unsure of what to say. I contemplated hanging up. A silence ensued, empty air waiting for something, anything. Probably me.

"Hi, my name is Colin Ruthy...."

I didn't finish my name. From the number I had called and the sound of my voice, all he said was, "Meet me at 'La Casa de Carne Fina' in fifteen minutes." I hummed and hedged, hesitated and explained something even I didn't understand about timing, distance, and inconvenience.

"I'm not sure if I can make it in fifteen minutes," I stuttered and was about to hang up.

"Listen, Cowboy, anyone can get anywhere from anywhere in Kingsville in less than ten minutes. I'd guess you've been needing to make this call for half a lifetime. So, you can answer destiny and get to 'La Casa de Carne Fina' in fifteen minutes or go back to what caused you to make this call." He hung up.

Jesus, he hung up on me. And he called me 'Cowboy'! I hadn't heard that since I was in flight training. Or maybe that nurse at the Naval Hospital in Japan. I sensed I was about to enter another kind of primary training. I was still holding the phone to my ear, listening to a strange, empty buzz. I looked at my watch and realized I had only thirteen minutes left to "answer destiny." Something about this guy got past my highly ingrained insubordination and urged me to obey.

It took me ten minutes to get to the restaurant. He was sitting in a booth at the dark end of the 'La Casa de Carne Fina,' the only place to go if you want decent Huevos Rancheros. Someone wearing an overcoat that looked like a throw rug had to be the guy I'd just talked to. The voice I'd heard on the phone was stamped on his face.

I sat down and looked across the Formica at a portrait of dissipated detachment and nonchalance. The server wandered over to our booth, gave me a fishy look, saw who I was sitting with and made the nod that said she would provisionally agree to serve me.

"Welcome back, Mister Garrity," she said, and placed a cup of coffee in front of both of us. "The last time you were here, we asked you to leave. I doubt if you recall. You had taken a nap in your Huevos." She walked away. She stopped, turned and said, "Also, you forgot to leave that huge tip, big spender."

I had not remembered, but I took her word for it. It was not the first time I had slumped forward into my food. "I'm really sorry about that, Verna," I muttered weakly. I reached into my pocket for a few bucks. I needed to make it right. She shook her head and smiled, nodding at my strange companion across from me.

"Excellent," the man said through a battle-hardened grin. "That's a beginning. You apologized to the lady. You're way ahead of the curve." He was fiftyish and had never, I will bet, performed the first push up; nor had he ever worried about it. His face bore the abuse of excess. Veins exploded on his nose and high on his cheeks. His eyes remained at half-mast, as if he had just woken up in this very booth. He had probably combed his hair, thinning and badly in need of a trim, with the flat of his hand. He was short and heavy but seemed strong, appearing to be tired but very much at peace. A light scruff of beard concealed, but barely, a double chin that fused fat to his neck.

I stared blankly into my cup of coffee. "Do people really drink this stuff at this time of night?" I asked.

"Get used to it. It's the universal elixir of the Fellowship."

"What's the Fellowship?" I raised my eyebrows and lifted my cup to reluctant lips.

"I'll tell you all about it." He put his cup in the air for me to toast it. I took a sip and raised my cup.

"Welcome to the Fellowship." He smirked. "The moment you took that first sip you were in."

That was about ten o'clock at night on the first of December, 1964. I've been "in" ever since. My God, what it took to get me here!

His name was Dick B. We finished our coffee. He left some money on the table and stood up. "Come on. I want to take you someplace."

I put a few bucks on the table and followed Dick out to his 1955 Pontiac. It looked strangely like that first car I had bought from Go Motor Company in Pensacola. Julian would have probably said there was something significant about that; synchronicity, I guessed. Dick's ride had every rusted mile of ten years on it, but it got us to our destination.

It was a converted garage behind a Mexican diner on East Santa Gertrudis Street. A double door had a padlock hinge to get in. The floor was old timber, dusted with a layer of dirt. A table occupied most of the center of the room, surrounded by a dozen chairs. A smaller table was covered with pamphlets and on the wall, two pictures of old guys with bad haircuts. A trio of platitudes plastered the walls, something about "First things first" and other phrases too simple for a problem as big as mine.

An elderly man in a soiled undershirt a full size too large came out of a room that looked carved into the wall. The room contained a set of bedsprings on the floor, covered in a blanket and a dirty pillow. I supposed this was the old man's home. It was just the three of us in the room. Two others drinking coffee and smoking leaned on the fence outside. Nobody said a word. A trace feeling welled up inside of me. It brought a faint remembrance, a bit of that part of me I knew I had lost. I was in Regina, Saskatchewan again, visiting my Uncle Jimmy in the friendly squalor he called home.

"What happens here?" I asked.

"It's already happening," Dick answered as he looked carefully into my eyes; "More than two of us are gathered together in His name."

"Who is this 'He'?" I asked, looking around the room.

He laughed like I had made a joke. "I have given you a taste. Be here tomorrow at eight p.m. for the rest of the meal."

Dick drove me back to the 'La Casa de Carne Fina,' His rusty Pontiac blowing dark clouds through a muffler riddled with holes as he pulled away. As dim as my understanding was, I kept feeling a warm, undefinable energy all the way back to the base. I thought about the genuine boyish laugh that came out of Dick's tired old face and that feeling I had in the shack with just the few of us there.

I arrived at the converted garage the following night with the same apprehension I had before my first flight in primary training. I was accustomed to attending mandatory muster in the home of a Commanding Officer dressed in a suit and tie, sometimes in formal dress uniform. I'd present my calling card and place it on a silver tray. This was the Marine Officer's protocol for arriving at a special place. On this evening I was so attired in coat and tie and prepared to present my card if asked.

A small cluster of men and women gathered around the door, smoking. They gave me welcome smiles from friendly faces. An array of hands rose into the air. I shook them all, some soft, others severely calloused. We made introductions, first names only. The crowd parted as I entered the little room. It was a chilly night, but warm just inside the door. An average age was mid-fifties, some twice my age, a mixed crowd of men and women, all with that same tired but peaceful expression. The people closed in behind me. The door closed. Once again, I was standing on timbers, only recently swept free from dirt.

I needn't have bothered with the coat and tie. It was sub informal. Two women and seven men attired variously in jeans, sports jacket, pajama bottoms and parkas. Most of them came from the King Ranch, cooks and cowboys, a bank manager and sanitation engineer for the city of Kingsville. I was the only Marine, long before Marines would admit they might be alcoholics.

I removed my tie. I looked around and wanted to take off the rest of my clothes. Anything beyond naked in this room was total bullshit, theater and pretense. And even if I had been naked, I had not penetrated the first layer of what was to be revealed. I looked around that evening at the quiet and very simple assortment of broken souls and felt that I had never stood on such sacred ground. I was totally at home.

They introduced me to a Truth that keeps growing every day, but only as fast as I can handle it. I would be on an inner journey that never ends, one of them said. I asked about the destination, where the journey would take me. They all said, in so many ways, that it would take me back to where I had begun and made the turn, where I had veered off the chosen path. Then, at the turning point, I'd be on a path to a life that works. I asked how long it would take and they told me, for the rest of my life, one-day-at-a-time. But no matter where I was on the Path, I would be at the destination for that day, and it would be enough.

"Don't try to bank this stuff and save a ration for another day. We do this thing one-day-at-a-time. And each day you will be given enough. Do not look for more." Her name was Jackie and instead of introducing herself as an alcoholic, she said she was a pillhead. Something deep was already taking hold, an understanding of something very fundamental about what I was doing. Before I had arrived where I could understand, I understood. This had more to do with more than my drinking.

An older man named Earl sat beside me. Halfway through the hour, I felt like the man had adopted me. He pulled me aside at the end of the meeting and we shared a late evening cup of "the elixir."

"If you make a beginning, you're as close as you can get right now. So, you're already there," he said. "Don't rush it. Easy does it."

The open humor and honesty were worth the price of admission. The price I had paid, they told me, was the desperation that brought me to my first meeting. "You've already paid for that seat you're sitting in. You don't have to go out there and try it again."

I said, "A journey sounds long."

Earl laughed. "It's better than what you've been doing. You'll have good times and bad times, but it'll be real. It'll be closer to the Truth than any place you've been that brought you here." His words resonated with something deep inside, an old sense I could not identify, nor could I explain.

That first night, Earl gave me a card he pulled from his wallet.

It read, "Until one is committed, there is hesitancy, the chance to draw back, always ineffectiveness. Concerning all acts of initiative and creation, there is one elementary truth, the ignorance of which kills countless ideas and splendid plans: that the moment one definitely commits oneself, then providence moves too. All sorts of things occur to help one that would never otherwise have occurred. A whole stream of events issues from the decision, raising in one's favor all manner of unforeseen incidents, meetings and material assistance which no man could have dreamed would have come his way. Whatever you can do or dream you can, begin it. Boldness has genius, power and magic in it. Begin it now."

"That's by a man named William Hutchison Murray. I want you to keep it. It'll probably have more meaning to you as each day passes. Just try to remember, when something seems too much for you, like the card says, 'Just goddam do it.'"

"It doesn't say that, Earl." I was looking down at the card. It reminded me of a Marine Corps leadership axiom: 'Ignore your fears. Just goddam do it.'

"Oh, but it does, Colin." He pulled his overcoat up around his neck as we walked out of the garage and stepped into a Texas winter night. "One day you'll give that card to someone else and you still won't be able to answer all the questions he'll have."

As I walked to my room down a long, darkened hallway of the Bachelor Officer's Quarters, I had an overwhelming sense that I would never have to drink again. This assurance prevails as long as I stay in the rooms and carry the principals they taught me into my life and the lives of others.

I've continued to return to any and every venue that can heat a pot of coffee and stain the walls yellow with nicotine. No one really knows what happens there. They'll explain how to do it, but nobody really knows what happens. There's Something Else there that does it for whomever takes a seat and stays in the rooms.

I awoke that first morning of sobriety without a hangover. Neither did I have the compulsion to drink. I didn't trust it. I kept waiting for it all to roll in on me and I would again be sitting at the bar counting down my drinks to four when the red blotch would paint itself on my face, and I'd order four more.

The desire to drink didn't happen that day, or the next; nor has it ever returned. But although I have felt the assurance of some new Truth guiding me, I was told by older fellow travelers that there were tough times ahead on the path to retrieving a life I had nearly lost. They were right. They were always right.

December 1964, with all of its treacherous holiday traps, passed, and I remained sober. I made a courtesy appearance at Sarah's parents' house, where the neighbors were drinking. I declined without temptation, but I did not want to test it. I left. It was the beginning of many events that I left with puzzled faces staring at me, wondering what had happened to the life of the party, the "Animal." Whenever I found myself in a place that might have previously offered a moment of artificial comfort, I repeated a mantra from the instructions, "I have no business being here" and I would leave.

While Sarah was attending a New Year's service at the Cathedral, I sat in a room at the Bachelor Officer's Quarters on the base at Corpus Christi. It's incredible how much time a person has on his hands when he's no longer drinking. I recalled the empty hours living the aimless life built around the compulsion, the meaningless time consumed in making arrangements! I had structured my life around the ceremony, the many diversions and distractions that took me to that fleeting and elusive place of ease and comfort.

Compared to the life I'd been living; I would soon be a monk on a private wilderness journey. I had given myself over to instructions that dealt largely with prayer, meditation and suggested disciplines designed to explore the inner life, that part of me that had not only been ignored, but I had shunned. Each day I turned more to the inward path.

But on this new-year's eve, as the year drew to its last moments, the room in the BOQ closed in with memories of the life I had just left. I became restless with the dangerous company of my unsettled mind. I left the room and took a long walk.

It had been a cold winter nine years earlier that I had been on this very base, living in the cadet quarters. On this new year's night, equally cold, I walked past a row of the old buildings to the edge of a pier that looked out over the darkness where the inky sky disappeared into an invisible horizon. In that essential emptiness, I calculated it was a quarter of a century ago when my family faced a similar prelude to a year filled with global uncertainty.

I was a week shy of five-years-old on September 10, 1939, when Canada entered the Second World War. My mother, father, and I lived in a small basement room in Calgary, Alberta. I recalled the familiar sounds of short-wave radio messages broadcast through a small cathedral radio into the crowded basement room. "This is the BBC, direct from London." Muffled static and British martial music followed. Then a voice that would become familiar in our home as the war years wore on told us of a war my parents thought might never end.

Unmindful of what war was, I listened to reports of the military situation from Britain. Military music and the crisp British accent broadcast the dour news as that country drew deeper and deeper into an almost hopeless situation. I did not know what any of it meant. It was nothing but a radio wave, mostly static, that brought a great weight of worry into our home. My parents were still shaken from the blow of the Great Depression. My father had worked at anything that would keep us fed. The memory of the First World War, the "War to end all wars" was still fresh in the minds of some who still carried the fragments of conflict in their bodies. Now here was another World War that must certainly have felt destined to defeat them.

On Christmas Day 1939, King George VI delivered a message to the people of the British Empire. Adolph Hitler was threatening to invade Britain. Times were decidedly uncertain. The King began his speech with the following words, "A new year is at hand. We cannot tell what it will bring. If it brings peace, how thankful we shall all be. If it brings us continued struggle, we shall remain undaunted."

He closed his message with a portion of the poem written in 1908 by the American Poet, Minnie Louise Haskins. Again, I did not know what the speech meant, but every home in Canada listened to it. I certainly couldn't grasp the gravity of the words with my limited understanding. What I did sense, though, was the leaden enormity of something that was falling upon my family. The King was urging through this inspiring poem that the people of Britain and the United Kingdom look to a Higher Source as the solution to imminent disaster.

The following year, a copy of Ms. Haskin's poem, printed on a small plaque, found its way into our home and into nearly every Canadian home. For most of my life, long after the war had ended, I saw this plaque hanging on the walls of our many homes. As decades passed the words registered and imprinted on my mind so that, on the beginning of this New Year, the early hours of 1965, as I stood on the end of a darkened pier, I could recall the message imprinted on my mind's eye. I remembered the small plaque so vividly that it almost appeared in the sky.

"I said to the man who stood at the gate of the year

Give me a light that I may tread safely into the unknown.
And he replied,
'Go out into the darkness
And put your hand into the hand of God
That shall be to you better than light
And safer than a known way!'"

Some people ask for a sign. I didn't have to ask for mine. I received it. In the first month of sobriety, I was spiritually bereft and blind to see it, but I was open enough to allow the message to move me forward into what lay ahead. It was the gate of a new year, 1965. A full month since my last drink. I had taken a long walk into a dark night and a message just came to me, petitioned from a deeper part of consciousness, the part I had found missing but was now speaking to me.

My polished cynicism attempted to block a fundamental Truth that I was blessed, highly favored and that all arrangements had been made. I was getting some badly needed help. The instructions were simple, but what it would take was difficult. "Put my hand into the hand of God." I just had to rearrange my entire life.

I had to be reminded that God does the rearranging. I just put myself in a position to be changed by following the instructions.

That first week in January 1965, I received orders to the Third Marine Aircraft Wing in El Toro, California. I was to report no later than 1 March 1965. I had less than two months to find clarity and hopefully make some healthy choices. From the chaos of that confusion native to early recovery, I had to come up with a rational decision. And in one of my earliest prayers, I asked for it. As my new friends promised, the answer to a prayer would not always be what I thought it should be or wanted it to be. In the beginning, I didn't trust that I would be guided, and I wondered if I could follow the guidance if it came.

"This is not about being good, Colin." Earl was a constant strength and presence in those first months. "This is about being real," he said.

"Trust the guidance, even though you think it might be wrong. Run it by a few of us first, then trust that God has it and go for it. Never go it alone."

Dangerous territory, I thought. But it was much safer than the place I'd been before I came through the garage doors.

In an instrument flight check, an examining pilot in the back seat will maneuver the airplane into an impossible flight attitude, maybe on its back or pointing vertical, quickly losing airspeed, approaching a stall that could lead to an incipient spin. The student pilot in the front seat keeps his eyes shut or is under a hood. Vertigo will tell the front seat pilot he is flying one way when the plane is flying in another. The instructor pilot tells the pilot to open his eyes and recover from the unusual attitude. The task is to go to the instruments, read them and according to the scan, against any bodily feelings to the contrary, or emotional sense the airplane is going in one direction, take corrective action based on the data in front of you and recover the aircraft to controlled flight. Go to the data and then recover.

I was comfortable and confident in my capacity to recover from an unusual attitude, no matter what a flight check pilot threw at me. But, in my current situation with Sarah, I was on my back, losing airspeed, fast approaching a stall. Earl and I went to the only data I had; and we read the hard, heartless facts together.

There was only one reason I had orders to El Toro. That was for eventual transfer to Vietnam, where the situation was deteriorating daily. I could marry Sarah and move us all out to California, but by the time we all got there, I'd be gone. It takes a special woman to be a Marine Corps Wife. They have it rougher than their husbands. At least Marines are doing what they want to do, often what they love to do. A wife has to wait, which is too much to ask of Sarah who once told me when we marginally broached the subject of marriage, "Just never leave me alone, Colin." Sarah was a very pragmatic woman, and what she told me carried a very honest assessment of how she could handle the absence of her man.

And, if there is one thing a Marine will eventually do to his wife, it will be to leave her alone, maybe for a year, to whatever options she is afraid she might have to entertain. I was not sure I could do that to her and when I was honest with myself; I did not want to do that to myself.

That forthright phrase hung between us. Had she said it in an unguarded moment, or was Sarah just as honest as she was sometimes cold? "Just never leave me alone." Aside from the suggestion that she might find someone else if I left her alone, there loomed another highly charged consideration. I understood what was going on in the world and, over and above any thought I had for Sarah, I selfishly wanted to be a part of it. I wanted to go to Vietnam and would have felt left out had I not.

When Dave Drewelow arrived in the squadron fresh from Vietnam the previous year, he related anecdotes from the first squadrons to fly into Danang. I was unconcerned about the effects that war would have on our country; selfishly, I was more interested in being a part of the fighting. Sadly, I was more emotionally invested in this than I was in Sarah. How could I possibly frame this without causing yet another blow to a psyche that was just now restoring itself to a stable orbit? If I was an instrument in her stability, how ironically cruel to be also the one to destroy it. She had taken a major hit. I did not want to inflict another. No entity in Nature can have an impact on another without reciprocal harm. It's like a planet's gravitational influence grazing another planet, however slightly. They will continue in their orbits, but both be altered in their course by the paths of the other.

In Her benevolent way, Nature brought two souls together who had barely a thin insulation against any further damage. She had conveniently matched us in our temperament. Silence fell upon us at the same time as did a signal smile cross our faces to the affectations of the world.

We had hinted at marriage. The inner counsel of women in her family, three intelligent ladies and a precocious younger one, had certainly put their heads together, and either organized or randomly conspired as to the future of Sarah and her child. Decisions that would alter the family balance hung in the air. Women cannot for long tolerate this kind of suspense. Their cycles unwind if one of their own is not bearing children or is at least attached.

In her advanced table of equivalents, Little Essie seemed to assume it would happen. I was already the replacement for her murdered father. Her innocent projections had it done, so why were her mother and Mister Ruthven not cooperating and immediately producing siblings?

Beyond these considerations was this Omnipotent Entity that was vital to both of our paths. The disparate perspectives we had on God were steering us in entirely opposite vectors.

Sarah's God was established firmly in two thousand years of doctrine. Every word that would direct her path derived from a catechism set in stone. Her instruction meant hours of reading, ritual and repeating, all time tested with little latitude from which to deviate. It was the rosary structure of counting beads and stations of the cross. The elegance of process and reverence had been fine-tuned and honed to an unquestioning exactness, all surrounded by the exquisite architecture and lovely stained-glass windows–esthetically wonderful, but still not enough to bring me in.

Essie thrived on the words, the music and the poetry of language, Latin and blind obedience to words uttered by a continuum of saints who had set in cement the work for anyone who would follow the path of the Carpenter. I went to the Cathedral with Sarah. The moments droned on interminably, my mind wandering to the back of a woman's head. She had taken a nap that morning and forgotten to brush her hair.

I was in awe of the sanctuary, the statuary, and the vestments. The walls of the chamber reverberated in perfect harmony, children's voices and the pipes resonating through every crevice in the folds of marbled drapery. Had I been bred in such a sacred environment; I would not have been able to break away from its imperious mandate.

I brought Sarah to one of my meetings. Nothing registered for her. She wanted to leave right away. We did. In that moment, I suppose we had made a good part of the decision we were facing.

I grew up with no religious orientation. My father, to all of our memory, had never attended church, nor had his family. Was it a Canadian thing? My mother's family had the same history, but somehow my mother could craft a spiritual ethos of her own. With her all-inclusive embrace of everything and everyone being a part of the One Big Thing doing the one big thing, my mother opened the door even wider for her son, who was just now exposed to a spiritual orientation. She gave me the latitude of total spiritual enquiry. Also, like my mother, I needed all the space I could get.

What other members suggested to my recovery was a 'designer God': everyone gets to have one of their own. In fact, if a person was really honest, he would see that he already believed in something, even if he thought it was the wrong thing. That was a beginning. With my options totally opened and no previous religious orientation to impede my path, I was an empty vessel waiting to be filled. I didn't have the stuff of a previous belief or religion that would need to be removed from the container. Mine was an empty virgin space, ready to be filled.

Once I had showed the willingness, however slightly, I could feel the shifting of the plates. The tectonic motion was happening to me. I was just presenting myself to the process, giving myself over to it so that it could happen. It was now beyond my volition. I believe that more is happening beneath the surface than in my conscious, material world. I only think I have dominion over some aspects of my life. I show selective competence in the everyday world and am deluded into thinking that I have dominion over all things.

My new friends suggested prayers, but I was told that the most powerful prayers arose from my suffering. I introduced Sarah to the fellowship. Her reaction to my sanctuary was as mine was to hers. We met in agreement on the most painful disagreement. We would go our separate ways, each driven sadly from a deeper place than our feelings for one another, supposed we would go.

The central fact I could not deny or overcome was that I was going one way; Sarah was going the other. Both at speeds coincidental, but in radically different directions. We only thought we had a choice. Her deliverance from her own vector onto another was as powerful. Who knows, maybe more powerful than my own.

I can't believe how cruelly easy it was for me. The words come in the moment if someone is in the presence of Truth. If one lives the unrehearsed life and allows the words to be drawn in the spontaneous moment, a radical Truth arises.

I left. In almost every sense possible, I moved away. I moved to another part of the country. I moved away from the person I had been to this unrecognizable entity, an unfamiliar form built from my formative years slowly reshaping itself into what this Power originally intended it to be. Nobody gets it all back–the losses of an entire lifetime. There's a tradeoff to every choice made on the path, markers on the timeline that leave an indelible scar on psychic flesh.

2

Return to El Toro

My orders posted me to the Third Marine Aircraft Wing for retraining in a newer version of the Crusader. The assignment that lay ahead was as yet undetermined.

The day I reported to the Marine Corps Air Station at El Toro, California, I drove down the winding Canyon Road to Laguna Beach to the "Canyon Club?" to check in with my fellow travelers on the Path. I would need sustained guidance back on solid ground.

As I reoriented myself to life in the Marine Corps, the specter of that flight violation arose with myriad other regrets. This would be only one of many ghosts that would haunt me as I gained traction in recovery. Consciousness would bring everything to the surface right on time. I was being refined while I retraced my steps back through time. I didn't have to go after any of it. It would come to me. All this I would learn as I found my place back in "the rooms."

When I first heard them, these words were like pouring fire into a paper cup, lost to me for a time. Others would be revealed as I went through my dark night of the soul. As the body remembers what the mind forgets, so the lessons that I might have forgotten would return to me right on time.

I finished the Crusader ground trainer syllabus and was about to get back into an airplane again. I was unsure if they would ever assign me to a squadron with my colorful history and that flight violation that would probably follow me to El Toro. Then one morning in

March 1965, an amazing set of dominoes began to fall in my favor. "It was to be the worst of times" for the country but "the best of times" for me. Our country was suddenly in a fighting war with the insurgent Viet Cong.

All officers and staff non-commissioned officers in the Third Marine Aircraft Wing were ordered to the base auditorium. They assembled the Commanding General of the Wing and his staff on a stage. Almost the entire complement of Wing personnel filled the auditorium, standing room only. The General announced that The Marine Corps was augmenting its strength and position in Vietnam. I was an immediate candidate for a fighter squadron.

As a comprehensive plan for the expanded Marine Corps presence in Vietnam took shape, it presented a secondary picture of how I might be favored. The increased numbers required every Marine in several specific occupational specialties. As it pertained to me, the Marine Corps needed experienced fighter pilots. And the current state-of-the-art fighter in Vietnam was the Crusader.

I was feeling needed. They placed training and preparation for deployment of critical elements on an accelerated pace. They gave combat readiness a wartime priority. Had I arrived a month earlier, I might not have looked so appealing. A month later, it might have been too late. I had snuck under the wire again.

During my early months of re-entry, I would continue to find friends from the previous years of my career who had seen me in various stages of professional undress. Competent Marine Officers with whom I had flown and who had witnessed my transgressions were all arriving right on time, exhuming a past that would need to be examined.

Lieutenant Colonel Ralph Conroy was the Commanding Officer of the Crusader training squadron. We'd been close friends in Kingsville. Ralph had watched me deteriorate over the last year of my drinking and was one pilot present when I was declared unconscious at "Tailhook '63."

"Colin, I need to talk to you." I had just entered the Ready Room, heading for my locker to change into my flight gear. There was a time when a call to the Commanding Officer's chambers meant a meaningful encounter with sometimes creative admonishments, none of which I took seriously. I had previously almost welcomed the occasion to be cashiered from this golden opportunity that had come out of a vacuum. Now, with my good friend calling me into his office, for the first time, a sense of responsibility visited me like an unfamiliar virus. I was apprehensive that at last the flight violation had landed in Ralph's incoming basket. Regrettably, it would be my good friend's unhappy duty to administer the kiss of death and jerk my wings. I could look forward to a desk job in Headquarters Marine Corps and early release from The Marine Corps, just when the balloon went up and they might want to keep me. And I badly wanted to stay.

"Colin, sit down," he said. I slumped in a chair and looked at the ceiling, trying to find a place to focus when he said the words. "You must be doing something right, Brett." He laughed and shook his head, recalling my infamous escape into the altar identity of Brett Garrity.

"I can't imagine what that would be, Colonel." I sat up as I spoke. "I'm waiting for my past to catch up with me. I fully expect Headquarters Marine Corps to cash me in and the only thing stopping them is a holdup in the paper traffic."

"You mean kick you out of the Marine Corps?" Ralph was nodding as if he would probably sign the charges on my court martial.

"Yes, sir." I dropped my head, looking back into a past that had very little to recommend in my favor. "That, and mainly that flight violation when we were in Kingsville. I thought I might as well preempt the strike and save you the trouble. I'll never be picked up for Major; I'll have to pack it in."

"Bobby Goodman has the captain assignment desk up in D. C. He has all your paperwork." Ralph leaned forward on his desk as if he were whispering and about to tell me a secret. "He called just as I came back from that massive Wing assembly. He wanted to tell me to put you on a hyper quick syllabus. They've already got you assigned to a squadron once you get over there. I don't think they'd be putting you on the fast track if they were going to release you."

I half rose from the chair. "Maybe I have some breathing room before they lower the blade," I said.

"I'm gonna call Goodman and ask him about your status." Ralph reached for the phone. "Pick up that extension." He smiled mischievously.

I lifted the phone from a small table. A few minutes later, I was listening to the voice of Captain Bobby Goodman, a contemporary with whom I had flown with the Red Devils in Hawaii. We had also attended the special indoctrination course in Quantico together. Ralph and Bobby exchanged Washington-speak, a language I never wanted to learn.

"Is he there with you now, Colonel?" Bobby's familiar voice sounded strained. He had a hell of a job, surrounded by senior officers with no breathing room from a constantly flooded incoming basket. Christ, a Captain at Headquarters Marine Corps, was like a private in the Army of North Korea, an insect underfoot.

"Sitting right in front of me, Bobby," Ralph answered.

"You are one lucky son of a bitch, Animal." Bobby laughed. "They have a file as thick as the bible on you and your antics. There's some bull shit report about you violating Mexican air space on top of the stack." I could hear him shuffling papers and probably talking to about three other people on a headset. His office was a crowded subway this day. "If you buy me a bottle of Haig and Haig five star, I'll start a fire with it."

"Christ, I'll personally deliver a lifetime supply of the beverage of your choice," I replied.

"Consider it done, Animal." Bobby sounded serious. "Major Dick Miller tells us that the grapevine says you've cleaned up your act. Turned into some kind a monk or something. Schlepping from squadron to squadron with a beggar's bowl."

All three of us laughed. I said, "Been sober nearly four months and have not seen the inside of an O Club, bar or loose lady's bedroom." It still amazed me I was not drinking, nor did I want to drink.

"Sold all his substance and given it to the poor." Ralph laughed. He shook his head, probably with relief for me. I wanted to cry. "No kidding, Bobby. Animal is no longer Animal. I don't have a name for it. I can't even talk to him anymore. Not the same guy."

"Jesus, nobody'll believe that." He laughed. "But somebody in high places seems to trust it. We're instructed to put your stuff in a pending burn file."

"Even the flight violation?" I couldn't believe what he was saying.

"That died the death it deserved when it got here. I didn't think I needed to tell you. Because of the size of your file, I thought it wouldn't make any difference. Shit, Animal, I figured you were on the way out when you stole Colonel Warren's sedan in Atsugi."

"Pennington wiped that car down. They had nothing on us." I used gangster speak, just kidding. "Christ, we dodged a hail of bullets in Atsugi. We should have been put to sleep."

"They didn't need your fingerprints. That heist had your name written all over it. I still don't know how you survived all your antics." He laughed out loud. "Hell, didn't they call you the 'Village Idiot' in the grotto?"

I didn't reply. Just lowered my head and nodded. He was right. It was as if I was pressing the very edge of the envelope to force them to release me. 'Here I am,' I thought, 'a high school dropout with a regular commission and I'm thumbing my nose at the very hand that feeds me. Again, looking for guidance from the finest leaders in the world but defying it at the same time.' It gave me a stomachache thinking about it.

"Colin, listen." Bobby was serious now. "After you finish retraining in the F8, you're going to be assigned to MABS until you go to West Pac."

"You can assign me to mess duty, guard duty or anything you want, Bobby." I was standing up, almost shouting. "I'll do anything at this point. I really understand my situation here and I do not take it for granted." I was lightheaded with relief. I sat down.

"Dick Tomlinson has MABS. He's asked for you. You were with him at Kaneohe Bay in '56. Right?" He was fluttering through some paper.

"Yeah, hell of a guy. I appreciate the slack."

"Well, you might not appreciate it that much, Colin." Bobby was all business now. "You'll be taking the MABS rolling stock and about a hundred Marines to Iwakuni, on an LST." I stared at the phone. Ralph Conroy burst out laughing. Coffee spewed from his mouth onto a desktop of paper.

"You're shitting me, Bobby." I could barely get the words out of my mouth. "I mean, you really are joking. Right?" I looked at Colonel Conroy, genuinely stunned. "Tell me: this is candid camera, right?"

"I'm not kidding, Colin. Tomlinson asked for you just for this project." He spoke as if he was reading data from a printout. 'Is good with the troops and will get shit done.' a quote from Dick Tomlinson's request.

"He says, 'If he stays clean, he'll be the only guy for the job. He'll be able to live with over a hundred Marines in close quarters for about a month and maybe quell a mutiny.'"

The big "If" would follow me for as long as I wore a uniform. I had the scarlet "A" woven thick onto every item of my uniform. I was willing to wear it. Hell, I will work naked. It could very well be the only checks and balances I might have. I still couldn't wrap my head around an LST all the way to Iwakuni. It sounded a bit like payback for something I had perpetrated against some fiend at Headquarters Marine Corps. I was okay with Universal Karma, but Marine Corps karma was probably going to be more immediate. There would never be enough restitution for my incompetence and misdeeds, no matter how long I stayed in the Marine Corps.

"Also, Colin, you're up for selection next year." He was serious? It fell on deaf ears. The idea of being promoted to major was ridiculous. Ralph and I both shook our heads and grinned.

I laughed. "There's no way I'll be picked up for major, Bobby." I calmed down. "I'm not thinking about that right now. I'll do anything to hang around as long as I can. I just want to get in on the action."

"Don't think like that, Animal." He was serious. "You should be here now. It's like we've hit a jackpot. They'll be watching everything you can do in a combat environment and forgetting everything else you've ever done. It's the current climate. Just act like you'll make major and it will happen." The line went dead. I looked at Ralph. He shrugged, grinning, and hung up the phone.

"Bobby's right, Colin." Colonel Conroy was serious. "If you hold what you got, I'll be giving you my gold oak leaves by the time you sail into Iwakuni. They're looking for experienced senior captains and junior field grade to fill billets in Vietnam. You are one of the most experienced fighter pilots in our stables. So, hang with it." He stood up and came around the desk. "Let's get you on the Crusader express track." He burst out laughing. "Jesus, an LST all the way to Iwakuni. Oh my God! Good luck with that mutiny." We both walked out of his office. He was laughing; I was in shock.

"Isn't that a flat-bottomed boat?" I whispered over his shoulder.

"Oh, hell yeah. You'll be one seasoned-assed sailor by the time you get off that bucket. Flat-bottomed and ancient as hell." He laughed. "They probably think you can prevent an uprising, because you once would have started one." He kept laughing as we walked to the Ready Room. A Ready Room full of younger pilots puzzled at us as we walked out to the flight line, both of us laughing.

Before I took a cruise on that flat-bottomed boat, there was something I need to.

I boarded the cattle car I had first ridden in 1954 around the base to the hangars at VMGR 352. The troops looked at me as if I was intruding on their territory. An officer, especially a captain, never rode in the cattle car. Nobody had stolen that hangar I used to guard. It was still there. I walked into the cavernous space, hoping to find Staff Sergeant Gilmore. I thought it unlikely he would still be here. But it was worth a try.

"Is Sergeant Gilmore still around?" I asked a young maintenance marine in grease-stained utilities. I was sure he had moved on, but I had to ask if he was still here.

"Yes, sir, Master Sergeant Gilmore is in the Maintenance office over there." He pointed to the same area from which the Personnel Clerk had emerged to tell me I had orders to flight school. Summer, 1954.

I had barely entered the office when he came rushing up to me. "Congratulations, Captain." He grinned widely. A spark of moisture shone in one eye. "I just goddam knew you'd make it." He was out of breath. I had hoped he could feel the part he had played in the entire experience. "Who you with?"

I explained my situation. He grinned wider and wider with each syllable. I became a bit emotional. I shook his hand, and he looked at me like a father who wanted to give his son a few bucks on his first date. I could see he wanted to hug me, but restrained himself according to officer, Staff NCO boundaries. Then I grabbed his shoulders and gave him the hug of my life.

"God bless you, Captain." He seemed about to choke. "You one of the best things I ever seen in an entire career."

"I'm surprise you're still here, Sergeant Gilmore." I poked him gently on the chevrons and said, "Also a few more pay grades. Congratulations."

"Oh, hell. I been to two other duty stations since you were here. I saw you once in Atsugi. It didn't look like you were seeing very much back then. You had a broken leg or something." He chuckled. "My God, everyone knew about you." He grinned. "The troops, everyone. They loved that shit you was pulling."

"Oh, my God. You saw me at my very lowest point, Sergeant Gilmore." I cringed at the thought. "Why didn't you stop me and kick my ass?"

"You looked like that probably wouldn't have done much good about then." He grinned sheepishly.

"Well, I'll always be grateful for that special, no shit, encouragement to press on and try it. I could have used some more of that in Atsugi," I said. "I don't suppose Booster Gallo's still around."

"Busted and discharged right after you left," he declared with some satisfaction. "Guys got no business being in the Corps."

"Well, you helped me dodge a bullet. I might have gone the same way he did."

"Oh, no, sir." He laughed just like Freddy Sellers had when he spoke about the glow and the auras. "None of that would ever happen to you." Then he blessed me with something I needed just then. It helped me think I might just do what was next. "You nothing like that shit bird. You gonna be okay, Captain. No way you anything like Booster Gallo." Again, his laugh reminded me of Freddy Sellers.

While I went through the Crusader syllabus, they assigned me to MABS, just as Bobby Goodman promised. MABS was the acronym for Marine Air Base Squadron, not the happiest assignment for a guy who only knew how to fly airplanes, who is not an administrator and worse, not a detail guy. It was not a flying unit, but most pilots had to spend the occasional tour in a squadron like this.

MABS just took care of the handling of a base in the field. It was the catch all place for assignments like the feeding and caring for troops in the field. I was the Nuclear and Chemical Warfare Officer. That's a guy who has to inventory hazardous clothing gear and train the squadron how to deal with defoliants or nerve gas when they hit. I was also the Legal Officer. I didn't need to be a lawyer to be the Legal Officer. I just had to know how to send a miscreant along the pipeline to office hours or a court martial or, better still, get his ass out of a crack. I'd been in so many cracks I could draw a map of the territory.

"Colin, I need to get you in the mill for a top-secret clearance." Dick Tomlinson was senior to me, but in some flying situations like dog fighting or advanced tactics, there's no rank and the guy who comes out on top usually holds most of the chips. Evidently, in his eyes, I still held some chips. I could not have been assigned to a better guy. "I'm surprised you haven't applied for a top-secret clearance before now."

"Skipper, you've got to understand." I was standing almost at attention in front of his desk. "I have just not given a shit about anything but flying. Hell, you know as well as I do. You watched me in Hawaii nearly cash in my wings. I never in million years would have thought about moving up the career curve or being promoted. But I'm willing to try anything now. And, for a guy who always kept himself at the level he saw himself, I would never have trusted me with a top-secret clearance."

"Well, Captain Ruthven," He smiled, "You had better get ready for just about anything." He shuffled a sheaf of papers, looked up and said, "Cause they're about to throw it at you."

"To be clear, again, just so you understand, I have never thought in terms of this as a career. I've just gone from day to day wondering if it would work. I have never put in for staff assignments that would augment my career or groom me for advancement. I have not requested service schools on my fitness reports; in fact, I have requested nothing. Another grim fact, I have never read a single one of my fitness reports. I just signed where it says that I read and understood without knowing what I understood." I stopped breathless, trying to remember anything else that I could lay before the altar.

"Well, you say I don't understand, Colin, but I do. I'm totally up to speed on your Officer's Qualification Record, plus a few other nuggets that I understand from Bobby Goodman have been deep sixed. Plus, do not forget I was with you in Hawaii and you were a train wreck there, but you could fly the shit out of airplanes."

He stopped breathless, looking at me for some kind of acknowledgement. I nodded, and he continued. "That's why we're applying for a top-secret clearance. We need to fill in some of the blanks if you want to salvage a career." I heard the echo of Jay Hubbard as he spoke.

"I think I know what an LST is, but what LST mean?" I segued into anything to give him air.

"Landing Ship Tank." He had my OQR and was on some of the last pages where all the heavy reading really began. "You've seen them in old World War Two movies, "Victory at Sea". The clam shell front gate opens up, and a ramp falls out. It's a flat-bottom boat that drives right up onto the beach. Tanks roll out with troops behind them. In your case, it will be squadron personnel and all of our rolling stock moving under your supervision to Iwakuni." He smiled across the table. "You'll do great. I've watched you with troops. And you're going to need a strong letter of appreciation from a Naval Command to fill in some of the blanks. You have none. That is: zero, commendations except for Flight Instructor of the Year, 1963." He shook his head. "That last one won't hurt you, Colin."

"There really has been nothing to commend me." I grinned.

"And," he continued, "hopefully we will go to war and we will be there for several years. You are going to need a couple of combat tours to scrub every bad memory anyone has of you. A good combat record forgets every mistake you ever could have made." He grinned. "Anything you do from here on can help to bury your previous crimes."

"Like a ride on an LST?" I offered. I was trying to fit myself into the picture. I'd been on four ships, all aircraft carriers. I was restless for ground under my feet from the moment I went aboard. The only relief I had was the couple of hours in the air every day. Without that, I probably would have thrown myself off the fantail.

"Okay, sailor." He pulled out an operation order. "Here is where you fit in." He turned a couple of pages and pointed at something to do with logistics. "You'll be our Logistics and Embarkation Officer and you'll accompany 117 marines and all our rolling stock from Del Mar, California to Iwakuni, Japan." He looked at me as if I were being consigned to the Gulag. "And soon."

"I'm serious, Major." I said, "I'll do anything to stay sober and I will do anything I have to do in the process. In fact, I have a suspicion this is part of the process. Everything that happens to me from this point forward is what's necessary to unfuck my career and resurrect a life."

Tomlinson had a quizzical look on his face. He paused as if he was waiting for me to add to what I had just said. "Process? What process? You said something about a part of the process."

"I have no idea, Major, but I think everything that happens is a part of the process." I was suddenly on an unfamiliar territory with Dick Tomlinson. What do I say? I realized I really didn't have an appropriate answer. "Everything that happens in my life now is none of my business. Something else is in charge. And this something is likely to throw anything that might work for it to happen."

"Get out of here, Animal. You're scaring me."

3

Learning to fly

As I had feared, I discovered that I first had to learn how to fly again. This time, sober, with a full understanding of what I was doing. I encountered the sudden onset of a very unfamiliar and uncomfortable awareness: I cared. It was a strange new mindset beyond caring if I lived or died, and how either of those happened. I suddenly gave a shit about a few more important issues in my life, like staying sober and salvaging a career and not falling out of the sky and wiping out an entire neighborhood. These new priorities cut across all the old considerations and gave birth to a new set of responsibilities. I didn't get as close to the edge as I had when I was drinking, which was where all my flying used to take place.

For someone who had previously held everything in renegade disregard, this new perspective on the major issues of my life was disorienting. There were now rules and edges, obedience to parameters. It was a new saner version of 'holding the line.' It would require a large adjustment.

When I was the Flight Line Officer in Atsugi, I was the very definition of incompetence. I thought I was exhibiting trust in the troops when I wouldn't even pre-flight my airplane. I would go out onto the flight line and just climb into the cockpit. Sometimes I had a Plane Captain start the airplane for me and then I'd strap myself in. True, on hungover mornings, starting an airplane was just too much work and took all my energy, energy I would need to fly the airplane and sometimes hang on a leader's wing through thirty thousand feet of cloud cover. With the outer layer of concern removed, or no concern there at all, I would very often feel an intuition take over. I realized now that this was a Higher Power buying me a few more days until He might have something more important for me to do.

My specialty had been air combat maneuvering, dog fighting, a largely intuitive exercise. During an engagement, there's always the chance that the fight drops into an overcast. I was attuned to instances like this. These situations sometimes required possible spin recoveries on instruments. It was the stuff that got me aboard the Forrestal. In a dogfight, I've had to recover from an unusual attitude and still keep my eyes on the other guy. ACM (air combat maneuvering) also requires a full scan of the more concrete matters, such as engine temperature, RPM and fuel management. In the past, I had done all of this second nature. I seemed to have a full read of any situation.

During this transition, I was disappointed to find myself uncomfortably cautious. Where once I would fly to the edge of the envelope at just the slowest airspeed, inverted with negative G and then apply a mental spoonful of rudder, falling off the wing to see my opponent drop in front of me and into my gun sights, I now kept the fight half a click this side of "the edge." I was addicted to winning all the time and maintaining a perfect record instead of doing the best you could with every situation. I would not allow myself to lose and face some critical presence that had always been in my life trying to tell me something. The lessons, as I was about to learn in recovery, most frequently derived from my mistakes. The upside to this new orientation was that I was willing to look at these mistakes and make a mature adjustment.

One afternoon, I separated myself from the flight and flew out over the water, close enough to Catalina Island to be rescued if I fell from the sky. I pulled the Crusader through everything I could give it. I deliberately stalled the airplane but would not allow myself to take it further into a spin. I was not there anymore. Maybe I was.

It just felt different. Everything felt different. Maybe I was feeling. Perhaps it was the first murmurings of the rational mind trying to assert itself. Something Else might hold the line for me now. These major adjustments were difficult.

But the matter of engaging head on in air-to-air engagement, one fighter against another, was soon rendered academic. Marine fighter pilots were to be retrained from the fighter to the attack mission-CAS, close air support for the troops on the ground. Giant chunks of hardware hung beneath the ordinarily sleek wings like ugly cinder blocks. Multiple ejector-racks and multiple bomb racks sucked the life out of high lift, supersonic weapons systems. The Crusader, the prettiest airplane in the Fleet inventory, became a grotesque caricature of itself. They had transformed the last of the Gunfighters into a very effective, but homely, attack platform.

Attack flying is a totally different animal asking for a different stick at the controls, a reframing of the ego and thinking for the fighter pilot. It required that the fighter jock, the very definition of arrogance, experience some unfamiliar humility. It was likely that the spiritual path I had adopted might have helped me give myself over to this new attitude. Happily, it took no time at all for me to learn that air to ground, close air support in the Crusader was as effective dropping ordnance on the ground as it was maneuvering air-to-air at altitude.

What turned my mind and caused me to see this brand of flying as sacred and worthy of all the attention I could give it was to be told I was not doing this for me. I was now flying and dropping ordnance as close to the target as I could for Marines, doing the real fighting on the ground. I turned myself into a bombing fool. As my thoughts turned to others in the deeper part of my consciousness, so I became more attuned to the troops on the ground and what I could do for the guys who were really closing with the enemy.

We spent several weeks flying from El Toro across the hills to the desert near El Centro, dropping anything that can hang from a wing and dig holes in the sand. This is not a one size fits all experience.

Every weapon: practice bombs, 250, 500, 1000, 2000-pound bombs, rockets, Napalm, strafing, all have their own very jealous delivery technique, dive altitude, release speed and bomb sight formula. It helps to have a small guidebook with the data and the dope, but once again, there is that element of intuition. There is no such thing as a purely mechanical pilot if he is going to fly a tactical airplane. It's a fortunate marriage between the mechanical and intuitive parts of the brain.

I thought I had it nailed, had almost memorized all the delivery configurations and worked out bombing patterns that best suited the guy on the ground, the person this was all about. Then, we started night Close Air Support. The words were familiar; I had heard them from that commander aboard the Forrestal, sharing his philosophy on carrier landings. He had said about carrier landing just what our bombing instructor would say during the ground school phase of night bombing, "Night bombing is just the same as day bombing, only it's dark."

Meanwhile, with an equal commitment that I gave myself to my career in the Marine Corps and as an attack pilot, I now applied myself to the spiritual Path. I was single and my time was structured exclusively around both endeavors. I gave everything I had to each. As I ran the required three-man track each morning, I alternately chanted essential parts of the ten-point spin recovery and the Twelve Steps to the Spiritual Path. "Retard the throttle to idle, blow the leading-edge droop, rudder against the spin, stick aft and into the spin." Running mates glanced at me as I muttered my self-crafted mantras in order to access a deeper dimension from which my healing was driven. "Pause when agitated or doubtful and ask for the right thought or action." The two aspects of recovery, my soul and my career, wove in tandem, separated only by a quick shower. People at my meetings looked at me with confusion when I would blurt out something about the ram air turbine to be used in emergencies, just as we were being instructed to ask for the best understanding of His will for us.

It was but a brief costume change from my uniform or flight suit into civilian casual. In less time than that, I was in my red TR4 Triumph driving through the main gate at The Marine Corps Air Station, El Toro. It was less than ten miles, and a few turns down Canyon Road to The Canyon Club at Laguna Beach.

The Fellowship flourished on the beach: Laguna, Newport, Huntington, Seal and Long Beach. A guy with a drinking problem had to hide from the solution. Help was everywhere. All it took was surrender. I turned myself in wherever I saw the sign and sipped from the dented tank of coffee and common sharing.

I'd have over a year to pull it together before they put me on the floating box with the clam shell mouth. Al Fontana and I had grown up together since we were in the first grade. We had watched one another learn everything there was to know about lying, cheating and stealing, plus how to engage with our fellow man in the harmless pastime of getting frequently Canadian drunk. Vancouver was the ideal training ground to board the express path to the bottom, to fall apart and make oneself readily available for Nature to put Humpty Dumpty back together again. If you were that lucky.

My reconstruction began at age thirty. Alfredo's would have to wait for a while. In the meantime, he and Gloria embraced me on the weekend and took me into their lives, providing a healthy balance from the monk's life I had crafted for myself at El Toro.

Gloria and Al Fontana thought it odd that a man, at the peak of his virility, living in one of the most permissive decades of the twentieth century, in a part of the country where free cross pollinating flourished, would choose to become celibate. I couldn't tell them–I was unsure myself–why I had incorporated this into my spiritual regimen. Maybe it was the stereotype I had of the spiritual man. With little religious training, I was beginning from the bare outline of what amateurs taught about God. Starting at near zero, I had a lot of room to grow.

Maybe I was receiving guidance from some deeper direction about a concept that would work for me. I had probably not fully accepted the fact that sex had been an inordinately important factor in my early life. One morning early into my recovery, when it felt like sex was going to be a distraction, I asked that the imperious urge be removed. Magically, it left and stayed gone for a long time. Sex would have been a distraction during my formative years of sobriety. I would need little else to occupy my mind but the reconstruction of my spiritual underpinnings and the rescuing of a career.

Inner Guidance had set me on a path of its choosing, understanding better than I the full dimension of my pathology. The adage, "We beg favors of the gods which the wise ones deny us for our own good" applies even we are seeking help. Something much smarter than me understood what I needed, more than I did. If I had confined my spiritual needs to my understanding, I would have constricted the path that this Power had intended for me. I would soon learn that the path I had chosen would look nothing like I thought it would be.

Alfredo's antics were alive and well. In the early morning, while Al and Gloria were sleeping off the assault of the night before, I slipped from his apartment and wandered Hollywood and Wilshire Boulevard with a clear head. As I had as a child, I explored the streets, a nuisance to traffic, observing with growing affection the vulnerability of the throngs that clearly believed they had a handle on things. Meanwhile, Alfredo suffered the miseries of the damned with a death throes' headache.

Committed to a uniform life of green or tan during a time of unbridled liberties, young people fascinated me with their new freedoms, dressed in flowering fabrics and sometimes nothing at all. Had the fates not arrested my incipient decline, how attractive it all would have been to me. Where would it all have taken me? I had unwittingly entered a world of order and been saved from my natural inclination to permissive indulgence.

Oddly, I felt freedom in my self-styled monastic life. Or was it self-styled? I had to have been getting help from somewhere. This was something that of myself I would not have done. The freedom I felt was in the few choices in the face of too many. I would one decide the number of choices he thinks he has available measured a man's madness.

My friends from Vancouver, Ernie and Barbara D'Amico lived in Long Beach. Ernie had become a professional student attending UCLA in the Philosophy and anthropology departments. Accustomed to seeing me drunk and out on the edge, it disoriented them to listen to my sophomoric railings about the vision I had of God. I supposed, with my rudimentary faith, that a bearded guy in the sky was keeping score. Ernie and Babs were the first to bring it down to earth and then literally back into the heavens again. They opened a large volume filled with pictures of the universe and exploding galaxies, colliding galactic bodies and enormous empty voids, "A Glorious Cosmology." I'm not sure what part of that helped what was already happening in my consciousness, but it broke me loose from the bearded guy in the sky and sent me back to the base with another book, "The Book" by Alan Watts, "The Taboo Against Knowing Who You Are."

The ice began to crack. I sat on a warm rock one Sunday morning at Laguna Beach, listening to waves and feeling the tide reach up to touch my toes mere feet away, while I read "Siddhartha" By Hermann Hesse. Something melted. I sat beside a man at a meeting who had spent a little time at the Esalen Institute. He spoke of human potentialities and alternative means of accessing higher levels of consciousness. All of this was entirely new to me and many others.

The Esalen Institute had just opened two years earlier. A new energy pervaded my mind as a fresh curiosity opened up. I felt the architecture of my alcoholism crumbling. I was unsure what to do with the pieces. I had to step back and allow a Higher Intelligence to put them back in Order.

It should have confused me, living in two worlds, one energizing the other. Not to say that I had it figured out. From these existential forays, I would return to the base, to that other world of dropping bombs and laying Napalm. I was told by the voice from inside: "If you want to know what We have given you to do, just look at what you're doing. Trust to the Grand Design. It has this thing."

And it was with deep satisfaction that I would fire a five-inch Zuni rocket into the cratered carcass of a tank in the desert. A deeper dimension of understanding was being installed in these two major areas of transformation: my work and my soul. There's room for it all. Further, I was taught to "Separate yourself from your subjective opinion of how you think things are supposed to be. Do what you have been given to do. Remove your judgment from the equation." I asked if there should not be judgment about my circumstances in order to decide. I was told: "There's a big difference between judgment and discernment. Judgment makes room for justification, rationalization and is fear driven. Discernment brings your higher faculties into play in order to make sounder choices."

My head whirled in a Vedantic vortex of Eastern studies. At the same time, I was falling in love with the concept of Close Air Support, delivering ordnance in support of the guy on the ground as close as I could to the friendlies, hurting as few of our own as possible. There would come a time when a Ground Commander would have to call in a can of napalm or five-hundred-pound snake-eye bombs on top of his own troops to save a position.

Peace movements around the world spoke of delivering death to an innocent, insurgent enemy. If I was to do this, I had to see it as supporting my own troops, rather than maliciously killing the enemy. They asked me to live with the apparent contradiction to the two parts of my life. On the spiritual path, there are even larger contradictions that I would be asked to face.

I had a short time left before I boarded the ship. I saturated myself with the presence of "fellow travelers" on the Path. Southern California was the perfect part of the world to make the transformation. An older conservative crowd in Kingsville, Texas, had embraced me with traditional concepts of God at my first meetings. "Just put the plug in the jug, trust in God and go to meetings" was their anthem. Laguna Beach broke me out of a rigid control and allowed me the latitude of total spiritual enquiry, all within the context of our chosen path of a few simple steps. I was fortunate in that I had not been exposed to religion as a child and was not fixed in a spiritual paradigm. I was an empty vessel ready to be filled, and I was thirsty for whatever might fill the space.

All that was needed was to give myself over to The Power, whatever that looked like to me. I didn't have to accept anyone else's power. I could choose my own as long as it fit. The designer God. The words, "broad and roomy, all-inclusive, never exclusive," warmed a cold and empty chamber. I allowed the vacuum to draw to it what felt right. All of this was familiar to the world of my mother. It confirmed my early reflections when I had been making the hard choices with Sarah.

I'm not even sure if I allowed anything. Everything worthwhile in the spiritual realm came to me. I had only to make myself ready to receive them. These lessons came to me by those who had preceded me on this path.

They said that my alcoholism was not a sin, but a disease. Ironically, the cure was to make friends with the disease; get close to my suffering and that of others. Get next to the problem and let God in. The closer I faced the problem, the closer this Power of my understanding brought the answer. All the work put me in a position for the Power to do the work on me.

I was to learn that love happened where the problem met the solution. And love was happening all around me. It's the only thing that's really happening. I had only to grow in understanding, to feel it and to know it. To be next to it, to lean into the problem and any of its symptoms. Then let God in. All of this to put me in a position for God to do the work.

"You have a top-secret clearance, Colin." Dick Tomlinson had called me into his office. I was his Executive Officer now, which for a compact unit like MABS meant I was also the chaplain, legal officer, chief bottle washer and father confessor. My office was next to his. "You've got a couple of schools in your Officer's Qualification Record now and your name has gone up to the selection board for Major." He looked up to see if I was shaking my head at the likelihood of making Major. It was. "Don't give up just yet, Animal. There is a lot of senior field grade on the board who know you and understand what you're doing. One of the most attractive features of the Marine Corps is its size. The Marine Corps Fighter Pilot community is very incestuous and insular. News travels fast in such a system. People who saw you fuck up are going to notice the difference."

"Thanks," I said, "I appreciate everything you've done for me, Skipper. Even if I don't get selected, I'm grateful for your efforts."

He nodded and took off his glasses. "And incidentally, your clearance is not what I was really wanting to talk about. They've moved up our departure date. Say your goodbyes and get all your shit in one sock." I nodded. "And anyway, who are those people you hang out with? They aren't drinking and they seem to have fun?" He had run into me and a group of my "people" at a restaurant in Laguna Beach.

"We're just a bunch of ex-troublemakers enjoying life and getting away with it." I was about to leave the room. And remembered something I needed to tell him. "I just had an interesting session with the Sergeant Major. He brought in Corporal Briggs with a fascinating fresh problem you might never have encountered."

"What's going on?" He asked.

"Seems Corporal Briggs has had to question some assumptions about his sexuality. Either that or he's looking for a reason to be discharged and not have to take this boat ride with the rest of us." I grinned.

"Jesus, what the hell is this all about?" He stood up.

"Corporal Briggs came to the Sergeant Major at muster sobbing and he needed to talk to me about something important. So, Sergeant Major brings him into my office. He's standing at attention. I tell him to stand at ease. Immediately he falls into a chair sobbing. I get up and walk around and put my hand on his shoulder to see if he's alright.

He turns to me and says, 'Captain Ruthven, oh, Jesus, I think I fucked a man.' Then dissolves into hysterical sobbing again." I shrugged.

"What the fuck did you do with this?" With this, Major Tomlinson sat down.

"Exactly!" I nodded. "Oh, Christ! I thought. What do I do with this?"

"I'm all ears here, Colin. This has you written all over it." He was grinning. He fired up a Pall Mall, sat back and crossed his legs.

"Well, according to his own words, Corporal Briggs was in Los Angeles last night looking for action. Apparently, there was a lot. He had attracted the attention of this lovely creature at the "Inside Track," a bar in North Hollywood. He says she was one of the most beautiful women he had ever seen. Briggs fell instantly in love as most guys do with whom they've had their first sexual experience." We both grimaced. "Yes, they bonded throughout the night in that very sweet and innocent way. However, a vital truth was not revealed until this morning when the new love of his life got honest with Briggs. She sat him down and confessed that she was not, in fact a girl, but a guy, incidentally, a busboy at Denny's on Sunset Boulevard. If that makes it any more innocent or poetic, however you want to see this thing.

"The girl was, in naked (excuse me) truth, a fucking guy! Now Briggs thinks because he has 'accidentally' had sex with a man that he might be scarred forever. He is, at the very least, gay, at the worst a pervert of the first order, a pariah who should be sent to a monastery, or wherever they send them." I folded my arms, challenging Major Tomlinson to come up with a better solution to the problem than had I.

"Okay, Colin, if you sanitized this, or convinced Briggs that this was not a fuck, I will personally fly up to Headquarters Marine Corps and see that they select you for Major." He looked at me and said, "Alright, Merlin, what did you tell him?"

"I did the Judo on it, Major. I transformed him from a perpetrator into a victim." I grinned. 'Corporal Briggs.' I explained, 'You are the victim of a criminal attack upon your innocence. She- he, excuse me-he has taken terrible advantage of your trust.' I told him to stand up and take charge of the situation. He then went on about her long hair and eyelashes, rhapsodized about her full mouth. I told him to calm down before I changed my mind. Besides, I wanted him to shut up before I hurled.

"I told him that technically this was not a sexual encounter, but, I repeated, a crime perpetrated upon him. She-He, excuse me again-had violated him and his trust. I sat with him for an hour while Sergeant Major stood behind him with his arms folded and a fishy expression, his head cocked, eyes rolling like one of these "Are you shitting me Captain?" looks.

"I urged Briggs to get angry about this situation and we would do everything we could to bring the perp' to justice. In the meantime, get your bags packed. We're on our way to Japan. I asserted vigorously, 'Briggs, as far as you are concerned, and as far as the Marine Corps is concerned, this did not happen.'"

"Jesus, remind me to call you when I'm arrested for anything." Major Tomlinson turned around and began arranging papers on his desk. "And it won't be for fucking a man."

"I also told him that nobody in the world will know about this except Corporal Briggs, Sergeant Major and myself. So, you don't know about this, Skipper."

"Jesus, I wish I did not." He shook his head. "Trust me, I'm going to do everything I can to scrub it from my mind. And, I was just about to have lunch."

He looked up at me as I was leaving and added, "And, good luck aboard the Sutter County, sailor."

4

The Sutter County

Alfredo drove me to Long Beach to board the Sutter County the night before she sailed south to Del Mar.

"Can you believe this, Coke?" His eyes burned behind dark glasses. It was pure heroics for him to bring me from El Toro to Long Beach with one of his thunderous hangovers. "Ten years ago we were running wild in the streets of Vancouver wondering where to make a buck and now I'm putting you on this ugly can. Jesus, it's ancient."

"Careful, Al. I don't think these sailors think it's so old and ugly. It's their home." As I looked at the ship, I had to agree with Al. It was not beautiful; and it sounded old just sitting still.

"Okay, my old friend. Keep out of the way of those bullets. I don't want you coming home in a body bag." He sped away in the TR-4 before I could hug him, his head averting mine.

"Permission to come aboard, sir." I saluted the officer of the deck and the National Ensign that hung limp at the fantail of the USS Sutter County. The ship was one of many LST's built during World War II to support amphibious operations. She hugged the pier like a wild dog looking for a hole in the fence. She was an animal that was only comfortable at sea.

There were two LSTs in the small convoy to Iwakuni, Japan. The other ship, USS Page County, would be the first to lead out of Long Beach for Del Mar, roughly 100 miles down the coast of California.

Our rolling stock and the troops convoyed from El Toro to Del Mar, where they loaded aboard the following day. They did not build the Sutter County for comfort. Designed primarily to transport tanks and rolling stock, the LST is structured around a tank deck capable of transporting vehicles across water and then unloading them through the bow of the ship onto the beach.

Since the ship was designed, they continue to use the procedures that were established with minor variation to those executed during the Second World War. The ship takes a running start onto the beach and deliberately powers aground. The clam shell bow opens, a ramp falls to the beach and everything loads aboard in a coherent logistical order. It sounds easy, but it took all the following day, the night and into most of the next morning to load, constantly adjusting for the changing tides. The ship literally ruts at the beach as the ship pulls and turns to keep the ramp straight for vehicles and troops to come aboard.

Embarkation is no chance exercise in coordination and preparation. We drew plans to load the tank deck months in advance. Once aboard, we secured trucks and support equipment to the deck with multiple heavy-duty lines. If a single line broke free during a high sea, a truck could break loose, resulting in a catastrophic domino effect of colliding vehicles and equipment. It would be impossible to bring order from the mechanized chaos. The contents of the tank deck would chew itself into a mangled wreckage by journey's end.

I shared a cabin with First Lieutenant Victor Friedman, my second in command. I assigned four section leaders, staff non-commissioned officers, to the care, feeding and monitoring of 117 marines. Symmetrically, as if to suggest a contest at sea, there were 117 sailors in ship's company. I went below to inspect the spaces where our troops were billeted together with the sailors.

"Captain Ruthven," The Skipper of the ship was with me as I toured the living quarters. "These sailors have lived on these ships, some of them, for years, and they know every hiding place your troops might think to stash their valuables. I warn you. It can get pretty hairy down here if there's a fight. I've had to clear the area and move everyone topside more than once when someone stole a Marine's wallet, and we couldn't find it." The captain of the ship, Lieutenant Pemberton, was orienting me to hazards endemic to his command. "I suggest you instruct the troops to put their valuable in the ship's safe or just give their wallets to the sailors outright."

It would be tight quarters for us all, a perfect climate for a riot if everyone didn't play well with others. In the short term, I didn't need to worry. Almost to a man. For the first few days after we were underway, everyone was too sick to think of making trouble. I made a tour of the troop's spaces twice a day. The stench of vomit permeated the atmosphere of the tight compartments, the fabric of the bunks and clothing. To make the situation worse, meals continued to be prepared. The nauseating aroma of freshly cooked meat wafted into the living spaces, challenging the most seasoned veteran, sailor and Marine to hold it down.

I was sick for a couple of days, as was the captain of the ship. He told me we'd get over it. "Everyone, including me, gets sick the first couple of days out," he said.

All of us lined the rails through our first days, the salt wash bathing and soothing wasted faces. When the stomachs finally settled down, an adolescent energy arose, looking curiously for the first place to direct a restless mischief. I would have to interrupt the first creative idea before it became an uprising.

I structured my plan primarily around monitoring the troop spaces, making sure I connected with every Marine each day. Somebody needed to know what was going on with everyone all the time. It was a benign "Big Brother" approach to leadership. Expecting the restlessness, we erected a boxing ring on the forward upper deck. I stationed a heavy bag and athletic equipment in the forward part of the tank deck, creating a small workout gymnasium.

As soon as I could detect the first signs of excess energy, I assigned the most potentially aggressive Marine, Corporal Ervin Goldstein, as NCO to maintain a continuous boxing card. We scheduled the matches for Saturday and Sundays to give the impression that we were still on the beach working a calendar week. We marked weekends instead of enduring an endless day at sea, interrupted only by occasional darkness. Early on, the sensation of time standing still set in. Within days it felt like we would be at sea indefinitely.

I opposed keeping Marines and sailors separated. I wanted to integrate everyone, so that there was none of the traditional polarization between the Navy and the Marine Corps. Nothing will foment conflict quicker than giving someone a reason to choose sides. I asked the captain if we could include the sailors in our activities.

Soon the fight card was intramural. A healthy competition grew not only between the two services but soon sailors were fighting sailors. If an actual disagreement arose, someone counseled them and then gave the two involved the opportunity to take it out on one another in the ring.

Usually after three rounds in a controlled environment, the two contestants left the ring, if not better friends, then much better acquainted. If they weren't done yet, we scheduled the two opponents against one another on the next card. There was always a way to work out differences. Some of the senior sailors and Marines who had experience fighting acted as trainers and seconds. Some of the older Staff NCOs wanted to box just to burn off energy. I ignored money being passed between rounds. I pretended harmless wagering was not happening.

Night and meals broke up the time. Flying fish, whales, dolphins and schools of sharks interrupted the enormous expanse of sea, a relief from an apparently infinite and unchanging ocean. Time soon took on the same character as the sea: endless. To break up the day, we tracked the path of the sun across the skies and observed the changing hues and values of the ocean.

Soon, a lassitude settled into all hands, more pronounced for troops who had been living a relatively riotous life in California. We broke the different troop sections down in time intervals for jogging in place for half an hour twice a day. I incorporated the two exercise sessions after both morning and afternoon meals. We inspected the spaces daily. Racks had to be made, linen surveyed. The captain asked us to rotate showers to observe water rationing. They broke ordnance out daily, fired off the fantail at floating targets, weapons cleaned and inspected. The troops practiced an abbreviated close order drill done standing in place on the aft deck. I filled the day with activities to avoid retreating below deck and never surfacing again. Meals were massively sufficient and well prepared. I watched people's perimeters expand, their uniforms tighten.

Lest the troops feared we would sail on forever toward an ever-receding horizon. our Staff NCOs delivered lectures about civilization and how to comport ourselves when we arrived at our destination. Those who had visited Hawaii, our only stop, spoke about liberty; where to find the joys and how to avoid the hazards. The older salts shared war stories of dread horrors and communicable disease on Hotel Street. Even the notion of something bad happening, as long as it occurred on dry ground, improved morale immensely and brought hope to those who eagerly looked forward to arriving at our first stop. The troops shone brass and shoes for inspection prior to hitting the beach.

Cheers erupted from the ship every time a loudspeaker announced passing another time zone with instructions to set our watches back an hour

This ship is not exactly a flat-bottomed boat, but it definitely does not drive like an aircraft carrier, a vessel many times larger that accommodates much easier to swells. The Sutter County felt every irregularity in the ocean and change in the wind direction. An uneasy ocean threw me from my rack four nights out. A television set in the wardroom that had been bolted to the bulkhead broke loose and landed on the other side of the compartment. I increased the one-on-one engagement with the troops between myself and all the section leaders. I gave every Marine individual contact at least twice daily. If there were any sicknesses or injuries, they got immediate attention and follow-up.

A day out from Hawaii, I received a dispatch listing the off-limit establishments. All four section heads read the message to their troops with the diabolical intent of making the upcoming stop in Pearl Harbor more stimulating, something to look forward to, like hitting the forbidden dark side of "Hotel Street" where they were told not to go. On 28 July, a Marine told everyone he could pick up radio stations from Honolulu. The incidence of birds and floating vegetation increased. We slipped into Pearl Harbor early the next morning.

The ship released the troops to a couple of days' liberty. I rented a car and drove over to Kaneohe Bay. I had seen Waikiki in 1956 and made the worst of it then. Ten years later, I didn't need to see that version again. My impression of the tourists who flocked to the Royal Hawaiian Hotel and other traditional interests was that they had waited too long to visit The Islands. They should have come when they were young. Old people with leis around their neck depressed me. Back then, I had been too young for the experience. I was awash in mixed feelings, mostly unsettling, remembering that tour. Some of it I wished I could forget, the wasted hours, lost chances, irreparable damage.

I drove through The Nu'uanu Pali Tunnels to the other side of the Island. They had completed the tunnels shortly after I had left Kaneohe Bay in 1958. I could once again feel and hear the impact of my fender hitting an opposing car, climbing up through the Pali as I was careening down. Drunk and unfeeling, I had not stopped to help or confess that I had crossed the line. Crossing the line had become familiar to me and to those who knew me. It had been my style.

My memories of flying at Kaneohe Bay were the few that I cherished. Thoughts of my domestic failure served only to dampen any good feelings I might have had of that time. A new mindset brought about by just these two years of recovery colored my thoughts with unwelcome regret. As time passed, cringe worthy moments became more frequent, a sign that I was more the ready to face my past and deal with the damage.

From a distance, I heard the sounds and saw the familiar shapes of Crusaders launching from the runway at the air station. Everything was as it had been, but I was seeing it with sober eyes. Why was I here? Because I had been there. I could not erase terrible memories, but in time they promised me I would see them in a more favorable light as precursors to making healthier choices.

I had to bring a sober presence to the place and possibly settle with the past. One cannot erase the past. We are our history. I was willing to let go, and live with what remained and deal with it. It all serves to Purpose.

I wasted little time at Kaneohe Bay or in Kailua, else I dwell in morbid reflection. I drove back to Honolulu in time to meet with a room full of my Fellow Travelers. They're everywhere. I drank dark coffee as if from a fresh stream after miles in the desert. I hung on the words of those who shared a mutual solution. As often happens, I took in the common plight and related to each searching soul as one with whom I might share a similar scar from the same blade. I scanned the faces and saw the default expression of fatigue and disappointment. Most of us arrive in "the rooms" more tired than drunk.

My eyes fixed on a woman, I guessed, in her seventies. But who knows with such ageless souls? She could be eighty or fifty. She seemed comfortable in her age. Her hair was white. Whistler's mother with a crooked smile. While everyone else much younger shared their stories, she sat at the back of the room and fondled a small white jar on her lap. She kept running her hand gently across the smooth surface of the lid as if it were a sacred talisman, bringing the air of sanctity to the space. The longer I looked at her, the older she became. She shared my mother's aspect. Mom had similar small jars on her table for ablutions where she would begin or end her day. Cold cream had filled an identical jar on her dresser. Much like this lady, Mother, in a moment that I knew was privately hers, contemplated her world as she spread the thick white stuff to her face.

The lady caught me looking at her. She smiled sweetly, almost seductively, as one who was caught in a private reverie. I wonder at a person's history, the experiences that have made them who and what they are. I will never know all of their secrets; they will never know most of mine. The woman wore a weary expression of resignation to time and circumstance. Her life might be nearing the end, and she was here to discharge any remaining duty or regret. She was one of those people whose face said, 'The hard part's over. I'm just here to wind down and watch what's left of the struggle.'

I slipped further to the rear of the room, my back to the wall. Then I drew closer to the woman. I studied her features with impudent relish. A slender swan's neck was a network of lines, skin dried and scarred by too many seasons in the sun. Hair, now more silver than white, was unbrushed and unruly at the back of her head. Her face matched her mussed hair. She had long ago surrendered any effort at cosmetic pretense. The woman, now older, bore the expression of the faces of those who've seen all they want to see and know there are no more big deals.

The small porcelain jar rested on her lap during the entire meeting. Her hand wandered across the ivory white lid, polishing its smooth surface with her worn hands. I fancied she was reciting ritual lines, long rote with repetition. Her narrow fingers presently rotated the lid, slowly. The last time I had seen such a jar opened was when I was a child. I would watch my mother's every act as if there were lessons in each motion. Light would strike the moist, glistening, whiter-than-white surface of the contents of the jar. With two fingers she would scoop the creamy, white cold cream from the jar and dispersed it across her soft features while her thoughts took her to some distant place. I could not imagine the woman covering her face in the middle of the meeting, but my assumptions held that when she opened the jar, I would see pearly white cold cream. She opened the lid.

Rather than a whiter than white cold cream, I stared into the densest hole of obsidian black. I experienced a jarring shift somewhere between clear cognitive awareness and total confusion. They were ants. My shock intensified as the woman dipped her long delicate fingers into the crawling heap of ants and conveyed them to her mouth. I took a stunned step forward. Were those ants she was putting in her mouth? Then I saw. She was dipping tobacco. Almost immediately I was hostage to an awareness that I could not escape. Just as my assessments of the woman and the jar had been skewed, so had many of the fixed ideas about my small universe been distorted.

I was unaware then, but it was revealed later that in this moment a part of me had been scrambled and then challenged to examine a lifetime of fixed assumptions. I explored the difference between my expectations, even the demands I had placed upon my world, measured against a current reality. Our reality changes with each moment. I did not know what was going on. Much of what I supposed I knew was being rearranged. Maybe I was drawing a clearer focus out of my confusion. It was a total rearrangement at depth beyond my understanding. A huge part of me was changing.

The last person I had seen who had put the small granules of tobacco under their lower lip was a grizzled, bearded, hook tender in a logging camp at Beaver Creek, British Columbia. This was not to be the last time Nature would charge me to examine how wrong I had been about everything or anything. She would ask me to be open to the absurd. And of these moments, there would be an abundance.

I returned to the ship a day early and relieved the duty Staff NCO. This allowed him to spend the last twelve hours on liberty. I settled into my compartment. It was very different, no longer in motion. The walls didn't sing with every movement of the ship. I inspected the spaces and helped prepare for the troops to return.

Everyone was present and accounted for at the appointed time. There were a few walking wounded. The military police delivered two sailors to the ship. They had to be spilled below and helped into their bunks. At least, the full complement of troops was here. Nobody had missed a movement. Although some jurisdictional charges might follow us to Iwakuni, it relieved me that I had not lost one.

We were underway again on the second of August. This would be the longest leg, the part of the voyage that would require the most attention. It would be easy to let up on our constant vigilance and fall apart on the last days. I could not afford to allow any of us, including me, to stagnate and take to the rack just as a healthy morale had been established.

The troops weathered the sea sickness in just a few days out of Pearl Harbor. General quarters on the first day came as a relief. I threw the Marines into routine activities with the sailors. The naval crew taught Marines how to stand a watch at sea. I asked Corporal Goldstein to set up the boxing cards again. I felt a sense of military order combined with a healthy mix of exercise and creative activity set in.

It might have become altogether too creative, when I looked back at it on how things went with the "skit."

I had asked Corporal Briggs, the survivor of Passion's throes with another man to write, produce and direct a skit. I wanted every man involved. He was allowed as many assistants as he needed, just about every Marine on the ship, to help design the staging, costumes and decorations and polish up his script. I supposed this would keep everyone busy, maybe even creative in the week I had given Briggs to prepare for the performance. He asked, with no small ceremony, that I make an amendment to the operation order and refer to the skit as a "Play" to lend weight commensurate with his "creative gravitas."

Almost regrettably, it revealed that Briggs was an English major. The moment I assigned him the project, he took on an entirely altered identity. I will swear he grew taller. He was instantly a better than Tennessee Williams version of Tennessee Williams. His dramatic transformation tied in neatly with the beard growing contest, a total departure from Marine Corps regulations. I overrode several prohibitions, the violation of which it would be difficult for Headquarters Marine Corps to police while we were in the middle of the Pacific Ocean. The relaxed atmosphere provided all the ingredients for a mutiny, which ironically, I found was the best way to avoid a mutiny. One needs to give the renegade soul the slack it needs to breathe and then apply the checks and balances of sound leadership.

We suspended recreation and other diversions for a couple of days as the ship passed through the roughest of the journey. Weather and long swells dropped the ship into deep troughs. Towering waves dashing across the decks wiped away anything that was adrift. If a soul was to hazard his way along a railing, he felt he was dancing on fresh, wet soap. Everyone was to travel at least in pairs, in case someone disappeared over the side.

After the storm, the troops crept out of their lair into a welcome sunlight. The first bristles of beards sprouted on faces I scarcely recognized. To restore a semblance of military bearing, we assembled the sections in formation for inspection. Fire teams distributed several clips of ammunition. They mustered by schedule on the fantail for weapons drill. They dropped targets in the water and fired at until they disappeared. Weapons were cleaned and inspected again. The troops had not seen this attention to military protocol since they were in boot camp.

Haircuts resumed, but the beards survived, sculpted to their owner's preference, revealing hidden facets of the personality. Corporal Briggs asked that his cast be provided with the latitude for longer hair to lend reality to his drama. I was questioning my decision. Should I have given Briggs such a wide berth to his creative abandon? Could he possibly be sublimating the abuses upon his sexual innocence?

The beards had awoken narcissistic inclinations in even the dullest of brutes. Never had there been more attention to the taming, trimming and combing of faces, some resembling lowland gorillas, others theatrical, even Shakespearian. I questioned my leadership style when I noticed some tonsorial fashions taking on a feminine aspect. Tragically, some beards grew less manly than others. Those with lesser growths, troops too shy to be seen with such a scant harvest, were allowed to shave entirely. Scant scruff offended their idea of military decorum. It insulted their image of Marine Corps' masculinity. It encouraged me to find some of the senior enlisted police the marginal styles and demand their fellow Marines "clean it up."

As I examined these specimens, self-conscious in the extreme, I almost regretted that I had come up with the idea. The beard growing contest was to be judged in several categories. In deference to those who had barely started shaving, we scrubbed the 'Heaviest Growth' category, for which Goldstein was bound to win. I scoured the ranks during inspection and spotted those minimally haired and suggested that they be a part of the skit that required the less hirsute, maybe female parts. Corporal Briggs was quick to see around my deception. He told me he had several roles available for players who could be female. I gave him the names of those who could barely sprout nose hair and they were allowed to shave under vital roles in Briggs' Play. By now, Briggs had fashioned a once healthy full beard into a Van Dyke goatee. I wondered if I should worry about Briggs and some others who were taking on the character consonant with their beards. Their whiskers were dictating how they behaved, a sadder than usual case of the tail wagging the dog.

That we might bring most of the Marines and ship's company into the scheme, I asked Staff Sergeant Leonard Thrasher, a music major, to assemble a choir. He could pick an assistant and write lyrics to whatever music would fit into the play. I did not know that I had just stirred Leonard Thrasher's dormant Gilbert and Sullivan. The choral rehearsals went from early morning until late in the evening. Some sailors asked if they could be in on the deal, many of them fine singers. Strange sounds rose from the troop spaces, causing the captain to look up from his evening meal and glance at me with a puzzled expression. We both wondered what I had wrought.

It was a puzzle to me where the galley personnel hid all the food. With so many to feed and so much of it served around the clock, it seemed, there had to be secret compartments in the bulkheads. Again, to convey the appearance of time passing, a cookout was scheduled each Sunday after worship services. Steaks to order on the fantail followed by a mammoth rehearsal for the play. We set a stage up and judges chosen from among the officers, navy and Marine, to judge the beards and some costumes from the dress rehearsal.

I worried that some of the Marines once released from military bearing in the slightest might spring all the way off the grid and never come back, especially with the wild transformation induced by the beards, never mind some of female cast now wearing dresses. Confined to the ship, there was little danger of anyone wandering away, but I could see a few deviations off center in the costumes during the contest. A few, including Briggs, had taken on a suspiciously attractive female appearance, even with their abundant beards. A few others had thrown caution to the wind and dressed as close to drag as the current crowd could stand. I drew the line at the female participants shaving their legs.

To bring us around again to a more masculine and military posture, we assigned everyone to certain of the vehicles, some of them to task-oriented assignments, others just as observers, to start all the vehicles and put them through periodic maintenance. This was a two-day endeavor that required inspections during and after. I made sure everyone got dirty. Mainly I wanted all hands busy for most of their waking hours. I didn't want them to vegetate below in their bunks. By the time we had taken a Marine through his daily regimen, he was ready to hit the rack. I was happy to notice an unusual enthusiasm for them to get out of the sack in the morning and get into preparations for the "play."

Our time passed between duty and recreation. The balance of both continued through the days. We crossed the International Date Line. That isn't exactly the equator, but it required we observe some ceremony, which was as good a time as any for us to cover the troops in ice cream and whatever could stick to them.

The International Date Line Celebration coincided nicely with final preparations for Corporal Briggs' production. The festive atmosphere of ice cream melting on sun heated bodies wove nicely into an afternoon of cultural diversion.

On the afternoon of his production, the "Judgment of Paris", all hands were assembled on the forward deck. The title Corporal Briggs had chosen was so grandiose, flying over most of the heads, that they ignored it. I, probably one of the few familiar with the original play, worried that Briggs' reach might have exceeded his grasp. He was still a little put off the troops continued to refer to the play as a skit.

He preceded the 'play' with a serious speech to all hands to assure the assembly, some squatting on the upper deck, others hanging on the rail, that this was a play, a modern adaptation taken from Greek Mythology. His protracted 'announcement' attracted more than a few puzzled expressions and a collective murmur that rose to a deafening din as Briggs left the stage with a suspiciously dainty step.

It was a calm day. The sun shone high overhead and leant a dramatic light to the stage and players. I was more than curious what Briggs might have conjured for this grubby lot that might resemble a plot from the classics. The heat of the day drew perspiration from the bodies, bathing them in a cosmetic sheen.

Three "women," selected for their inability to grow a beard, perched with an affected allure at a bar. They were clearly hookers from their sinister makeup and scanty costumes. Their seductive postures, legs immodestly opened, revealed too much thigh, several of which were, against my express order, mysteriously bereft of hair. I was wondering if I should have reviewed and approved the play, at least the costumes, certainly some bodies, before the performance.

Staff Sergeant Waters, an enormous black man, far beyond the acceptable Marine Corps fitness standard, dressed even larger than he was, in padded decorative clothing. The cover from a Chief Petty Officer's hat was draped over his head in spangles and patterned paper in what I supposed to be a pimp's headwear. When the play was translated days later, Sergeant Waters was supposed to be the current version of the God Zeus and the women were the goddesses, Hera, Athena and Aphrodite. Each of several selected actors were to approach Zeus and challenge him to tell why he thought one goddess was the most beautiful. Briggs had exceeded his own, and certainly my, expectations. The larger part of the audience, with scant acquaintance with the referenced classic Greek Mythology, easily missed, or more probably ignored the serious nature of the entertainment. They rather made of it what they wanted it to be, not what Briggs had intended. It was a riot hit of their own conjuring.

At intervals there was a brief pause between acts as they shifted scenery. A chorus broke into a Gilbert and Sullivan style choral under Staff Sergeant Theodore's direction, followed by another brief pause. Then when silence was restored, less the ambient running of the ship and its company, plus small murmurs of appreciation, the play resumed. Corporal Briggs cowered nervously behind the stage set, assessing the crowd's reaction to his creation, clutching a clipboard to his chest, frantically leafing through his script.

Sad to see, Briggs, who had also fashioned himself a decorative headpiece from a Chief Petty Officer's hat, darted amongst the crowd, clipboard pressed to his body, explaining what everything was supposed to mean. Nobody really appreciated the hidden subtleties that Briggs had written into the script with which only a few, I would have wagered, were even remotely acquainted. Staff Sergeant Theodore's choir was given a standing ovation and asked to perform an encore.

Zeus, played by Sergeant Waters, who in real life could have been a pimp sent down from central casting, had the audience in stitches. Unfamiliar with the origin of the plot, the audience could not care less, and filled in their own projections, as did the actors. The production soon dissolved into a melee of extemporaneous confrontations with Zeus, the pimp, about the quality of his ladies, opposed by heated rebuttals from the goddesses Hera, Athena and Aphrodite, or whoever they were. Ship's company was in hysterics. The play ran into several additional unplanned scenes and had to be shut down with the ship's loudspeaker. It was an enormous success.

As the days passed after the play, there were about six of the choir that would meet in a corner of the aft upper deck and practice singing. The captain of the ship could not contain his laughter days after the production was over. Every time he ran into me on deck or in the wardroom, he would shake his head slightly and chuckle.

On the days that followed, Corporal Briggs moped around the ship addressing a multitude of questions and complaints about his production and explaining Greek Mythology. By the time he was in my cabin, he was close to tears. I explained that he might have extended his reach a bit for a limited audience, but his production was a hit. I suggested he might work his twisted homage to "The Judgment of Paris" and show it in another more sophisticated venue. I added it was brilliant.

I was tiring of rescuing Corporal Briggs from himself. He had survived his sexual misadventure with a man, but I was not sure he would ever get over his play. He went into a sort of post-play depression that lasted until we arrived at our destination. Iwakuni would eventually rescue his sense of self and restore his challenged heterosexuality, a very reassuring time for us all.

A few days later after everything had calmed down, and I was satisfied that the troops had fallen into a manageable routine, I was close on to taking a nap when the captain of the ship, no less, and the officer of the day loomed over my bunk.

"Could you come with me, Captain Ruthven?" The Skipper asked with false amiability. I followed them down into the tank deck, the troops glancing curiously at our small party as we strode by. We wove our way through the trucks, trailers, and starting equipment forward to the very bow of the ship.

"I invite you to look in the bilge, sir." The skipper said. The bilge is that area between the ramp and the clam shell bow that routinely collects water as the ship plows across the sea. I stepped up onto a railing and peered over the ramp.

Inside the bilge were three of my Marines "swimming." I stepped down and, over the roar of the ocean pounding against the bow, asked the captain, "Is there any way we can open the clam shell so they can almost fucking drown?"

"I appreciate your mischievous intent, captain, but no, the sea would probably suck them out into it's wake."

"Is there any way we can do that, then, Captain?"

He grinned. "No, this is not the USS Bounty, Captain Bligh. But might I suggest we put them on permanent mess duty until we arrive in Iwakuni? We're almost there."

I climbed up over the ramp and above the ship's collective roar, shouted, "Okay, kids, take off your swimsuits and pick up your aprons. You're all on mess duty." The three faces twisted immediately into the air and so recently exposed to Greek mythology, they might have assumed I had appeared like a Delphic god, consigning them to a current version of whatever the Gods required.

I awoke early pre-dawn to an unfamiliar activity. There was a stir among the ship's company that suggested a fire drill. The captain was having a cot taken up onto the bridge, where he would stay for the rest of the trip. We were getting close to our destination. Troops lined the railings, hoping to be the first to sight any sign of land. Someone spotted a sock floating swiftly past on the starboard side and claimed that he had won the pool. There was a small discussion which turned into a dispute which told me that there was some book making going on down below. I would not go into the troops' quarters to search for the floating poker game at this stage, nor was I going to break up a wager as long as their minds remained occupied.

The last big storm hit. Down in the galley a pile of something threw itself off one bulkhead and hit the other, erupting like a hundred pie plates falling on a metal deck. When we awoke after the storm, we were approaching the Bungo Channel between the island of Kyushu on the Port and Shikoku on the Starboard. Small islands on either side of the ship closed in on us. A long peninsula from Shikoku reached for the bow as we steered through the Channel into Iyo-nada Sea. Between the Iyo-nada to the Inland Sea, a complex of islands creates an impossible navigation passage.

Small boats and some larger commercial vessels suddenly surfaced, making no effort to avoid the Sutter County. There seemed a deliberate effort to ram or be rammed by the larger ships.

"They're trying to induce an accident. There's more money in a claim against the Navy than they can make in an entire year, and sometimes a lifetime," the captain explained. I was with him on the bridge. I joined him for the better part of the last full day.

Suddenly, we were there. The metal hangars of the Marine Corps Air Station Iwakuni glinted in the sun. Two Crusaders flew overhead to the entry point of the duty runway. Their familiar scream drowned out the now familiar vibration and voice of the Sutter County.

I was back in Japan.

5

Iwakuni

Iwakuni Air Station was established in 1940 as a Japanese training and defense base with assorted aircraft, including 150 Zero Fighters. Nearby, the Etajima Naval Academy opened at the same time. After the war, Marine Aircraft Group 13 became a unit of the First Marine Aircraft Wing at the Marine Corps Air Station in Iwakuni. It operated there until September 1966, when the Wing deployed to the Republic of Vietnam.

Marine Air Base Squadron's mission was to support MAG 13 units operating at the Iwakuni Air Station. Until I could be assigned to a tactical unit, I was the Executive Officer of MABS 13, a position that entailed close contact with the troops, often processing them for Article 15, which is minor disciplinary action and sometimes more seriously for court martial. It's easy to rubber stamp a problem Marine and put him on the conveyor belt to his doom and dismissal from The Corps when he could otherwise be rescued from his errant ways with a little creative leadership. The Executive Officer's principal job is to run interference for the Commanding Officer so that he can do his job, which is leading the efforts to support the tactical units.

Iwakuni is an ancient city, famous for its many monuments and historic landmarks that identify periods of the country's honorable history. The immediate district of Iwakuni surrounding the Marine base was a complex of traditional Japanese enterprise, small shops, an Onsen, or hot bath, a hotel or two, and a complex of bars and clubs, far more than I could remember in Atsugi five years earlier. The bars had entertained the troops since the end of the Second World War and through them, an economy had flourished. Familiar with the recreational needs of Marines, the Japanese had made it an entrepreneurial art form, providing female companionship for the troops from nearby Iwakuni Air Station.

As time passed, the clubs kept up with contemporary music and the needs of the servicemen who rotated in and out of Japan. Principal to the entertainment and the economy were many hostesses, young, alluring and immediately available at a price just suited to an enlisted man's meagre budget. Very often, one of these ladies would be that woman who gave a young man the first bit of female attention he had ever experienced. Further, one of these women might be the first with whom a Marine had been intimate. Explosive, blind love, as that man had just come to know it, would likely follow. This was not innocent, high school, first love, but a skilled apparatus designed to subtract money from the troops' wallets and possibly break a few hearts.

If there was trouble to be had for a young Marine barely out of high school and suddenly exposed to the allures of the Far East, it was in the proliferation of these small bars traditionally situated outside any military installation. I had made a recreational study of many of these places in Atsugi in 1961 during my tour with Marine Fighter Squadron 312. Of those that I had encountered in the Orient, the clubs in Iwakuni were the most nefarious and exploitative. So, any Marine who had found trouble in this part of the world could not have found a more sympathetic listener. And listen, I would do.

Nothing was free. Any time a Marine spent with a girl cost him money. He paid the girl, and she paid the bar. Although very young, the girls were skilled in the craft of stealing a young man's total attention, often his heart, and shortly after that, some of his money. To be fair, some serious long-term relationships grew out of these encounters; some married, but they were the exception. If a young man became so captivated that he wanted to rescue a young woman from her circumstances, the owners required him to "buy her out" from their bar. Again, nothing was free. The cost to take a woman from a bar was usually all the money a young man had. If he had no money, there were ways he could borrow it.

"Captain Ruthven, Corporal Redfern needs to see the Commanding Officer." It was Sergeant Major Reed. "I think it's a Code Seven." He smiled wryly.

Code Seven was marine-speak for something that I could handle and keep out of the Skipper's office, and it would require a measure of subterfuge and duplicity, a skill I had turned into an ugly craft during my formative years in Canada.

Corporal Redfern was a slight, dark, part Native American Marine, about five foot four, just above the minimum height for the Corps standard. He looked like he was ten. His cheeks were rosy, his eyes like large black buttons. What he lacked in height, he made up for in his enthusiasm when he stepped outside the main gate into the seedy streets of Iwakuni. His service record book reflected frequent engagements with half a dozen of the seediest bars in the town. I can't reveal the entries in his medical record.

"At ease, Corporal Redfern." I smiled. I had an immediate affection for the young Marine. "Tell me about it."

"I need permission to go up to Atsugi and borrow money from the Marine Credit Union, sir." He raised his eyebrows, expecting I might ask him what the money was for. His expectations were half warranted.

"How much money do you need?" It was not an impertinent question. A good part of the responsibility of an Executive Officer was to provide guidance for just such young men as Corporal Redfern, who often made choices that an officer might help him avoid. Spending beyond their means was a constant problem, a distraction to a young man who needed to stay in focus. These troops would move south very soon. They needed to bring everything they were with them. This was difficult when one's heart was trapped in a seedy bar in downtown Iwakuni.

"Two hundred dollars, sir." His eyebrows raised, expecting that I might guess what he was going to buy with just such a sum. He was right again. Two hundred dollars was the standard hit a Marine took to buy a girl out of a bar.

I picked up a stray stack of paper and shook it gently in the air. "Do you know what this is, Corporal Redfern?" I looked at the blank pieces of paper, studying them seriously.

"No, sir." He was squinting now, a bit puzzled.

"Just a minute, Corporal Redfern." I held up my hand as if I had something urgent to take care of. I buzzed the Sergeant Major, and he came in the office. "Sergeant Major, will you take care of these? They were supposed to have been at Wing Headquarters two days ago. What are they still doing on my desk?"

"Sorry, sir," The Sergeant Major nodded at me, trying to guess what I was doing.

I helped him. "If those orders to Danang aren't on the Group Operations Officer's desk today, we'll all be AWOL for the move south. I don't want Corporal Redfern to miss a movement." He had been on the Sutter County with me and had been indoctrinated by the Navy as to the seriousness of missing a movement.

The Sergeant Major looked at Redfern and nodded. "I'll take care of it, sir."

"We're all going south in a couple of days. You, me, everybody. And we cannot allow key people like yourself to leave the base. Hell, I can't leave the base." I looked at him gravely as I lied. "You know, the only reason we're here, is to support the troops in this air group and most of them are down there already."

"I can't leave the base, sir?" His face was growing from pink to purple. I had the distinct sense that he was about to jump over the desk and choke me. I nodded and looked him in the eye. I didn't break lock for a full minute. Presently, tears sprouted from his eyes and his arms fell at his side.

"Grab a seat, Redfern," I said, still maintaining an edge to my voice, and walked around the desk. "There are a lot of sacrifices men are making in this war that are sometimes as painful as taking a bullet." I sat in a chair beside him. "Your name is on the advanced party to Danang. We need you down there. Maybe in six months we can send you R&R to Atsugi, but now we need you in country. It's the only reason any of us are here. There can be no distractions."

He stood up, wiping his face with his cover, reluctant, I was sure for the Sergeant Major to see him crying. "I get it, sir." He squeezed a smile and then shook his head. "I get it."

I wondered if he had "got it." My cunning would be rewarded in my particular hell when I had my final reckoning. I buzzed for the Sergeant Major. "I need to get Redfern on a set of orders real soon, Sergeant Major." I scanned a stack of papers involving Marines with whom I would have to deal with that day. "We need to get him out of Dodge now!" Over one Marine had jumped the fence when he had lost his heart to the first lady to let him get past third base.

"No problem, Captain." He smiled. "Already taken care of, sir. Looks like we're all moving down there real soon."

"I hated to do that. I like Redfern. Need to get him out of here before he thinks he has to marry one of our local ladies."

"Oh, that one's been red flagged, sir. A Pro. She'll just dump Redfern, roll half that two hundred back into the club and keep the rest." He shook his head. "We can send him down in a couple of days to make it look real. Meanwhile, I'll keep him busy this side of the main gate."

"I think he's onto us." I shook my head. We'd been here for a month now. I was about to be reassigned to Marine Fighter Squadron 235. The squadron had just rotated back to Iwakuni from Vietnam to train replacement pilots and add a few experienced new ones. I was one of the new guys.

During my first week in Iwakuni, I was parched for spiritual sustenance of any type. Although in no way religious, I was more into the broad and roomy, all-inclusive school of feeding the soul. The Path I had chosen required I engage in community. I sought the comfort of the base chapel, usually the clearing house for all variety of spiritual outreach. I explained my needs to the chaplain and my main orientation.

"I think I know just what and who you're looking for." This was the least likely chaplain to address my requirements. He was well beyond retirement and his nose was the size of his fist, bright red, doubtless swollen from an excess of spirits. He had stayed too long at the fair and had fallen into easy choices. "A man comes here two nights a week and waits for anyone who might be looking for the kind of company you seek." I returned to the chapel the following night.

He was there.

It was Tuesday evening and Brownie was the only thing in the room besides a few chairs scattered around him in the event others might arrive. He had the settled appearance of one, knowing that they might not show up and hoping that they would not. Accustomed to solitude, it surprised him to see another person in the room. He sat snug into the chair as if he and it were one thing. Huge. I guessed he was nearly sixty, about three hundred pounds, and tall. A great shock of white hair might have added to his height. An intense focus stared at me through heavy lenses with thick, dark frames. He removed his feet from one chair, and he placed a copy of "Doctor Zhivago" on another.

"I like the poetry." He nodded at the book. "It's a wonderful book, but the poetry is exceptional." He pointed to a chair. "Brownie." he said.

"Colin." I replied, not quite as laconically as he. There was something mildly defensive about his manner. His introduction told me more than he probably preferred to reveal. I would bet he was the person who could convince anybody to do anything. He looked like someone who had never felt it necessary to apologize. I wanted to apologize for interrupting a routine with which I supposed he had become enamored. He was reading me as if I were a poker opponent.

I learned in our early meetings that Brownie had been a part of the Marine forces during the Second World War that had worked its way up the Pacific Islands with plans to invade Japan. He had been a member of the Marine band. During combat operations, musicians were stretcher bearers. He retired after the War and stayed in Iwakuni. He had no desire to return to the states.

His heart had been broken long ago. He did not want to go anywhere near that pain again. He married Hisako Otani, a young woman who had been working as a cashier on the base at the Marine Corps Exchange. They moved into a small house in the hills of Iwakuni. They had two children, a boy and girl, then ages six and five.

"Look." He was quick to set some ground rules before we shared the first words. I had barely warmed the chair. "The last guys who were here were all into talking about a 'Higher Power'. You know, God as they understood Him." He leaned toward me with an expression I confused with menace. "Can we not talk about that stuff?"

"Sure." I smiled and opened my arms. "I'm just looking for company. I've got to put myself under house arrest. Back there…" I nodded the general direction of the Officer's Club, "a whole gang of my old buddies are doing what I used to do and that's all I did. I have no business anywhere near that anymore. I don't want to do that." I nudged my chair a little closer to his. "And, I'll do just about anything to avoid it."

The remote suggestion of a smile rippled across his face. "Would you even eat home cooked Japanese food?"

"Hell, yeah." I sat up, smiling. "Show me the way."

He drew me a crude map with large bold strokes. I took a circuitous route through the town into the hills across the Nishiki River. Then up another steep hill into a small neighborhood of small homes surrounded by iron fences. I arrived at a tall fence necessary on the Brown's property to keep two German Shepherds from bounding over the railings and eating a small child.

Brownie's own harsh bark brought the animals to heel and stationed at his side. I peered over the fence and was welcomed by this pretty child's face. He had sent the smallest, Jackie, an adorable little girl bundled up in padded Japanese attire, to open the gate. As I stepped inside, she said in a clear English pronunciation, "Welcome, Colin san."

Through several weeks, while I avoided the fighter pilot theatrics and songs at the Officer's Club, the familiar ring of camaraderie and bonding marinated in alcohol, I became a part of this small family. I had more than my share of camaraderie and bonding for two of me. And I knew where that would take me.

I would run the gauntlet of their raised voices and rows of bars as I pedaled my way to the quiet sanctuary in the neighboring hills, a tranquil comfort and retreat from demons I had sent into exile. I would have plenty of time to walk across the famous Kintai Bridge, see the castle, and maybe hike Kintai Mountain. Right now. I needed to attend to deeper matters. Brownie and his small family fed my body and, with it, my soul.

Hisako was about forty, I guessed. She had been in her teens during the war and worked at the Japanese Officer's dining room at Etajima Naval Academy. Her family lived on the Island of Itsukushima just south of Hiroshima. On August the sixth 1945, she had just returned home from her shift and was going to take a nap. Hisako went to the upper room of her home. Resting her chin on her hands, she looked out the window across Hiroshima Bay when suddenly! "Blue ball in the sky!" She ran downstairs to tell her parents what she had just seen. When she stepped onto the bottom floor, the roof blew off their house.

The Browns were not an ecstatically happy couple. He, it developed, was not a person who got excited about anything. Early on he shared a fragment of his very simple, yet ironically complicated philosophy. "Colin." He always waited until he was sure he had my attention, as if he was only going to say this once. "Take nothing so serious, but that you can't just get up and walk away from it." There lay the icy simplicity. His creed. The mechanics of his belief, to me, were not that simple. It was something he could do readily, but that would challenge my nascent understanding. "The only thing that's happening is what's happening right now. Pay attention to that, and only that. Be present and don't get attached to anything that doesn't fit." I would reflect on Brownie's ethos as I cycled back to the base, trying to find room for it in my burgeoning spiritual context.

The evening when I had called Dick B., on the first of December 1961, I knew I had lost my soul and would do anything to retrieve it. Now, with but a bare beginning back to innocence, I was with a man who had evidently parked a good part of his soul and still stays sober. I would learn much later that Brownie's soul had gone nowhere. Who and what he really was. His soul was speaking directly through Brownie. I just had the wrong idea of what that should look like.

He understood that most of us mortals could only see ourselves in relation to someone else or something else. They needed a human context. I don't think Brownie really needed any of that. He was his own context. Hugh Brown had animals and children to complete the masquerade. He saw the world, cynically, as a joke. Yet he had a reverence for the creatures within it. He spoke often of the symbiosis between the animals and the world, how it all supported itself in an exotic ecosystem. He spoke of matters and used terms which I had not yet encountered. I would need what he was teaching me to mediate a very naïve set of spiritual references. My problem was then as they would continue to be: how things are bounced against how I think they should be.

I met Brownie two nights a week while I settled into the squadron. In the meantime, I invested myself in self-appointed spiritual studies. I would not bother Brownie with the mention of God. It wasn't necessary. I felt it was implied in everything. God is everything there is and everything there iis God. He didn't need an explanation. I think this bothered Brownie. People trying to tell him what he already believed and understood. It needed no words. I didn't evade the topic, but the space I had left provided him with an opportunity to bring it up by himself if he wanted. He was like many so-called atheists, who only thought they didn't believe, but were in fact just angry that they were being asked to believe in a man-made definition of what was irrefutably there and needed no explanation. "Do you know, Colin, that in some religions, and many of the Eastern teachings, it is forbidden to use the word, God?" That was as close as he got to talking about it for a while.

He had been talking about the size of the dolphin's brain and how sophisticated its thought processes were. He thought they had deeper access to the intuition than other animals, certainly humans. Humans had layers of artificial context built into their already limited understanding. All of this blocked access to intuition and the vital sixth sense. He read vastly. That was all he did except to take care of the two large dogs and his children. "About this power greater than me?" He began one day weeks into our friendship.

I nodded, feeling we were about to step into deeper water and plumb the depths into which I might submerge.

"Me, sitting in this chair is bigger than me." He looked at me like he was looking for permission to leave the room. "Me plus the chair is more than me. That's a power greater than myself. Right?" He beamed.

"Absolutely." I looked at him a bit amazed at this barebone simplicity coming from such elegant intelligence. "If that works for you, that's all that matters. It doesn't matter what anyone else thinks. You can believe anything that works for you." That was the end of any conversation with Brownie about a Power Greater than Himself. I added what I had been taught on the beach, "All that was necessary was a willingness to believe. The willingness brought your belief to the surface from where it had always been."

I had never seen before, nor have I seen since a more sincere willingness to believe than this genius asking a novitiate permission to believe what was unavoidably installed in his old soul.

I was pedaling back to the base. I crossed the bridge and glided down the slope of a hill lined with soba shops and tofu parlors, small crowds of Japanese. They went simply and quietly about their business without a single military uniform in sight. I was ruminating on my conversation with Brownie. The thrum of the bicycle sprocket ran a rhythmic riff to my thoughts. I suddenly had to stop and sit on the curb. I felt myself getting emotional.

The total innocence of one of the most intelligent minds I had ever encountered. His willingness to believe anything beyond his disbelief for license to believe. He was asking me, a kid compared to his intellectual stature, for permission to believe his simple belief. What had hit me the hardest was the faith of such a brilliant mind to believe in something so rudimentary just so he could be allowed into the Deal. It all spoke to an enormous but childlike willingness. God would do the rest. He had more faith than I did. He was also infinitely more honest.

I sat in a ready room chair of Marine Fighter Attack Squadron 235's newly renovated spaces. Major Carl Olsen, an old friend from VMF 312, was the Executive Officer of the squadron. He was trying to wrap his brain around the picture of me not drinking, nor pressing the edge of what I could get away with. He said it one day, "It's like you don't have to try so hard anymore, Animal. You used to work so hard just to be seen."

I replied, "Yeah, everything's happening for me now. I just have to let it happen."

Paul Sigmund had expressed it better than anyone shortly after I had stopped drinking, "Colin, what the hell happened to you? Three months ago, you were a poet. Now you're an old man."

"That's the deal, Carl," I explained, "I'm not who I was, I'm who I am. Haven't had a drink for nearly two years." I hesitated, wondering if I could explain the factual truth. "God's truth, Carl, is that I wasn't who I was back then. I was who I thought you needed me to be."

"That's too deep for me, Colin. You just lost me." He held up both his hands. "But who you are right now is easier to be with. It feels real." He rustled through some papers on his desk. "And you don't even want to drink? Like, not even at happy hour?"

"I won't be going to happy hour, Carl." I shook my head. "And I have no desire to drink, at all."

"Jesus, what the hell will you do?" He looked totally confused.

"Oh, I'll be just fine," I said. "I'll just be."

Carl gave me a fishy, side-long smile, holding a hand in the air, quietly asking me to stop. He smiled. "The Skipper will not like it at all. He wants all hands at the bar. It's where he does most of his business. Nothing makes sense outside the sound of rattling ice cubes and rolling dice." He was shaking his head. "He has you slated for S-4, logistics."

"Isn't that a field grade position?" I asked, mulling over the deal about happy hour and occupying a key department head job.

"That's right." He was smiling.

"What?" I asked, totally puzzled.

"Well, it's not my job to tell you, but your name is on the selection list for Major. Skipper got an advanced copy of the dispatch. It's also one reason you're in the squadron. We're weak on field grade and we really need previous F8 experience. You also went through the attack syllabus at El Toro and they say you've forgotten how to drink, but you have not forgotten how to fly."

The orders to leave MABS 13 and be transferred to Marine Fighter Squadron 235 came in at about the same time as my promotion for Major. Dick Tomlinson handed me the warrant and his gold oak leaves, just as he had promised.

"You must have sent a hell of fitness report to Headquarters Marine Corps." I said and thanked him. "I'd buy you drinks all night if I was still a drinking man," I added, staring down at the document that made it official.

"You also got a letter of commendation from the Navy for your job on the LST. The gang up at the Captain's desk in D.C. has been sitting on a lot of your history and put it in someone's lower drawer." He was shaking my hand. "You pulled it off, Animal."

If I had learned nothing from my ten years as an incompetent officer, it was that somewhere in the pipeline of whatever job you have, there's someone who knows what they're doing. And they'll cover for you while you grow up. And it's usually the senior Staff

NCO or a Warrant Officer, or one hell of a special field grade officer like Colonel Jay Hubbard. The secret hidden behind the lesson of incompetence was that these men were experts in their specialty to make choices, and they usually made the right ones. They often understood you did not know what you were doing, so they would make the right choices for you. As long as you brought something to the party, they would take care of the rest for you.

There was no secret that I could fly, which was the primary mission of the squadron, the point of the spear. If I took care of that, a senior Staff NCO or Warrant Officer would take care of my collateral duties, but it was unfair to assume that this would happen for an entire career. I had to show up eventually if I was going to wear gold leaves.

They assigned me the S-4 position, Logistics Officer.

I had a conference with Warrant Officer Barrister, who had been immersed in aviation logistics since the Korean War, and I clarified I saw him as the expert. I had the head job; I would keep my eye on things, but I trusted entirely that he knew what he was doing. It's one tenet of big business: hire the experts and let them do their job. Then stay out of their way but be cognizant and available. This formula fit in perfectly with The Gunner's idea of how logistics was going to work in the combat zone. But I was no longer hiding. I flew the hell out of the airplanes, but I was also there. I was present to do the job.

Lieutenant Colonel Ed Rogal was the Commanding Officer, a veteran of the latter part of the Second World War and the Korean War. Major Don Dilley was Operations and Fred Vanous, Intelligence. Rocky Plant had the admin desk. I felt like I was back in the Checkerboard Ready Room, only this time I could see what was happening and I was invariably on time.

I didn't know what Carl was talking about when he said the squadron needed Majors. VMF 235 was already top heavy with Majors. Then it occurred to me that the rank equated with experience, and we were all loaded with training in the Crusader and were dying to try it out for real. The Marine Corps was going to get a return on what she had invested in us, and we were all slathering dogs wanting to get 'in country.' Sadly, there was a war, but while there was one, I wanted to be in on it.

The squadron deployed to Okinawa for a tune-up on our bombing procedures. The airfield at Kadena closed if a U2 was taking off or landing, but the air base at Naha was ideal for our operations. We were the only squadron on the flight line. Operations were swift and uncomplicated. After three weeks bombing a hapless little island in the ocean, we were almost over trained and eager to go south.

The people in my world and many of those in the squadron had known me in a previous life as renegade, with no sense of duty or ethics. They had kept me around because I could fly and draw anecdotal cartoons of everyone else's misadventures. Now they were seeing me in a new moral structure with ethics and values and did not know where to put me. Had they never known me, it would have been easy. They would not have had to get around the previous picture that had of me in their memory.

Anyone with even the slightest spiritual orientation would have presumed that I had become religious. Members of assorted churches spoke to me in an ecumenical baby talk hoping to win me to their congregation. With one religion so like the next, I could easily be flipped, they supposed. I was thus co-opted to the closest bidder, the one that most closely resembled our mutual belief.

In my home, my mother taught me to be irreligious. She embraced all faiths. She believed that if I chose one specific belief, I automatically had to exclude others and joined them in the war to make their god better than others. Her anthem was to embrace it all as leading to the one large Truth. Religion did not have the monopoly on God. If you looked closely, you'd understand: everything we see and know implies the very Presence of God. Mother believed that religion and science, philosophy, psychology and all other disciplines were all incomplete without one another. "One day there will be a synthesis of all these disciplines. Everything is God, Colin."

Bobby Turner, one of those who had never entered an Officer's Club and so had never attended happy hour, assessed that my conversion closely inclined to the fold of his Forever to Be Unrevealed Evangelical Church. All I required was to be taken through the occluded motions and the forbidden rite of passage that made this church unique. My behavior already spoke to many of their tenets. The only adjustment required to turn me from my hedonistic ways was to learn the secret handshake and utter the incantations.

I did not know that this was Bobby's intent when he invited me to the home of this Army family on Okinawa. I would do anything to avoid the magnetic force field of the music, songs and laughter emanating from the Officer's Club, so I gave no thought to Bobby's invitation to a dinner and harmless fellowship. I liked Bobby. He was easy to be with.

Okinawa was a floating military installation: Army, Navy, Air Force and Marine occupying every square acre of the Island. It was a critical piece of U.S. Government leased real estate and we were not going anywhere. The town of Koza sat at the heart of the Island. It was here that I was introduced to the Vincent McCormicks. Their home literally creaked beneath the burden of more visitors than could safely fit in the house, their weight lightened by the belief that their denomination rose above all others.

I couldn't help but notice the hush that fell over the throng when we arrived. Equally, the special deference given me of a preferred seat. They drew my attention to a large plate of assorted sandwiches and an unidentified mealy dip. They invited me to refresh and nourish myself. As if to announce royalty, the muffled chords of music emanated from a hidden space behind a thick purple curtain. A freakishly tall man wearing a lavender to purple robe and tall hat sprang from behind the curtain. At this point Bobby disappeared as if he were but transportation and would wait for me at a later hour once this guy pulled something from his hat or I disappeared somewhere into the fold.

Four children scurried from beneath the curtain and assembled a fold up screen. The tall man advanced to the center of the room and stood hugely taller than he was in the very tall hat. The music was reduced to an eerie white noise, with something that sounded like muffled screams in the background. A telescopic pointer suddenly sprang from the sleeve of the reverend's robe, the end of which tapped upon the screen and the show began.

I was given a guided tour through Biblical times according to the understanding of the Forever Unnamed Evangelical Church of Koza. I was not entirely uneducated in religious matters. I was aware of the Virgin Birth and Christ's mission and the further adventures of Paul. However, I was amazed and newly edified to discover additional players previously held secret and known only to the Forever Unnamed Evangelical Church of Koza. Some of their numbers had been on the planet since before Christ. One of these, the main protagonists apparently, still lived and would always live. To my utter disbelief, the guy in the tall hat was one of them. I had barely time to absorb this arcane data before he began activating a secret clicker that changed the slides.

It took two hours, plus the replenishment of a stack of sandwiches and dip onto my plate for the presentation to conclude. For the vast number of people in attendance, the Reverend McCormick's breathing was the only other sound in the spaces, except in the distance the unearthly and awful ripple of running water.

At the conclusion of the presentation, there was a collective sigh of reverent awe from the multitude, followed by an atmosphere of imminent revelation. The silence lasted the time it would take to get this assembly of the devout across the Red Sea. The void seemed to elicit some response. I looked around to find all eyes on me, anticipating that the Reverend McCormick's revelation should overwhelm me. Instead, I had a question.

"What is that sound I keep hearing upstairs?" I asked, unsure if I was allowed to enquire. I had an intuition of what his reply would be.

"It is your baptism being prepared, Brother Ruthven."

I turned to Bobby Turner, who was now standing breathless at the periphery of the multitude, anticipating my imminent immersion. I said, "I have another question."

"And that is?" The Reverend McCormick's eyes were half closed, anticipating the definitive question of innocence that would elicit from him the wisdom that he had been prepared through all eternity to convey.

"I wonder if I may ask Brother Turner to please get Brother Ruthven the hell out of here?"

The Brothers Turner and Ruthven drove back to Naha exchanging only occasional conversation, none of it religious, awkwardly directed to matters professional, primarily our departure for Danang, The Republic of Vietnam the following day.

6

Da Nang

I led a section (two planes) out of Iwakuni early one morning in June,1966. My wingman, First Lieutenant Jim Lucas, (Luke) and I filed for Kadena Air Force Base, Okinawa, a very busy runway during that time in our history. They forecast the weather for a broken overcast at about fifteen hundred feet, with occasional thunderstorms, common for that time of year.

We made a section instrument penetration, the same approach into Kadena where we lost Bill O'Rourke back in 1961, during that infamous tour with Marine Fighter Squadron 312. True to weather prediction, the runway had just been lubricated with a generous film of rain from one of their famous thunderstorms. We broke out of the overcast at about eight hundred feet. The sun broke out with us and reflected its glare off a one-inch layer of rain that had not quite drained from the runway surface. I should have let Luke land first and taken it around and landed behind him. Instead, I asked and was cleared for a section landing, a performance that both we and the tower will probably remember for a while.

Our planes touched down together, pointing in the same direction. We stayed off the brakes, allowing the momentum of our approach to keep us heading in the same direction and decelerating down the duty runway. We were slow enough, and I hoped we could come to a stop without applying brakes and thus inducing a skid.

We will never know for sure which one of us either applied a little rudder or just the breath of a brake, causing the other to adjust, sending us both into a slow gentle turn toward one another. Neither of us broadcast a word as both airplanes turned three hundred and sixty degrees around one other, gliding on the invisibly wet surface. Somehow, purely by divine chance, we avoided colliding. I will never forget the size of Luke's eyes, nor will he forget mine as we passed one another in a lethal pirouette to a miraculous safe stop at the end of the runway. Our wing tips barely missed colliding during what felt like two complete turns. As we taxied to the chocks, I looked up at the tower to see a small crowd giving us an enthusiastic thumbs up. We shut down and sashayed to the Operations shack, as if this was nothing out of the ordinary in the lives of Major Ruthven and Lieutenant Lucas. We did this all the time.

It was one of those moments where I was aware of how uncertain it all is. What was wrong with me to be in the throes of dangerous possibilities about which I had no control and feel afterwards that I had just had fun? I suppose that this was the beginning of it all. Welcome to the combat zone, Colin, and you haven't even arrived yet.

That afternoon we made an uneventful section landing at Cubi Point. We planned to remain overnight and to fly into Da Nang the following morning.

The near collision on the duty runway at Kadena might just have whetted my appetite for more adrenalin inducing action. I had barely removed my torso harness when I felt the magnetic pull of Olongapo. What viable business does a guy barely into recovery from a once and always incurable malady have going into the heart of all darkness again? The only thing happening in Olongapo was very loose women, dangerous men, and a lot of booze. But for the booze, it all still sounded very appealing. I had lost the compulsion to drink, but evidently not the need for a bit of excitement. We burn some appetites into the bone. In some areas of my life, I continued to test the edge.

Maybe it was more curiosity than compulsion that drove me to the Roundup Bar in the very bowels of Olongapo. I remembered exactly where it was, although my recollection came from a dark period when every moment of that time was the return to a bad dream. I only thought it had been fun. I sat at the bar and ordered a coke. I looked at the mirror across rows of assorted alcoholic beverages. An unfamiliar face looked back at me. I was no longer that guy.

As I was looking through the mirror, a figure stood up in the background. It stood still for a long time, then loomed slowly toward me from a darkened corner of the room. I turned and looked at an old woman. The eyes were familiar, but the rest of her was dissipated and almost destroyed, barely a vestige of who I knew was in there.

"Captain Ruptan," it said.

"My God. Rita!" I tried to gather myself. I pulled it together and searched inside for something that would lighten the moment. "I hope I haven't missed the fish fry."

"You have come back," she said, it sounded as if she really believed that after all this time, I had returned to be with her. I had not the heart to convince her otherwise. As artfully as possible, I tried to veer the conversation away from any such illusion. I inhaled a lung-full of a familiar dark cigarette from across the room.

"What have I missed, Rita?" I smiled. The line on her face that was once her mouth broke into a semblance of what used to be a vivacious grin. "What's happened in here since that guy hit me in the head with the chair?"

A stream of uninterrupted Tagalog and broken English gave me the condensed version of the bad dream that was her life. Translated, and I will always remember: "Please don't come back and tell me I have no life at all. Life goes on the way it always has and always will for me. And here you are after being out there around the world and deep into a life that has meaning."

She walked away. I left The Roundup Bar, wishing that I had not come.

Fifteen minutes inbound to Da Nang, Air Control handed us off to The USAF and Combat Reporting Center (CRC) Call Sign, Panama. This was the agency that controlled all fighter operations in I Corps, theZ northernmost portion of three segments of military operations in South Vietnam. My first view of Vietnam came out of a mist, most of it from rising smoke and brown dust. From thirty thousand feet descending, the land looked totally intact as if its smooth moss-like surface had never been touched. The closer we flew toward the entry point to the duty runway, the more I could see what we were doing to this land that was not ours. So why were we here?

It was a different country, a strange language. It would be a very different place when we left it. Once a verdant paradise, Vietnam would become a cratered panorama of scorched forest and brown earth.

Leaving aside the implements of war, the hardware, tactics and feet on the ground, Vietnam was more an attitude than a war. It was an ugly, unpopular war that had the opportunity to look good if it had ended when it could have. It might remind a prizefighter of a match that he needed to win in the early rounds or not at all. But it went to the full fifteen, a tedious contest of attrition until our fans in the States and some of our own troops were cheering for the opponent.

Operation Rolling Thunder, the code name for the extensive aerial operation in Vietnam, began on the 2nd of March 1965, and, although it was only meant to last eight weeks, did not end until the 2nd of November 1968. It was our war, the war that many of us had trained for since Korea and could not wait to fight. Ask most fighter pilots, Navy, Air Force or Marine and they would have told you that if the government had threatened to shut down hostilities before they had their chance to take part, the pilots would have been disappointed.

If you were from firebase Mai Loc, you had a secret handshake; if you were on a River Patrol Boat, yours was different. It took half a day for members of a fireteam in the jungle to go through their private ritual. The emphasis was on distinction and not much on unity. Division among the units flourished as the war drug on. An uglier than most statistic crept into the narrative: not how many of theirs we killed, but how many of our Staff NCOs and junior officers were being fragged by their own troops.

A national narrative wrapped itself around "In-Country" culture. It had a hard time shutting down. It was only a matter of time before it replicated in Vietnam a sentiment widely shared in the States. At home, they protested what they could not see and so had everything to fear. Those in the combat zone, close to the conflict, provided a more detailed picture that was worthy of their worry. It was, after all the Sixties, a time when a country badly needed something to protest as the fabric of the "establishment" was fraying. The Collective Consciousness just needed to say something-anything. Vietnam was an ideal context in which to say it.

For guys like me who spent the war largely in an air-conditioned cockpit, delivering ordnance to troops on the ground as close as I could get to the bad guys and hoping I would not hit one of our own, the war was relatively easy. I did not see the same war as did the Marine on Firebase Rendezvous. I did not see the whites of the enemies' eyes. I did not carry torn up bodies to helicopters that were taking fire. I would not become a number in the grim body count. I left Vietnam without a scratch. Every night I slept in a cot and I remained relatively clean; I don't think I missed a twenty-four-hour period without a shower. I shaved daily and ate in the Officer's mess. With apologies to those who suffered and still do, I enjoyed the hell out of two combat tours. I'd trained for over ten years to get there, and I was willing to be used in any capacity.

This is not about how I fought the war, but mostly how I did not. It was not an especially heroic tour, nor was it unheroic. I was there, and I went home with the "I was there" collection of medals and awards. I did my share. I'll save you the heroics that those who were at the point of the spear, many who felt the opponent's spear, have already written. My name is not on the long black wall of 58,000.

This is about the inner engagement I had with myself- my private Vietnam before I got to Vietnam.

I remained clean and sober throughout the entire tour. If I had put my hand outside the fence long enough, someone would have handed me some good dope, maybe high-grade grass laced with heroin. My war comprised an antiseptic straight line from my hooch to the flight line, with no detours to the club. I could hear the voices from my ugly past every night. The oldies and goodies I had sung in Beaufort, Atsugi, and Kingsville. I had worn out the Far East Asia song book until I shut down my game. I focused on what was going on in my small part of the war, which was plenty for a wounded and clouded mind. We had more trouble keeping the troops out of trouble than we did keeping the airplanes in the air. As recreational as most folks kept their leisure moments between missions, I'm surprised we didn't get swept into the sea long before it happened.

Vietnam wasn't going anywhere. There was something about both the inner and outer workings that kept it just where it was until something else happened. On the inside, someone way up the line would not let us shut it down. On the outside, at home, the pundits juggled the balls till they fell to their political advantage. There was something happening more important than what we were doing, and few of us knew what that something was. It has always been the way of wars that they are a device that serves nothing to its own purpose but is the instrument of other concerns. In our little corner of the world, which largely comprised close air support missions for our Marines on the ground, we operated in a relatively small sector and received a small ration of the daily frag from Saigon.

From the cooks to the Commandant, everything that happens in the Marine Corps is for the guy on the ground, the Marine with his face pressed against the fire. Most of us fighter types were trained in air-to-air combat missions for which we were infrequently scheduled, unless you call fighter escort for Buffy Arclight missions of three B 52s or Barrier Combat Air Patrol missions along the coast between North Vietnam and a carrier air group a fighter mission.

We flew no further north than a southern portion of North Vietnam designated Route Package One, and occasionally into Laos. Most of our work was in I Corps, close to home, which, for fixed wing Marine aviation, was Da Nang or Chu Lai. I never saw a MiG. I was never in a turning fight. In this tour, I forgot what fighter aviation was all about. I learned to love air to ground in any flavor: napalm, bombs of all sizes, rockets and strafing, cluster bombs. The troops loved the Crusader for our four twenty-millimeter cannons. We would get down to tree level and spray the enemy. Day or night and in all weather, they called us in. I wondered if there might not be more that we could do. For the small trickle of smoke rising above an enormous jungle, I often thought that our bombs could do very little. The troops loved our airplanes because they were pretty. As if daring to have them shot out of the sky, we painted their noses red with white stars.

Our gunsight was designed for a solution against a maneuvering airplane but readily adapted for air-to-ground close air support. We worked out our own handmade set of rules, pipper-drop and lag formulas. Testimony to the diversity of the F8 Crusader, it could carry two tons of assorted trash beneath one of the finest wings ever designed for air-to-air combat. Bombs in all flavors and sizes 250, 500 and thousand pounds with straight fins or snake eye for low altitude delivery. Napalm was a favorite close-in weapon, as were 2.75- and five-inch Zuni rockets. The squadron stood on a twenty-four-hour hot pad, as well as the usually scheduled daily missions. Once we had set up shop, it was business as usual. The Wing established a predictable routine. The troops counted the days on their short timer calendars.

I shared a hooch with three other pilots. Rocky Plant whom I had flown with in VMF 312, and Ed (Mofak) Cathcart. We had enlisted at the same time and attended flight school together. Also, Hondo Ondrick, all of us majors. Many of the experienced company grade pilots (lieutenant and captain) early in the war were transferred to postings in the ground component: air liaison and forward air controllers. It mattered little that there was a plethora of majors in the squadron. What they needed was experience.

Very early one morning, we heard the first familiar howl of Russian rockets coming in at us from the surrounding hills just outside the perimeter. It took little coaxing for the four of us to dig a small bomb shelter beneath our hooch. It was never a direct hit, but close enough to dislodge our insulation and send the four of us piling out of the hooch and into the underground condo. Small flairs on tiny parachutes fell constantly, illuminating Da Nang throughout the night. These flares, very plentiful, packed in large Styrofoam boxes that were discarded in the logistics dump. Enterprising to a fault, Hondo commandeered a six by six truck and transported enough styrofoam boxes to insulate the upper inside of our hooch. Rocky Plant got a small air conditioner. I wired in Armed Forces Radio music. Donald Trump had never lived so well.

Housekeeping arrived weekly to tidy up. The ladies felt insufficient to the task when they were met with a hut filled with Styrofoam cartons piled on the floor from the previous night's rocket attack. They just walked away to clean up the next hut. We would have to re-install our ceiling. The only injuries I incurred during the war were from falling styrofoam.

The officer's living area was a complex of sturdily built hooches in a neat circle surrounding a large community latrine. Central to most of our memory, but infrequently commemorated, was the singular stench of human waste burning in large drums. That, and of a strange pungent fair common to the Vietnamese palate floating across the barbed wire perimeter. There was some discussion about which aroma carried the biggest punch. Vietnamese women cleaned the spaces, ranging in age from teen to late octogenarian, judging from the condition of their teeth, which were different shades of black from incessant chewing on betel nuts. The ejected aroma from these nuts released a mild narcotic, a substance I would have taken had I lived in these climes, totally unsuited to a boy who grew up in Western Canada's temperate ambiance. Background to the atmosphere inside the compound was the staccato riff of the Vietnamese language, harsh and oddly musical, like someone beating on a hollow brass bowl while humming.

Avenues constructed out of metal packing pallets lined the space between the hooches. These led to the showers and other conveniences, like the laundry and commissary. I experienced not a single shortage of anything I needed except drinkable water, which was substituted for by vast warehouses filled with carbonated beverages. Some represented an assault on the blood sugar, while the secret ingredient in the sugar-free Diet Rite Cola removed the enamel from the sturdiest American teeth.

I was wide awake and eager to get into the action. I now had a clear head and could retain the intelligence brief each morning. I ate up as many of my missions as I could and some others of the pilots who were indisposed. I wanted to fly because that's what I did. I never considered it combat. Again, apologies to those who still have shrapnel in their bodies. After three quarters of a century, I can confess that whether I was in the worst night emergency mission beneath a low overcast or standing on the hot pad, I enjoyed the work.

I was debriefing in an intelligence hut after one of these missions. I looked across the desk at a face that I seemed to recognize. He was not wearing wings. We had gone through the debriefing process, a routine that lost meaning with its mechanical rote process with little significance to report in our small corner of the war. I stared across the table and said:

"Angie, is that you?" I didn't want to waste the Intelligence Officer's time. He had another flight waiting for him in the next tent.

"I wondered when you'd wake up, Colin." He laughed and came around the table. We gave one another an awkward hug, with my wingman looking awkwardly on. "The story has it you've become a warrior monk or else you've taken on an alternate identity." He stepped back. "Goddam, I don't know what it is, but you are really different."

"Yeah, I've got some of the old guys confused. Shit, I'm confused." We both sat down. My wingman excused himself and left the room. Angie was clearly an intelligence officer, otherwise he would not be working on the other side of a debriefing hut. "What you doin' over on that side of the table?" I asked. They restricted most Intelligence Officers from flight status because they were a security risk if captured. They knew too much.

"I turned in my wings, Colin," he said apologetically. "I can't seem to make myself drop bombs on these people." Angie looked at his watch and glanced into the other room where a couple of flights were waiting to debrief. "I know where you live. Why don't I drop by your hooch later and we'll talk? Okay?"

Could this really be the Angie who was present when Hastings slipped us the Absinth and we all slid into an alternate state of consciousness? He was the guy I'd talk to after a long bender late into the eleventh hour when everyone else was sleeping or had found better friends. He was the original twilight guy, the one you'd be talking to after the action, and you'd cut through all the bullshit it took to get drunk. You could no longer get drunk but could talk about why you were still trying. We had become close, call it intimate. I could have pretended to be a poet, but Angie was a poet. Very well educated, spoke a couple of languages, and usually had his head in the classics while I had my face peering at him through the prism of a vodka blurred glass.

Angie was also the guy who called on the first of December 1964 to tell me he was flying into Kingsville on his way to Beaufort that afternoon. That morning, I had planned to quit drinking once and for all. I had tried countless times before, but on this day, I was determined to quit drinking. I knew I would have to drink with Angie if he came through Kingsville. I couldn't disappoint him. We'd hopefully engage in that evanescent dialogue that most drinkers look for. The words and their meaning disappear as soon as they're spoken in those early hours of the following day when two guys are alone or with a special friend, looking at the rays of a new day coming over the sidewalks of a strange early morning street. I had vowed to stop drinking that day. Now I would have to drink because Angie was coming in.

Later, he called to say he couldn't make it. Predictably, I was at the bar that night counting the drinks.

That was the night I called the used linoleum salesman. I've not had a drink since. Angie had to have been what the gurus were calling a divine catalyst, an instrument to synchronicity. He had been an agent in my transformation. He had been with me during my worst drinking and had arrived at the turning point. Someone real smart told me that from life to life these same catalyst agents show up in a different guise to effect major shifts on one's path. Without these entities, we would not have a life.

Now, almost five years later, we were meeting halfway across the world. Tell me Nature does not have Her own agenda just to keep us confused. The rest of the hooch was at the Officer's Club. The familiar songs and chants floated across the compound as we sat across the large round table where I drew cartoons.

"It was that exchange tour I had with the RAF, Colin." Highly intuitive, he had known 'Animal' never fit. "I was flying The British Electric Lightning at Coltishall in Norfolk, England. Later we deployed to Singapore."

"Fast airplane, Angie." I nodded enviously. "Over and under Rolls-Royce engines inside the fuselage."

"Right. You would have loved it, Colin. Mach two and a hell of a rate of climb. An interceptor, not a fighter." He laughed. "They would have loved you. I see how honestly you come by your thirst for the brew. There was another Ruthven in the squadron. Pronounced his name Riven."

"We're all disgusting drunks with the morals of a transsexual pedophile." I took a long pull on my Diet Rite Cola and ran my tongue across my teeth.

"The Brits have a very objective and a totally realistic view of our so-called war." He sounded bitter and was no longer apologetic. "I spent over a year in that squadron with a lot of intelligent people who do not have a dog in the fight and can see past all the rationalization behind the war. I took their premise on entirely, Colin." He shook his head. "Then, of all ironies, I got orders to Vietnam."

"They didn't threaten to release you when you turned in your wings?"

"Oh, hell no." He replied. "There's a gang of us. All with too much experience to waste. Most of us went to the Intelligence branch. They put me behind a desk until I cease to be useful." He smiled wryly. "So much for my dreams of becoming Commandant."

Like Jim Angleton, I had no pretensions to promotion, so had not groomed myself for advancement. I didn't look at the flights with an idea of promotion or prestige. The missions were sufficient unto themselves. I could think of nothing I would rather have been doing. As a single man and free from the desire to drink, I stood the hot pad when some had party plans. It thrilled me to provide for the current version of an old Colin Ruthven, some amusement. I realized that anyone who still had wild oats to sow would sow them. With the possibility of being blown out of the sky, be as crazy as you need to be.

They asked me more than once if it wasn't a lonely place, isolated, just outside the herd. I'd listen to "The Stones" and songs from the Far East Fighter Pilot Song book rising from the Officer's Club, just beyond the Skipper's hooch near the Intelligence compound. I had learned the difference between loneliness and aloneness. Brownie helped me find the guy who could be alone and find that sacred solitude. He was a mystic. Brownie taught me how solitude is the sanctuary of spiritual unfolding.

Angie and I spent one night exchanging the maps of our different paths since that tour in Japan. We had taken diametrically distinct vectors into a place where we could no longer find the friendship we had. Our previous selves fit into that time when I could fall apart in the night, and he would help me get it back together again the following day. We were not who we were. He agreed we could not ask ourselves to be those guys again. Angie convinced me we could not find a context without it insulting what we had. It seemed cold, but it was real. We parted ways and just nodded at one another during debriefs and dinner.

Unless I was flying or working around the squadron area, I sat at a round table in our hooch surrounded by my drawing materials. I drew cartoons, sometimes caricatures, for which they would know me more than they remembered me for my flying. The pilots would likely forget me for any heroics I might have exhibited or for my flying prowess, but they would remind me of a particular cartoon I had probably forgotten I had drawn.

By 1966, Rock-and-roll had fully established itself "In Country." Of course, the constant chant, "I just got to get out of this place, if it's the last thing I ever do," was an incessant, tiresome anthem. I had my own music, a fan of Armed Forces Radio in Vietnam and a fast-growing Rock-and-roll enthusiast. Like several of my younger squadron pilots, I had a small cassette tape player and a growing collection of music. It was a simple task to patch my cassette deck or Armed Forces Radio into my headset. Shortly after takeoff, I'd turn on my tape and for the rest of the flight and during ordnance delivery listen to the Rolling Stones, Jimi Hendricks, Bob Dylan, The Doors and others. Often when a pilot was rolling in on a bombing run talking to a forward air controller, anyone else on the frequency could hear the faint beat in the background of Bob Dylan singing, "All Along the Watchtower."

"There must be some way out of here"
Said the joker to the thief
There's too much confusion
I can't get no relief."

There would be no relief for a while. Still a while to go to get where it had to be. Everything leads somewhere. Ask the Great Constant. We're always at the end point but never done.

My priority was my squadron duties, plus I would fly all my missions and any others. I became a scavenger, sometime volunteering for some unpopular flights like late night and early, early morning missions. I'm in a sound sleep, but barely, for the sound of artillery and a gunship in the distance. The steady thrum of a heartbeat is coaxing me deeper into the forbidden realm of unspoken secrets. Then a soft shake awakens me to the wide-awake reality of a driving monsoon on the hooch's tin roof. A corporal in a rain hood, rain dripping onto my bunk, wakes me for the 3 a.m. launch. Cold and wet, still half-asleep, I am driven in the rain to the flight line. Rain was a constant, then a steaming jungle heat with daytime hot pad temperatures at 120 degrees. Adding to the emptiness, it can be freezing in Vietnam during the winter. In December, I huddled in the night for warmth or to stay dry. The drive to the flight line dipped into ruts of mud and puddle rain flying up onto a flight gear, steadily getting wetter and dirtier. Uncomfortable, sometimes miserable, but as I remember it, I miss it.

We launch into full instrument conditions until the flight breaks out over a moon lit cloudscape. The thick layer, like a half-darkened mattress, will not share our concern for what's happening below. We break back down under the overcast, the small bubble of air between my wingman and myself pressed against the underside of my wing. I can feel him so close. The bubble between our wings pushes against me. We drone around beneath, sometimes breaking into the flossy underbelly of the clouds, laying ordnance to the static cries of the ground or an airborne controller. We completed our mission. I think of the ones down there, left with the rest of the night and an enemy, a constant presence who might or might not even be there. Fully awake, we RTB (return to base) on instrument approach after a nameless, meaningless rain of wrath onto the jungle canopy. I break through an overcast to find the runway immediately before me and barely visible. Rain sweeps across flooded asphalt. I drop the hook and allow the rest to happen without me. I clear the arresting gear and I watch my wingman take the gear as I taxi back to the fuel pits.

Taxiing in a monsoon is more difficult than flying in a blinding overcast and dense fog. They mandated Da Nang tower and ground control to man the facility with Vietnamese and English-speaking personnel. More times than I could remember, a Vietnamese controller was directing me somewhere, but I did not know where. The language is a foreign song that could take me anywhere. If I asked for an American controller, I got nobody and very often had to fight to get clearance to cross a runway I couldn't see.

Our squadron was in Da Nang on the night a Vietnamese controller cleared a Marine A6 Intruder for take-off just as a giant Air Force Transport filled with acetylene was cleared to cross the active duty runway. The explosion brought the entire compound from their sleep into the night. We thought the VC had nuked us. One more time, I awake to an explosion and a rain of Styrofoam boxes.

Secondary to the squadron mission, but primarily to the long-term saving of my soul was establishing my spiritual regimen. I had no contact with another similarly wounded soul. Contact with others was an essential ingredient to the maintenance and growth of what amounted to a total transformation in consciousness and being. I received regular tapes from friends with whom I had grown up in the West End of Vancouver. The dispensary had a reel-to-reel recorder and player. This became an alternate headquarters and a frequent haunt where I became recognized and identified as someone who might help another floater among the players. As Nature has a way of doing, she soon brought someone to the help.

A certain Staff Sergeant in our motor pool who we will call Wally was best friends with another Staff Sergeant we will call Roy. During the hours of daylight, they were the best of friends and had been for as long as they had been in the Marine Corps. At night with alcohol added to the friendship, they became instant enemies, attempting to settling differences sometimes real, but mostly imagined. The longer and the more frequently they fought, the better, or worse, they became at it. My inner shrink imagined they were at war with parts of themselves they saw in the other. I was thinking way outside my paygrade. I needed to leave that alone and concentrate on what I could do.

Most of the older pilots could recall me from the bad old days when I used to have to drink to start an airplane. The rumors and fables still prevailed within the squadron. Other rumors revealed that I had discovered a miracle cure. I was in my office one day when Wally rapped on my door and wanted to talk to me. He stood in front of me, almost in tears, and confessed, "I bit Roy's ear off last night, Major." At which point, the full confession produced actual tears, and he had to sit down.

It tempted me to tell him I was not a plastic surgeon. Wally spilled his guts, sobbing in short bursts he had just about had enough of himself. He was seeking counsel. He allowed, as if he needed to quit drinking before he ate the rest of Roy's body.

"I heard you used to drink a lot and you quit. Someone said that you got a way to stop drinking," he said. Bill Ridings, who knew me in Atsugi and in Kingsville, had told him that if I could quit drinking, anyone could. He had directed Wally to me.

Usually there's a boundary between officers and enlisted in their private hours. In some venues, they discouraged fraternization, but almost tolerated it in the combat zone. The boundary is less defined between officer and staff non-commissioned officers. We did not go into the enlisted living area, nor did they go into ours. This has nothing to do with protecting an officer's snob status but protecting the enlisted area for privacy. The quote from unwritten regulations: "They need to know their area is safe and sacredly theirs."

I told Wally to meet me in the dispensary where they had a big reel-to-reel stereo and Hi-Fi set up where we could have meetings and listen to tapes. So, for the duration of that tour, we met twice a week. I ordered literature for him. Soon Roy joined Wally and me. We had our own little crew, the only such group in I Corps.

Vietnam, 1966 and 67 were the years where my past came to visit me and ask, "Who is he now and who was he then?" I was standing in line at the officer's dining hall, wondering at the overweight amongst us, now crowding one another at the latest diet craze: a mountain stack of bacon on a bed of fat grapefruit wedges.

I had almost reached the tub of scrambled eggs and was up to my elbow when I heard a voice I should have remembered. "Ruthven, is that you!!?"

It was Lieutenant Colonel Steven Fairburn, my first Commanding Officer from VMF 232 in Hawaii back in 1956. He was standing in line with several staff officers who had flown down from Wing Headquarters for the requisite two days "In country" to satisfy the requirement to collect combat pay.

"Ruthven, I thought you had been court-martialed." He fumed and placed his tray on a convenient table already filled with lieutenants. He walked up to me about three inches away. "I personally endorsed the recommendation to have you and that other troublemaker put in hack pursuant to court martial in Atsugi." I think he quivered; I could feel the full weight of his invective inches from my face. He almost shouted above the din of tin trays and chewing mouths, "You stole the Group Commander's sedan, for crissake!"

His words reverberated around the dining room, blending into the mild cacophony of chatting and chewing. But there was something else going on with Lt. Col. Fairburn. He was not digesting food, but masticating memories, visions of Second Lieutenant Ruthven wrestling in a drunken heap with one of his staff non-commissioned officers. Now I was a major, the one who got away, the nemesis woven into the fabric of all his woes. None of this made sense in his reality. I was living outside the realm of all probabilities, a field grade officer, insulated and safe from the grim consequences of outrageous exploits.

Lt. Col. Fairburn's burning glare was arcing across a tin plate of food. It seemed to say, "When you were a captain in Atsugi, you blasted the outer edges of what you could get away with and now you're a senior officer in a fighter squadron? Help me make sense of this."

Carrying my regret with me, I almost followed Fairburn to his table to volunteer for whatever punishment he deemed necessary. He could walk across my back on the way to his jeep.

He was right. The heist of the Group Commander's vehicle and many other offenses he could have witnessed in Atsugi sufficed to send me into a civilian life long ago. Of course, there was my behavior in Kaneohe that had Colonel Fairburn poised to seize on any untoward behavior to justify his charges of fraternization. I can still see his face about the middle of the third round when I was boxing, then wrestling with Staff Sergeant Julio Hernandez at the beer bust smoker in Kaneohe. This would not be the only cringe worthy moment I was to have for the duration, recalling toxic vignettes from my previous life insisting I feel or answer to the crimes.

I had more to worry about than whether Colonel Fairburn could digest his meal and further stomach my presence in the Marine Corps. Here I was promoted to major and still in fighter squadrons while he occupied a staff chair up at wing. He had to snivel flights to Da Nang to satisfy the requirements of at least two days in the combat zone to earn combat pay. Something held me in a giant protective bubble with myriad consequences lurking just outside. I had put myself on house arrest, a short leash, and needed to stay there. The war zone was a good place for that to happen.

I returned to my hooch. Nobody else was there. As I did first thing each day as I awoke, I again fell on my face to thank whatever was in charge that I was overpaid in every department of my life. I asked for one more day on the planet to do whatever was necessary for whatever purpose that was beyond my understanding.

7

Ubon

December 1966 the Wing ordered the squadron back up to Naha to conduct live ordnance training for FNG's ("fuckin' new guys") and ground support. For a solid week, the planes directed bombs, rockets, Napalm, and strafing attacks onto a small target island. Unknown to the squadron, a fishing crew had sought shelter from a wrecked vessel on and inside the coral hollows of this very island. There the unfortunate survivors huddled, unseen by daily, round-the-clock bombardment by ammo' laden Crusaders trying to destroy their only dry land.

The procedure for bombing the target island provided for a preliminary low altitude flight past the island for a visual check to assure it was safe and there was no one on the island., it required that we check for the very remote possibility that shipwreck survivors might have sought refuge on an uninhabitable rock and be waving frantically at menacing planes screaming by. That there could be people on an island we were terrorizing was so impossibly remote that normal precautions were all but ignored for nearly a week. It was unlikely we would have seen the survivors if they had been dressed in international orange flight suits.

Possibly the only pilots to have the integrity or the ingenuity to abide by this procedure were the Fucking New Guys, those pilots we had come up to Naha to train! On an early morning bombing flight, an alert FNG glanced at the island as he passed at eye level and a relatively slow speed. It shocked him to see figures on the broken surface of the reef, on their knees, frantically waving their arms, begging to be rescued. The mission was aborted and help immediately summoned.

In a previously published narrative, this event, which nearly started an international incident and kicked the American Forces off the Island of Okinawa, was given the honorific, "The Battle for Torii Shima," for which an irreverent anthem was composed at the Naha Officer's Club by the squadron choral group. Ed 'Mofak' Cathcart has expertly chronicled this sad episode, a record of which is in his Google archives.

While the Navy and Ryukyuan authority investigated the island incident, and with the squadron still in Naha, my life took a minor detour. If I had believed in an avenging and punishing God, seeking retribution for the target island survivors, I would have acknowledged His punitive presence one morning when I awoke to find the inside of my shorts filled with blood. If I had thought further of an avenging God, or current life karma, I would have wondered if the situation related to all the sexual indiscretions in my past which were admittedly on a par with bombing hapless survivors on an island.

I was scheduled for an afternoon flight, so I delivered myself and my soiled shorts to the dispensary for an early morning sick call. They gave me preferential attention in that we were officially still a unit in the combat zone. The doctor was not all that alarmed, but he said I would have to provide a specimen to determine if I had a problem other than bleeding from a bodily orifice.

I went into the little room at the dispensary purely out of obedience to the corpsman's instruction. When he explained it would require me to provide a sperm specimen, I asked him how I was supposed to do that. His answer was, "The way you always do, Major."

At this point in my sobriety, I experienced not my first, but one of many spiritual crises. Against all wise and loving counsel from the sages of Laguna Beach who had traveled my chosen path to recovery, when I first began my recovery, I had decided that to adhere to a more spiritually sanitized path to the principals of recovery than anyone else, I should become celibate.

Celibacy, by my uninformed standard, was a stricter adherence than the Holy See inflicts upon their clergy. I denied myself even a "self-release." I would, with even clinical caution, wash my private parts lest I violate the personal prohibition I had set on the "imperious urge." Fanaticism is historically a secondary problem to addiction.

The American Medical Association defines alcoholism as a disease. It further explains that the disease is incurable. We are promised only a daily reprieve, contingent upon the application of spiritual principals. I had no religious training. Sacred or Sunday church services had not been a requirement in our home so there was no cumbersome religious architecture that I had to disassemble to erect a pristine spiritual path, as there is say, with fundamental Baptists who have a difficult time departing from their principals as they launch upon a different spiritual journey. The disadvantage in a total absence of religious training was that I was leaving it up to me to fill in the blanks. I imagined that it required an equal and opposite effort to something as enormous and imposing as an incurable disease, that further, only a Power greater than myself could arrest. I thought I would have to go the extra mile and do at least that which had been required of the spiritual giants. I thus applied myself with similar enthusiasm as had those insane saints down through the centuries.

My part in the spiritual scheme of things would require I sacrifice that which represented my very being. I would quit screwing, or anything else I thought might resemble "the deed." In very ancient times, people used to sacrifice virgins to a live volcano to expiate for their transgressions. Wasn't there something like that I could have done instead of celibacy?

Fast forward to the moment. I went into the little room to produce a specimen. This minor emissary from God in hospital scrubs released me from my self-imposed celibacy and the death grip

I had on my sobriety. My spiritual structure was being rearranged; but I didn't have time to celebrate. There was a problem.

The specimen I delivered to the medic was not the clear and creamy fluid that delivers millions of healthy sperm to swarm the single submissive egg. Rather, the sample was approximately two tablespoons full of an inert black substance. I handed it to the corpsman, and he almost dropped it.

"Jesus Christ, Major. What the hell is this?"

The doctor's version of this was milder, but more clinical. "You might have cancer, sir. That's an ugly specimen. We're going to send you up to the Naval Hospital in Yokosuka and let the real doctors up there look at you."

Early in my Vedantic studies, I would have entertained the idea that this was a karmic debt I had to pay for my last visit to the Naval Base at Yokusuka. Pennington and I had spirited a full case of Haig and Haig five-star whiskey from the Officer's Club, never mind several raincoats. There was probably no karmic compensation allowed for the ties we left behind in the nurse's quarters, but there was the ghost of our unclean presence that would probably need to be expunged.

They placed me on a medevac airplane the following day. Lest I generate undue drama, I fast very far forward to the last scene. I'm in an operating room where they're prepared to enter the passage to my bladder and examine the damage. I have gone all "doomsday" in my thinking. My eyes wandered to find the scalpel that stands sanitized to remove my entire package, plus a few related organs. How far into my viscera will they have to go to 'get it all?' Is this a good time to ask for a transsexual conversion?

I remember his name vividly because I remember the event vividly. Doctor LeBlanc came at me with a cystoscope about the diameter of a wrestler's thumb. He explained, as they always do, that this might be a bit "uncomfortable." He sends the probe through the head of my penis and down the tube. Halfway through my urethra I hear him utter the urologist's version of "Eureka, I think I've found it." and he pushes the scope in one quick thrust all the way into my bladder. I fainted briefly from the "uncomfortable" thrust of metal cutting through flesh to its destination, and I awoke to his smiling face and cavalier pronouncement:

"It's just an urethral stricture." He distanced himself from his unhappy work. "That blood was an enormous backup collecting in front of the prostate." Then he looked at me and said: "You're going to have to have that dilated every couple of months for about a year. Also, it looked like you hadn't used that thing for a while."

"How do I have it dilated in the combat zone?" I couldn't imagine flying up to The Naval Hospital at Yokosuka every two months for Doctor LeBlanc to have his way with me.

"Oh, hell," he replied, ripping his surgical gloves off with a snap like they do in movies. "You have the best medical facilities and doctors in the world down there. You just need to get a ride to any of the hospital ships. Probably the Hope or the Repose."

For monks and priests who are mandated to a life of celibacy, the idea makes some kind of sense, but for a man who has been sexually active and compulsively accustomed to ejaculating on a regular schedule, celibacy is probably unhealthy. In the words of the battle-hardened female surgeon aboard the hospital ship Repose on my first visit, "You need to run a round through that thing on a regular basis, Major."

I returned to Da Nang to discover they had transferred me to another Crusader squadron. Marine Fighter Squadron 232. The Red Devils needed more field grade officers. I didn't have to move my living quarters or change my routine. I moved my flight gear to the hangar next door. The Skipper, Lieutenant Colonel Vince Crosby, was younger, and it seemed more energetic than my previous Commanding Officer. I was the Logistics Officer in VMF 235 but had spent most of my time when I wasn't flying, drawing cartoons and caricatures. It satisfied colonel Crosby to have me just draw cartoons, but in a strange twist, my collateral duties took an unusual turn.

The last time I had seen Corporal Redfern was in Iwakuni. The Sergeant Major of MABS 13 had to hold Redfern from jumping into my face and choking me to the floor. Now down in Da Nang I had just landed from a mission and was stuffing my helmet into a canvas bag when I looked up and there was Corporal Redfern right in my face.

"Major!" The moment was more exciting and fraught with consequences than the mission from which I had just returned. "Corporal Redfern, sir." He saluted. "I don't know if you remember me, sir."

"Oh, I remember you, Corporal Redfern." I put my helmet bag on the tarmac, laughed, and held up my hands as if I had to defend myself. "It looks as if that broken heart didn't kill you, after all."

"Oh, God! No, sir." He looked down at the ground like a punished schoolboy. "I just wanted to thank you for what you did." We walked toward the hangar. He took up a pace about half a length to my left and to the rear. "You helped me save a bundle of money, but mostly, Oh God!" He was almost overcome with emotion. "I nearly made a huge mistake. God, I was going to marry her. From what I heard, she was back in that club and someone else was buying her out."

I interjected, "I would have made a mistake if I had let you get taken by the girl and the bar maid scam." We both smiled. "Are you here with 232, now?"

"Yes, sir. Flight Equipment." He looked down at my helmet bag. "It looks like you need a new helmet bag. That one has 235 a patch on it. You need to get one of ours. Let me fix you up."

Somewhere between Joseph City, Arizona and Oklahoma City, Freddy Sellers taught me that the kindest thing you can do for someone is to allow them to do you a favor. I handed Corporal Redfern my bag. Flight Equipment made helmet bags, clothing bags, anything with a sewing machine.

"I'll get it to you this afternoon, sir. Are you flying real soon?" I told him I was not. He almost trotted to the flight equipment spaces.

He turned around and gave me an emotionally charged salute. In the hangar area, saluting is customarily unnecessary.

"What was all that about, Colin?" It was the Skipper. He had been watching as he walked down the flight line behind us.

I explained everything as we walked into the Ready Room.

"I've got to debrief here and at group intelligence, Colin, but I'd like to talk to you about something." We poured dark fluid from a giant tankard. I was pretty sure it was coffee. Skipper turned to a small table to debrief his flight. "Drop by my office after you finish debriefing."

I was in his office about an hour later.

"This won't take long, Colin. I've got a meeting with the Group Commander, so I'll make it quick." He told me to sit down. He came around his desk and sat beside me. "We need field grade officers here mainly for their flight experience. You've got plenty of that. But we filled all of our billets for collateral duties." He shrugged. I had the feeling he was going to transfer me to Group. An officer's career is based upon his performance in a unit's collateral duties. The more important an office–Operations, Intelligence, Logistics, Maintenance–the more weight the grades on a fitness report bore on his suitability for promotion. To be in a unit and not assigned to a collateral duty was commensurate with an accusation of incompetence.

"You seem to keep busy drawing those cartoons, which I have to tell you are terrific and they're helping morale." He reached behind him and picked up a folder.

"Colin, you probably don't remember me when you were in Atsugi." He grinned sheepishly.

"I remember very little about Atsugi, Skipper." I shook my head. "Except that I was there and little of that." I was visited again by a cringe worthy moment. My sheepish grin was better than his. "No sir. I don't remember you in Atsugi, Skipper."

"Oh, I was there." He grinned widely. "I was very busy up at Group. But I was also watching, relatively sober from across the pool, when you showed up dyed blue." He laughed out loud. "And– you climbed into that goddam tree." He laughed. "When you joined the squadron awhile back, I didn't recognize you." He looked up, trying to remember something. "And you kept the entire grotto awake all night long, playing that goddam Nazi Marching music. I would watch you when you had that cast on your leg, totally shit faced, falling on your face."

"God, please stop." I grinned, but really hoped he would stop.

"I could go on. You were a production, you, and your sidekick. Who was it? Pennington?" Then added nonchalantly, "He was court martialed flying choppers. Did you know that?"

"Jesus, no!" my head dropped into my hands. "I lost track of him after our ignominious departure from Atsugi."

"Yeah, he was all shitfaced and landed a chopper down at Rosy Roads; it rolled over and thrashed itself to death. He walked away from the wreckage. Some of the crew swear he was totally hammered on Boilermakers. A wonder no one was killed."

He walked around his desk and sat in the chair. "Okay, Colin. It's no secret what you're doing. Although I hear it's supposed to be anonymous. You're a totally different person. Even if you dyed yourself blue again, I still wouldn't recognize you. Also, I saw how you were talking to Redfern. He responded to you. I can't do that. And, my XO really can't do it. He wants to hang Article Fifteen on everyone that comes into my office." He seemed to contemplate something that caused him to frown.

"I think you know the biggest problem we have in the squadron, and it's not keeping airplanes in the air."

"Keepin' the troops off drugs?" I offered.

"And alcohol! Or anything that will help them forget they're in the forgotten war." He sat back and fired up a cigar. "If we threw the book at every one of these kids that comes in here high, hung over or unavailable or in a deep state of 'don't give a shit,' we'd have to shut the squadron down."

"What do you do with them now?"

"Truthfully, we do nothing." He opened the file and handed it across the desk at me. "There's a list of offenses and repeat offenders. The Marine Corps has no protocol to deal with this recent problem. Really, it's an old problem. It's just got worse. These kids are a different version of pathetic; and there's nothing we can do about it but put them on report or fuck up their service record book with multiple offenses or worse, mark them down on their performance marks. We're applying an old solution to a new problem." He shrugged and took a long pull on the cigar. "We ignore it."

"I can't do for them what happened to me. It's a kind of magic."

"All I need you to do is talk to them the way you were talking to Redfern out there." He pointed his cigar toward the flight line. "It's a skill most officers don't have. And, my XO definitely does not have a clue how to win their hearts and souls."

"How about the Chaplain?"

"He knows less than shit. Tries to convert them to something or other. Sides, the troops don't trust him. Think he's weird. You know? No, I need someone to talk to these kids so we can keep the airplanes in the air." He shrugged. "I wish I had a more altruistic motive. I saw how you talked to Redfern and I know what you're doing in your private life. And my XO loves to put them in the brig. Thinks that's the only solution.

"I'll give you a small room off the avionics shop to talk to anyone who comes in fucked up on this junk the slopes are pushing through the fence. Group commander thinks it's the Vietcong selling kids grass laced with heroin. Sends them to a place where they do not give a shit."

"I've been to that place."

"That's what I'm talking about, Animal."

So, I opened up a new department in the Squadron. We didn't heal the multitude, nor did I have a "visitor" for over a week. Then came a small trickle of repeat offenders. We met individually and sometimes as a group.

"I can't tell anyone here how to not drink or stop taking drugs." I looked around at the puzzled faces. "That's not what this is about." There was a group shrug and more puzzled expressions. "It's not about fighting the compulsion to drink or take drugs. It's about doing something else entirely. And, while you're doing this, you stop drinking. It just happens."

The thrust of the "visits", sometimes an hour, often more, was to describe to them what I had been doing for over two years. They did not become pristine and microbe free, but the incidence of alcohol and drug-related offenses decreased dramatically. Surprisingly, there was a heightened performance in most of the departments that previously had the worst offenders. Not only did I have visitors from our own squadron, but a few from other units in the air group as the word got out that there was a different approach to the high incidence of work and man hours lost to alcohol and drugs making their way into the compound.

This didn't curtail my flying. Operations sped up in Marine Fighter Attack Squadron 232. For about a month, I stood on a permanent night hot pad. I had yet to know many of the younger pilots in the squadron. I took some of their watches while they deposited their scent at the bar. We launched every night, sometimes on missions close to Da Nang. The attacks by Russian Rockets into the base increased.

On just such a night, my wingman and I were returning from a mission. We were on final GCA approach into Da Nang. My wingman Lieutenant, Dick Forrester had about a three-minute separation behind me. Sometimes on final approach at night, a scattering of small red projectiles flew up in the path of landing aircraft. I could ignore the small arms fire, but the brilliant flash and explosion halfway down the runway arrested my attention and my descent. The tower operator waved me off; and they diverted us to Ubon, an Air Force Base just the other side of the border into Thailand.

"Maggot two, this is lead, in a port turn at about your ten-o'clock. Close on me, we'll get a vector to our alternate." We changed channels to Panama for clearance from Da Nang and a vector to Ubon. He pulled up on my wing. I advanced power, and we climbed to our cruise altitude. It didn't break my heart we were going to Thailand. Ubon was the preferred destination while a flight crew waited for things to cool down at Dan Nang and any repairs to be made. The diversion usually amounted to a mini-R&R and a change in perspective.

We were met in the chocks as we stepped down from our cockpits by a welcoming committee of two Air Force Captains eager to entertain us while we waited for Da Nang to open, which would be the following day. I thought at first that they were looking for any excuse to escape to the Ville for shadowy fun and games. It was later revealed that they were assigned to us as an escort so that nothing bad could happen to us, or more, that we could do nothing bad to the Ville and thus reflect adversely on the Air Force. They had more than once experienced Marine air crews who had been in Vietnam too long and were looking for something on the beach to break.

Our escorts spirited Dick Forrester and I, still in our flight gear, into the small town of Ubon. As with most military bases overseas, there was a small strip of bars almost immediately outside the main gate of the Air Force Base. The strip amounted to nothing more than a small shadow community of several bars and houses of questionable reputation. We could enter one and be bathed, steamed, and serviced by any of a multitude of indigenous girls, all with no name, but a number. I still had my gear healing and in hock, so I suggested that Lieutenant Forrester take advantage of the rare opportunity to have someone walk barefoot on his body. He declined, and we stayed with the tour.

I was thirty-two, an old guy compared to the average Marine in Country. Dick Forrester was twenty-four. Each of us grew up in different musical generations. Although I imprinted with the Big Band music of the Forties and really locked on to progressive jazz with Dizzy Gillespie, Chet Baker and Miles Davis, there was something about the music of the Sixties that hit my musical sweet spot. As we dismounted from the jeep, I could hear a din of different music pulsing out of as many venues. To escape the dissonance, we slipped into the first joint on the block. The music evened out into a familiar sound that had been flooding the combat zone through Armed Forces Radio, the only show in town aside from our personal tapes.

They guided us through darkness blacker than the night from which we just left, except for psychedelic images blowing up and changing on the black lit walls. The tables were wedged together and jammed with young men and even younger women. Some of them appeared to be children. We took a table and tried to talk to one another over the deafening music of "The Doors" and the mixed ambiance of two languages, each trying to understand the other.

This was not a recording or a tape. This was a musical group of local musicians, every one of them mimicking to perfection a member of The Doors. Not that they sounded like The Doors. They were The Doors. They riveted me in my seat. It could have been Jim Morrison, this small Asian kid dressed in whatever he could find that might replicate the costume of Jim Morrison, although Jim Morrison didn't keep his clothes on all the time.

"It's incredible," I screamed to my escort. "They sound just like..." My comments were interrupted by the arrival at our table of four children. On closer examination as I squinted through the dark night and across a candle-lit table. They were local women, all weighing about eighty pounds. On even closer examination, they were seriously worn, but highly drunk or drugged escorts copping a drink and hopefully some extracurricular action that they said would be "plenny cheap."

"Yeah," my escort yelled back at me. "Every one of the joints on the strip specializes in a popular rock group in the States. You can't tell the difference." He leaned down to a child, kissed her playfully on the side of the head, and slipped some local currency across the table. I reached in my wallet and he stopped me. "No, don't leave any of that Bot or American. You can pay me back. These people are black marketing American currency."

"So, I could go into any of these bars and there would be a band for a different popular rock group?" I put my arm around a set of little brown shoulders and collected a series of playful nibbles on my neck. She played with my hand, like a small animal examining food she had never seen.

"That's right." He yelled and then spoke loudly as the band shut down for a break. "What do you like?"

"I'm a relatively old guy, so this might surprise you. I was around at the beginning of the decade when the Stones showed up. I like a lot of their stuff." I took a sip of soda and collected some more nibbles on my neck and felt a small body gluing itself closer to my body. "But what I like now is a new group that's just showing up. CCR. It's almost country rock. If I was still drinking, I could really get lost in this sound."

"CCR?" He gave a shrug that only slightly impeded by the small body hanging from his neck.

"Creedence Clearwater Revival." I shouted again as the diminutive Thai equivalent of Jim Morrison poured out a modern dirge.

My escort stood up. A child fell off his body. "Come on." He nodded toward the door. "We don't have that yet, but The Stones are just down the street."

We stepped from the club into a darkness softened by low wattage bulbs hanging on lines draped across the street. The half-light painted our bodies in a mid-range monotone gray. The girls hung from our arms. I had a feeling they were necessary for our safety. Like, you couldn't walk down the street without a child hanging on your body. Apparently, they were a part of the deal because our escorts didn't object to their presence. In the light of a barely lit night, I could see they were still youthful women, but packing some cruel mileage.

We stepped into a constricted, psychedelically saturated room. The place was relatively quiet. There was no music, just the singsong chatter of indigenous female voices trying to sound American. We found a table in a corner where two different images met on respective walls. Exploding bubbles, melting drapery, varying colors and patterns suddenly moved to the beat of an explosive music that filled the small space. It was the unmistakable opening chords of "Satisfaction" trying to blow the walls away. I sank back in the chair.

It was here that I experienced one of my earlier moments of clarity. It was as vivid as Julian's voice. From an atmosphere of complete abandon, release and escape from all constraints, everything fell into a quiet focus. Something entirely aligned me with the beat, the pure live music, the fidelity of the voices and strings, the black lit psychedelic explosions all around us. Floating, melting abstract patterns painted the walls and faces. Sweat saturated, grotesque grimaces looked back at me from the dark. Trays of drinks rattled by our table. The happy brown urchins at our table stood and sang along with the quasi-Mick Jagger. I sat all the way back and found the same center I find in a cockpit when it's just right. I asked myself, "Colin, after 32 years chasing after it and trying to get there, have you ever found it, and did you ever arrive? I never knew what the 'it' or the 'there' was, but I felt as close I had ever had, that this was probably both the 'It' and the 'there.'

I leaned across the table filled with drinks. Smoke drifted toward the ceiling.

"Dick," I yelled.

Lieutenant Forrester leaned in closer, still stroking a small brown arm. "I'm thirty-two, you're twenty-four. I feel younger than you look. I think I've been in a holding pattern since I kicked the sauce. And I think I just caught up. I had to get sober to find a place like this that I'd been looking for drunk."

We returned to Da Nang after an altogether too brief night and no sleep. I was as wide awake as if I had slept for twelve hours. As we walked back to the hangar, I looked at Dick Forrester grinning. We had stayed up all night hitting all the bars on the strip. I changed some money with one of our escorts to slip to the child that had hung with us throughout the night to all the bars. We even found a crew that was working on a burgeoning Creedence sound.

"That was great!" laughed Forrester.

"Yeah," I responded, and thought for a few steps. "Honestly, there was an old part of me that didn't want to leave." We both laughed, and I added, "I'm afraid if we diverted any time real soon, I wouldn't come back."

After years in fighter squadrons, I was being consigned to a staff job at the Naval Base in Millington, the boneyard for Naval officers about to retire, but a career move up for Marine officers. This was about as far away as a Marine Aviator could get from any of the moving parts of his occupational specialty. Again, someone up in headquarters, Marine Corps, is filling in the empty spaces of my misspent career. Over and above that, I was convinced that there was something larger than all of it that was drawing the lines, establishing the rules. I didn't care if they sent me to the center of the planet, I just wanted to continue to find myself no matter where I was or what someone asked me to do.

8

Millington

I was in no hurry to get to Millington, or anywhere else in Tennessee. It suggested a Southern Tundra of empty sameness. Neither could I imagine a place where there were six-thousand feet of runway and no tactical airplanes droning around the airfield, and Colin Ruthven not operating at the working end of a Crusader. My squadron days were over for a while. This was the staff billet Jay Hubbard had said was waiting for me to beef up my career profile.

With thirty days to get there, I could take my time. I had no children to visit. Beth was happily married again; I had concluded our business just before I left for Vietnam. Before I had boarded the USS Sutter County, I explained to Steve, my spiritual advisor, that I was about to go to the combat zone. Before I left, I thought it might be a sound idea for me to make a tour of all the broken spots in my life. to make amends for harms done. I would start in Vancouver and work my way across Canada to Ottawa, where Beth was living with her new family. My Farewell Tour, without bumper stickers, t-shirts and souvenirs.

"Colin, you've been in this work for less than two years. Do you really think you understand the full magnitude of your madness?" Steve peered sagely through a cloud of smoke. He chain-smoked but had been off booze since the early forties. He knew his stuff, and a lot about mine.

I replied, "I think I've taken a pretty thorough look at the carnage and where I did the most damage." I hadn't had a smoke since that day Jack Ruby got shot. Breathing the same airspace as Steve was like smoking again.

"Colin, I've been doing this work for half a lifetime and every day it seems I get a clearer picture of how really crazy I am, and definitely how crazy I was. The more I understand myself, the more I think I should leave people alone. It will take a long time for you to see clearly how nuts you've been..." He took a long and dramatic drag, "... and still are."

"Well, I hope I don't sound too dramatic, but I'm gonna visit Beth and the kids–just in case I buy the farm." I stared at him, looking for something. "Do you have any advice?"

"I don't give advice, Colin. I share my experience. I will tell you what I think, though. Only you can make your own choices. What I'm saying is that it might be a while before you really know how much damage you've caused, and it might take even a while longer to dig deeper into the causes and conditions that drove your alcoholism to realize how much damage you can still do."

"And?"

"My question is: 'Do you want to contaminate her domestic system with your crazy ass just when she's trying to start a new life with a new husband?' You made a conscious choice when you were drinking to be absent in the marriage, and now you're going to show up all heroic and shit and bring wonderful you back into her life. Just think on these things and then make your own choices."

Steve's wise and loving counsel was prescient. When I suggested to Beth that we might try to start some sort of dialogue and visit with the children, she told me emphatically to keep my distance. In her words, "I think it would be best for all concerned if we kept our distance."

It was ironic that when we parted during the divorce; she offered some well-meaning counsel based on the picture she had of me. "Colin just don't go out and get some teenager pregnant. Okay?"

It was excellent advice. She could have had a hint at what future had in store for her. Shortly after her divorce, she married again and immediately had another child.

Someone once said the best amend is to say goodbye and mean it. I owed her and the girls some distance. My madness was still a potential nuisance to her life. I never knew when I might return to its default drunk position.

Now I had returned from Vietnam, and I guess I was going to make a victory lap across Canada before I reported to Millington, Tennessee. I spent a few days in Vancouver, then took a train across the Rockies. The CPR had transferred my father from Chapleau, Ontario, the northernmost point on the Canadian Pacific Railway, to Calgary, Alberta. He was now working in Ogden, an outskirts CPR facility a few miles out of Calgary.

It takes a while to adapt to random, recreational time after a year of concentrated on-point focus. Uncrowded by the cares of the combat zone, thoughts long dormant seeped in to fill the void. I could not stop thinking of Sarah and the unhappy goodbye we had exchanged when I left Kingsville in March 1965. It was now September 1967. Our paths had diverged, but she had always been on my mind.

One pre-dawn in Da Nang, when thoughts of romance often returned, I awoke with Sarah on my mind. In the distance, the thump of artillery and the faraway thunder rumble of an arc-light bombing reminded where I was, the percussion of a still unsettled war, an incessant gray noise. I risked writing to her, expecting to be rebuffed, or at least scolded for leaving and now, after all this time, trying to reconnect. I did not have reconciliation in my mind. I just had Sarah on my mind, and so had she been thinking of me. I received a friendlier than expected answer to my letter.

The closer my train came to Calgary, the slower it seemed to travel, not to Calgary, but to Corpus Christi, Texas. My stay in Calgary was brief. Archie and Jean just needed to see that nothing seriously changes a person when they're out of Canada for more than a year. By now, my arrivals to wherever they were living had become unexpected, my departures swift. My father and I had fewer words than usual to share. All my mother required was a booster shot, the three-day stay every few years, exchanging the private language we had shared since I was a child.

Neither parent could visualize me flying fighters or in any way involved in combat, so to them, it just hadn't happened. They could not fit who I had become into the picture they held of who I was. I still had that problem. Like my parents, I couldn't fit what I had been doing for the past thirteen years into the limited picture I had of myself, so I just behaved as if it wasn't happening. Again, that's probably how it all got done.

After only an obligatory visit, I left Canada again.

I'd been in the Free World less than ten days when I landed in Corpus Christi and rented an automobile. What is it about a tour in a foreign country, engaged in a life-changing experience, that made me think that a place like Corpus Christi should have changed as had I? My narcissistic notion was that those people and places in my world should have kept up with me in my frantic race across life.

Corpus Christi hadn't changed, but according to Sarah, I had. She was also markedly different. The distance we had provided in just a couple of years had allowed a transformation in us both that might otherwise not have occurred had we been together. With the combined needs we had for one another, we would have obstructed the passage to our individual truths.

So invested had she become in her new Catholicism, and so warmly was she embraced in the church, that she was now working as a secretary for the Diocese of Corpus Christi. She had taken the express track to conversion; and was thoroughly installed, in love, with Christ and with her church–more than she could have been with me. I felt no loss from this. I celebrated her victory. Was it a selfish part of me that experienced a certain relief? How could I compete with this kind of love? I would measure any love that

I could exhibit against the relationship a person was having with Christ himself.

A beautiful thing happens to those who find Christ later in life. Often, they arrive on the wings of a wound and can more readily experience the Power. Practically, a person recognizes the validity of the experience; emotionally and spiritually, they feel the Power, the enormous difference between what life had been and what it is now—with Christ. With more of life's lessons behind them, they are more suited to the experience and more refined. A sometimes blazing, personal relationship occurs that eclipses anything that could have occurred when the Christian was younger.

No man can compete with the Jesus a woman has just recently discovered, and if he is not happy with the love she now shares with Christ, he will create a very dark experience for all three parties. As they say in The Marine Corps: either lead, follow or get out of the way. When an outsider is engaged with a true Christian, he needs to either get on board or get out of the way.

I got on board. Immediately and clinically to the point, there would obviously be no sex. She was thoroughly committed to the Church's mandate that sex must be a part of the marital contract and further to the production of offspring. I felt no pressure to oppose this. I had been celibate as a warped part of my spiritual conversion, so I had no immediate sexual agenda.

I was "on board" because I missed her and wanted to see her again, lest having not, I would always remember and regret the one I allowed to get away. There are those who worry about this too late, long after they have fallen in and out of love. They think they had the choice, then walked away. Those are the stories about which poetry and bad country songs are written. Love calls the shots. You disappoint this lady at your own risk.

After about ten days, the conversation naturally matriculated to marriage. Realistically, for Sarah, it was the next step. We could try to talk around it and not address marriage directly. It would have been an awkward and deliberate detour around the topic, leaving more space for the elephant that was already in the room.

"I couldn't marry you as it is now, Colin," said Sarah. She was making a sandwich. She spread the mayonnaise precisely, as if it were a necessary emphasis to such a serious comment. At first, I thought this was to dispose of the idea altogether so we could get on with lesser matters, like a picnic or a 'just for old time's sake' trip to Padre Island. I gave it a cursory reply.

I said, "Probably not." I wanted to move the conversation along without knowing why we couldn't get married. Maybe it was because she had read "no intention or desire to get married" in my words and actions.

"You're divorced; and the Catholic Church will not sanction our marriage," she said, slipping potato chips between the bread of her egg salad sandwich. It was uncanny. She was saying we could not get married and already she was using the term "our marriage" as if we had been planning it for years. I had better catch up. I was way behind the curve here.

"Not much you can do about that, I suppose," suggested that frightened boy, hoping it would all go away. Somehow, when I really wanted to be with her, I felt the mention of marriage wedge a familiar distance between us. And there was no civilized way to say, 'Look, I believe I have powerful feelings for you, but I know I am incapable of being married. In my bones, I know this. I am unsure of several suppositions, but I am sure of this.' My marriage to Beth had pretty well proven I couldn't be married and still stay sober. I would very likely have to drink. It was the ultimate bad contest between marriage and alcohol.

"Well, there is something we can do about it," she said, carving the air with a mayonnaise smeared knife. A small fragment of potato chip fell to the floor.

I was this close. I could turn around and take the short flight up to Memphis and the bus ride to Millington. A deeper wisdom listens to the heart's first signal and obeys. But I was here with Sarah on her turf, and worse, that of the Roman Catholic Church. If I stayed a moment longer, I would fall in lockstep with two thousand years of inertia. I might as well go all the way. I'd been talking about it and now I had committed to go all the way. If I would not go all in, why the hell was I here?

"There's a process called a Pauline Privilege," she said. "The Church investigates your background and examines the previous marriage and the nature of the divorce. Very often the Church finds a way." She looked at me hopefully.

If I said another word to show I was even curious, I would be all the way in. "Well, how long does something like this take?" I asked.

One thing I knew about the Catholic Church, it loved detail. They had paper piling up on the desk of the Vatican for two thousand years. It would probably take forever to get past the hurdle of my divorce. And I was not a member of The Church. And yet, over the centuries, The Holy See had become very adept at finding loopholes. The Inquisition's office was still open and waiting for a reason to crank up the Strappado for just such recalcitrant subjects as me.

"I think a Pauline Privilege takes at least three years," she continued. Sarah became very professional, as if we had already drawn up the papers and all that was needed was for me to set the investigation in motion. I thought she was going to ask me to take a chair in her office, "The Bishop will be right with you, sir."

She was no longer eating the sandwich, but having presented the topic, she now stood at a very correct attention five feet away from the lunch counter as if she needed a pointer for her training aid, and an answer right away.

What the hell. With three years to work with, I'd probably come full circle and might even start attending church with Sarah. At that moment, I had no inclination toward her church or anyone else's. I'd found my own spiritual path. When I thought of the changes that had taken place in my life in the past three years, I realized I could not realistically predict what would happen in the next three. That was a long time ahead. I figured I might as well set the ball in motion so

I wouldn't regret any time I might lose. In the meantime, after three years, if I was still undecided, I could express my reservations. 'Of course you can, Colin.' A cynical voice said.

These thoughts and a crippling inability to disappoint a woman checked me from taking an effective distance from the topic. I made no direct statement. It was vague to such an extreme as to allow anyone to step in and make a choice for me. It was the old 'silence implies consent' thing.

With Sarah, as beautiful as ever, standing in front of me, and the church looming up behind her, I would probably have taken any direction they suggested. I had at least listened to the data, and that was enough to give her assurance. I had yet to learn that 'No' is the shortest sentence in the English language and probably the most honest, and in the long term, the kindest.

I spent a week with Sarah, scouting out different ground, avoiding the familiar old haunts so much a part of what had brought us together. The new context was turning a fresh and unfamiliar earth in which to plant an unknown seed. What I needed was clarity, the kind that only distance can provide. It was time to return to work, to an equal but less ambiguous unknown.

The Naval Air Station at Millington is nineteen miles north of Memphis. For professional Naval officers it's called 'the bone yard', the last resting place of career naval officers. I could kid myself that I was being handpicked for an assignment as Marine Liaison Officer for the Naval Air Maintenance Training Group. History showed that my predecessors had been assigned because it was just time for them to serve a staff tour in the wilderness. The biggest problem with being a staff officer is that flying is restricted to basic minimums to maintain proficiency. Also, once a person becomes a staff officer, he is probably never going to be anything else. If he ever went back to tactical flying, he would never be the same.

I thought I knew what heat was. I had just returned from sitting in a cockpit at the end of the runway at Da Nang beneath a hundred and twenty-degree sun. But there's no excuse for a Memphis summer. Uniform of the day in Da Nang was a flight suit or at worst dungarees, both suffering an incessant saturation of sweat. My Millington uniform of the day stuck to me like a loose layer of humid skin. I was sitting at a desk. They finally got me. This was the ninth circle of hell from which all of my drinking had kept me hidden. Now almost three years sober, it was time for me to spend the next three years in purgatory.

The Naval Air Maintenance Training Group Headquarters oversaw anything that had to do with trainers wherever there was a Navy or Marine airplane. A trainer is a facility equipped with schematics, mockups, full-blown operating systems to train aircrews and maintenance personnel on the care, operation or feeding of any aircraft in the U.S. Naval Inventory. At Millington, we trained the trainers, the educators, the guys who wrote the training manuals and taught the personnel. I was the Marine Liaison officer for the unit and was a kind of commanding officer of all the Marines at NAMTRAGRU Memphis.

The Marine Instructors were Staff Non-Commissioned officers who would not be in Millington very long; just sufficient time to be trained as an instructor and then assigned to one of many facilities all over the States, mainly in California and the two Carolinas. While they were attached to the Group, they answered to me in terms of how they structured their time and satisfied the organization. There were only minor problems with these men. They were seasoned, highly vetted Marines. My collateral duty was Assistant Training Officer. My immediate reporting senior was a Navy Commander, the equivalent of a Marine Lieutenant Colonel.

All went well, until I encountered the civilian counterparts in the Group, several of them female. Every office had a secretary. If there had only been one woman in the building, it still would have blown my fundamental orientation. Until now, it had been boys only. But the place was running with women, principally Beverly Weber, who kept getting in my way. I had the immediate sense she was deliberately trying to collide with me. And there was a lot of her, everything perfectly in place, with which to collide.

"Major, I been assigned to he'p you with these reports."

The very stereotype of Southern innocence sat across from me, folding and unwinding eight feet of legs beneath her like a newborn colt. I could not recall seeing this much inner thigh in one sitting.

"How long do these usually take, Beverly?" I examined a heap of paper with words and numbers, none of which made sense.

"Well, when Major Everett was here, we could finish it up in half a day." She looked at the heap as if it was confetti, she had to reassemble into meaningful copy.

"Whyn't you come out to the place tonight. Me 'n Jimmy's cooking catfish and eatin' Sarah Lee. We'll watch Gunsmoke." She conveyed this like she and her husband were going to kill the fatted calf and that I had no choice. It would happen.

"I go to a meeting at seven, Beverly." I had hooked into a small group at the Baker Community Center in Millington.

'S'right. You go to them meetings. Jimmy otta go too, I reckon." She uncrossed and crossed her legs. It took fifteen minutes. "So, you comin, then?" She began shuffling the papers into something that Beverly could convince me was order.

"Okay, I'll be there. What time?" I picked up a sheet and compared it with another sheet, pretending I knew what they meant. This shouldn't be too hard, I thought.

"You come anytime you want, Major. We'll be there. We never go nowhere but there."

People from Mississippi differ from anyone I had ever met. I was to learn that if they like you, there's nothing they will not do for you. If they don't like you, there's nothing they won't do to you. Jimmy and Beverly Weber were from Booneville Mississippi. It turned out they liked me. I arrived at their home in Raleigh, a suburb of Memphis, around nine in the evening. Too late, I thought for anyone to let people into their homes. They welcomed me as if I were a favorite uncle. Beverly handed me a dish of heated Sarah Lee pastry, melted ice cream spilled across her fingers and onto the floor. She languorously licked her fingers. Oh, God.

"You missed the fish, but we waited the Sarah Lee on you." She held the screen door while I maneuvered myself and the plate of raw glucose around her perfumed form and into their tight little two-bedroom home. The glow of the Andy Griffith Show flickered its light across a dimly lit room onto nicotine stained wallpaper. Jimmy reclined a dreamy forty-five degrees on a La-Z-Boy. It looked like they had tailored it to his three-hundred-pound frame. Smoke curled up from an ashtray. He had a second cigarette in the same hand that held a can of Schlitz. The other hand was going for the cigarette in the ashtray.

"Bev give you yer 'zert?" He asked, his eyes not leaving the episode where Goober takes over the Sheriff's duties. It would require Jimmy's total attention. "Bev," he shouted, "tell them kids to keep peanut butter off the screen. Heah?" He butted a cigarette. "Can't goddam see what's happen'n in fucken Mayberry even. Jesus Crise."

I sat on the couch. Beverly sat too close to me. I was afraid she'd awaken Jimmy from his torpor and bring him out of his recliner in a jealous rage. But nothing could keep him from Goober's plot.

"Wha' they do at them meetings, Major?" Beverly had curled up in the folded Llama position, her body leaning in my favor. I could see how she was built to bear children. If she ever seriously opened her legs, a child would emerge. "Sit around talking about not drinkin' 'n stuff. Right?"

"No. They don't talk about not drinking. There's nothing they ever say about not drinking. They talk about doing something else." It was the paradox of 'The Deal.' There are no instructions on how to stop drinking. They tell you to do this other stuff instead. And you stop drinking. It just happens.

"What's that sumpin else they talk about, then?" Beverly's hands played in the folds of her apron, bunched up on her ample haunches. "Gotta be a lot of sumpin else, I reckon."

I thought for a few seconds, wondering how to frame the process. "It is. You're right, Beverly. Everyone shares their experience when they were drinking and talks about an alternative path to a better way of life." I sounded sufficiently enough like Norman Vincent Peale to turn her away from anything she might want to do.

"Sounds pretty dull, Major." She looked across the room. "You hear all that–what he said, Jimmy?"

"Yeah." Jimmy stared at the screen, annoyed at the interference. "Sumpin about a path. I can't hear the show, Bev! Crise!"

"It is dull, Beverly." I broke into the marital interlude, mostly to patronize Jimmy. "Very dull unless you really want it."

The Andy Griffith Show ended. Jimmy eased himself forward on the Lazy-z-boy and rolled off the recliner. He headed for the bedroom with a grumbling apology. He worked at the DuPont Chemical plant halfway to Memphis and needed to get up in just a few hours. I left before Beverly licked the ice cream off my face.

Women hate to see an unmarried man running around enjoying his life and getting away with it. I could tell that the girls who worked at NAMTRAGRU seriously considered me an eligible bachelor. Beverly was at the head of the phalanx of women who seemed to need to get me married even if I were to marry one of them, Beverly included. For this reason, I did little else to discourage Sarah and her Pauline Privilege. I still had well over two years to go for it or decide that I was not marriage material for one of the pope's flock.

I set aside my thoughts of Sarah, Beverly Weber, Sarah Lee and marriage early Monday morning, October 30, 1967.

"Major, one of your troops is missing." The administrative officer loomed into the room, reading from an early morning muster report. "Staff Sergeant Chester F. Duncan. You want us to report him AWOL?"

"No! No, not yet. Give him 'til noon." I shook my head. This Naval Officer seemed thrilled to find a Marine about to get his ass in a crack. Chester Duncan had just returned from a tour in Vietnam and was still getting acquainted with his wife and family in Jonesboro, Arkansas. "Keep me advised please, Lieutenant Whitlock."

"Gladly, Major." He skipped down the hall, chasing after the anti-submarine warfare department secretary.

Noon had not quite arrived when Commander Shields nudged me with a whisper, "Major Ruthven, you have a call." I would not have paid much attention, but it was rare for the executive officer of the Group to come tell a Marine major he had a phone call. Also, the raised eyebrows and slow nod from Commander Shields might have tipped me off that this was something different. I punched the blinking light of the open extension and answered the phone. "This is Major Ruthven."

"Major, my name is Frosty Williams, Captain–Memphis homicide." He gave me a second to let that settle. About the time it takes a martini to hit your system. It allowed me to stand and then sit down and listen. "We have one of your Marines living rent free in our hotel."

"Is his name Duncan?" I asked. He probably got nailed for impaired driving, coming back drunk from Jonesboro, I supposed. I wondered why these guys didn't get all their drinking done before they got back from Vietnam. Or was Vietnam the reason they drank when they came home? "Catch him sleeping in a ditch?" I joked, worried about why this was a detective from homicide calling me.

"Very good. You guys look after your boys." I could hear him butt one cigarette and light another. "You need to come down here or send a rep. He's in a bit more trouble than sleeping in a ditch."

This puzzled me. This was a captain of detectives. Homicide! It had to be something more than drunk driving. "So, can I ask what he's done, Captain Williams?" I almost wished I had not asked.

"He is alleged," he emphasized the word, 'alleged' and waited for another martini minute, "that is, alleged to have murdered a woman."

"I'll be there in an hour." I realized I was standing up again.

"Don't break any o' our speed reg's, Major. He'll be here for a while. He ain' goin' no place soon." This was not Captain Frosty Williams' first day on the job and, I found out, not his first murder.

Had I not been so intent on arriving at Homicide within my one-hour estimate, I might have otherwise been able to study the rustic panorama between Millington and downtown Memphis. This part of the country is an oasis of varied trees, wonderful old oaks, and an array of deciduous, all that shelter the city from above by a billowing canopy of green. The back road out of the Air Station travels through a deep bottom populated by a couple of trailer courts and remote homes. There's a church every mile. A river defines a county line and leads through several gullies, poor neighborhoods, and a small airport. The suburb of Raleigh abruptly interrupts and funnels several roads through a low-income neighborhood into the city.

I had called base security and told them my situation and that I was requesting a siren in front of me. Military police are trained to respond to an extreme of violence but are robbed of the opportunity to do their worst by pesky minor offenses. So, they were delighted to put a military vehicle escort in front of me with the siren on full all the way downtown. Purely for effect, I asked them to escort me into the building.

"Jesus, you weren't kidding. We're you, Major?" Captain "Frosty" Williams glanced at his watch. I needn't have had the military police escort into the building. My uniform with wings and the current collection of ribbons from Vietnam sufficed to gain entry to the inner chamber. The MP's thanked me, grinning, and departed. They'd wait for me outside while I found out what was up with one of my troops.

"What happened, Captain Williams?" I asked, still standing.

"Frosty, please. And sit down." He pointed to a chair. "I think you'll need to be seated, Major." His chair squeaked as it turned to face a small burner by his desk. "You want some of this?" He poured himself a cup of something very black and thick. He was shaking his head 'no' for me. It looked bad. I shook my head 'no' back.

His desk and surrounding area for ten feet was a drifting dune of files beneath which you could have hidden a body. Papers piled up to the edge of his desk and folders, pictures and diagrams spilled from the top of the heap. A couple of large display boards behind him were smothered with pictures, notes, and diagrams. I asked myself, 'How many cold case files are buried in that mountain?'

He screeched his chair up to the edge of his desk and handed me a worn, sepia and nicotine-stained folder. I suppose this was Duncan's new file, but wondered how many old murders it had held. I was about to open the folder when a hand reached across the desk.

"First, Major, are you at all squeamish? I know that's a dumb question to ask a major of Marines just back from Vietnam, but I gotta tell you there is very little Disney in that file."

I sat back and opened the file. There was a standard form on top filled out in hasty pen and ink, the dull sort of bureaucratic document that discourages thorough examination. I disregarded the paper and flipped it. Right away, I wanted to cover the pictures. There, obscenely displayed, was the grotesque image of a naked woman taken from the feet up. Her legs were spread to their extreme. At their apex, where once there was a crotch, a vagina was torn open with what I supposed to be a rock emerging as if it were a baby's head crowning. I closed the file and looked across at Frosty Williams.

"Thanks for the warning." I wished that I had not quit smoking. The cigarette from which he had just taken a drag looked good. "I would have been seriously pissed if you hadn't warned me."

He nodded and looked at me in a way that I'd forgotten, but with which I had once been very familiar. It's that expert, critical examination of someone reading you, attempting to find a point where they can begin: where to enter, what to hit first? It's the jeweler's loop of the con man examining a mark. I realized that I was probably just another in a long string of residents who had occupied this chair.

"That top picture enough for you?"

"There's more?"

"Oh, yeah." He stood up and came around the desk and took the file. He flipped through several more pictures and then dropped another on my lap.

"Jesus!" I whispered. A dark mantilla scarf wrapped around the woman's face and draped across her torso, partially obscuring mutilated breasts. "Duncan did this?"

"A butt load of evidence shows, with little to convince us otherwise, that Duncan was seen with Martha Hetherington Styles, age 53, at a bar on Jackson Avenue, the heart of Memphis, on Saturday night and he was the last one seen with her when they left together early Sunday morning."

He was reading from the second page of the report that I had set aside. "That Sunday morning his car stopped at a "Steak, Egg and Deep Fry" restaurant on Summer Avenue. He went to the restroom without ordering food. In the restroom they found a sink covered with blood, fresh washed from the hands of the accused. A few blocks later up Hi Way 51 on the way to Millington, his car was stopped driving thirty miles an hour over the speed limit. We found him obnoxious, more hungover than drunk, and brought into the drunk tank, still covered in blood."

"His blood?" I asked innocently. It was the beginning of the naïve effort to find extenuating information about a man I had barely met. He had been a member of our command for less than a week. He had not even started his training.

"No, that was someone else's blood, Major. Not his type." He looked at me with a professional pity, realizing what I was doing. "And one guess who we're pretty sure it belongs to."

Benjamin Hooks, Tennessee's first African American criminal judge, presided over the trial. It lasted less than a month. In the first week after Duncan's arrest, he attempted to kill himself with a ballpoint pen. He told his family to forget about him. They assigned him a barely competent public defender who made only one objection and went to a movie with his mother when the jury went out for deliberations. Duncan was convicted and given a life sentence in the Tennessee State Penitentiary in Nashville. It contradicted everything I believed happened in murder trials. Swift, furious and virtually no resistance from Perry Mason springing from the bench.

What was equally surprising, while I focused in one direction, what came at me from another, was the historically accelerated approval of the Pauline Privilege. It had been approved within a year of its execution, inconveniently one year ahead of my schedule. The Pauline Privilege did in no way fit into my current agenda. By now I had been brought into a spiritual framework in my meetings so diametrical opposed to Catholicism that it would have sent me to the stake during any decade of the Inquisition. I would be their first execution in the twentieth century for my beliefs; I would have been burned at the stake twice for many acts I had committed or thoughts I had before breakfast.

I had not been attending these meetings long in Millington when one of its senior members approached me and with an expression of the sincerest gravity, said, "I've been listening to you lately. I think you need to go downtown to Memphis Rainbow House. It's run by Fred Haynes. He's crazy too."

Perhaps my madness, or the appearance of my "craziness," could have been the product of enforced celibacy for the past three years. They had thoroughly indoctrinated me in the fundamentals of the current gold standard for alcoholic recovery. I had been at the mercy of my own devices for a full year in the combat zone. Both allowed me the latitude to explore alternate ideas that crept their way into my comments. In the deep south a ruminating style like my own translated to 'crazy' if it did not align closely with the New Testament and, most emphatically, the Old.

Decades before substance abuse recovery facilities required certification, just about anyone who had a novel idea that would stifle the alcoholic urge, could open a half-way house. A facility could realize funding from local and state governments without having to prove they were doing anything but serving sandwiches and dispensing esoteric verities intending to curb addictions.

Obedient at least to this senior member's guidance, I went into the city and sought out this Fred Haynes person. He held classes in a halfway house he had opened. It contained space for twelve residents. His sessions, held twice daily, amounted to a syllabus that was, to my rudimentary analysis, the synthesis of the Readings from Edgar Cayce, The Urantia Book, Psycho-Cybernetics and a suspicious suggestion of the teachings of L. Ron Hubbard. For an open and empty vessel eager to be filled, arid and ready for spiritual sustenance, this amalgam was as irresistible and addictive as the substance from which I had been separated for three years.

I attended the classes on Tuesday and Thursday evening also meetings on Saturday and Sunday morning. A small cadre of about twelve of us grew out of an average attendance of forty that showed up on Sunday. We twelve had early tired of just the basic pap fed to the multitude and were seeking deeper teachings. Having scoured the bare surface with Fred's alloy of esoterica, a select group of us went to Fred and Vera Haynes' home on Sunday after the ordinary meeting for the real meeting.

We had already been fully primed with an earlier hour at The Rainbow House and were postured to go deeper. The twelve of us gathered in a circle at the Haynes home. We meditated for an hour or at the first rustling of a restless supplicant, which was usually fifteen minutes. Then we broke up into small groups and explored different dimensions of the transpersonal and paranormal.

I was in the automatic writing group to begin with, not ready for table tapping, conjuring of spirits or past life regression. I would later be led to these other disciplines. I was on an ad hoc disciplinary board that needed to be assembled whenever Heather McDermott was caught using the Ouija Board. The Ouija Board was out of bounds. Heather walked in her sleep. We all attributed this habit to the direct results of using the Ouija Board without authorization. One night she awoke still asleep and walked into her giant circulation fan. It's called current life Karma.

I had been regressed several times, to as many centuries of past incarnations, and was vigorously accessing my twelve guides through automatic writing. I was also about to finish a small paper I had written on the writings of Carlos Castaneda. I cross-referenced these with my Rosicrucian monographs. And the people in Millington had the nerve to think I was crazy.

What loomed counter to all of this was the possible approval of the Pauline Privilege, followed doubtless by a marriage to Sarah. I wanted to be with her, but there was something in me that could not embrace her Catholic Church. Sarah was completely and comfortably ensconced in Catholic doctrine. I could not have reversed the inertia of my growing beliefs, totally out there on the fringe, flying further beyond the perimeter. The gulf between Sarah's religion and my spiritual vision was growing deeper.

I was soon at the crossroads of difficult choices, which were complicated by an evening with the Webers, watching early episodes of The Andy Griffith Show. You know: the one where Ernest T. Bass joins the Army. Jimmy had eaten too much and gone to bed early. Beverly waited until we were hearing deep, submersible snoring from the bedroom. Suddenly, she stood up and planted herself straddling a small rug in front of the television screen. All I could see through the transparent print dress were those legs and where they met, bereft of under panties. I stood up, and her dress fell to the floor.

It was at this point that the very real and ancient part of me that had stood by while I committed the rest of me to celibacy came fully alive and made a command decision. In an instant, the screen door slammed so loud I was afraid it would wake Jimmy. I bolted to my car with the television flickering behind me and a totally naked Beverly Weber still standing there on the porch.

9

Choices

As I gave myself over to alternative studies, Julian surfaced again. He became increasingly more present in my meditations and frequently in my waking life, occasionally through "interior locution." A constant presence, he assured me he would never intercede or interrupt my choices but would visit with friendly counsel when indicated. He was not here to protect me; he would support me.

"Colin, you do not need to be pursuing these exotic alternative means to stay sober. Much of it will help, as long as it is an augmentation to the simple method that has arrested your compulsion." Julian was singing from the same songbook as the heavy hitters in sobriety. They watched with patience as I pressed the paranormal edge, looking for answers other than those I already had.

Julian continued: "You need not restrain a natural spiritual curiosity, Colin. You will continue to look for God wherever you might find God. This is the definition of the mystic: one who seeks to know and understand God. Continue to look wherever you are drawn and to whomever you are attracted. Be spiritually receptive to whatever is happening, but do not abandon the simple path that has brought you this far."

"Julian, how do I know what to be drawn to and what to avoid?" I asked.

"It's all vital." The voice was a distinct, intuitive knowing, not necessarily a verbal statement, more a presence felt throughout the mind-body. "Everything. All of your life is sacred, no matter how painful. Sometimes, the more painful, the more sacred. There's always a reason you are in any situation. Try to see God in all of it."

A comfortable full minute of silence followed to remind me that the message is not always contained in the words, but the moments between the words. Although Julian would not provide direct answers to a problem, he would occasionally ask questions. "What would you want to erase, Colin?"

"The year 1968."

From the end of January until mid-September 1968, the North Vietnam Army and the Viet Cong waged one of the largest military campaigns of the Vietnam War. I should have been there. I missed the Tet Offensive, but the DMZ would have been a safer place than any proximity to Beverly Weber, both of us bathing in the flickering light of a Gilligan's Island rerun. I count it a miracle that we did not collide in rodeo, furniture breaking, sex that would have woken her husband and brought him into the squalid scene, shooting blindly from the hip. With a heroic effort of the will, I had fled into the night. The image of a flickering light shining in and around the outline of Beverly's open thighs stubbornly fixed on my retina. The memory would linger throughout the year.

Hovering above all this was an overcast of uncertainty. I had some serious unfinished business with Sarah and, lesser, hopefully finished business with Beverly. Most immediately I fled the Weber's living room and sought the privacy and safety of my quarters. Then I looked for Julian.

In the matter of Sarah and the Pauline Privilege, I had attempted to illicit Julian's presence. Then one night during an automatic writing session Julian revealed he had been communicating with me through all my experience long before I had uttered the prayer, "My God, what am I going to do?" He was a part of everything I had done, every choice I had made, all that had happened to me. Why would he not be with me during this troubling time? "Look for me in all your transactions. I reveal myself in all your experience."

There was a higher level of influence than direct communication with him. It was experiential, not verbal. "The verbal word is the lowest form of guidance given to man. Direct experience informed the Path," he once said.

Julian had explained that he was not my only guide; I had thirteen. I had contacted twelve of these guides through automatic writing and other devices but could not access the thirteenth guide.

Julian explained, "Colin, you are the thirteenth guide. There is within everyone a deeper understanding that constantly informs you. It is ultimately the most accurate unless occluded by the many distractions to your authentic path.

One of my guides had told me I would meet a soulmate soon at an unlikely location under unideal circumstances. It's common for unevolved minds, exploring the paranormal, to create or look for circumstances they believe might be the circumstances they would the answer to a guide's suggestion. One of these soulmates, I supposed, or rather wished, would show up certainly within twenty-four hours. So, I sought this person in the most unlikely locations, expecting to find her. I searched, focusing on the response from every female I encountered. I almost ran off with a cashier at Kroger.

Julian often reminded me not to look deliberately for outcomes from prayers or other spiritual intentions. If we do, we often craft the outcome to our preferences. It's called "Outlining." All would come in Nature's good time. And you could look forward to an outcome definitely different from your preferences. Trying to seek a specific outcome sometimes obstructs God's idea of what it should be, which I would discover is more often than not different from I wanted it to be, or had supposed it should be.

After looking at every woman for several weeks, supposing this would be the one, I just gave up and went to see "The Graduate" again, hoping I might get lost in someone else's confusion. I had released myself from the possibility of my soulmate arriving for but a few days when she showed up.

It was a historic fourth of April 1968. I was driving the back road into town to a meeting with some friends at the Carousel Restaurant on Union Avenue. It was shortly after six in the evening and without trying to overdramatize the event; the sky was quite literally a blood red. I thought we were going to have tornadoes, which occur quite often about this time of year. Then, just as I was thinking how strange the sky was, I heard the first siren. The nearer I drove into mid-town and the closer I drew to the Carousel, the louder the sirens grew until, by the time I arrived at the restaurant, it seemed that every police car was in motion and had their sirens pegged to the very loud and never turned off position. The streets were a chaos.

As I parked my car and walked to the restaurant, I notice all of my friends standing outside on the sidewalk.

"Who got shot?" I chuckled.

A black man wearing an apron and holding a broom said, "Doctor Martin Luther King." He choked back some tears. "And just last night, he said it would happen." The man turned and walked back into the restaurant. The rest of us followed him. We sat in a booth, looking out the window at a frenzy of traffic.

Five minutes later, a police car wheeled up to the restaurant, and a cop came in. He announced, "You have a choice; you can all either go home right now, or you'll have to stay inside this place for an undetermined period. It could be all night."

Reba, a young woman I had only seen a few times before, looked at me and said, "Do you want to come home with me, Colin?"

Reba was thin and short with tight wavy blond hair that hugged the crown of her head like thick moss. She wore no makeup and had the slightest scattering of freckles only across her nose. Her features were curiously Roman, like those early busts with thick-bridged noses and high cheekbones. Her eyes were flat gray. When they looked at you, they wouldn't stop. It was a constant read. She was a person born to wear denim skirts and walk barefoot through

Macy's. Her voice was hoarse, like she had just smoked a full deck of Camel cigarettes.

Unaccountably, I said, "Okay."

So, they closed the Carousel, and Reba and I went to her apartment to watch wall-to-wall coverage of the assassination of Doctor Martin Luther King. Soon our attention turned to matters that trumped anything that was happening outside the little mid-town apartment. I had supposed, and Reba did not discourage the notion, who seemed very much taken with me, that we would stay where we were all night until things cleared up the next day. It was the late sixties. Morals and ethics had developed considerably from my Victorian underpinnings. Sex was no big thing anymore. Reba, more closely aligned with the new frontier of free thought, just assumed that I would "sleep over."

I slept over. And that's all I did. I awoke twice in the night to feel someone looking at me. Reba was lying beside me, her head resting on one hand, her elbow on the pillow, a small breast exposed. Later I awoke to the smell of cigarette smoke and fresh coffee. I dressed and went into the kitchen. She was wearing a white slip, sitting on a high stool, her knees pulled up around her, an eerie thin rope of smoke rising from her hand. There was a cup of coffee placed beside a bowl of granola and fruit. Milk and sugar sat beside the bowl.

She pointed at the table with her cigarette. "That's for you, Colin."

Neither of us spoke for a while. And then she spoke. "You're different, Colin. In a lot of ways, you 're different." Her legs spilled out from beneath her slip. She stood and walked around the table to sit beside me. "I'm really glad we didn't have sex last night. I know it's not because you don't like me or don't find me desirable. That shit doesn't matter to me."

"I do like you," I said between bites of granola. I sipped some coffee. "I'm not into sex right now." I had also explained to Reba about the Pauline Privilege and how unsettled all of that still was with Sarah.

She lit another cigarette. "None of those matters, right now. You're practicing a spiritual celibacy, aren't you?"

"Yes. It doesn't follow any discipline. I've just had the intuition since the beginning of this ongoing inner rearrangement that it was necessary."

"It has been necessary, Colin. And it will continue to be necessary until that intuition or circumstances tell you to come out again." We both nodded as she spoke.

She had a small altar: a shrine with assorted images and items, pictures of people she had known and historical events. I pointed to the dominant image. "That's Kali, isn't it, Reba?"

"That's right, destroyer of evil forces," she said almost protectively.

"Also worshipped by devotional movements and tantric sects variously as the Divine Mother, Mother of the Universe," I smiled, reciting something I knew about the Indian deities.

"That's right, Colin. I'm not surprised you might know that. But, how do you know that?"

"Oh, God, ask me what I have not been studying for nearly four years." I laughed. "You've got books on your shelves that I've read. We're kind of into the same stuff. You know–Gurdjieff, 'The Fourth Way.' Right? Jung, Alan Watts, and Kerouac. We've been on the same journey, Reba." I stood and took my cereal bowl to Reba's sink and began rinsing it. "We've both had our Journey to Ixtlan."

She smiled, then planted herself on the stool again. She pulled her slip back over her knees, her eyes still fixed on me.

It was early morning still; and I needed to get back to the base. I heard traffic moving on a side street. I supposed things had calmed down overnight. I was leaving.

"Look, Colin," she said as I was stepping down the stairs from her apartment. "When you decide to come out of this celibacy, come see me. Really. I know it has to last as long as you need it, but when you decide, you'll probably need someone like me." I was at the bottom of the stairs, and she added, "And I want it to be me."

I drove the back road back to the Naval Air Station, feeling very safe and very refreshed, as if I had just stepped out from beneath Kiyomizu Temple's "Otowa no taki," "Sound of Wings" waterfall. Misogi is one of Japan's ancient ritual purification practices, probably the only thing I didn't try while I was in Japan.

Less than a week later, it happened. I thought I had reached the nadir of confusion with Beverly's sexually frenzied front room antics and further, with Reba who was about to send me into existential wonderland, when Sarah called and opened a trapdoor on the bottom of uncertainty.

"Colin, good news." I could have crossed the Golden Gate Bridge in the pause. "Guess what?" I knew what she was going to say but remained mute for the second it took her to keep the news to herself. "The Pope has approved our Pauline Privilege!" It didn't help that she had borrowed the Holy Father's celebrity, also she called it "our Pauline Privilege."

She was giddy. I tried to be her version of giddy. I'm not sure how convincing I was. She said she had things to do and hung up. It relieved me I didn't have to hold the pretense much longer. I wondered what it was I had to pretend and how I was going to pull that off. I had just stepped out from beneath the freezing waters of Shinto purification in the presence of a soulmate nymph. How much further could I be from Sarah, and further from the traditional tenets of her church?

The gathering assumption for Sarah and her family was that in a short time we would get married. I knew, on every level then, conscious and subconscious, that it would never work. I had already hurt Sarah terribly the first time when we broke up in 1965. Now I knew I was going to hurt her again and there was no soft way to do it. So instead of stating it in a single painful sentence, I composed an agonizing and endless essay of anything I could think of that might convince Sarah she should not marry me. I set it aside and thought about it.

I called her that night. She sounded thrilled to hear from me. I sensed she was about to launch into a litany of things we would have to do before we got married, and I stopped her. "I think I need to talk to you about my reservations, Sarah."

All she said was, "Uh Oh." And she hung up.

I sent the letter. It was a coil notebook full of rationale, not all of it real. Sarah did not reply. I didn't hear from her again. She was gone. I didn't lose her twice; I let her go twice. I immediately fell into the abyss.

What followed was a prolonged darkness. I had never known depression. Faced with everything that I had done to make life unbearable for myself and others, I had never felt depression at this depth. It fell upon me and grew darker and would not go away. I shivered beneath an overcast of cold self-hatred. I could have told her up front I could not marry her. But no. I had to wait for the duration of a Pauline Privilege delay. Long enough to install in any woman the implied promise of marriage.

I knew the underlying psychological toxins that forbade my honesty to women: I cannot disappoint her, I cannot hurt her, I can't inconvenience her. Reason, an effort of the will or Carl Jung himself, could not get past this thing with my mother. I just needed to get away from myself. There had to be a better place on the planet than my consciousness. But I knew that there's no way to get away from what stands obviously in the way. I had to be with myself until I was done.

Sarah vanished for good. I could never have redeemed the moment. I should have consulted Julian or even Caesar before I crossed this Rubicon. She was no longer there, but Beverly was waiting for me every morning as I rolled in to work.

A loneliness rolled in on me like a flesh-eating virus. I felt literally like I was dying. Then a strange thing happened. One day as I awoke, dreading another day in the land of the living dead, I strangely felt very much alive. I spent a full day finding myself, not quite trusting that I was not only alive, but oddly more alive than ever, as if I had been reborn.

I waited a few days and then, late one night, I made the call.

"Reba, this is Colin."

"Where are you?" She asked urgently.

"In my quarters, out at the base," I replied. "I hope it's not too late. I've been thinking of you." I looked at the clock. It was one in the morning.

"Colin, I want you to come over here right now." She was talking as if she were standing up.

"It's not too late?" I asked.

"Colin, if you wait any longer, it will be too late. Not for me, but for you. Come over here now! The door's open." She hung up the phone.

She was sitting on the same stool with her knees up around her chin when I walked into the apartment. As I stepped toward her, she came down from the stool, took my hand and led me into the bedroom.

Three hours later I lay beside Reba, watching her smoke, trying to find the rest of me that was gone for so long.

"Not everybody gets to lose their virginity twice, Colin."

"What do you mean?" I asked, half understanding what she was going to say.

"How long have you been celibate?"

"Over three years," I replied. "A minor eternity."

"Three years without sex in my world is a major eternity. Whether you realize it, Colin, you are a very carnal creature. Much of your creativity is tied up in your sexuality. If you shut it down for any length of time, it will speak to you in a very uncomfortable way. You were dead. Now you're alive. I have a feeling that sex sober is different from sex while you're drunk."

"I've never had sex like we just had it, Reba."

"It's because you're a different person. Like you have just had sex for the first time."

It had been so long that I had forgotten what sex really was. It was no longer what it used to be. Reba knew more about it than I did, as if she had been watching and taking notes during a lifetime of my misadventure. Through the night we went through exhaustive exploration, fell asleep and awoke to frantic lovemaking, then fell sleep again. We ate cereal in the middle of the night and made love again.

And so, I stepped out of the darkness of a puzzling celibacy that had been sucking the life and creativity out of me.

Julian explained what I now realized: "It's impossible to shut down one aspect of one's Being without effecting it all, including the resident soul. A person's sexuality is a vital component so native to the creative force. If a person deprives himself of such a force, the rest of that person will gradually wither and die. A wound in one major part of consciousness propagates across all vital lines and wounds the rest."

As with much of Julian's wisdom, I asked why he didn't tell me about this stuff before I made such dangerous mistakes.

"You only learned through the mistakes of your own choices. Feel it happening in your body. The brain does not provide the information you need. Again, I will never tell you what to do, or what not to do. You have that first freedom: to your benefit or otherwise, the freedom of the will. You make your own choices. I'll say it again, I am not here to rescue you from your choices; I'm here to support you."

In the morning, Reba and I went to the Carousel. We had waffles. Just the thing for famished lovers. We had finished our breakfast. We were quietly watching the traffic run up and down Union Avenue. I looked across at Reba and had the feeling I had known her before I knew myself.

It was a Thursday. "I have to go to Nashville."

"What's happening in Nashville, Colin?" She reminded me of a child eager for a road trip.

"I visit this Marine every month. He's in prison," I replied. I waved at Phineas to bring us some more coffee. He was the man who was there the night Martin Luther King was assassinated, "He's in for life."

"Wow. Wha'd he do?" Now she was really interested. I told her about Staff Sergeant Chester F. Duncan.

"I don't think he got the best defense. He said he couldn't remember doing it. Then he shot himself in the foot when he took the stand. Told the court he could have done it. The evidence was damning based on his military record which had some offenses for violence with women in Japan." I thanked Phineas for the coffee and put a five in his apron pocket. "I don't think they pay him in this joint. Do you?"

"You know, Colin, they find a way." She watched Phineas walk away. "I mean, it's good that we tip him. I do all the time, but do you know what?"

I looked up at her. I just wanted to look at her. She said, "Even if people like that don't get paid, they find a way."

"People like what, Reba." I knew she wasn't talking about race. She hated racists and was a card-carrying member of the NAACP.

"Some people are just closer to the answer than others. There're some folks who learn to live with poverty just knowing there's a power. And that knowing attracts the Power. If they're suddenly provided even a minor wealth beyond what is minimally necessary, it disturbs their spiritual equilibrium. They are robbed of the experience.

"If you take a person out of their circumstances, you take them out of their life. The only thing they've been given to do. In the marginalized world there's power in their circumstances. If a person gives himself to what he is evidently given to do, he accesses a power greater than anything he could find in property, position or money."

Wow! Here was the embodiment of Julian, sitting across from me, drinking coffee. And we had just given our bodies to one another.

"I agree." I had probably read it in one of my mountains of books. "Sometimes I think their wealth burdens people with a lot of money. It often insulates them from the answer. Money becomes large in their life early and they can't get away from it. They don't get close enough to their suffering," I offered. "But they are drawn to suffering in different ways. Where did I read that man cannot forever avoid his own nature and therefore his own suffering?"

"I read the same thing someplace. Same place as you, probably." She smiled. "So, can I come with you?"

"I want you with me as long as you can stand it."

"I think we'll be together, just a little longer."

I smiled; she wasn't smiling.

Seventy years had done a number on the building since the Tennessee State Penitentiary had opened in 1898. Its grey, august architecture lent no sense of hospitality as we passed through the outer gate and were ushered into a strip search room. I could almost feel the history of the place, the thousands of convicted prisoners and their lives, some who had died in this very building. Nothing much good can happen in the prosecution of law enforcement in a maximum-security prison.

When Reba came out of the strip search, I regretted having brought her here, but was soon cheered by her coy smile and immediate proximity. We proceeded to the visiting room. I had been coming here once a month since they had sentenced Duncan to life. In the beginning, I had visited every week.

I thought that Reba's presence might brighten up his day. His family had ceased visiting. His wife had divorced him. It was a crap shoot. Maybe Reba might demoralize him, knowing that he might never be with another good-looking woman again if he lived.

We were sitting at a table when a guard brought him in. Duncan was thinner, and his face had lost much of the life force. It had, as some said it would, taken on the lifeless tone of the prison walls. After he had been seated, he spoke right away, as if he had been rehearsing a speech. He looked at the guard first, as if he and the guard had discussed what he had to stay.

"Major, I really appreciate you coming up here, but I don't want you to come anymore." He had not even looked at Reba. I didn't say a word, but I waited for him to clarify his request. He looked up at the guard, who gave him a barely perceptible nod. Then Chester F. Duncan stood and walked back into the prison, his guard a step to his rear and a step to his left, which, I was reminded, was the position a junior officer walks behind a senior officer in the Marine Corps.

We had made our way out of Nashville traffic and up to speed on I 40 before Reba talked about it. "I think I know what that was all about, Colin." I had been dwelling on Duncan's demeanor and his statement. I was probably too occupied and had said little about it as we left the prison. Exiting a maximum-security facility does not lend to deep or intimate dialogue.

"How long you been drivin' up here?" Reba was watching the trees blur by. She wiped her fingertips across the window, leaving thin wet lines in the condensation.

"It'll be a year pretty soon," I answered.

"How long did you intend to visit?" She turned to look at me.

"Jesus." I shook my head. "Forever, I guess," I said.

"How long does it take for a favor to turn into an insult?" Reba often spoke from a place beyond her years.

We had driven a few mile markers before I spoke. "I think I understand, Reba." I glanced at her and then back at the road. It was raining, and we were entering a series of turns. "But I'm not sure."

She spoke. "So, here's a guy who's gonna be in the joint for the rest of his life. He's probably been told by that very guard that he needs to decide he's in there and not going to get out. So, every time you show up, it does a couple of things to him. It reminds him of a life he will never know again. He's probably saturated with guilt as it is. Now he has to feel guilty about never being able to pay you back for visiting him forever, even though forever hasn't come yet." She undid her seatbelt and slid closer to me, putting her arm over my shoulder. "The only way a guy like that can say any of that is, 'I just don't want you to come back again.' I think he was returning the favor by setting you free."

"That poor soul. What does a person have to do to make that adjustment?"

"Some never do." She looked out of my window over the vista of the valley passing far beneath us on the left. "There's some people walking the streets trying to make the same change. They're walking around in their own prison and can't get out."

"I guess I was that way." I looked at Reba. She looked older sometimes than she was. "I had to find a way out."

She laughed. "Think you're all the way out yet, Colin?"

"Evidently not. From the inside it doesn't feel that way yet." We didn't talk until we were passing through Jackson.

The Pancake House on Summer Avenue served us waffles. I ate them and drank coffee like I had just been released from prison. We drove home and sat up in bed all night. We didn't make love. In the morning she was awake just as I had found her months before, sitting on the high stool, her knees up around her neck wearing the same white slip. There was coffee and granola waiting for me. As I ate, I knew what was going to happen.

"Do you know, Colin, there are people in the world who wake up in the morning and can do anything that comes to their head. There's nothing in their way. It's not that they're sociopaths or anything like that. They've just built a life where there's nothing in their way. Nothing stops them; things get out of the way for them."

"I don't guess I'll ever be one of those people." I stopped eating. "Jesus, far from it."

"Yeah, I think you need structure, Angel." She looked at me. "You might think you need freedom or that you're free because you run free sometimes, but all you're doing is running around wild inside a self-imposed structure."

"Like I need my own prison, but I need all the maneuvering room available inside the walls," I said, nodding.

"Yeah, like that." She smiled almost maternally. "That's about as close as it's going to get for you."

"Why do I have the feeling I won't see you again, Reba?"

"Because you're not going to see me again Colin." She wasn't smiling anymore. "I hope one day you will be happy or free, or both."

I would never be that person. Reba was telling me I didn't have to be anything other than who I was. She agreed with me; I was in my own prison, like Duncan. Most of my plight was caused by trying to be the guy who woke up in the morning and did whatever he wanted. But she was right. I would always need structure. I had to visit Reba's world for a while to find out that I could not be her, or any part of her. I'd be whatever my life had made of me. Even if I'd been set free, I would need to build a structure around it. I'd run around inside it, breaking its rules just to think I was free, but I would still be inside the prison. I'd run back to what was holding me hostage.

We had talked through the night. Reba spoke of her Tantric training and even explored Santeria, which did not stray too far from Sarah's Catholicism. She was drawn to it all, not because she wanted to become any of it. Reba was free to explore, without feeling she had to do any of it. She could wake up in the morning and do whatever came to her. She was one of those people she was talking about. I would be bound by a deeper, indefinable adherence to a growing belief, always changing but never knowing where it was going. I would have to make friends with this, she had told me, or else I would be at war with everything. I would never be happy in the sense that people define happiness. Now and then I might experience the absence of conflict, but I would always seek, but never find that place that fits. It was the seeking itself that satisfied.

"Will I ever cease from seeking?" I asked her.

"If you live to be an old man." She offered her sweet, dimpled smile, probably referring to our previous conversation about me surviving another tour in Vietnam. "When you're in your eighties, you'll probably look at your shelf of books and wonder why you had been seeking and what you had learned. You'll probably say, 'I've finished looking.' Then you will have consolidated all you've learned into one, private learning and not have to think about it"

"A sort of Ruthvenism?"

"Yes, call it that." She laughed lyrically.

I said, "But you'll get up every day of your life not tied to any belief and do whatever you want to do. I don't see you ever being married to any person, never mind any belief."

"That's right, Colin, I'll probably never be married to anything." She laughed, nodding that I had landed on a fundamental truth. "But you'll probably marry someone real soon and it won't matter who, but it will probably have to do with what you currently believe in or that you are seeking." She was shaking her head as if she had thought of something, but was reluctant to share it. With a resigned smile she said, "And when you marry this person, it will prove one thing: no human power will provide you with what you want or need."

She finished a cigarette and lit another. "You're an artist, Colin and a poet. The sad news is that all of this is going to show in your art. Your poetry will be stiff and your art constricted in tight lines, trying to find their way in words and shapes that others have already formed, but you'll never find your own line as long as you are looking for it in others'. It will always refer to something else and never be itself. Derivative. One day late in life it will fall in place, but in the meantime, you are going to be very restless."

I didn't see Reba again. She went away. I don't know where. She would be no one's bride. She would always be her own person. I would have to go back to Vietnam. But even short of that, I would have to go back to the base. I would have to climb into a uniform every day. None of it fit her Tantric shirts off, free-for-all soul. You don't develop that kind of soul. A person is born with it. I had to make friends with the soul I was born with. Right now, it was wearing a uniform, and I had to show up somewhere every day and a part of me had become totally at home with that. Just as Julian had repeatedly told me, "If you want to know what your path is, look at what you are doing. If you want to know what's going on or what God would have you do, look at what you are doing."

All at once, I entered a vacuum where nothing existed or could enter. I was beyond alone. I had severed ties to a friendship with Sarah. Reba had created a fullness of life and then vanished, creating an even larger emptiness. The daily proximity of Beverly emphasized the very real need to find some place to put this newly awoken sexuality. I was peeled and ready for the first possible piece of a puzzle that could fit into the vacant shape.

On the fifth of June on this strange 1968, Robert F. Kennedy was shot dead, barely two months after Martin Luther King's assassination. Had the heavens been rearranged? Has the planet swapped poles? All the major chaos plus my own, lesser problems recalled "The Second Coming" by William Butler Yeats:

Turning and turning in the widening gyre
The falcon cannot hear the falconer;
Things fall apart; the center cannot hold;
Mere anarchy is loosed upon the world,
The blood-dimmed tide is loosed, and everywhere
The ceremony of innocence is drowned;
The best lack all conviction, while the worst
Are full of passionate intensity.
Surely some revelation is at hand;
Surely the Second Coming is at hand.
The Second Coming! Hardly are those words out
When a vast image out of Spiritus Mundi
Troubles my sight: somewhere in sands of the desert
A shape with lion body and the head of a man,
A gaze blank and pitiless as the sun,
Is moving its slow thighs, while all about it
Reel shadows of the indignant desert birds.
The darkness drops again; but now I know
That twenty centuries of stony sleep
Were vexed to nightmare by a rocking cradle
And what rough beast, its hour come round at last,
Slouches toward Bethlehem to be born?

What else could happen with the year only half done?

"Major, take a look out this window." Daphne Cottingham, the secretary for all helicopter systems, was indicating the crowd that had assembled for the NAMTRAGRU picnic. I looked out the window. "No, take a look through these." She handed me a pair of binoculars. I looked through the window in the direction she had shown and saw a slender woman with two little girls. "That's Kim, Billy Earl's sister, down from Pittsburgh for a visit." She took away the binoculars. "You should come visit tonight. We ha'n a cookout, me an' Billy Earl. And them too. They're comin'."

I knew they were rescuing me from Beverly Weber. Everyone could see the force field, both of us drawing together in a hot arms, legs, and elbows collision.

Kim was everything Sarah and Reba were not. She was singularly unattractive, very thin, with a prominent aquiline nose; she was angry and aggressive. I drew myself toward her so that I could not fall off and into Beverly, who was very wide open. Maybe I could avoid Beverly Weber plus fill the void left by Sarah and Reba by engaging with their opposite. I had been taught that everything in creation refers to everything else in creation. We are inexorably related to All of It. In a small way, I saw it happening locally. Everything and everyone were referring to something or someone else. Reba was right again. In no way could I just get up and walk away from anything. I stepped into it; and let it happen.

I became acquainted with Kim. Real well and soon. We were immediately intimate the very night we met, right after the cookout in the back of my car. She moved to Memphis. She was divorcing her husband who in her words was, "Not worth a tinker's damn;" and there was some other stuff about his anatomy.

Barely two months passed. I was automatic writing and wrote the question, "Mokurra, should I marry Kim?" Mokurra was the most ancient of my thirteen guides. He used language that reminded me of the Native American idiom. Also, he would never tell me what to do, but ask questions that drew a solution from my own consciousness, the closest to the deepest part of our inner Selves. After I asked him if I should marry Kim, he waited for the usual minute and the familiar scrawl replied, "Does Colin love 'nose and ankle, girl?'"

I asked myself, "Does that matter?"

When a person asks someone to marry him, he should ask himself a few questions about the person he is about to marry. I veered clear of these questions lest they dissuade me from my mad purpose, which was very close to no purpose at all. Had I asked the questions or paid attention to the data that was flooding in at me, I would have heard Daphne when she took me aside one day and said, "Major, I just don't want to see you get hurt." I didn't ask her what she meant, but pressed on.

When she visited Memphis from Pittsburgh, Kim would spend a lot of time at the Chief Petty Officer's Club "entertaining the troops" according to Chief Petty Officer Dempsey. He also had tried to feed me information when he heard I had asked Kim to marry me. Even Kim, when we had been getting acquainted, made the statement, honest in the extreme and as cautionary a comment as could be offered. It was something that Sarah had once said and any honest woman who needs a man most every night would say, "Colin, just never leave me alone."

We were married in a very informal ceremony at a church in Munford, Tennessee. Prior to the ceremony the minister took me aside and asked me as a friend and not a clergyman, "Do you really know what you are doing? Do you really want to marry this woman?" Not that I could be dissuaded. I was just not listening and proceeded as if I were being guided by the same forces that allowed Reba to do whatever she wanted with each day that she awoke.

It's important now that I add a vital player to this strange mix.

Sheldon Elliott was a resident in recovery at The Rainbow House. He had come to Memphis that summer in 1968 to join an advertising agency as a copywriter. When he was sober, he was an amazing talent for creative copy, voice over and comic impersonations. But, like most alcoholics, he was a total pain in the ass when drunk. It had taken a few months for him to lose the job he had come to Memphis to fill. He bottomed out on a spare bed at The Rainbow House during a time that I frequented the place, sharing my experience with the residents.

Sheldon Elliott reminded me of one of legions of people I had known in the smarmy ranks of Vancouver's grifters. We became fellow travelers. He reminded me of home. I became his sponsor in recovery. When he was released from The Rainbow House, he got a job at another advertising agency. He had seen some of my drawings. He told me he could get me work freelance, illustrating for one of his accounts at his current advertising agency. Each Sunday an ad appeared for Pidgeon Thomas Iron Company on page A2 of the Commercial Appeal. Sheldon wrote the copy. I drew the cartoon. We were a team. It was my first job as an illustrator while I was still in the Marine Corps. With but a surface relationship with the man and an equally surface, or at least ambivalent commitment to my imminent marriage, it made sense that Sheldon would be my choice for best man at the wedding.

The morning of our wedding, Sheldon told Kim that if she were ever weary of me, he would be available.

10

Sheldon

There is a certain personality for whom people will make undue allowance in the face of enormous insult, offense, and other evidence that would recommend caution. An unwary soul is blinded to the wiles of such a person and will show enormous charity even when the cost is onerous. At just that point where a sane person might recognize highly schooled duplicity, this personality will say just the right thing, and with such skilled humor as to elicit a laugh and an effusion of forgiveness from the victim of which he had thought himself previously incapable.

Sheldon Elliott claimed to be from Cleveland. He had been in no place else if you were to have read his legitimate life itinerary. However, if you were to hear first-hand the litany of cities in which he claimed to have lived and the celebrities with whom he had socialized, you might suppose you were entertaining red-carpet royalty. It begged the question of why he had landed in the very provincial town of Memphis, Tennessee. Five minutes with Sheldon would convince you he had rocked their world as a voice for the "Flintstones" at Hannah Barbara until they became too small for him and he had to move on.

He arrived in Memphis at the behest of a large advertising agency that would find out too late that his style varied vastly from his resume. Organizations often dismissed him before he received his first paycheck. When I met him, he was standing in the dayroom of Rainbow House in a dirty undershirt, shaking off minor Delirium Tremens and sipping decaffeinated coffee, loaded with condensed milk and three heaping tablespoonfuls of sugar.

He was barely five feet tall, shorter without his elevated shoes, athletic, chubby, but not fat. A bushel of hair surrounded an uncanny resemblance to James Cagney. A thousand different voices would spring from his mouth at will and an endless reservoir of jokes and anecdotes. He composed sorrowful eulogies for anyone with whom he had scant connection and for whom he had less understanding. He had an Irishman's appetite for sadness and fell to grief at the demise or even minor sickness of a remote acquaintance.

If he could stay sober, avoid benzodiazepines and opioids, he was the single most talented copywriter and voice in the city. A long and interrupted resume spoke to the capacity of the man to find work and just as quickly lose it. If it could be an even deeper fault, he was Irish to the bone, and although not actively religious, he was conveniently and devoutly Catholic if it were to his theatrical advantage. Drama was his forte, on and off the stage. A credit to his talent was his successful portrayal of, ironically, the Great Ziegfeld in a Memphis Dinner Theater production even though he was the smallest person in the cast. He could convince the audience that he was as tall as the role required. An amazing memory assisted him with scripts, names and events, although he might have forgotten where he had parked his car.

One of the unnerving qualities of this personality was his charm, a device that readily got him into trouble and just as conveniently out of it. This attribute was never used to greater purpose than in Sheldon's ability to network with total strangers or celebrities. Once engaged, he could schmooze indefatigably and convincingly. Shortly thereafter Sheldon would announce to nobody's surprise that he had once again landed a new job. One could set his watch and wait for the day his new employer would discover that Sheldon was sleeping in his car or at the job and was invariably impaired and uninspired. An annoyance to anyone for whom he worked for any length was

Sheldon's generosity with positions that didn't exist on a firm's payroll. He had but to know you for a few minutes and he would offer you a job for a skill you might not have but that Sheldon would convince an agency you did.

Originally, when he saw my drawings, he suggested I retire immediately from the Marine Corps even though I had only seven years left on my twenty. "Come to work with me at Ward Archer and Woodbury," an agency that had just hired him, only provisionally. Fortunately, I had grown up in a larger city that flourished with such personalities. I regarded his invitation with affectionate skepticism. The West End of Vancouver cultivated this character type. I had sat with the best in the beer parlors on Granville Street as they discussed the finer points of separating a mark from their money. So, I was not only comfortable with Sheldon, but in a sad, sentimentally exploitive way, I used his company to assuage a mild home sickness.

The seriously unfortunate aspect of his Irish-ness was a superstition bordering on paranoia. This pathology does not sleep well with matters relating to the paranormal, and to that topic Sheldon often suggested caution. I spoke to him about the private meetings our group had at the home of Fred Haynes, the founder of Rainbow House. He would throw up his hands like a fishwife and mutter superstitious incantations of cleansing, while wringing his hands in his apron.

Fred Haynes had established his paranormal confederacy long before Sheldon appeared at The Rainbow House. With his capacity to ferret out key people and their "game," it wasn't long before Sheldon found out about the "closed" group and the arcane nature of our gatherings. Although he wanted nothing to do with the group, he just had to know more about it.

Ace McVey, who had worked for the Pepper Tanner Media group as a jingle writer, had died earlier in the year. Sheldon had met him once as a very irrelevant part of a group that was listening to jingle samples. Sharing but bare cursory words with Ace, Sheldon still assumed that he had established an intimacy of blood brother magnitude. He wept at Ace's funeral and rendered a eulogy usually reserved for high clergy or exhumed saints.

About a month after Ace's death, while I was practicing my automatic writing and seeking counsel from the damnably inscrutable Mokurra, I began getting a strange series of messages on my writing. The entity identified himself as Ace Mc-Something. I couldn't quite make out the last name. But I later assumed that it was Ace McVey, and I showed the writings to Fred Haynes. Fred urged me to make contact during one of our Sunday meetings. I did this and, in the force field of like-minded nutcases, the entity identified himself as Ace McVey. Further, the entity Ace McVey confessed he had failed to leave a will for his family, believing, as most musicians do, that he would live forever. Much further, Ace McVey allowed that if I was strange enough to have contacted him, I would take it to the next level. If it was, in fact, Ace, the entity asked me to write a last will and testament posthumously from the grave through my automatic writing.

I consulted Mokurra. Of course, kill joy as ever, he provided no counsel at all; he just asked a key question. "Is this allowed in your world? Is it legal?" When I tried to contact Ace again, he wouldn't talk to me. He had left the room. These guys, on the other side just can't take a joke. The truth I supposed was that I had blown Ace's cover and he could not stand a snitch. Or, as often happens, entities on the other side appreciate and even enjoy the innocence and gullibility of Earthlings who are more interesting about life to come than the one they're in.

It's not so much that delicious data travels fast, but that Sheldon had a way of mining information before it had arrived and making of it more than it could be. If a rumor was alive, Sheldon could sniff it out and turn it into a sellable, highly embellished copy. Then, his very imaginative thoughts could conjure a soundtrack, costumes and a stage setting and take a harmless rumor to melodramatic fact. The guy fed on drama.

"What the fuck's this stuff 'bout you talking to Ace McVey, Colin?" Sheldon had slithered up to me undetected and was whispering on my neck in this clandestine fashion, common to espionage players in Cold War Movies. I was in a scene from "The Third Man." A full cubic liter of smoke billowed from his chain-smoking face. A cigarette, to Sheldon Elliott, was a major accessory, a prop to his incessant histrionics. It also helps maintain a raspy broadcast voice.

"Sheldon, you don't want to get involved with this. It involves psychic phenomenon, most of which is a projection and has no basis in fact." I was reading chapter and verse from the cautionary introductory statements on the paranormal. All I needed to do was introduce a pathologically superstitious energy like Sheldon to the works, and it would draw all the dark forces of the other side. Just because they're on the other side does not mean they're free from psychic baggage. A dark entity will enter a session for nothing more than mischief. The other side is populated with the same variety of idiots as is planet Earth.

"That's bullshit, man." He sat down on a couch at Rainbow House. When he sat down, his legs were not long enough for him to sit in a classic masculine posture with his legs crossed. He'd slither up on the edge of the seat and allow one knee to touch the floor. The rest of him sometimes slid to the floor. He squat-sat dragging frantically on a cigarette. Sheldon had dentures that frequently lost their grip when he was excited. His teeth would involuntarily clack together when they lost purchase with the surface of his gums. In a touch of drama, he deliberately teased his hair into a reckless male bouffant redolent of a scene from "Streetcar Named Desire." This was his favorite pretend place to go, Marlon Brando his favorite pretend person to be.

"Sheldon, these people are practicing a dark art, summoning, and exorcising demons at the same time. They don't know what the fuck they're doing. Forget about it." I was running out of ways to discourage him. Knowing he would probably spurn my invitation, I suggested he come out to the base and I would demonstrate. In the business world, they teach a person how to say just enough and know when to stop. I missed that lecture. I should not have invited Sheldon out to the base to watch my show.

Night on the back road from Memphis to Millington is eerie enough without Sheldon's Shakespearian expectations, rendering it darker. He was about to conjure the dead from a sleep that should not be interrupted. He arrived early. There was a tentative tap on my door. If a knock can be nervous, Sheldon's was psychotic. I suppose the Navy was saving on their utilities. Barely lit, the halls of the bachelor officer's quarters were a dull dark grey, blacker than the night. To lend a lurid ambiance that needed no help, I delayed my response for several seconds before I opened the door. I let it fall open, as if by a ghostly hand, revealing a lesser darkness but for a few low watt bulbs.

"Jesus Christ, man. Turn on a fuckin' light! Mother of God!" He was shuddering. I think he was smoking two cigarettes. I had arranged my automatic writing material at a desk where a fifteen-watt light shone down, barely illuminating the paper. I told Sheldon to be quiet if he really wanted this to happen. He squat-sat at the edge of the bed, one knee pressing into the floor, his hand teasing his hair into Marlon Brando disarray. His eyes wide open like eggs.

"It's best to pray before we attempt to contact the other side." I side whispered to heighten the tension, as if it needed anything else done to it. "On Sundays we meditate for half an hour before we explore the outer dimensions."

"Shit! Don't meditate, man." He took an enormous dramatic drag that caused him to grip the side of the bed. "Christ, just goddam do it." He lit another cigarette. I was unsure he would have enough for the evening. Following my protocol, spiritual or superstitious, I wasn't sure. I prayed and then sat down at the table. Then I spoke in somber petition.

"I am open to the presence and response of the entity Ace McVey. The request on behalf of the sitting entity Colin Ruthven." I could hear Sheldon muttering prayers or curses on his breath. His teeth clacked twice. The insufficient light of the small lamp reflected beads of perspiration on Sheldon's face. I placed my pen to paper and allowed a loose hold to take the pen where the entity showed. Nothing happened for several seconds, then the pen quivered and began to write.

"Jesus, Christ, Colin. Tell it to stop. God dam!" Sheldon was standing, his superstitious energies gone full paranoid, surging to psychotic. The room began to spin with energy. He was breathing hot smoke into my hair. A part of him was nudging my chair closer to the desk.

"Sheldon, there's no way this can happen with you doing that. Just sit down and we'll start all over." I gradually coaxed him into a chair. He sat across the room, peering at me, squinting and blinking. After a swollen minute of silence, I continued.

"Ace I'm here with Sheldon Elliott whom you might remember from Vernon Caldwell Associates." Sheldon had moved on to a third agency that had already fired him, and he was looking for work elsewhere now. From across the room Sheldon's voice whisper shouted.

"Yeah, Ace. Hi. I was the guy in the green cardigan. I had a mustache then, but I shaved it since. You probably wouldn't know me now." I glared at him to stop. Then he added. "So, how you doin' Ace?"

I gave him a 'you've got to be shitting me' look. The pen moved again. Sheldon jumped in the air and scurried to the opposite end of the room. The pen kept writing. As with most automatic writing, I wouldn't even watch what was appearing on the paper but let it continue. As it kept on writing, Sheldon slowly crept closer, looking at the paper, his eyes attempting to focus on the blurred images. Eventually he was looking over my shoulder. His eyes finally landed on the writings. He was reading them before I read them.

"Mother of God, Jesus Christ all mighty." It was a hushed whisper. I felt Sheldon's grip on my shoulder like a vice. Smoke blew down onto the paper. I had written a full paragraph:

'I Ace McVey, being of sound mind and body, do willfully make this my last will and testament. I leave to my wife Freida the entire substance of my estate, except for my power tools that I leave to my good friend Stephany Spurlock.'

Sheldon screamed. The writing stopped. He reached for the phone and was dialing a Memphis number. "Ernie Bernhardt's got to read this shit, Colin." Sheldon could barely dial the number. As soon as there was an answer on the other end, Sheldon almost screamed, "Ernie, Jesus Christ, guess who I was just talking to?"

The night wore on for a few hours, Sheldon phoning anyone who would listen. Each time he made a contact he put his hand over the speaker and would say to me, "Ask him if…" Or "Does he want me to…?" At no time after Sheldon made his first outburst did I hear from Ace McVey or anyone else again. It was happily the end of my adventure into paranormal correspondence.

Because of his association with the spirit world, Sheldon lost the job for which he had been lobbying, but he readily found work again at a dwindling roster of advertising agencies. Just as quickly, he got drunk and lost another job. People in the industry lost interest in Sheldon Elliott. They regarded him as almost a fictional character. I could take him in small doses, so it was a relief that my duties at NAMTRAGRU required my attention most of the time. Sheldon was a full-time job. When I was with him, it took all of my attention. So, I took frequent breaks from the man. But he will remain a permanent fixture until the very last page of this story.

Naval Air Maintenance Training Group had a hefty travel schedule. It visited and inspected several detachments and their personnel across the United States annually. The trainer, or the hardware used to train aircrews, represented a large component of a contract with manufacturers like Grumman or General Motors. Contractors and sub-contractors from all over the country signed on to manufacture parts of a weapons system. Someone deeply involved NAMTRAGRU in writing the training programs for all weapons systems. Some of the personnel spent months at a time at the factories writing outlines for the training and allowing for the maintenance of the trainer.

In a single year, I traveled with inspections groups and logistics management planning teams to Bethpage, New York, El Toro California, Beaufort, South Carolina, Key West, Florida, Jacksonville, Florida and Whidbey Island, Washington. While I was on Whidbey Island, I took a few days leave, departed from the team and flew up to Vancouver.

During the Vietnam War there had been a huge influx of Americans migrating to Canada, most of them to Vancouver where they were welcomed, not as draft evaders, but kindred souls of a common political belief. The largest percentage of those who found their way to Vancouver ended up in the West End. This will always be the spiritual center of the city, the neighborhood where I discovered every way to make a mistake.

I had no intention of seeing any of my relatives. My parents were in Calgary and my sister was busy raising a family and didn't need my help. Although the West End was my destination, my main reason for being there was to visit Ernie D'Amico. Ernie and I had been friends since the first grade. In 1966, just before I had departed for Vietnam, I had visited Ernie and Babs in Los Angeles. It was here that he introduced me to his concept of the Ultimate Power of the Universe in his pictorial essay, A Glorious Cosmology. Ernie's words and the book had stirred me off dead center from a rudimentary, sophomoric idea of the God of commensurate punishment and reward for deviation from or adherence to whatever was the current Word for all the ten thousand paths to the same destination.

In the intervening few years, Ernie and Babs had parted company, both with as vastly divergent beliefs as those of Sarah and me. They divorced on a much more honest platform of understanding and an intelligent basis for a continuing friendship. Ernie had become a monk in an obscure Middle Eastern discipline that had required a lengthy apprenticeship. He accompanied an Easter Swami across Canada with a begging bowl. He held a vow of silence and obedience to whatever the world asked of him. I had heard that he was now a junior adept teaching meditation and yoga in a rooming house in the

Kitsilano district across Burrard Bridge from the West End. I had been having repetitive dreams of Ernie urging me to seek him out. The dreams stated that there was a "foreign entity occupying his body."

I rented a car and drove into the West End. At this point in my sobriety, it would be a good idea to avoid my crowd at the Austin. After a morning meeting with friends who had sent me tapes and letters while I was in Vietnam, I drove across Burrard Street Bridge to the Kitsilano District. I had to slow down for the mobs of pedestrian traffic, all young men probably between twenty and thirty who had found refuge from a war in which they didn't believe. The streets were so full nobody seemed to notice crosswalks or traffic lights.

Ernie's ashram was the place Angie should have sought instead of suffering the disdain of some of his old squadron mates. It took me awhile to find the house. The place was at an obscure address, run down beyond repair. They had built it at the end of the previous century. An enormous set of wooden stairs led up to the main floor. Beneath was a vast basement where an ancient sawdust furnace, that might work, but probably did not, sent heat through two floors and into an attic. Here, a constant drip of water seeped through a ceiling that had not been repaired through uncountable previous tenants.

I had no trouble finding Ernie. He was the main event. The first floor, except for the load-bearing walls, were stripped to accommodate a single large room. In the middle was a raised platform upon which Ernie sat upon a discarded automobile seat and stadium cushions. He wore a sheet that had been white about ten washings ago and a small rope-like rag around his neck. A chela had tried to shave his head that morning. There were slight cuts where his apprentice had got too close to his work. Otherwise, his head shone, back-lit from a large window. It reminded me of a scarred orange.

Thirty young men occupied the periphery of a stage surrounding Ernie. They were silent, intent on something he had been saying. His supplicants sat akimbo on the floor with no cushions and notepads in front of them.

I was sure Ernie had not seen me. I entered and remained at the edge of the room. Ernie had not looked up and seemed to have been lecturing with his eyes closed. Presently he said,

"That's my dear friend Colin, over there at the door. Please let him into the circle." A path parted in the crowd and I walked down to the front row. Curious eyes looked up at Ernie all the while, wondering where to fit me into their framework. How many times Ernie and I had run down the alley on the way to school, stopping long enough to pluck the fat and ripe Bing cherries from the trees. In high school we had drank together and fought together. The years passed. We had found each other in Los Angeles. I recalled our happy hour trip to Tijuana with Sharon. In later years he drifted away, he would have said, further apart but in fact closer, "arriving where we started," as T. S. Eliot suggests and, "knowing the place for the first time." Today he was nowhere near any of the places I had known and nothing of the man I had known. But I could see he was close to what he had always tried to be. All his life he had been trying to get back to this place.

He had walked away from his total history. I didn't know him now, but he was offering me the courtesy of a favored place in his temple.

"Colin is a major in the Marine Corps, a fighter pilot." Some eyes looked at me, wondering that they had just allowed a field grade officer of Marines into their ranks. They relaxed as Ernie read my resume. "We went to school together, and we were in the Marine Corps together. Colin was in Vietnam in 1966 and 1967 and is going back in a few years. Right, Colin?"

"Perfectly right, Sir." I didn't know what to call him. It was no longer Ernie. I turned around and faced the men. "I have no opinion one way or another about your decision. That's not why I'm here. But I do respect whatever decision you've made. Many of us do." I was mobbed by shaking hands and a few hugs.

"Let's break for the day," Ernie proclaimed and rose a hand for invocation that everyone recited. They all left the room. Ernie and

I were alone. With the absence of the others, I felt at once in the presence of a stranger. The others had insulated us from the distance that had grown between us.

After the room cleared, Ernie came down from his mound of cushions and hugged me. I said, "I was in Vancouver, so I thought I'd drop by and see what you're doing over here."

Ernie laughed and scratched at the rope around his neck. "Oh, Colin, that's such bullshit." He bent over laughing and sat on the curb of his platform, rubbing his naked ankles. "I'm supposed to be dying, right?" I was surprised and didn't answer right away.

"Well, to tell the truth and clear the room of the bullshit, I had these dreams, and you were in them, and something seemed to show that you were not well." I stopped, too self-conscious to add the bit about foreign agent occupying his body.

"I have this tumor, Colin. In the brain. Doesn't that make sense?" He started laughing again. "Do you know that the doctor had to find some reason for it? People just have to make sense of everything. They can't allow things to just be. The doctor says it might have to do with multiple acid trips. I can't tell you how many hits I took when I was down at UCLA." He laughed some more. "If I had been a doctor, I would have used that one." He smiled. "And if he's right, I'd still go back down to the campus and drop as much acid as I did then."

"What do you think it is?" I asked, as naïve as any of those doctors.

"I don't think about it." He laughed and could not seem to stop laughing. "It just is, like everything else. Everything just is." His face became serious. "It's a part of me, so it's sacred."

"Sounds like it might be your ticket out."

"Oh, Colin, that's perfect. Oh, yes. My ticket out. And I can hardly wait."

I was not sure what came next now that Ernie had become this Eastern monk with a dirty rope around his neck and a tumor in his brain. I looked around the room, bare with no people in it and almost naked, with just Ernie and me there. I was about to say something, anything, just to fill the air space when he suddenly spoke. His face was no longer Ernie D'Amico, but an unrecognizable old man.

"I must sleep now. You'd better go." With that, he stepped behind the broken car seat and, pulling a sheet over his body, rolled over on his side. I never saw him again.

When I returned to Memphis, Kim was waiting with a scattered stack of messages from many of my Memphis friends. "Your fucking public has missed you, Major Ruthven," she said.

"How about you? You miss me, Kim?" I asked as I went through the messages, most of them from Sheldon, a few from the people at Rainbow House, and several from our study group. The group had moved on to Edgar Cayce and his "Search for God Study Books" almost exclusively. "Kim, why don't you join our group? We could do this together and when I'm out of town, you can be with that crowd." She didn't answer but was watching an episode of "All in the Family."

"I get bored when you're gone, you know," was all she would say. I supposed that while I was gone, she was bored and found other things to do that had little to do with a search for God. I couldn't blame her. I gave her all the room she needed to be just who she was. It was like Reba had said. 'We must make friends with our own soul and not try to be anyone else. We are who we are and none of that is bad. And the only actual sin is to stand in the way of another person's path and further, to interrupt our own. We must allow them to be who they are, allow ourselves to be who we are and to find out who that is.'

I took care of some calls and returned to work the next day. A heaping incoming basket awaited me, the barrier I wanted to keep between me and Beverly Weber. She was there and seemed to send the constant semaphore that she was available and was still not wearing any panties. I buried myself in my work, my marriage, the study group, and whatever summons I received from the city. It didn't take long.

It was nearly five in the evening, and I was wrapping things up around the office when my private line lit up.

I picked up the phone, "Hello, Ruthven here." Nothing. "Hello. Anyone there?" Then I heard a hoarse whispering followed by a series of familiar coughs. "Sheldon, that you?" I knew his cough, knew it better than his voice. I heard a lighter fire up another cigarette, and then he spoke.

"Colin, you gotta get out here." I could barely hear him.

"Why the fuck you whispering, Sheldon? Where you at?" I pressed the receiver closer to my ear. "Speak up for Chrissake."

"Okay. Come get me. I need you to bring me some stuff." He was speaking in his stage whisper voice now. God knows what kind of drama he had created. I think he was doing his James Dean. "Go to my place. You got a key, right?" I nodded at the phone and said nothing. He continued, "Get my typewriter. It's full of blood and shit! But get it anyway."

"Blood! Your typewriter is full of blood? Jesus Christ, Sheldon, what the fuck you talking about?" Beverly was leaving, but she was staring at me as she left. She waved and lifted her dress so I could see she was wearing panties after all. Thank God Sheldon was on the other line. "Sheldon, tell me what's going on. This is too strange for even you."

"Cynthia's old man found out I was fuckin her and he paid me a visit." Sheldon had swiftly lost one of the best jobs he ever had and was now working for a dorky in-house advertising agency for a real estate firm. He had taken up with Cynthia Costello, one of the sales team, and her husband had evidently found out. "He busted the place up."

"D'you call the police?" It was an obvious question. I expected a left field answer.

"No! No, shit no. No police. Too many questions and shit. Fuck! You should know better than that, Colin, Goddam it." That was Humphrey Bogart, his gangster, tough guy voice.

"Okay, never mind that shit. How about you? You okay?" I asked, knowing what he was going to say.

"He busted me up pretty bad, Colin. He opened my head. Hit me over the face with my own fuckin' typewriter! God damn! I need that fuckin' typewriter. I got this freelance piece for Drusilla Jewelers."

"Well, where the hell are you, then?" I pulled out a pad and a pen, about to copy the address. It was a place in Horn Lake, Mississippi. "What the hell you doin' down there?"

"Shit, Colin. I'm in fuckin hiding." I was about to hang up when he added with urgency. "And, oh, wait. Bring us a couple of Big Macs and two vanilla shakes?"

"Two!" I groaned. "Oh, God, who's with you?"

"Cynthia, of course. We're getting married." He was doing Lawrence Olivier on me. His wrist stuck to his forehead. He had to protect his illicit love interest.

"And what about their three kids?"

"I'll marry them too."

I stopped by the house to change.

"Where you going?" Kim was standing at the bedroom door while I changed. She was wearing 'Gogo boots' and had just come home herself.

"I've got to go to Sheldon's place and rescue him from himself." I was pulling on my loafers and looking up at her. "He's got his ass in a crack again and needs help."

"You know that little prick tried to fuck me, right?" She pulled a cigarette from her lips with the indignation of the total female domain. She spewed smoke across the room. I thought it was going to bounce back off the wall. "You need to let that little shit crash and burn." She took a drag that could have sucked half the air from the room.

"I have no doubt he tried to fuck you," I replied. "And he does not need my help in the crash and burn department. It will happen all by itself."

"Aren't you going to ask me if I fucked him?" She pulled the cigarette from her mouth and spilled the room full of smoke again. I had never known a woman who could get so much smoke and velocity out of a cigarette.

"I figure you'd tell me if you did. And quite honestly, Kim, I have never thought that you might fuck someone else while we were married. I kind of trusted we were not fucking anyone else while we were married. Please correct me if I'm wrong." She turned and walked downstairs into the den, dumped herself onto the couch with a crash and turned on the television set.

I drove into Memphis to Sheldon's current address, which he changed as often as he did jobs. The Capri Apartments was a converted motel with soundproof concrete block walls. He lived on the second floor. I accessed his room from the outside on a balcony that faced Linden Avenue off South Bellevue Boulevard. I walked up the outside concrete stairs and followed a trail of blood. It led from his apartment to a place on the railing. Sheldon had evidently jumped for his life into a privet hedge pursued by an angry husband–again. I didn't need the key. The door was ajar and inside there was a carnage of books piled upon books, a broken coffee table and a hole in the television screen. Dead center of the room was his little blue portable Royal typewriter, several of the keys clogged with blood and a few clumps of hair. Shit. I missed all the fun.

I curled a handful of M&M's and peanuts from a small bowl, tossed them into my mouth and inventoried the place while I munched dinner. The walls were wedged edge to edge with pictures, all of himself, some of them studio photos for movie or television portfolios. I had a sudden ache of sorrow for the man who had tried all his life but could never quite get beyond himself. I wondered how much of that sorrow I was having for myself. But this was a man who had spent most of his life trying to be other people. I had bought into the myth, hoping it might be real.

I went by McDonald's and filled a bag with Big Macs and two giant vanilla milkshakes. This was not exactly central casting, on the lam fare for lovers in hiding. It was another day's march from downtown Memphis to Horn Lake. I should have bought the burgers in Mississippi. By the time I got there my Memphis McDonalds were cold.

Sheldon's directions were surprisingly accurate for a cowering lover hiding from a jealous husband. A driveway was invisible, swallowed up in darkness. The lights all over the house were out. Sheldon and Cynthia, the lovers, had gone dark. I hoped I could find the numbers for the address. It was on the mailbox at the street. My knocking drew frantic whispers from the other side of the door. I could have predicted what was next.

"Who's there?" Two voices asked- a boy's voice and a girl's voice, then heavy breathing.

"It's the big bad wolf and I've come to blow your house in." I was shaking my head, visualizing the two of them on the other side of the door staring at one another, wondering if it was safe or was I the husband coming to finish Sheldon off.

The door cracked, and Sheldon peaked out. He looked beyond me and to both sides, as if there could be anyone else there. He was taking a scene from "On the Waterfront" for openers. I pushed my way in and handed him the bag of food.

Cynthia Costello was curled up on a couch, her hair a pile of broken hay scattered in all directions. She had on a short dress that kept rising around her hips as she pulled herself further up the couch.

"Close your fuckin' legs, Cynthia," shrieked Marlon Brando, his skivvy shirt torn a Stanley Kowalski askew. One of several differences between Sheldon and Brando: Sheldon had no muscle, hardly any sinew at all. Stella Kowalski kept riding up the couch, as did her skirt. Stanley threw himself at her feet and covered her exposed calves with his cowering body, whimpering and screaming. "Jesus, he can see all the way up to your fuckin' navel. Close your legs, Cynthia."

Oh my God! Sheldon had taken ownership of another vagina.

"Who could have possibly let you into their home?" I enquired.

"I take in strays," a voice said through a thick billow of smoke. From around the corner stepped Frieda McVey. "Look, if you kids are not gonna eat them burgers, let me at 'em," The widow McVey turned to me with her hand out. I shook it. "I understand you been speaking to my old man."

"Sheldon told you, I guess," I replied.

"Yeah, that little shit got in touch with me as soon as he heard you was talking to Ace. On the other side, fa' crissake." Frieda pulled up a kitchen chair, sat at a dinette table, and pulled an ashtray toward her. She nodded to a place on the other side of the table. I pulled up a chair and sat down.

"Did Sheldon even know you before then?" I asked, knowing what she would say."Shit no, the manipulative little prick thought he was going to comfort the bereaved and get in her pants." She smirked.

"That's about right." I nodded and looked across the room at the couple folded up on the couch like one person.

"Could you fire me up?" She nodded at the cigarette in her hand. A man size hand on a woman handed me a lighter; and steadied my hand while I lit the cigarette. She smiled seductively.

'Oh, Jesus,' I thought.

"And then he calls and asks if he can bring little miss tiny tight pants over here." She pointed her man's hand at the two piled up on the couch, trying to crawl into one another's clothing.

"So, I'm to understand he calls and doesn't even know you, trying to romance you at your lowest moment." I show with one finger. "And I'm to suppose that you tell him to take a hike in several flavors." She nodded. "Then he shows up anyway with his current romance interest, both on the run." I was running out of fingers. "With the likely possibility that a jealous husband might be half a league aft and headed for your door."

"All of that is correct, Inspector Harthstone." She laughed a mouthful of smoke into the center of the room.

"Sheldon, you know you're still bleeding." I pointed to his head. "You really should go to the hospital with that." Neither of them acknowledged a word I was saying. They sat huddled together, gnawing at a burger like gerbils and alternately sucking on the shakes and kissing one another's foreheads. Their faces and hair were covered with food and milk. "And I doubt if that typewriter is going to work. It looks pretty jammed with your blood." I got up to go outside and get his typewriter.

When I returned to the room carrying exhibit A, Frieda McVey was standing over Cynthia, wagging her finger at her and speaking maternally. Sheldon had excused himself to tidy up. He came rushing in the room.

"Jesus Christ, I'm still bleeding. There's a fucking hole in my head the size of a dinner plate." He was circulating the room trying to get our attention, one person at a time. The rest of us had to look inside his head. He had fed us enough drama that by now we were drama dope sick.

"Cynthia! Goddamit cover yourself!"

"May I enquire?," I asked. Sheldon returned to the comfort of the couch and his love monkey. He had her examining the dinner plate sized hole in his head. "Do you kids have a plan?" They looked at me with a blank stare, as if I had asked them to recite the Third Law of Thermodynamics. I waited for about twelve beats of their pounding hearts and added, "Because if you do or if you don't, you're going to have to do it without me."

"Why?" Sheldon asked, his mouth full of burger. "What do you mean, man?"

"I've got orders."

11

Orders

"What do you mean, orders?" Sheldon was alternately fondling the keys of his typewriter, the hole in his head and the remnants of the cheeseburger. His teeth were clacking.

"I've got preliminary orders to report to El Toro, California, for retraining in the Phantom and further to report to Headquarters First Marine Aircraft Wing, Danang, Republic of Vietnam." I was reading from the body of a dispatch I had been carrying around since early that afternoon when the administrative officer handed me a sheaf of messages, one of them releasing me from the Navy and back to the Marine Corps.

"Well, shit!" shouted Sheldon. "Where does that leave me?"

"What the fuck, you two married or something?" This time it was Cynthia. She pulled herself away from Sheldon's tentacles. "Never mind, you two. What about you and me, Morris?"

"Morris!?" I asked

"Yes, that's his real name." Cynthia looked at Sheldon with a proprietary glare. "It's Sheldon to everyone else, but Morris to me."

"Nice to meet you, Morris." I was staring at Sheldon again, trying to pull himself out of Cynthia's love lock. "I'll ask again. You guys got a plan? Because you got this furious husband and I don't think he's done yet. And, Sheldon, I do not belong to you. I belong to the Marine Corps first. And second: I belong to a wife."

"That's too bad." It was Frieda McVey.

"What's too bad?" I asked.

"That you belong to a wife." She smiled. "And what's a Phantom?"

"The F4 Phantom, it's a Marine fighter. Actually, it's an interceptor. Goes faster 'n shit and carries four Sparrow missiles in the fuselage cavity, plus anything else you can hang on it." I was probably getting too excited just talking about it. I could hardly wait to get out of Millington and back in a cockpit. If Frieda hadn't stopped me, I was about to recite a total disassembly and nomenclature of the Phantom's fire control system. The message had me sufficiently charged that I had myself back on marine property and free of the Navy's constraints.

"Jesus, a Marine fighter pilot shows up in my kitchen and all I can offer him is a cup of coffee?" Frieda looked around the room. "And I didn't even give him that."

I reached across the dinette table and held both her hands. "Frieda, it's all about timing. We only think we're in charge. Time is fate's insidious mistress."

"And a philosopher, too! You better get out of here, sweet pants, before I do something you and I would probably enjoy but eventually regret." She took a Kim Ruthven drag on her smoke and added, "We could probably show these two goons a few tricks."

"Frieda, I hate to leave you with all this. Is there anything I can do to help you out?" I looked over at the groveling lovers on the couch, kissing the milk shake and blood off of one another's faces.

"I can manage these two clowns, no problem." Frieda stood up from the table and was leading me out of the house by my elbow. "You had better leave before it's too late. I'm not sure I can manage myself."

"Incidentally, did Ace leave a last will and testament?" I probably shouldn't have even brought Ace up at this point.

"Hell no. Are you kidding, Colin? He was a fuckin' musician. He could barely sign his own name." She closed the door and left me to the night.

It would not be the last time I saw Sheldon Elliott. He's pivotal to the plot. I was to learn that catalysts enter our lives to affect major adjustments along the path, changes we would otherwise not have made on our own unaided will. Where one would expect catalysts to be major figures, these catalysts often appear as comic anomalous figures who might be summarily discounted as irrelevant.

My orders were not an immediate problem with Kim. I could take my family to El Toro while I was going through familiarization with the Phantom and training. The big problem was that I had told the trio in the love nest about my orders before I told Kim. By the time I returned to the house, Sheldon had called enquiring about a few things he needed me to bring them the next day. Incidentally, he mentioned to my wife that she was going to be a Marine Corps widow for a year, but the good news was she was going on a trip to California.

"So why don't you take the little shit to California with you, Major?" If she called me Major, she wanted to kill me.

"I'm sorry, I should have told you earlier." I turned down the volume on the Hi-Fi. It had been playing "Hey Jude" on a continuous loop. She grabbed the volume knob, turned back on full loud, then dropped the arm of the needle onto Hey Jude with a horrid screech. Smoke followed her from the room as she turned and stomped away.

"So you go to Viet fucking nam, I suppose." She dropped her body onto the lounge as if she wanted to break it.

"You suppose correctly," I replied quietly. "It seems from your tone, that you would be glad to see me out of here for a year."

She stood up and stormed out of the room. I could hear the front door slam. I looked out the window, and she was marching up the street. Jimmy and Daphne lived a block away. She would stay with them tonight. Maybe she'd talk to me next week.

Three weeks later we piled Kim's two girls and our baby, Phoebe, almost a year old, into the Plymouth station wagon. We crossed the Hernando de Soto Bridge on I 40. Our destination: The Marine Corps Air Station at El Toro, California.

The Phantom was, as I had explained to Frieda, an interceptor. I had flown the last of the gunfighters, the Crusader. I would never fly it again. The Phantom was an entirely different animal. It was the beast. This time there was an air-to-ground bomb sight, and there were a few more bells and whistles to give you half a better chance in the combat zone. Its principal difference was the GIB, the "guy in the back," the brains of the radar and intercept machinery. A monkey could do front seat. It took brains to occupy the rear seat, and he was a passenger. He had no control stick and, if I wanted to eject him, I could. And did I say that the Phantom had two engines with afterburners?

Kim and I rented a small apartment in Santa Ana. I began a six-week transition training into the Phantom, attending the very training that the Naval Air Maintenance Training Group provided. I knew the Staff NCO instructors. It was my first experience with a multi-engine fighter with twin throttles and a whole new feel from the engine and the controls.

After nearly three years attached to the Navy, I sank into the Marine Corps environment as if they had released me from prison. I took a new passion into the training. I ate it up, adapting to the Phantom as if I had always flown it. My only hang up and one that I had to get over was the GIB, (Guy in the back). When I pressed myself back into the ejection seat to find my 'hold the line' center of axis position, I had half a feeling that I was sitting on the Radar Interceptor Officer's lap.

I was a major, so all the RIO's were likely to be junior to me. However, in the beginning, it was like Archie was sitting behind me, my old man waiting to blind side me every time I sat in the front seat with someone in the back. I had gone through this same trauma bond all through flight school and thought I was over it. There are some patterns a wounded consciousness never scrubs from its primal layers. Someone once said that fundamental orientations to life do not yield to manipulation.

I flew with a different RIO every flight. Until I told Archie to leave the airplane, he would always be back there. I had to fly with him through about twenty training flights, waiting for him to hit me upside the head. When the wheels lift into the well and the beast breaks ground tracking upward in a twenty degree climb in afterburner, the two of us are in our own environment. It's just us, the RIO and me, and it can be very intimate, especially if we flew into marginal weather, a night intercept and a near midair collision. Night in-flight refueling with no lights on the tanker, simulating combat situations is a true bonding experience. Of course, I had the communications with the outside agencies, tower, air traffic control, ground-controlled approach. But throughout the flight there is a hot mike marriage between two guys, flying one enormous machine. We were a tiny corporation every time we briefed, left the hangar, and walked out to the airplane and back to the hangar.

It happened on a night bombing run in the desert. On such a procedure, the RIO usually reads out each thousand feet of altitude. For each weapon and dive angle, there's a release altitude that we designate before takeoff. Naturally, the pilot monitors the altimeter in the dive, cross checking his instruments with the readout he's getting from the RIO. I had achieved the dive angle for the delivery and had maneuvered the pipper onto the target. I knew the altitude for the delivery, critically specific for pull-out to avoid getting hit by the "beam spray" or any broken chunks from my own explosion. Also, and even more important, to avoid flying into the ground.

I was anticipating the "Mark" from the back seat and was about to hit the pickle, but there was no transmission from the back. I pulled out of the run with enough altitude to recover and not dive into the target, creating just another crater.

"You back there, Archie." The minute the words came out of my mouth, I laughed. There was no reply from the back. I looked in the mirror and I saw First lieutenant Barry Thurmond waving his hands frantically in the dark. In a minute, I heard the familiar click of the hot mike.

"Jesus, sorry, Major, I lost the connection back here."

When I replied, I was still laughing. We climbed back up into the bombing pattern and I said it again, "You okay back there, Archie?"

"Say again, sir." the puzzled reply came from the back.

"No problem, Barry. I'm just having a serious breakthrough moment. I'll be okay as soon as I can change my diaper."

"What?"

"Nothing." I was almost in hysterics. I hit the afterburner twice in a row and did a night roll. I thought Barry was going to eject. Archie was never with me again.

Flying the Phantom was a breeze. It flew itself and was a very stable platform for weapons' delivery. A pilot could almost fly hands off in formation. Things went smoothly as I brought myself back into the Marine Corps and even deeper into a cockpit.

But it was another story at the Globe and Anchor Apartment Complex.

For some families the apartments were temporary accommodations, but for others they were permanent quarters. Most were Marines and their families attached to the Air Station or the Helicopter Facility at Santa Ana. Permanent families develop small communities and engage in activities creating neighborhood social systems. While the marines are at work, and often deployed, the wives and the children gather to occupy their time and take care of the children, get them to school and socialize in small groups.

It took only a few days for Kim to connect with a small group of wives in our section of a large apartment complex. Customarily, every unit in the Marine Corps has an Officer's Wives and Staff NCO Wives Club that create activities to account for free time, organizing generative activity. This component of Marine Corps structure is crucial to officer and troop morale. The group that Kim joined had a steady rotation of new families. There was no structure; it had also become locked in party mode. The children basically took care of themselves, getting to school and coming home. A few of the more responsible women took up the slack and covered for a few of the women who were engaged in recreational activity. Those who are so engaged are very often at the frontal edge of the leadership and the rest of the crowd follows.

The good news of the bad news, or the upside of the downside, was that when I arrived at the apartment in the evening, instead of a customarily angry Kim blowing smoke across the room and finding the first flaw in every detail, she greeted me at the door with a smile. Some kissing and amiable conversation followed as I wound down from my day. The girls were old enough to take care of themselves, get fed and watch Phoebe. Meanwhile, the festivities continued into the evening. Eventually Kim went to bed, often with amorous intent.

I was gone by sunup in the morning, so I only saw the afternoon side of the activities. About the third week of our six weeks there, I noticed the crowd growing. When a certain element senses a good thing, they seem to find traction and their numbers increase. In the world of Officers Wives Clubs, the women organize charity events, tours, student activities and sober gatherings like coffees and teas. They join civic groups and contribute to their community. It would have been well for Kim to have found this community.

At the Globe and Anchor Apartment Complex, the party grew in numbers and the hours increased long into the night and early into the morning. The activities were not exactly civic minded or charitable. To give it a positive spin, they became seriously recreational, oriented to particular appetites native to the West Coast of California in the early seventies. Children were not getting to school and husbands were skipping work.

I'm convinced that Kim did not take drugs. She was simply a part of an original group of wives who enjoyed an afternoon glass of wine or two; then she'd come home happily shitfaced. In 1970, Southern California was flooded with an exotic substance that The Globe and Anchor crowd washed down with Orange Julius. I was the senior officer in the building and knew nothing about what was going on. I should have suspected something when my wife, usually an angry person, had become oddly amiable when I came home at night.

The investigation arm of the Military Police loves to explore anything radically outside the normal course of events. They thrive on matters suspicious and subversive.

I was tying up business one afternoon after flying a couple of flights when a corporal came up to me and said there were a few guys in the parking lot who wanted to talk to me. The couple of guys were military police from the Criminal Investigation Division.

"Major, we were wondering if we could convince you to take your wife and kids on a small vacation this weekend." The older man, in civilian clothes, about my age, showed me a badge. He reminded me of Frosty Williams, Homicide, Memphis.

"Can I ask what this is all about?" I enquired.

"You can, sir, but we cannot tell you what this is all about." He smiled wryly. "We know you're living in the Globe and Anchor and that you're only there temporarily, so you probably are unaware of what's going on." He butted a cigarette on the asphalt. "Can we ask you when you're due to leave and rotate back In Country?"

"I'm finishing up here in a week and taking my family back to Memphis. Then I come back here for another ten days of training, and I rotate back to Vietnam."

"It would be best for everyone involved if you could take the family to Disneyland or down to the San Diego Zoo. Just get out of the complex this weekend." They got in a military police vehicle and drove away, leaving me with several questions that I was rapidly answering in my head with paranoid alacrity.

I told the skipper of the squadron that I needed to take the weekend off and give my family a brief vacation. He was evidently in on the deal and told me it would be a good idea. The kids were thrilled that we were all going to do something as a family. We took the weekend off, drove down the coast, and spent two days in San Diego. I finally saw that fabulous zoo they wouldn't let me see on the way to boot camp. We returned to Knott's Berry Farm and spent a day on the sand at Laguna Beach. The whole time Kim fumed in her brooding best, wondering when the organized fun and festivities would end so she could get back with her "friends."

We returned late on a Sunday night so I would be up bright and alert Monday morning for an early briefing. Kim was very excited to return. We had barely unloaded our bags and souvenirs when she left the apartment and went down the hall. She came back in five minutes, slammed the door and blew smoke all the way across the room.

"Those motherfuckers busted the place." She stared at me as if I had been the motherfucker who had "busted the party."

I went down the hall and rapped on a door. A younger man whom I had seen in the squadron answered the door, just barely opening it a crack. He looked behind him and barely whispered. "Major, the police raided us on Saturday. About ten of the guys and five women are in the Santa Ana can."

"What the hell were you raided for?" I thought everyone had just been locked in a harmless party mode and couldn't get out.

"Oh shit, the place was loaded with drugs." He looked at me suspiciously. "Didn't you know about this?"

"Trust me," I replied, seriously puzzled. "I knew nothing about this. I am totally stupid and stunned but very grateful we were out of town."

He looked at me for a few seconds and then shut the door. He didn't believe me. I don't blame him. I guess I knew about the raid, but didn't. I had just been warned because they didn't want a field grade officer getting pulled in on a routine drug raid. I was also allowed some slack because I was about to return to the combat zone.

On the way to Memphis, Kim sat low in the seat, her mouth tightly shut. She scowled all the way to Barstow. She finally cracked when she spotted the "Desert Redoubt Roadside Antique Discount Warehouse." They were selling stuffed Gila monsters and snake-skin ladies' pumps at an alleged discount. I stopped. The girls wandered the aisles while I waited on a wooden bench beneath the outdoor sign of the "Redoubt". I commiserated with other husbands while their wives searched for expensive animal skin to cover their feet.

As I sat beneath the shade offered by an enormous overhanging buffalo skin awning, I thought that I could probably start a support group for men like us who wait outside emporiums, berry farms and discount outlets for angry wives. I could offer tours, now that I know how to get to the San Diego Zoo, Sea World and Knott's Berry Farm.

But what came to mind over and above anything else I should have seen was something that had never occurred to me. In my self-centered, totally self-absorbed attention to meaningless details, I had failed to understand why Kim had been so happy at the Globe and Anchor Apartments. She had been with her people, doing what her people did. I did not think she was in on the drugs, but I realized that she was a drinker, and it was in her nature to drink. Just like Reba was telling me. People are who people are–good or bad. In a real world there is neither. People just are. Drinking made Kim happy. And the horrible irony of her life was that she married a guy who could not drink, and so she had to "not drink" with him. I had married a female version of myself. God help us all.

On two counts, Kim had every right to be as angry and hot as the smoke that spewed from her tight little mouth. She needed a drink now and then. She might not be an alcoholic, but she needed the palliative that allowed some souls to get through their day without it becoming a problem. Without this small mercy, they'll be angry at anything and anyone who stands in the way of the only thing that makes life bearable. I would be angry with myself if I were married to me and could not drink because of me.

And hugely, there was this next year while I would be in Vietnam. The woman who told me not to leave her alone would be left alone. While I was not around, she could again find a small community, however harmless, to make life as easy as it can be for someone for whom life has always been difficult. I think it's called a "free hall pass" in our new world. And for the rest of our marriage, which I expected would not be until death did us part, I would grant her a "free hall pass," whatever that looked like.

I had barely pulled the station wagon into the carport, but Kim was out of the car, striding up the street to her brother- and sister-in-law's house. She had endured as much of all of us as she could stand. The girls and I emptied the car of luggage, Phoebe and the box filled with strange colored rocks that the woman at Desert Redoubt promised us had arrived with the first asteroids four million years ago.

We were all watching Gunsmoke re-runs when Kim returned upbeat. She was in a mood strangely redolent of her general deportment when we were living in the Globe and Anchor Apartments. I was happy for whatever concoction Jimmy and Daphne had prepared for the transformation.

I had been assigned only temporary additional duty while in El Toro. I had to return to NAMTRGRU to tidy up some loose ends, which was a treacherous prospect in that it involved taking inventory with the training officer's secretary, the ubiquitous Beverly Weber. Beverly suggested we do this after hours, but I protested lobbying that we do the job in the middle of the brightest daylight and surrounded by everyone on the base. She couldn't manage, so I relented and agreed to arrive after dinner the following night.

It was well that I did not arrive in my pajamas or anything suggesting to Beverly that we finally bury the hatchet, or whatever she wanted me to bury. I walked in the front entrance in partial darkness and was blown back by the lights suddenly illuminated and a hundred voices screaming, "Surprise!"

I felt safe at last except for the wild Fifties bouffant of blond hair that kept lurking at the periphery of the mob surrounding the punch bowl, assorted lunch meat and dip. At one point the crowd parted and there she was with her dessert dish up around voluptuous lips, made moist by the frequent ingestion of ice cream. She grinned and waved a spoon. That would have to be as far as we went with our goodbye.

When an officer leaves a unit, he usually walks away with at least a coffee cup bearing the unit's emblem baked on the outer surface. NAMTRAGRU presented me with a large plaque with the Group's colors and below engraved on a strip of copper, a legend, doubtless composed by any of the chief petty officers who could have read and felt the heat between Beverly and me. They had the cunning to couch the language in sufficient ambiguity that I could concoct an explanation for anyone of a number in a broader universe. But to the present crowd, there was no doubt what they meant.

"To Major Colin J. Ruthven for exhibiting restraint and resistance in the face of temptation beyond that which ordinary man would have succumbed and for which we will always say he was 'One of the Few Good Men'"

"What's this?" Kim was holding the plaque as far away from herself as she could without dropping it, looking at it as if she had just retrieved it from the sewer. It was barely after breakfast, and I was packing.

"Oh, they gave that to me at the Group for being able to restrain myself at the bar." I was stepping over one of several bags that littered the den. The kids were watching Sesame Street. Kim didn't seem to know or care that the kids were in the room.

"That's bullshit, Major." She dropped the plaque. I heard a chip fly across the floor. She lit a cigarette. I waited for the funnel of hot smoke to fire across the room and break against a wall. "This is about that Beverly Weber cunt." Kim stepped over one of my bags and kicked another. "That bitch has been trying to sit on your face ever since you got here." She walked out of the room. "Daphne told me about it, asshole." Her words faded as she strode deep into the house, deeper into her own darkness.

I glanced at the girls. They were fast approaching puberty and were well schooled in the ways of boys and girls. Their mother had not put a gag on her feelings or language, ever. By the time they arrived in their teens, they would have a sadly accurate but cynical perspective on life. Phoebe was barely two, but big enough to know when her mother was off the page. She had that 'will an adult please show up' look on her face.

"And another thing, Major." Her hand was on her hip and the other elevated on the door jamb. "I know that the only reason you married me was so you wouldn't fuck Beverly Weber and get court martialled or have your ass handed to you by Billy Earl." She threw the cigarette at me and charged out the door. I thought she was going to march up to Jimmy and Daphne's place, but I heard the station wagon start and tires leaving rubber on the street. It turned in the base's direction, most likely the Staff-Non-Commissioned Officer's Club.

She was half right. One reason I married her was to get away from Beverly and invest my testosterone in my home instead of someone else's. The other reason was Sarah. I had put myself so far away from marrying Sarah that I married the first woman that crossed my path. More to the point, the first woman who represented the polar opposite of Sarah.

It was not a happy goodbye. Most farewells for military families who will not see one another for thirteen months are sad, but at least warm and soft. There was none of that. I just left.

There was the actual possibility that I would return to the same house and the same family if nothing happened to me in Vietnam, but that was hardly a certainty. And then suddenly the odds increased they would all be there when I returned.

Kim was pregnant.

She drove me to the airport. We stopped at the gate. I jumped from the car and unloaded my gear from the trunk. I waved at her through the curb window. Kim didn't wave back. She burned rubber like she was blowing smoke across the room.

I would be at El Toro for a week while I processed for further transfer to the Far East. I rented a car and sped down Laguna Canyon Road to 'the Place.' Many of the same faces were there. Although there's a freshness to the skin, the default expression in every one of these rooms is the face of fatigue. We arrive more tired than drunk. I didn't have to talk to anyone. I just had to be in the room. I was there every night until I left.

"You were here about five years ago," she said. I turned to see a full length, to the floor, muu-muu and long curly hair. The dress hung on a woman I supposed to be about fifty. Acne had ravaged her face in her miserable high school years, probably. She looked like a woman who had every reason to seek comfort in a substance or activity. A constant barrage of nicotine and alcohol had ripped her voice. The combination creates a female baritone that's unmistakable. "You were a pilot. You were going to Vietnam."

"I still am. Both." I pulled a chair over so she could sit beside me. "I remember you. Shorter hair last time and a shorter skirt." We both laughed.

"What's it like?" She nodded upward toward the ceiling. "You know, flying and dropping bombs." She had fired up a cigarette. Her hands shook. She leaned back as if she should wear glasses.

"Can we go outside?" I suggested. "I feel odd talking about it in here. The place is crawling with people who are decidedly not on board with what I do." I smiled. "As if I'm trafficking in child slavery."

"What makes you think I'm on board with it." She looked at me sideways.

"'Cause you're talking to me, for one. And you're asking how it is." I shrugged. "You've got no idea how some people avoid me altogether."

"'Kay, let's go outside." She shrugged. I followed her through a couple of rooms to the back of the building. She was a tall woman, and she had been a tall girl who had tried to look short by leaning forward when she walked. I detected a slight scoliosis and a limp that she preferred I had not seen. We sat on a bench by a small, coy pond.

"It's not really what you imagine. Tactical flying is like a lot of highly dramatized things in life that are nothing like they are portrayed in movies. Maneuvering into position is very physical, often violent, and then, like they say, it can be hours and hours of utter boredom punctuated by moments of sheer terror. The moments of sheer terror drain every ounce of adrenalin from the body and leave you totally exhausted." I was waiting for it to happen. "A pilot often looks forward to the hours of boredom after those moments of excitement."

I had expected to have run her off by now, but she was leaning forward, hanging on every syllable. "They really make carrier landings look like a ride around the racetrack. Every landing's different. At least it is for Marines 'cause we don't do it very often. Night carrier landings have totally 'come to Jesus' events." I looked at her, supposing she wanted to talk or for me to stop. She nodded for me to continue.

"The plane I fly is a fighter, but for our purposes it's academic. They converted most of us fighter pilots to attack, close air support." I stopped and began over.

"We drop bombs, rockets and napalm as close to our troops as we can, hitting as few of our own troops as we can. It's called close air support. It's almost a leisure activity. I could do it in my sleep. At night or in the soup, it can get pretty hairy. Night air refueling is pretty hard as well. But it's work. If you don't love what you're doing, you'll die. I just know that. Love it or you'll forget what you're doing and you'll buy the farm."

"So you love what you're doing?" She nodded.

"I love what I'm doing." I knew what was coming next.

"Do you love killing all those children with fire-bombs?" She stood up and walked into the clubhouse. I sat there for a moment. I asked myself the question, 'Do I love killing all those children with fire-bombs?'

Of course, I didn't. There was no feeling to it at all. I had learned naturally to shut down all feelings when I left the ready room and walked out to the airplane. I wondered what other feelings I had to shut down at the same time. It would not be the last time they reminded me you cannot just selectively shut down one part of yourself without affecting the entire system.

During our orientation prior to departure, we were told not to wear our uniforms at the airport. A group of Marines just back from Vietnam had pizzas thrown at them as they went through the terminal wearing their uniforms. I could tell there was going to be more of me to shut down in this experience than I had expected.

12

Vietnam

American Airlines was far more hospitable than the civilian passengers that saw us off at the L.A. terminal. I ignored the cat calls sent across the rope. The flight attendants were apologetic, politely compensating with assorted beverages for the mob that tossed insults and few other items across a bright red cordon that surrounded our boarding area. We changed into our uniforms in a small dressing room in the waiting lounge. I engaged with Brett Hamilton, another major with whom I had gone through the Special Indoctrination Course at Quantico in 1959.

Thankfully, we were soon in the air. There was an unusual haste to get us aboard. I had the distinct sense that the terminal wanted to get the uniformed personnel out of there before someone started a riot. I was numb to it all. This was my second trip. It had been worse when I had landed in the States back in '67, when a kid in his teens who did not know what Vietnam was all about threw the remnants of a cheeseburger at me as I walked through the terminal.

The processing center at Camp Geiger, Okinawa, was a congested hive of camouflage and green utility uniforms, filtering in and out of Vietnam. Those on the way out wore faded utilities, but renewed purpose. I was in a large auditorium with the inbound, a lethargic lot filling out standard forms that cleared us into the combat zone. A Marine private first class was in charge of the process. He tapped loudly on a microphone, producing the obligatory screech that usually precedes a bad talk. The room was packed, mostly with officers. I recognized a bird colonel I'd flown with in Atsugi a few seats away. We nodded at one another and then looked obediently at our form in response to the young marine in charge. He spoke with exploratory confidence as one unaccustomed to authority, but fiercely protecting the scant charge he had.

"Attention to the block of items at the top of the page." He looked up to see if he had our full attention. He looked down again. "Name, Rank, Home of Record and Date. Block number one. Please spell your name correct." The colonel and I grinned weakly at one another, shook our heads, and sank into our chairs. Welcome back to the combat zone. The Marine tapped on the mike again as he would before every line item.

A Marine C130 Hercules transport flew us from the Air Force Base at Kadena to Danang. I sat down next to Brett. The hypnotic, dull drone inside a C130 is distinct and unforgettable. The vibration was enough to put me to sleep, but sufficiently annoying to keep me awake. We looked across the cargo bay at a dozen brand new Second Lieutenants. Brett and I apparently shared the same thoughts. We glanced at one another sorrowfully. The life expectancy of a brand-new platoon leader in Vietnam was grim. One reason there were so many replacements on the airplane. The darker side of that grim statistics were the numbers of our own Staff NCOs and officers who would be fragged by their own disillusioned troops.

This war had worn on tediously too long. There was just too much going against it beside the Viet Cong and the strengthening forces of North Vietnamese Army, NVA. Civilian protests back in the States had spread an infectious seed across an ocean and into the ranks. The troops were fighting on three fronts: in America, in Vietnam and among themselves. In some units that were evidently not too occupied, troops had formed alliances similar to a union and were threatening to go on strike.

It was a strangely uncertain time to arrive in Vietnam. The war was winding down as far as those at the peace tables would try to convince themselves, but the looming numbers of NVA about to swarm south were growing and gave the troops little to celebrate, but more to fear. There had been a considerable force withdrawal, diluting the numbers of our troops fighting a growing threat. Nixon had ordered an additional 150,000 troops to be rotated back to the States this year. Ho Chi Minh had died the year before. My amateur political analysis told me that without his mature presence, a serious nutcase would fill the vacuum and all hell would soon break loose. Something bad was about to happen if an adult did not soon show up.

"Nixon is no dummy, but his decisions are purely political. He could give less of a shit about the body count as long as he looks good." Brett spoke from some authority. He had just spent a year at the intelligence center in Arlington, Virginia. "He's accelerating this Vietnamization too soon. We won't have enough of our forces in Country pretty soon to fight the build-up of NVA about to pour south."

"Those kids don't have a chance," I replied, nodding across the cargo bay. There could not have been a more dramatic study in contrast: two second lieutenants fresh out of Quantico were eagerly grilling a jaded captain about what awaited them. The Captain looked across at us with a blank stare beseeching us for some word of encouragement for 'those soon to die.'

As the Hercules droned southward down the coast toward Danang, I looked out at the familiar terrain. In Okinawa the paddies were terraced, the ancient topography carved from the rich and abundant hills of fertile growth, a verdant explosion, miles of unmolested agrarian order, untouched through centuries of grooming. In tragic comparison, the cratered and tortured terrain surrounding Danang was flat and dull. Even the dirt was dead.

Large swatches of vegetation had been burned, breaking up the order of once healthy growth. I could see where Agent Orange had done its work. It would be decades before we could count the damage. Those hills that might have yielded a harvest were broken brown slopes, a disordered moon surface of cavities and military positions. They had scraped entire hill tops of vegetation, but for a few broken trees, everything was a dull beige going to black.

A cluster of exhausted majors in weathered utilities the same color as the hills were waiting at the off ramp to welcome the junior lieutenants with smiles, as if they were offering a free weekend at luxurious condominiums, no obligations to buy. Nobody was looking for Brett and me. Brett grinned at my humorous impulse to get back on the 130. Our orders were to report to Wing headquarters. A small van shuttled us over to G1 Administration. They stamped our orders and told us to grab some lunch in the officer's dining room, then report to G3 Operations for assignment. We were theirs now.

"Which one of you is Hamilton?" A full colonel appeared next to our table. We had barely dug into our lunch. The dining room at Wing Headquarters was table after table with back-to-back bird colonels chuckling like they were in college trading boasts of the night before. Brett raised his arm; which is probably a dangerous thing to do anywhere in the combat zone, even in the officer's dining hall at First Marine Aircraft Wing headquarters.

"That's me, sir." He wolfed down what was left of some rare roast beef and a strange-looking thing with antennas poking out of a small sump of mashed potatoes and gravy.

"Don't rush, Brett." The colonel waved at us and walked away. Yikes! The guy even knew his name. "Your desk is waiting for you a few buildings away. You know the way." He walked back to another table and added, "Give me a nod when you're done. We have a lot to do. That desk has been empty for a couple of weeks."

"What's all that Brett?" I hazarded, not usually all that curious. "You gone totally spook on us?"

He nodded. "Yeah, I won't be doin' much flying this tour. They've got me cleared 'cosmic beyond classified, burn before reading, top secret. I'm worse than a fucking spy."

I cringed. You don't even go near a plane with that many secrets planted in your skull.

"They will not take the risk of me being captured and spilling what the bad guys probably already know and the Washington Post is eager to reveal." He grinned.

"Now, you," his smile broke into a laugh, "you're up for grabs. I hope your missions don't take you too far up north. They've got fire-can radar anti-aircraft under every tree in Route Package One now. North of that, they're totally built up. Trust me." Something about the colonel's instructions for him to report to his desk had ruined Brett's lunch. I reached across and speared some of the beef left on his plate.

"You know about Freddy Hart?" I asked. I had a hunch these intelligence guys traveled in packs. Freddy Hart, with as many dark marks in his jacket as mine, had turned in his commission at the end of his tour while he was 'In Country.' He signed a contract with Air America, which the world knew was the air arm of the CIA. He had gone to the same school from which Brett just graduated and was loaded with lethal clearances. Freddy knew too much to have a good night's sleep. He had only flown half a dozen missions with CIA when his picture appeared in a copy of Time Magazine. Everyone who had known Freddy recognized him, his hands raised over his head, being led into the jungle by a crew of small people in black pajamas. Nobody had heard from or about him since.

"Yep, got the full story on Hart. He passed through the school while I was at Quantico." He nodded and was wiping his chin and standing up. "Hell of a guy. You evidently don't have the full story on Hart, do you?"

"I guess not. From what I understood, he was dead. Wife collected insurance and everything," I replied, noting a wry smile come across Brett's face.

"No. There's something fishy about all of that. He's really got his ass in a new crack now. I'll tell you about it." He laughed. "Drop by my office before they send you down to Chu Lai."

"Your office!" I laughed. "Shit, you just got here."

"Oh, I've been here before. I know where they buried all the bones. And I've got a map to the secret chamber."

"What makes you think I'm going to Chu Lai?" I chuckled. "You just fucking got here. How could you know that?"

"Like I said, I'm cleared 'come to Jesus, super-secret.' From my rudimentary analysis, it just makes sense with what's happening and what is about to happen. I think you'll be happy here." He got up and walked out of the mess hall, tapping the colonel on the shoulder on the way out.

I'd been waiting in Colonel Conroy's office for two hours when he arrived. I had lots of time, like another thirteen months, left to wait. I stood at attention. He looked at me as if I was late. I'd seen it done before. I'd done it before. The switch. If you're wrong, make the other guy look worse than you. I pretended I was the one who was late.

He was looking at my officer's qualification jacket and scowling. A scowl usually makes you look like you know what you're doing. "You've been here before. Looks like you know your way around the country." He slammed my jacket shut, looked across at me, and smiled for the first time. "You're just what they've been looking for down south." He turned around in his desk chair and pressed a button that summoned a voice in the other room.

"Yes, sir."

"Sergeant Weber, we need to have a chopper get Major Ruthven down to Chu Lai this afternoon." He didn't listen for an acknowledgment.

Colonel Conroy went through a few more papers and then hefted his six-foot three, two eighty pounds, into the air and left the room. The unmistakable bouquet of martinis with very little vermouth wafted behind him. In a few minutes, Gunnery Sergeant Weber came in the room, smiling. "Could you use some coffee? It's terrible. I think you'll like it." He examined a clip board fluttering with papers. "The chopper'll be at the Wing pad in an hour." He handed me a packet with my OQR, orders, and a small locked satchel attached.

"The Colonel asks that you deliver this to G2 at MAG 13, sir." At which point, without giving me a moment to protest, he locked the satchel to my wrist with a long chain. He gave me an apologetic smile.

With an hour before my chopper arrived, I found Brett's office and rapped on the door. "Permission to come aboard, sir."

He was on the phone, but waived me in. He hung up and laughed, pointing at the briefcase on my wrist. "Who'd you piss off? They got you on courier duty now?" He chuckled and pointed at a chair. "Sit, down. Goddam we got a lot of time, both of us. We've got twelve months and twenty-days left. In case you're counting."

"I was curious about Freddie Hart. You said he had his ass in a crack or something." I sat down and gave the appearance of being all ears.

"They kept all this very classified. So secret, you can't find a record of it. It's one of those 'if you tell, you go straight to hell' classified deals. This is so classified that it's beyond hypothetical." He looked at me in a mock mysterious way. "You get that, Colin? Hypothetical?"

I perched on the edge of my chair. "I dig. Ultra-hypothetical. This conversation is not happening and if it ever did, it would have been total bull shit. I've already forgotten what you haven't said yet."

"Okay, then." Brett lit a cigarette from a miniature blow torch on his desk. "When Freddie was attending the school in Virginia, we can suppose, he fell in league with some bad people. He had a gambling problem. And when you owe bad people money bad things happen to you." He looked at the door and told me to open it.

"Don't you want it closed if you want to keep it hush-hush?" I asked.

"Oh, God no." He frowned at me. "Evidently they didn't send you to top-secret school. Basic secrets 101, leave the door open so you can at least see who's listening to you. Someone's bound to be snooping. You might as well know who it is."

He toyed with the lighter and waited for me to open the door. "Anyway, back to Freddie. He owed some thugs a lot of money, so he scored some orders to Vietnam, hoping to hide from the mob." He shook his head. "Yeah, taking a runner on government money."

"And the mob turned up the heat at home," I added.

"Exactly. They threatened to do bad things to Freddie's wife and three kids if he did not come up with the money."

"So, Freddie dies in Vietnam," I add again. "And his wife can collect the insurance money and pay off the mob." I was enjoying this too much.

"Exactly. Because his clearance was too high, he wasn't actually flying over here. But while he was working in Intelligence G 2, he found friends in the intelligence office who flipped him to the CIA. Air America almost dumped him because he had almost forgotten how to fly. But at least the record showed that he was flying shit in and out of Laos, in ancient C 47's."

"But he was captured by the Viet Cong. I read the piece in Time Magazine," I puzzled. "I saw a picture."

"Let's say, for instance, that this was all bullshit. This would be the secret beyond hypothetical part. Officially Freddie is dead, and his wife has the insurance money, and so I suppose, does the mob have their money." He was shaking his head. "It pays to have friends in the system. You know that if it has to, the Marine Corps can be just as crooked as the mob."

"Do you mean that picture and the story I saw in Time Magazine was a plant?" I shook my head in genuine disbelief.

"I'm not saying anything. I didn't say a thing" He shrugged with an innocent and stupid grin. "I was just conjuring a pretend story that makes for cool fiction. You fill in the blanks."

"So, if this were to be true. Where is Freddy now?" I grinned.

"Officially, he's dead, Colin." Brett pretended to browse through an incoming basket. "But I can imagine a million small places in the world a thug outfit like the United States Government could hide someone and make him show up somewhere else as someone else."

Brett opened a red folder that had just walked in the door and landed on his desk. "You know, a crooked corporation like this that can keep a war going just so our president can win the next election is crafty enough to make one of us vanish in one room and show up in another."

A first lieutenant from The Marine Aircraft Group 13 G-2 office was waiting to relieve me of the courier satchel when I landed in Chu Lai. I reported to the G3 operations office to find the flip side of Colonel Conroy. He was on his feet, standing at a waist level desk. I had only seen one of these before. An entire wall had a ledge that stuck out and down at about a thirty-degree angle for about four feet at the level of the average guy's navel. Lieutenant Colonel Frank Sellers stood in camouflage shorts and a sweatshirt, marinating in his own perspiration. No socks and shower shoes. He was half bent over my OQR, alternately shaking his head, and wiping the beads of sweat from his totally shaved dome with a green towel.

"Ruthven, I'm doing my best to find something redeeming about you." He tried to laugh good-naturedly. "You've attended no schools, nor have you attempted to earn any college credits to beef up a GED test you took—in boot camp seventeen years ago! You've had all the opportunity to groom yourself for senior field grade, a regular commission and have not done a goddam thing, Jesus!" He stepped back from my record and took a few steps further down his mile-long desk as if to get away from a foul steam emanating from my officer's qualification jacket.

"You have what we need in terms of tactical experience. Been in four squadrons, two of them in the combat zone, plus a butt load of F 11 time as an instructor, which does not hurt. A lot of flight time in several models." He returned to my OQR. "What I find amusing is that you have served more time with the Navy than with the Marine Corps. Three years in the training command as an instructor, three years in Memphis at some non-descript desk job. Shit, you even sailed the high seas in an LST, once. Never mind the years it takes to earn a set of wings."

I interrupted him cautiously. "That was a staff tour in Memphis, I think, Colonel."

"A desk job with some Podunk Navy unit is not a staff tour, Jesus!" He laughed then returned to examine my OQR. "A staff tour is with a Marine Corps or Marine Corps affiliated organization. You have not had a single staff tour. I'm surprised you made Major, Major."

"As am I, sir." I opened my hands and got clear with him. "I spent that first ten years of hopefully a twenty-year career, drunk and disorderly and, as you have just reminded me, doing anything I could to discourage anyone from taking me seriously."

"Oh, wait! Just a minute! Oh, shit!" He thought for a few seconds, looked at me closely, turned a page on my jacket and then closed it. "You were the fucking animal! Atsugi,1961!" He grinned for the first time since I had entered the room. "They were going to hang you from a tree for stealing Joe Warren's vehicle. The fucking Group Commander! Jesus! You had a rap sheet growing at base security. You and—what's his name? I forget. Don't tell me." He nodded and tossed my OQR at me. "So, you been sober how long now?" For the first time since I had met the man, he plunked down in his chair across a desk from me.

"Since the first of December 1964."

"How the hell'd you do that?"

"I didn't. Something else did."

"That don't make sense, Animal."

"To a good Marine like you, it wouldn't, Colonel."

"Still makes little sense. Main thing is, you're sober enough to have a conversation at least. Sit down, Animal." He was massaging one of his knees and began examining a callous on his left foot. "That's a long time between drinks for a guy who, from my memory and as legend has it, drank all day and all night."

"I had a few involuntary rest spells in the hospital, drying out in Yokosuka." I bent down to look at the callous. "But I pretty well had a constant level in my system most of the time. I was officially the Atsugi village idiot."

"You guys were on four carriers during that tour. That's what saved your ass. You were critical personnel and highly qualified. You certainly didn't drink while aboard the Forrestal."

I grinned and shrugged. "A drunk will find a way, sir."

"Jesus," he whispered. "I was the executive officer of MABS 11 when you were doing your number down in the grotto. I attended some of your parties at the Quonset huts. Not bad." He shook his head. "If you had put half the energy you spent organizing those parties into your career, you'd be a bird colonel by now." He laughed at himself, examining the other foot. Looked back up at me and shook his head. "Colonel Fairburn was once your commanding officer. Right?"

I looked at him with that 'we were in the same club' expression. "He was my first skipper in 1956 with 232."

"I know." He stood up again. "He was doing everything he could to write you up at Kaneohe Bay and Atsugi. Fairburn was not a very popular guy. Most everyone on the staff would have liked to make him look bad. It was to your advantage that he had a hard on for you. Everyone else was doing everything to make him look paranoid." He looked around as if to see if anyone was listening. "Which he probably was."

A corporal entered the office with a stack of papers and three different message folders, one confidential, one secret and above, the other routine. We didn't speak as the corporal organized the paper in several locations on the mega-desk. I was grateful for his presence and the time he allowed for the conversation I had with Lieutenant Colonel Sellers to distill and maybe harvest a decision, hopefully to my advantage.

"Ordinarily, I'd try to find some situation that might fill in some blanks in your career profile. But it looks to me like this is just about your twilight cruise and you'll get your twenty years in and retire." He looked at me from a squat position, crouching in his chair, both feet bare now and flat on the floor. "That sound 'bout right?"

"Yes, sir." I nodded. "No way I'm gonna make Lieutenant Colonel. Miracle I made Major. There are people in Headquarters

Marine Corps that saw my act back in the bad old days and they have an excellent memory. And as you have pointed out, if I was going to groom myself for senior field grade, I should have done that about ten years ago. As Skinny Lamar used to tell me back when he was skipper of 312, 'Basically, Animal, you're dead.'"

The Colonel laughed. "Vintage Lamar. You've got a lot of flight time and, if nothing else, a good flight instructor. In fact, "Instructor of the year" in an Advanced Training Command squadron. We need that right now, more than you need to polish up your portfolio." He stood up and went to the far end of the desk, a day's march away. "I'll send you down to 115."

I almost dropped on my face and kissed the floor. Marine Fighter Attack Squadron 115 was the only Phantom squadron in Chu Lai. The Silver Eagles. I would have surrendered either or both of my gonads to be in that squadron. "I appreciate that, sir. I really appreciate it."

"Your reputation has preceded you, Ruthven; not only from the bad old days, but also your last tour." He handed me my orders with his comments scribbled across the bottom. "Good luck. I wish I was going with you."

I didn't thank him again. I was feeling obsequious, and that's a bad look for a Phantom pilot. I left and walked down the flight line to the Marine Fighter Attack Squadron 115 ready room.

"You've got more experience than most of the pilots in the squadron, and the RIOs are really new." Lieutenant Colonel Kip Snyder was the skipper. "Most of these kids are first tour out of flight school and familiarization in the training at El Toro and Cherry Point." Snyder was an unlikely-looking fighter pilot. He was short and not in very good shape and seemed to give me the feeling that he was shy. It's a mistake to judge a Marine from behind a desk. Size does not matter in the cockpit. In the air, it's not size of the dog in the fight, but the fight in the dog. You would have thought Kip Snyder was John Glenn.

"We won't be here very long, probably 'til September, then the Group's folding its colors and going back to El Toro. 115 will be going up to Danang and join MAG 11. The squadron will operate better up there. More room. This place is shutting down. The base has a short timer's attitude. You can barely get anything done." He stood up, all five feet six of him, and came around the desk.

"The maintenance officer is leaving for test pilot training. Guy's almost too smart to fly. I'm giving you his job, but mainly I'd like you to be den father to some lieutenants in the squadron. I saw your name on the inbound roster and hoped they'd send you to us. The kids heard some stories about you, and I think it would help if you mingled."

"Oh, hell I can mingle, Skipper. One thing though." I opened my mouth to speak.

"I know. We won't be seeing you at happy hour. And from what I remember of you when I was in Beaufort in 1960, it's just as well." He walked toward his office door. "Come on. I'll show you around and we can get you on the flight schedule right away." He grinned, his hand on my shoulder. "You didn't forget how to fly on the way over, did you?"

Chu Lai by the Sea was a perfect spot for a beach resort. Surf, white sands, and clear ocean waters. In May 1965, when the marines arrived and first established the air base, they planted a miracle 1,200-meter runway on soft sand. They built it from the classic aluminum surface of interlocking lightweight metal alloy planking, to accommodate a SATS system (Short Airfield for Tactical Support) which amounted to a catapult and a carrier deck-type arresting gear. The first squadron to arrive flew A4 Skyhawk attack planes. By 1970. The engineers had built a 10,000-foot concrete runway, more than sufficient for every inventory of Marine Corps fixed wing to operate.

The party was just about over at Chu Lai now in 1970. Like Kip Snyder had explained, they'd be moving the remnants of MAG 13 up to Danang to join MAG 11. Chu Lai had all the major food groups of an operating base. Firebase Cunningham just inland from the beach and constant traffic of helicopter support. Since 1965, with predictable Marine ingenuity, Marine Aircraft Group 13 had established a small city with every convenience, including a more than sufficient medical facility. A small trailer with a porch and potted plants stood at the end of the runway. It still accommodated the group commander and anyone who wanted to spend the night with him. The base employs some local, female housekeepers, most of it friendly, others they warned, Viet Cong.

Eric Thompson, the Major I was relieving as maintenance officer, was loading the back of a jeep with a bottle of wine and a couple of steaks he had commandeered from the officer's dining hall. He had a date with a nurse. So, I had arrived long after the party was over. But long enough to get back into the cockpit, become totally enamored with the Phantom and the way it delivered everything you could hang from its distinctive polyhedral wing.

I shared a house on the beach with Floyd Harding, another Major, who I had known more for the bar he and his wife owned in Santa Ana. The home we occupied had belonged to a wealthy Chinese merchant who had thought it a good idea to purchase a holiday villa in South Vietnam. It was the most unlikely living quarters I could have imagined, unless it was the apartment villa I eventually moved into at Danang, a two-room luxury home I shared with Diego Cortez, the operations officer.

The move to Danang took less than a week. I would have a very ambiguous relationship with my roommate. In our new quarters, Diego Cortez and I were the best of friends, but in the working spaces, we were minor enemies. Usually, the operations officer is at war with maintenance because maintenance can never deliver the number of airplanes necessary to satisfy the daily fragmentary order. In our case, I let my assistant, Captain Evan Barker and Diego, work it out. I tried to spend my time in the guts of the maintenance spaces, connecting with the troops, getting a sense of the current attitude.

The Phantom is a reliable airplane and relatively easy to maintain if it's in a hermetically sealed desert environment. However, the jungle heat, humidity and other exotic agents in the air are a nightmare for the electronic and radar compartments. The potting compound melts in the cannon plugs allowing the many connections to send random signals throughout a system that response to electronic signals. Without it, nothing happens, or worse, stuff happens that shouldn't. The engines are reliable, and the airframe is like a tank. It can carry more bombs than you can count and it's deadly accurate if you can fly the airplane to the right place in the sky with the right airspeed and dive angle. Which, to me, was the recent version of a fighter pilot maneuvering to a six-o'clock kill position.

Even with all of this reliability, there still came a day shortly after we arrived at Danang when we asked for a full day of maintenance to catch up to checks, inspections and service changes. Never mind a backlog of gripes on some planes that we were letting slide. The skipper gave us a day for maintenance.

On that day, with several of the officers restless and looking for something to kill, a few of us organized a squadron vasectomy. One of the most resourceful of us arranged with the doctors at Marble Mountain for a group procedure. We were to come in at half-hour intervals. Of course, they required us to prep ourselves, at least the shaving part.

Two doctors manned the operating table, one for the left nut, the other for the right nut. At the end of my surgery, as I watched over a large sheet covering most of me, I witnessed the youngest doctor, the one dealing with my right nut, throw his hands in the air and yell, "Calf rope!"

For the following week, half the squadron, who had already had children and were at an age when they desired no more, walked slowly to our airplanes, and required some help strapping in. With matters uncertain about Kim and myself, I didn't want to run another child through her frail body and psyche. We had one–Phoebe, and another on the way.

Targets that had so occupied our entire intention for my previous tour, like Khe Sanh and the Rock Pile, were a desolation of brown broken hills, pocked with pits still filled with the remnants of military trash. There was a constant stream of missions up in the northwest corner of I Corps, near Khe Sanh, around the Ho Chi Minh trail with an obvious build-up of northern forces. Now we flew a lot of hot pad missions around the Danang perimeter. The sense was that there were more of the bad guys and fewer of us to watch the store. Night emergency missions became almost routine. I had probably become complacent and all too casual with rote checklists and procedures. I almost had it rubbed in my face to prove it one night. Fortunately, it was but a warning and not the end. I got back, but my RIO almost did not.

It was a night napalm mission, which is a blast, but murder on the night vision with bursts of fire billowing behind us, illuminating the inside of the cockpit and mirrors with every release. And I was getting altogether too much out of the adrenalin on these missions, attempting to bring the plane as close to the deck as possible before pickling the tank. With each run I brought it closer to the treetops, a sense of something almost touching the leading edge of the wings. I'd pull up and perform a wing over on instruments into a low layer of clouds and then roll onto my back and in on another run, timing the run from the fallen flairs that lit the target area. I could hear the hyperventilating of a relatively new RIO from the back seat.

Danang was intermittently socked in. Return to base was an instrument approach. The low cloud cover had moved in around the field. I was on the downwind of a ground-controlled approach, landing south and instructed to turn left ninety degrees onto final. I had been hypnotically on instruments the whole approach, but as I began my turn onto final, I surrendered to just about every pilot's temptation. A seduction that could be fatal. I glanced out of the cockpit to see if I could go visual.

There was nothing but my reflection on the inside of the canopy. I turned immediately to my instrument cockpit scan, and the world turned with me. I had fixed on the instruments and was alarmed to see my gyro horizon showing almost a ninety-degree turn. I immediately corrected, but I was correcting to my misread of the gyro horizon. I was suddenly inverted with a serious case of vertigo. I heard this pounding coming from behind me and thought I might have a flight control emergency. Somehow, I brought the plane back to straight-and-level flight, and I turned as instructed onto final, avoiding the looming high terrain of Thua Thien Hue, a mountain straight ahead.

The pounding I had heard from the back seat was my RIO, who will go nameless, trying to reach the face curtain and eject. We had been on our back pushing negative g's and I was in the landing configuration. I had to go to full power and afterburner for the maneuver. After we landed, the RIO requested never to fly with me again. I couldn't blame him.

I was never quite the same on a Ground Controlled Approach again. A few days later, the RIO said that he might have made an emotional decision. The more he had thought about it, no matter how bad I had read the gauges, I had to have performed secret maneuver to get us out of it and onto course and then glide slope. He might have felt better about it, but I could not. I had forgotten the lecture about night carrier approaches or anything else in an airplane that deserves my total focus. I was losing my edge. For a full instrument approach in minimum weather conditions, I had forgotten to hold the line. Something about me was changing. And I was unsure what it was. But it would gradually reveal itself to me.

There was a time when I could hold the line intuitively. Something from a deeper place had been doing it for me. Now I had to work at it. I was losing interest. Something about me and my career was clearly winding down.

13

Winding Down

Night barrier combat patrols were requiring a lot of attention for a mission that seemed to deserve none. It was becoming apparent that a very important part of me was no longer interested. A racetrack pattern for three hours in a piece of air between North Vietnam and the Fleet. To date, not a single BarCap has encountered the first Mig. Midway in the flight, we find the tanker, a KC130, and only our radar to find it. All aircraft who flew in the area of hostilities at night traveled with their lights out. Once I merge plot with the tanker, that is: almost collide with it, I find the eighteen-inch circle rotating erratically in the air defined by radium buds on a drogue basket. My probe comes out on the left side of the plane. I can't see it. But years of plugging in, muscle memory and a quart of adrenaline flies the probe into the circle, I hope. Sometimes I miss and the drogue is hammer beating its way into the cockpit. I pull back and try again. This one night I tried and failed four times. I expected we might not make it. We would run out of fuel over a dark and hostile bottomless ocean where the friendliest species we would encounter were sharks. Lenny Fuchs, my RIO, had talked me off the ledge until I plugged in.

We were returning to Danang. I was as tired as four tries at that tanker, and three hours on the BarCap track could make me. I was becoming very disinterested in the war. This had been my second mission of the day, not counting an emergency scramble on the hot pad the previous night.

"Lenny, I'll give you a hundred dollars for any reason to divert. I don't care if we must fly into Hanoi International. I need to get out of Danang." I left it on open mike. Of course, I was jesting; I thought he would laugh. He heard my fatigue. Like any good RIO, he came up with a solution.

"Well, Major, today's my birthday." Lenny's was the voice of pure innocence. He didn't drink. Nor did he have a mercenary or hostile bone in his body. He was the very definition of core goodness. He had talked me off the ledge at night more than once as I tried to find the basket or on final approach with the weather down to minimums. One night, we had a full load of bombs and attempted to air refuel. I was hanging in the basket on the other side of the power curve with a maxed out heavy beast, going in and out of afterburner to stay plugged in until we had a full load of fuel. We exchanged heavy breathing for the duration of the refueling.

"Well, Happy Birthday, Lenny," I replied. "We're going to Ubon." It was a driving rain at Danang. We had a few Zuni rockets hung on each side of the plane. It was the extreme of the latitude we could take to divert. Danang could be being rocketed or there could be a fouled runway. The last of all resorts was rockets hanging with the possibility that you might have to make an arrested landing in a monsoon rain. The rockets might jump out of the launcher when I grabbed a wire and they would fly down the runway toward an ammo revetment. Definitely an excuse to divert. I declared my intention. There was no objection when I made the request to operations. The Group was drawing down. Things were not as urgent as they had been.

I was not the only one who had lost enthusiasm for this losing war. I witnessed the fruits of American discontent in March 1971. We'd been sharing a lot of the missions with the Air Force and their Specter and Spooky missions along the Ho Chi Minh trail. During the intelligence briefs, hints came in about what was going on.

Fifteen minutes west of Dong Ha and less than half an hour on the 330 radial out of Danang, across the border in Laos, sat Tchepone, a fat NVA supply and ammunitions depot, a vital transshipment point. It had been of crucial strategic and logistics importance to the Ho Chi Minh trail in the sixties. It had been heavily fortified with an enormous, overkill anti-Aircraft defense.

During my previous tour, Tchepone was a treacherous area in which to operate. Whenever a plane had been shot down in the area and a Jolly Green chopper tried to rescue the pilot, they launched every available plane in the inventory to support the rescue.

Now in 1971, I Corps was unsure if NVA even occupied Tchepone; but in line with Nixon's policy of Vietnamization, they launched Operation Lam Son to cut the Ho Chi Minh Trail in Laos and possibly taking Tchepone. It was a total ARVN operation, as per Nixon's policy of Vietnamization. Supported by American Air and other factors, the operation targeted different parts of the Viet Cong and NVA infrastructure. These included the Ho Chi Minh trail supply route, which ran through Laos and Cambodia. It was a total failure. The ARVN troops were routed. They retreated wholesale, leaving their entire ground support inventory, plus helicopters and other logistics treasures. Nearly 8,000 ARVN troops were lost, and over 100 U.S. helicopters. They abandoned a fortune in military equipment as ARVN forces fled Laos in a near-rout.

They directed the increased missions we were flying around the Ho Chi Minh trail at our own equipment, including tanks and helicopters lest the losses from Operation Lam Son get into enemy hands.

For the first time in any of our careers, we were bombing our own tanks, helicopters, and equipment. After return to base during the intelligence debrief, we were asked how many American tanks, choppers, and C Rations we killed. The aircrews asked that they forward this data to Hanoi so we could be written up for North Vietnamese Army decorations?

I was feeling like a spoiled brat. I had worked myself up into a patriotic furor in order to convince myself that we were making a difference. Now, with the unavoidable fact that even the Air Force, the command that was writing the frag orders, could not keep a straight face and were in confusion coming from several directions, I became distracted. I could not give myself to this job with the same enthusiasm I had in the beginning.

Once I lost enthusiasm for what we were doing, I noticed the fissures in everyone else's morale. Rather than the fight we were having with the enemy, as time ate away at the moral fiber, it became apparent that we were either at war with ourselves or one another.

The high point of this combat tour occurred on the first day of January 1971 when my son, David, was born.

"You gonna tie one on at the club tonight, Major?" maintenance chief Master Sergeant Turf Shore, a legend of more hangar decks than I had hot meals, was grinning as he read the dispatch over my shoulder.

"During two tours in DaNang, I've never seen the inside of that club, Turf," I grinned. "But have a six-pack of Smirnoff for me and don't come in tomorrow. Go out and be foolish. It always worked for me."

"That's right. You're no longer the Animal, are you?" He nodded. "I was at Kaneohe Bay when you were a second balloon. I saw a bit of your act back then." He walked away. "Don't need to see no more of that. Do we? Congratulations, Major, on both counts, sobriety not being the least."

There was no secret in the entire group about my drinking, even less about my sobriety. I'd turned my office into a counseling chamber, improving on the method during my previous tour. I didn't have to go out hunting for candidates. They came to me. It surprised me that there was more aircrew in the Air Group interested in getting sober on this tour. I wasn't sure how much my efforts kept airplanes in the air, but I felt the troops more approachable to a drinking solution.

David's birth was auspicious. Hopefully, it would be a good year. I could work a lot as Maintenance Officer, which occupied most of my time–managing several interior departments that made up the effort. I flew probably more than my share of missions, although the stress was on giving the younger aircrew the opportunity to get more missions, and possibly awards, with an aim to promotion possibilities.

Their dungaree still caked in mud, their faces weary from facing a different version of war than my own, troops from Firebase Mohawk or many others, visited the hangar to thank pilots that had delivered ordnance on just the right spot at just the right time. It could have been on any night when to me it was routine and return to base, but to them was critical. Given the opportunity to crash for a day and rest, they would sometimes rather visit the squadron and thank an aircrew for "saving our ass." For me, that kind of reward was more than sufficient. But there were those who sought and deserved additional recognition.

"I've got an endorsement to Division from our Battalion Commander for your flight that night, Major." It was an infantry captain. I'd seen them in Hawaii with the Brigade and then with the Division at Camp Pendleton. They were the ones who took notes and absorbed the lessons of Marine Corps history and continued to make it what it is. They would write history themselves. The captain had competence written on every feature of his face and every stitch of his uniform. He thanked our flight for "Getting our ass out of a hot crack". He was the officer who would worry about his troops and support them at every turn. If they were to be commended, he would acknowledge it in public. If they were to be reprimanded or censured, it would be in private.

I recalled the night well. It was an emergency mission, dead in the middle of the night. We were flying beneath the overcast. I had a full wing of napalm, my wingman, snake eye bombs. I was having to lay the napalm at treetop level. Vinnie Powell, my wingman, gained sufficient altitude to drop the snake-eyes. Snake eye bombs have umbrella fins that deploy when the bomb is released, thus allowing an airplane to drop at a lower altitude with resultant greater accuracy and to avoid being hit with the beam spray.

I never heard from the captain again, nor anything about a citation. There was no doubt in my mind that his endorsement for a decoration had been sent somewhere, but very often they were lost. It was the combat zone. Ground commanders had more to do than ensure someone received a medal. My wingman had been scoping this process ever since the captain visited us and told us we were going to be cited for this flight. Nothing happened, and I forgot about it. But my wingman would not.

"Major, if we get a way to find that ground officer, we could speed up the citation. How about asking the Group to frag us a helicopter and we visit the grunts?"

"I will not do that, Vinny," I replied as clearly as I could without showing my revulsion to the idea. In my previous tour, I'd seen it happen where a helicopter was taken off missions that could have been vital to other operations just to fly a pilot to the find a ground command who might write a citation, but probably would not.

"If we're supposed to get a DFC it will happen without us doing anything more than flying the mission, Vinny." I was probably too firm in my resolve. They awarded neither of us a Distinguished Flying Cross for this or any other mission. I might have shot down Vinny's opportunity for DFC with my pristine attitude to honesty.

"Vinny, you can do that. But I don't want my name or my scent on any part of it." I had found his hootch that same night. "It was unfair of me to impose my new discipline on you, when I've barely got a handle on it myself."

"What discipline is that?" Vinnie was alone in his hootch. The rest of the squadron was at the O Club seeking a sense of ease and comfort from the realities of our life. I knew the feeling very well. I'd done that a lot.

I explained to him what I was doing. "We measure success in the effort, Vinny, not the results. Just do what you are told to do, fly the missions for which you are scheduled, and forget about the results. They'll roll in if they're supposed to." I was about to leave the hut when I added, "As much as possible, I try to live my whole life that way. Just do the best you can at anything and forget about the results. If you have some idea what results are supposed to look like, you'll try to make them that way. Something else knows what's supposed to happen. The things that I think should happen are often far less favorable than our lives really have in store for us. No matter how you see it, Vinny, everything is working in your favor."

A light went on in Vinny's eyes. I left the hut. Several days later, he showed up in my office. "Sir, the night you came to visit me, I was doing my best to stay away from the club. I had been going every night that I wasn't scheduled." I told him to sit down and continue. "Then one night, the night before you visited me, I asked them to take me off the schedule. I told them I had an ear block and needed to go to sick bay." He paused as he saw it all register in my eyes. I knew what he was going to say, because I had done the same thing many times. "Sir, I didn't go to sick bay. I went to the club. I not only wanted to drink," he paused as he saw me nodding, "I needed to drink."

Vinny joined our small group. It was growing larger. He said he had a desire to stop drinking. The group spoke of the solution to the compulsion. They didn't talk about drinking but spoke of other matters: The state of mind that was the problem and the Something Else that was the answer.

The air war or the air-to-ground war, continued. The story is chronicled in dreary duplicated sameness. But little is told about the war between the agencies who kept the airplanes in the air. I let my assistant maintenance officer deal with the conflict between operations and maintenance. There was the occasional screaming contest on the hangar deck between our Operations Officer, Major Diego Cortez and my assistant Maintenance Officer, Captain Perry Baker. These became frequent enough to be routine and regarded as some of the sad and sometimes entertaining transactions of war.

The frag orders arriving from Saigon were based upon a sometimes-unrealistic picture we had provided of our readiness. The danger in conveying a glowing report to maintain a sterling appearance is that it becomes necessary, when circumstances and aircraft readiness are less than desired, to employ a creative exaggeration of our capabilities. How many romances have been destroyed by one party presenting an appearance or conveying a capacity that cannot be sustained? It's difficult in a system that is rewarding for high performance and appearance to remain honest.

To the point: squadron operations often provided an unrealistic assessment to Air Force Command of what we could do. If I had been the operations officer, I'm sure I would have asked for more airplanes to be available for a schedule that I had to write. The maintenance department could only provide so many planes. The operations department had to satisfy the frag order that was based on an unrealistic assessment. In short, maintenance could only provide the airplanes we had, not the airplanes for a dream schedule.

So, the AMO had it out daily with operations about what was scheduled against what was available. The two, unevenly matched, created a polarizing energy in the squadron that radiated out to the troops and, critically, within the ready room.

On the upside, polarization between the maintenance department and operations created a convenient atmosphere in which parties, frustrated with anything that moved: the war, their roommates, or bedbugs within the squadron, could vent their emotions.

The combat zone is an ideal place to generate frustrated feelings and emotions that will look for a legitimate target. Most of the enlisted body was in the maintenance department, so our numbers favored those of operations. Neither did it hurt that several of the junior officers occupied billets within the smaller departments of maintenance, like flight equipment, the engine shop and avionics.

I made it my practice to contact most of the troops daily, to visit every department and derive a realistic assessment of aircraft availability. Usually the maintenance department delivered, but as the months passed and the schedule accelerated, the hardware suffered and needed attention, like engine changes and addressing the constant fatigue upon the system from just living in an environment that was inimical to optimal operations. A parallel attack on the human component was happening with the troops and officers. Fatigue and emotional exhaustion expressed itself in small and sometimes deadly demonstrations of the human predicament.

A large irony of the minor war between operations and maintenance revealed itself in the living arrangement: I was the maintenance officer, and I shared a fairly comfortable bungalow with the Diego Cortez the operations officer. Our small space with two bunks provided enough room to create a compatible atmosphere for a couple to live in under conservatively unnatural circumstance. The two of us got along reasonably well. However, the complaint maintenance had with operations somehow crept from the hangar to the officer's club.

At the end of a very drunk night and early into the morning, a person yet unidentified left an ugly statement on our porch as a symbol of his enmity. The package, a hefty and fresh mound of human waste, had been delivered from an individual who preferred to remain anonymous. A card showed unequivocally that the insult be delivered directly to Major Diego Cortez. The person who had left the package deposited it directly from their body a short time prior to discovery.

When I stepped out onto the porch on the morning that the anonymous party had delivered the package, the operations officer was fortunately in the air on an early morning mission. I was not about to permit the foul gift to remain on the porch any longer, and I was certainly not going to allow Diego to arrive after an exhaustive evening and find his gift waiting for him. No one had evidently considered the reaction of the recipient, which I could guarantee to the world would be swift, ugly and totally commensurate with the offense. The war had landed on our front porch.

I was also not going to get close enough to the package to determine who could have placed it there. I had perpetrated similar, but decidedly not as gross and ugly, mischief in a previous incarnation. The deed had the signature of a new "Animal." So, I could not but feel a private empathy for the deed and the perpetrator. Crude and not very sophisticated, it still bore slightly the stamp of the Animal. How do I scold a man who is only doing essentially what I had done? I rationalized it was not me, personally, who had to do the reprimanding, but what my position and rank insisted I do. I employed the detective's craft of not asking if a miscreant had perpetrated a crime, but telling him he clearly had.

"Hog body! You crapped on my porch?" Lieutenant Paul Evans had earned his sobriquet from his squat and unathletic body. He was not an unattractive person, just unathletically chubby. I would not accuse just anyone of taking a dump on my porch, I had watched Paul Evans for several months and with an affectionate amusement observed that Hog body, as everyone from commanding officer to mail clerk called him, had the same style, however crude and hardly as elegant, as The Animal in Atsugi.

"Oh, God, Major!" His reply wasn't just fear, just stool softening (no pun) terror. "That wasn't for you, honest."

"But you realize that I live there?"

"God, I wasn't thinking." His body hung limp and seemed to ask to be punished. A classic characteristic of the Animals and the Hog Bodies of the world is that their capers invariably have very little long-term thought given to them.

"I get that, Paul." I almost wanted to put my arm around his shoulder and comfort him, but I realized this would only sanction the deed. My problem was that Hog body worked for me as the flight equipment officer. "I very nearly stepped in it. You realize that had the Operations officer stepped in it, excuse the metaphor–but it seems to fit, you'd be in deep shit. But worse, knowing that you work for me, he would think that I was implicated with the deed."

"Oh, God, sir. Is there anything I can do to unfuck this?"

"Well, not to get too gross. You can't exactly "unshit" on my porch. But, before Major Cortez lands and returns to the tranquility of his hootch, that area had better be sanitized, as if it had never happened. I don't want to have to re-install that crap back where it came from, Hog body." I tried not to laugh. I was dead serious. I could have and might have become too theatric with my feigned anger. "Do it. And I mean in the next five fucking minutes." I gave it a few seconds. "And you owe me–a big one. Major Diego would have a set of orders cut for you to Division as a forward air controller before you could remove your G-suit".

Paul nodded vigorously and disappeared. I ruminated over my present compared to my past. I couldn't allow myself to become too pristine, too antiseptic in my thinking, to demand of others that which I couldn't deliver myself. I couldn't make allowances in the present for my behavior in the past. Allowances became moot late one night in the fueling pits.

Chief Warrant Officer Tim Rice was the squadron safety officer. We were equally friend and adversary in our mutual confederation to keep the airplanes flying and the missions completed. The cartoons and caricatures continued to fly from my hut, 'wry and humorous' to use the plaudits of the Aircrews, and usually related anecdotally to flight operations and directly to flight safety. In this respect, I was Tim's huge ally in his very aggressive pursuit of optimal flight safety.

As maintenance officer, I sometimes found that he would get in the middle of my equally aggressive efforts to maintain aircraft. I had to deliver as many airplanes as possible as quickly as possible to flight operations to satisfy the frag order. My efforts, although equally aggressive, were not as competent as those of Chief Warrant Officer Tim Rice. This was dramatically showed on this very particular night after I had, for some time, shown a blatant disregard for his program.

"Major, you realize the troops are not installing the safety pin on the wing fuel tanks during hot refueling." He wasn't asking if they did not do this. He was telling me in no uncertain terms that they were not installing the safety pins on the wing fuel tanks. We should install them before the airplane enters the fuel pits. He was shorter than I was but looked up at me with a bulldog determination that felt six foot six tall. "And, when they hot refuel, there has to be someone in the cockpit. All one of those plane captains has to do is accidentally hit the wing fuel tank jettison switch and both those tanks filled with fuel will be jettisoned down onto the tarmac at a high explosive velocity."

"Thanks, Gunner. I appreciate you reminding me again. The reason we hot refuel is to save time and not have to tow the aircraft to the fuel pits after every mission. I save a shitload of time." Even as I was saying it, I felt my reply insufficient to the warning. Trying to save time at the expense of safety was a recipe for disaster.

He turned and walked away.

I don't think I deliberately ignored Gunner Rice's warning. I don't think I would have. However, I did nothing to reinforce the policy to install the safety pins in the wing fuel tank immediately upon landing. Operations continued at a vigorous pace, and I did not take sufficient time to create a safer environment. It was one of the many small details I would ignore in life that garnered larger consequences that I will always regret. I was no longer holding the line in the air, and sadly, on the ground. I had been here too long.

It was about three in the morning, the hour of the wolf when a person is most paranoid and likely to read the worst into the most innocuous moment. I was on the night hot pad. Operations had recently accelerated. There were more emergency missions than routinely launched on the night hot pad. I thought I heard a muffled thump, like artillery not too far in the distance.

"Major, there's a fire in the fuel pits!" A breathless plane captain was leaning into the hot pad trailer. He turned around and ran back toward the flight line.

I called the ready room and told the duty operations officer to send another pilot to take my place on the hot pad. Hog body came running and panting into the hut, pulling his torso vest together.

"There's been an explosion out in the pits, Major." I ran toward his jeep, my g-suit and torso harness still on my body.

By the time we'd passed the revetments and were turning onto the flight line and the fuel pits, an emergency fire crew had arrived. Less than a minute later, I heard three consecutive explosions. I could feel the jeep jump beneath us as one of the two sidewinder missiles and the four sparrow missiles cooked off beneath the airplane's wing. Fire billowed up from behind a revetment. I jumped from the jeep toward the inferno that had once been a Phantom fighter attack aircraft. Light from the fire reflected and flashed on the faces of terror and confusion that surrounded the conflagration. On the periphery of the crowd that he should have been running from, but was rushing toward, strode the grim figure of Colonel Al Pomerenck, our Group Commander. Someone's bloody t-shirt clutched in his hand. Then, I felt someone immediately beside me.

It was Chief Warrant Officer Tim Rice. I looked down at him. He didn't say a thing, but his sad eyes said, "What did I tell you, you stupid son of a bitch?"

Two weeks later, I stood before the accident investigation team and told them they could put my name, rank and serial number on the report and send the bill to Major Colin Ruthven. I agreed to be one hundred percent culpable for losing an entire airplane, but worse, the lives of three firefighters.

I wasn't the same for the rest of my tour. I wouldn't have to be. One day, the cosmos or some benevolent force realized that I had enough.

"Major Ruthven, you have a message from the Red Cross." The Chaplain delivered it to me while I was standing on the hangar deck. I was examining a fist full of potting compound that had drained from the radar cavity of a hulking Phantom.

"The Red Cross?" I said. "That doesn't sound good."

"No, Major, it isn't. Never is." He replied, reading from the message. "You have a family emergency and your presence is required at home as soon as possible."

It was the same process I had walked a few enlisted men through during two combat tours. If there was a crisis at home with the family, nothing would resolve it faster for a wife or whoever was having the problem than to call the Red Cross. If there were sufficient grounds to determine that a man's presence was critically required at home, The Red Cross would expedite the request through channels and a man would be given emergency leave to attend to the problem at home.

Kim's letters had grown increasingly remote and hinted of a problem she would not identify. There was an increased reference to an original statement she had made when we had first been together, "Do not ever leave me alone." Some people cannot tolerate a certain intensity of loneliness. They might translate it as abandonment.

The previous week, I had received a small package from her. There was no letter attached, just a cassette recording of a popular country western song by Sammi Smith, "Help Me Make It Through the Night," a sad and passionate plea. Or was it an ultimatum? "Come and lay down by my side, til the early morning light. All I'm takin' is your time, help me make it through the night. I don't care what's right or wrong. I won't try to understand. Let the devil take tomorrow, Lord tonight I need a friend. Yesterday is dead and gone and tomorrow's out of sight, and it's sad to be alone. Help me make it through the night."

Some women are built for the task. Kim was not. And she had honestly warned me she was not. I could not blame her for her loneliness. I certainly couldn't blame her honesty. I would have been the same way and would not have cared what I had to do or who I had to be with to make it better.

I did not want to know if Kim cashed in her hall pass and found someone to help her through the night. This was not the index of fidelity to me when I had left my wife alone with four children for over a year and she had essentially warned me that she could not do it.

I had known officer's wives who were structured to make it through the year and through their husband's entire career, never mind through the night. They had to take care of the children and the family business with ease and dignified aplomb. They did it as though something had naturally equipped them for all that this would entail. Their husband's career was their career. They went through the deployments and the combat tours as if they were there themselves. These are the heroes of the Marine Corps, a very distinct brand of warrior. When you ask someone to do something that you know, and that they know they cannot do, you can anticipate a large trade off and it should not surprise or trouble you when it happens.

I became a hot potato in Marine Aircraft Group 11. Nothing gets the command's attention faster than an appeal from the Red Cross assisted by their ninja emissaries, the Chaplain Corps. In less than a week, I had emergency leave orders back to my address of record in Memphis. My combat tour was just a month short of over, so the orders were permanent change of duty pending reassignment after I had settled whatever catastrophe met me when I arrived in Memphis.

Getting into the combat zone was a lot easier than getting out. Saigon Airport was a crush of dirty brown and green uniforms on myriad priorities of exit orders, R&R and leave papers. No matter what rank you were wearing, they leveled the playing field here. It sometimes had more to do with levels of intimidation and graft. I could see the friendships being cashed in at the counter as small groups pushed their way to the front of the line. Those not so hardened to language and conditions of the trenches slipped to the back of the auditorium. Small clusters of troops, now released from the immediate combat front, showered, and dressed in clean starched utilities. They'd brought their edge back from the firebase and were pushing the envelope. They exchanged complicated fist and hand greetings that had the stamp of the street. I recognized a dangerous mischief still alive, loaded with something still left to be killed.

I ignored the intimidation and pressed past several layers of gang ritual up to a harried clerk who looked at my generic face, trying to find anything about me that made me different besides a piece of paper bearing the operative word "Emergency." These orders barely got his attention, but enough to stamp them and hand me what amounted to a ticket on an American Airlines flight to Hawaii with connections to Los Angeles.

Once I got to California, it wouldn't be this chaotic. I wondered while I was waiting in the departure depot what it was going to look like when Nixon reduced the troop size to a force deficit. The panic of the many at the back would crush the few at the front. It was only chaos today. Tomorrow it will be anarchy. Like so much that had happened in my life, I seemed to slip in just under the wire, barely qualified for the positions and the skills I would occupy but allowed in. And here I was again. Slipping out under the wire before it all fell apart.

14

Cherry Point

Three days later, I was looking down onto Union Avenue as my flight made its final approach to Memphis International. Lest I had forgotten that I lived in the bible belt. The most prominent, but not the highest, feature visible from my window seat is the tall and graceful white steeple of Second Presbyterian Church on Poplar Avenue at the corner of Goodlett. Further east on Poplar, a giant American flag flies on Clark Tower, the tallest building in the city in 1972.

Memphis sits on a natural aquifer, the source of some of the purest and most plentiful water in the country. No small benefit derived from this is a proliferation of trees. It's an arboreal oasis. The city's giant oak and assorted deciduous, flowering dogwood, magnolia and countless others make of Memphis an oasis, a verdant umbrella, explosively alive in spring. A Memphis spring is gentle, vivaciously alive. Where the south and spring meet, it demands that life bloom wherever there's an opening. Azalea proliferates. If you were to stand still long enough in the same spot just off open concrete, kudzu would seize, smother and cover you in place with its enormous, lush leaves that grow as you watch.

The four of them were waiting at the arrival gate: Kim, her brother, and sister-in-law. And Julian. I could feel him there as if he were a buffer to anything that might occur and my reaction to it. It was unnecessary. The entire scene was benign, a non-drama.

I loaded my bags into the trunk of Jimmy's car. Julian, Jimmy, Daphne, Kim, and I pulled into the familiar Memphis traffic. Kim and I piled up in the back, fogging the windows. A sitter was with the children.

I had missed Julian's reassuring presence while I was in the combat zone, particularly during my last tour as my energy waned. I found it interesting, but uncomfortable, his obvious absence during my most difficult moments, as if he were allowing me to find my own resources and recognize more readily my skills, but mainly my limitations. He had said that our limitations largely defined us, not as a negative measure, but as they determine the parameters within which we most effectively function. Just as the Grand Design had built genius into consciousness, so had it planted limitations. As we discovered these, then we would find and focus our genius into a positive purpose. With each new discovery, we adjust our boundaries.

The war was winding down; so was I. I could no longer find that part of me that was required to be there. My part in Vietnam, like everything I would experience, was vital to my spiritual realization. It's how our life plan is structured. Each piece is like a stone in the mosaic that would define a life's passage.

Julian had no small part in the influences that would show me the way: new people, events, and readings crucial to my unfolding. He told me to be alert to the underlying forces that guide us through a single incarnation and how that one lifetime weaves itself into the Whole. I had been informed that there would be a large surge of events as my career in the Marine Corps ended. It had all been vital, but I was going to make a course correction more closely aligned with my authentic being. There was not much room for someone dropping napalm where I was going.

Just a few years before I went to Vietnam, a dear friend was seriously ill. His disease was believed terminal. I visited him in the hospital on several consecutive days. There were moments when I thought he was about to expire. I was reluctant to leave his room. His illness required that the fluids in his peritoneum be exchanged daily.

The peritoneum is a lining that covers the organs in the abdomen and acts as a filter. Someone, usually a nurse, or sometimes his wife was required to exchange the fluids daily. One day, I arrived in his room and found my friend standing on the floor, hovering over the exchange vessel that contained the peritoneal fluids. He was very cheerful, energetic and optimistic. He told me he was trying to figure out how to do the exchange himself. The nurse came into the room and urged him to get back in bed. She would take care of the exchange for him.

Leaving, I passed the nurse's station and remarked how nice it was that my friend was coming around, apparently recovering from his illness. He seemed to be doing so much better.

"Oh, no, Mister Ruthven," the nurse said gravely. "That was a bad sign. I don't know how many times I've had a patient deathly ill one day; and the next day, they try to get out of bed and take care of some chores. In a very few days, he would die. This is a death surge. I don't want to discourage you, but he might not be here tomorrow."

The next day he died. I thought of my friend as I felt my career winding down in the Marine Corps, that I could probably look forward to a last surge before I made a transition, a correction hard right, or left onto a new vector.

It was clear what had precipitated the emergency. Kim was desperately and passionately lonely. Our old friend Dick Gastineau, a retired Marine Gunnery Sergeant, had told her how to arrange through the Red Cross to get me home before she did something she might have regretted. A doctor signed an affidavit that she was a suicide risk. Her brother was required to write a note from the family that endorsed the doctor's diagnosis. Jimmy said in his attachment that his sister was a "nut case." Jimmy's diagnosis, very basic, was closer to the truth than I allowed. I only thought I understood how troubled she was. She didn't know. How should I? We would all find out how far a person must go before they say I can go no further.

My welcome home was much warmer than my departure. As we drove home from the airport, Kim's sister-in-law, Daphne, looked back at the two of us piled up in the back seat. "It's amazing what a girl will do to get a hard dick."

Kim laughed. Jimmy punched Daphne playfully on the shoulder. I wondered at the rest of the squadron and half the Marine Corps still in the combat zone. Here I am in the back seat with my sex kitten wife with a note from my chaplain that I'm no longer needed in our war. My presence is required at home. It was as well that I was here. For the last months in Danang, I wasn't totally there. And, that job would require my total presence.

Some years later, too late for me to have benefited now, I was friends with a man who had been in prison for three years. He had been billeted with another man who was in for life. My friend spent a good part of his day looking out through the bars beyond the razor wire at the free world.

One day his cellmate told him, "You're not gonna make it."

"What are you talking about, old man? I'm getting out in a couple of years, but you're in for life."

The seasoned prisoner responded, "You're spending most of your time in confinement with your head out there. When you get your head where your ass is, you might make it.

I needed to get my head out of Vietnam and take care of business in Memphis. I had the feeling I was going to be busy. I needed to get my head where my ass was.

Returning to Memphis. my feelings returned. Dreams and intuitive thoughts brought me closer to Julian, who had evidently been waiting to really lay it on me.

He insisted that there is a Higher Authority in charge of the scheduling and our several movements. Every hair is counted, every motion monitored. It all might seem random, but Julian reminded me one night, as I walked in the darkness of our backyard, that it was necessary that I respond obediently to the moment just as I had. He had tracked my every move and mistake, although in the grand scheme of things, no mistakes are made. The pieces were moved about the board in a manner unfamiliar to the puzzled player. It required that he give himself over in faith, not knowing what was next. No man will ever know how the game is structured. He will only be handed his script in the play for that day-that moment and asked to step into it.

"Don't try to figure it out, Colin. It's all a mystery, a holy mystery. Horrendously brutal at turns, but elegantly, unspeakably beautiful." It was a relief to feel Julian's presence once again. More a relief to know I didn't have to figure it all out. As if I could.

Many of the troops returning from the combat zone checked in to the Veteran's Hospital or their psychiatrist to deal with post-traumatic stress disorder, agent orange contamination, confusion, and fatigue. I felt the need for none of this. I was disappointed with myself for not sustaining the enthusiasm needed to be present. I felt worse that I got out without a scratch with none of the mental torment many Vietnam veterans would always live with.

I did not have to adapt to a peaceful environment. I did not experience oppressive combat fatigue or PTSD. I had grown up with all of that in the West End of Vancouver. I found the combat zone a comfortable and familiar place to live where people were doing things that closely squared with my early upbringing. I was reminded again of the adage that skills learned in danger require danger for them to be effective. Hopefully, I would learn quieter skills and be directed on the Path that more closely comported with my Native Being, not my upbringing.

I worried that my behavior had not tracked with Julian's vision of me. He explained that all the discord, the alcoholism, the nervousness, irritability and often demonstrations of a naturally unhealthy disposition were not illnesses in themselves, but the expression of a soul engaged in the work required to the struggle back to his authentic being. "It's like a drowning man fighting to return to the surface." A greater part of the refining required that a soul go through a life that seemed alien to who and what he essentially was.

I was more than ready to come home. There was some resistance, but I gradually settled into the domestic pattern. Like many who had come out of the combat zone, I began to look for things that were not there. But this soon diminished. Mine was a minor transition from the potential dangers of flying projectiles to the occasional episode of flying dishes.

At Danang I had been insulated from the immediate impact of bullets against my body, looking into the whites of their eyes and the black of their teeth. My stress was lessened by my distance from the actual fighting below on the ground, the comfort of a supersonic fighter bomber inside an airconditioned cockpit. I was sheltered from the immediate impact of combat. I lived in an enclosed base surrounded by barbed wire and a company of Marines guarding the perimeter. I slept in a cot and soon adapted to the constant pounding of artillery and rumble of bombs in the distance. In Memphis, I strangely missed the ambient noise of Danang. My sleep was often interrupted by the silence of the night. I would awaken to an exaggerated quiet of the bedroom, the soft breath of my sleeping wife, a dog in the distance, a horn's feint honk. A siren. Then, a smothering, unnerving quiet.

Kim and I became a couple again. She wanted to get away from Memphis as soon as possible. She kept asking when I was going to get orders anywhere else. At the same time, she was receiving unwelcome phone calls, some she refused to field and told me not to answer. I put it out of my mind and thought that she might have created a life in Memphis while I was gone that she needed to get away from, something akin to the community she had joined at the Globe and Anchor Apartments. At least she didn't get raided. She wasn't in jail.

Someone about my age showed up one evening. Kim hustled him out to the curb and told me to stay in the house. I heard her yelling. A car burned rubber up the hill toward Raleigh Egypt High School. I didn't want to know what that was all about. Thankfully, I received preliminary orders over the phone that required no paperwork. We could soon pack the station wagon and leave for Cherry Point, North Carolina. I would be happy to stay out of Kim's business and get out of her city.

"Colin, how long you been in town?" It was Sheldon Elliott. He sounded different. The hole in his head had hopefully healed by now, covered by a full Marlon Brando growth. He had apparently escaped from the jealous husband and lost the interest from the object of their mutual affection. "When d'you get in?" I heard him drag on a cigarette, put his hand over the phone and yell at someone in the background.

"Sheldon, how did you know I was in town? I've only been here for a day or so." I got no response. He was obviously talking to someone else at the same time.

"Where you at, Sheldon? You sound real busy."

"I'm at work, Colin." Another drag. He was whispering to someone else in the room.

"You getting out real soon? I got a job for you," he said in the middle of a drag. I could visualize him sitting down now, his feet crossed on a desk. He had his theater voice, all confidential, with his hand over the phone so nobody else can hear us. "Kim told me you were coming in. So, when you gettin' out?"

"Oh, hell, I've got a couple of years at least until I retire. I can get out on twenty with retirement in January 1974. That's about two years away"

"That's too bad, Colin," he sighed with exaggerated histrionics. "I could get you in here at Archer Woodbury and Associates right away. There's an office waiting for you when you get out though. Okay?" It all sounded too optimistic. In the background I could hear him say, "Darling, grab me a cup of speed. Okay? Thanks. You're incredible, darling." Oh, my God, I guessed, he's in charge of something, somewhere. God help us all. I could hear him circling, ready to strike and take possession of another vagina.

"Sheldon, we're leaving tomorrow for Cherry Point. It's in North Carolina. I'll drop you a line when we get there and talk more about this."

"Okay, count on it, man." I could hear furniture moving around, his hand on the mouthpiece, muttering to someone, probably the closest secretary or mail clerk. "Plan on it, Colin. When you get out, I've got you a job."

I had put the house up for sale and left the arrangements in the hands of Jimmy and Daphne. If they realized a profit, they could have it. On the way to the East Coast, I thought again as I drove the long I-40 through Tennessee, that Kim had probably found her way into another small community where she could be more who she was than she could when she was with me. I recalled how relaxed she was after visiting her 'friends' in the Globe and Anchor who certainly could drink, while she couldn't while she was with me. I'd entertained the idea that she was an alcoholic, not a bottomed out drunk, but someone who required alcohol to cut the edge of her angry, irritable, and discontent disposition, her four emotional food groups.

A person's temperament naturally figures in behavior. Kim was who she was. I no longer expected her to be any different from what everything inside her told her to be. Kim was fiery and short-fused. It was just how she was. If I'd been that way, I'd probably find some way to ease it. Then it hit me. I am that way, or at least when I was actively drinking. I was that way exactly. I required alcohol to allow me to live with myself. It had occurred to me more than once, but now I realized. The awareness landed so hard that I almost stopped the car to breathe. Kim was a female version of me. I had married myself. Jesus! I recalled my behavior as an active alcoholic in my first marriage. I quietly commiserated with Beth, my first wife. And now I was having the same feelings for my second wife, Kim. She left me with a tremendous sadness. I could not get angry with her. I had the feelings that sometimes she wished that I could. She often seemed to press me to the edge. She was furious if I didn't respond.

In every way: our marriage, the Marine Corps, and my sobriety, never mind my personality. It had all put a demand on Kim that was over and above her emotional paygrade. I thought again of the free hall pass. Maybe with just a few years left on my twenty, she could either hang on or make the change. But I'd learned that I could not deny my essential nature for too long. And if I was not aware of it and accepted it, who I was would sneak up on me. If it was true for me, it was true for Kim. But I had the advantage. I was aware of who I was, but Kim was still denying who she was. And, at more and more frequent intervals, who she was creeping up on her and everyone around her. It was at this point that I realized that I really liked Kim, but I was unsure if I could live with her. She was very much like me. Again, If I had been a woman, I would probably be a Kim.

I checked in to the Second Marine Aircraft Wing headquarters, Cherry Point. G1-Administration. The Personnel duty NCO stamped my orders, and they immediately sent me to the G3 Operations Department. I had barely walked into Colonel Stern's office when he whisked me away to a room that had six desks, all occupied but for one.

"Here's your new fighter officer, Burke." A tall and imposing Lieutenant Colonel rose from a desk at the end of the room. Kent Burke, heavy and boisterous, walked around the desk, his hand held out to me.

"Major Ruthven, we've been expecting your arrival. Your reputation precedes you." He gripped my hand and didn't let it go. Instead, he walked me around the room introducing me to the attack, helicopter, air control and electronic countermeasures officers. "Here's your desk," he added after the introductions. "It's been empty for a while, but your incoming basket is full. If you can make your way through that stack of pending messages, you'll learn what this job is all about." He grinned as if I had just delivered another of his children. "From what I hear, you'll figure it out in an afternoon."

So, this is what a staff job looked like. I wished I could tell Jay Hubbard, who was now a Brigadier General, that I'd arrived. I was told to take a couple of days to get settled in housing and arrange for household goods to have my effects shipped. It took me a day. I wanted to get back to work. I checked in with the Phantom training squadron. Paul Sigmund was the commanding officer. We had been in Training Squadron 23 together in Kingsville. He kept showing up during my Marine Corps career, a critical creature in the mix. He's the one who pulled me aside after I had been sober a month and said, "Animal, what the hell's happened to you. A month ago, you were a poet. Today you're an old man." He had been right. That was that first month of total confusion, disorientation, a fighter pilot by day, a monk by night, a wandering generality, looking for a place to be something that had not yet been defined.

"You've come back to life, Colin," he said after we had finished a cup of coffee and spoken about the passage of about eight years since I had seen him. "I was worried about you back then. We all thought it was alcohol poisoning."

"It was," I replied. He said I could fly with his squadron if I kept it to a minimum. They barely had funds to direct to the student training.

I was back in a Phantom that week. I thought I might have forgotten how to fly. I had. In the States, I had difficulty adapting to the restrictions of air traffic control again. I did not know what a luxury it was taking off, checking in with one facility that directed all air traffic and pressing on to a target. I felt constricted with the ground rules and the area of operations, the several agencies with whom I had to check in. Combat operations had spoiled me.

As I looked back not that far, barely months, I recalled I was falling out of love with tactical flying, which to me was falling out of love with flying. When I was totally honest with myself, I didn't enjoy flying. Flying from point A to point B without wringing the airplane out for all the g's available and dropping a full load of assorted ordnance from her wings was not flying.

A couple of pilots with whom I had been in other squadrons approached me one day. "Hey, Colin, I know you've got a few years before you retire, but why don't you get out and come with us. We're going to Memphis to get on board with Federal Express."

"What the hell's a Federal Express?" I asked. They explained that a former Marine had come up with a thesis in Yale business college for a logistics model and was applying it to nation-wide package delivery.

"They're flying Falcons. It's a small transport. The pilot loads the plane, files a flight plan, flies it to the destination and unloads it then brings back cargo to a central loading hub in Memphis."

They were on fire with the idea and wondered why I didn't jump in. It would have been a death sentence. I could barely discipline myself to fly Phantoms back and forth between the flight line and the restricted area for an air intercept exercise. The idea of droning a plane straight and level for more than an hour put me on the verge of a panic attack. I could feel the end rapidly approaching. It was a tough admission. Where once there was romance, now there was none. Peak combat operations employing all the skills a career of tactical flying had taught me had jaded me. I could not return to basics. I was like a drug addict who has been taken off cocaine and put on decaffeinated coffee and that there was no going back.

It was a perfect time to take to a desk. I became an administrative fool. I was composing messages that should have won awards. I had established liaison with fighter squadrons throughout the Aircraft Wing, routinely flying down to Beaufort, South Carolina, where I had been in a fighter group in Marine Fighter Squadron 312, the Checkerboards.

We moved into base housing. Kim's two girls, now almost in their teens and savvy in matters of the world, started school. David was still a baby, Phoebe about three. I drove a Volkswagen Bug, Kim, our station wagon.

We'd been in Cherry Point about six months. I came home from a day and a half absence. I had been inspecting a squadron's operations down in Beaufort. The station wagon was gone. All the children were in the house, but the station wagon and Kim were gone. The girls seemed to know something that I did not. The oldest girl informed me that her mother had left and might not be back.

For about a month, I was alone with the four children, going to work every day and depositing the children at a babysitter's home. Kim's brother called and told me that Kim was with them and that she wanted to come back to Cherry Point. I told her to come back. I didn't ask why she had left. I believed again that I had just forced her into a lifestyle that was inimical to her basic nature. Kim had wings she needed to spread.

Within a month of her return, she left again, this time with the babies. She left me with her two girls.

I settled further into the Wing Fighter Desk, composing orders, new air traffic control routes for the aircraft flying in and around the Cherry Point air traffic control space. The FAA representative became a close friend. I was flying to and from Headquarters Marine Corps in Washington, D.C., arranging and planning parades and ceremonies, coordinating and controlling air shows. I was a serious player. The world knew me in Wing Headquarters, and at Headquarters Marine Corps, in Washington DC. They got out of my way when I storm down a passageway. They called me into the General's office a couple of times a week. I grew deeper into the furniture and became one of them, whatever they call them.

Not entirely blind to my future when I reported to the Wing, I thought of what I would do when I retired after my twenty years, about two years away. Sheldon Elliott, although a total flake, had suggested I had a new career as an art director, waiting for me in Memphis when I retired from the Marine Corps. I had not forgotten his habit of promising job opportunities for people who had no talent. It didn't matter that he was promising them jobs that didn't exist. My last memory of Sheldon he was wearing a blood soaked, torn skivvy shirt. His face was buried in a married woman's lap. I set my doubts about Sheldon aside and made plans to train myself to be a commercial artist. While I was still in the Marine Corps, I immersed myself in a correspondence course. I would like to have half a clue what I was doing when I stepped into the job.

One night after Kim had returned home again, a strange thing happened. We had been there about a year. I sank deep into a futon, watching something meaningless to get my mind off a hundred messages I had pending in my basket. The doorbell rang, saving me from being swallowed up in administrative quicksand. I answered the door. It was my boss, Kent Burke.

He came in the house balancing a highball in his hand. Ice was making its familiar soft ring inside the tumbler. He'd been drinking most of the evening. He came into the living room holding papers I recognized as a three-page message. I was having a vicarious trip on his buzz. At the same time, I wondered if the papers in his hand were a handful of mistakes I'd made in the day or additional matters for me to attend to right away.

"Congratulation, Colonel." He spoke. I thought he was going to go into some kind of drunk routine. I did not know what he was talking about. He said it again, "Congratulations, Colonel." I frowned, and he handed me the pages he had been holding. It was the selection list to Lieutenant Colonel. I looked at about the last page and there was my name. They had selected me for promotion to the grade of Lieutenant Colonel.

I came out of the futon in an Olympic jump, landing on my slippers. I stood for a while, staring speechlessly at the message.

"How the hell does something like that happen, Kent?" I was shaking my head, stunned. For the last year I had been planning and directing air shows and parades, visiting fighter squadrons, rewriting plans for the air traffic corridor for tactical aircraft in and out of the Cherry Point air traffic flight pattern. I was also the master of ceremonies for a roast they held for General Tom Miller. They gave it to me because I had the least to lose if it turned out the general had no sense of humor. If something needed translating from unreadable headquarters Marine Corps speak, I could convert it to baby talk. None of this would compensate for my colorful past. So, what had I done to be promoted to Lieutenant Colonel?

"Nobody gets promoted to paygrade O-5 by accident, Colin." Burke finished his drink. I felt bad that I could not offer him another double shot. "You'll probably have to show them you deserve it though."

"What do you mean?" I asked.

"They'll probably give you an assignment that's Lieutenant Colonel level, difficult." He finished the ice in his glass and walked to the door. "Don't worry. I think you might underestimate yourself. You brought a good reputation back from two combat tours." He sipped at the empty tumbler. "And you have done nothing this last year to disappoint me or anyone else."

15

Blue Axe

As if I would ever turn it down, a condition that I accept the rank of Lieutenant Colonel was that I would serve at least two more years of active duty from my promotion. I had no problem with that. I was in no hurry to go anywhere but where I was pointed next. Julian would often say, "If you ever have any question about what you should do, just step into whatever is next and see what is evidently there. Trust to the Grand Design."

With this stipulation, if I retired after twenty years, I would only be adding about nine months to my original release date. I would retire August 1974, a month before I was forty years old, young enough to begin another career. With every expectation that Sheldon was locking my position into his advertising agency, I continued with the correspondence course and looked forward with a renewed vision to become an entry level commercial artist when I retired.

But there was this thing Burke was talking about, the Lieutenant Colonel worthy project. What the hell would they ask me to do. I felt like I was about to go through an initiation before I could pull the sword from the stone. I didn't have to wait long. I had barely pinned the silver oak leaves on my collar when Colonel Mitchell called me into the Operations Office for my ritual circumcision.

"The Marine Corps is adding a full inventory of AV8A Harrier attack aircraft. Headquarters Marine Corps has charged the Second Wing to test the aircraft's suitability in training and combat operations." Colonel Mitchell, the Wing Operations Officer, stared at me, supposing that I might have translated his statement into digestible form. His look demanded that I already come up with a solution before he had presented the problem.

"Your job, if you choose to accept it," he smiled and chuckled privately to himself and then said, "As if you would turn down anything General George Axtell would ask you to do." He continued smiling. "So, your job is to plan and write the operations order around the surge and sortie rate validation test of the AV8A Harrier. He wants a Wing wide operation. Support from all elements, fighter, attack, helicopter." He fired up another cigar. His office held a constant gray overcast at about eye, ear, nose and throat level, sufficient to cause you to sit down without invitation.

"Coincident with this, we will test the new field command-and-control center for the operation." He sat down as if what he was going to say next would require that I be restrained. "Also, they fragged full filming from the Marine Corps Motion Picture Lab' in DC. They want this operation documented and strung into a film suitable for promotion and training. And I have every confidence that you can do it."

"Is that all?" I asked if I could move from the sitting to the prone position. My immediate response was to bolt, find a phone booth some suitable distance away, and tell them to give my silver oak leaves to someone else. I had done none of this. Everything Colonel Mitchell had just described was new to me.

The thick gray overcast, and this remarkable challenge was making me dizzy. I should have asked if I could find a quiet corner and cut a vein. This is the reason Marine officers go to command schools as they are promoted up the rank structure. This is what Colonel Weber was talking about when he said that he could find nothing redeeming about my record: I had never been formally educated in the processes necessary to the task before me. I did not know how to write an operation order. But they had promoted me to Lieutenant Colonel, and I was going to show them I deserved the new pay grade. And how the hell do you document an operation and make a movie?

I spoke with the Wing Chief of Staff, Colonel John Weaver, who gave me the keys to the kingdom. "You have all the resources of the Wing at your disposal. We want everyone and everything involved in this. Also, you have all the real estate we own." He laughed out loud. I didn't know if he was my surrogate hysterical self or if he was on his way home for some lunch time romance, for which he had become refreshingly notorious.

"Operation Blue Axe" would be a tribute to General Axtell, World War II flying ace, and a Navy Cross recipient. During World War II, he was the youngest commanding officer of a Marine fighter squadron and was now Commanding General of the Second Marine Aircraft Wing. The man was seriously severe, imposing, tall and gray, perpetually preceded by a cigar and fleeing staff officers.

I employed my graphics gravitas to create the cover, an actual axe, painted blue, sunk in a piece of driftwood against a dark blue background. I had charts and graphs which many other op orders that I had read did not. I "rented" all the real estate of the Second Marine Aircraft Wing for a month to account for the build-up, the operation and the clean-up.

There's a standard format for an operation order that does not allow much creative latitude and still keeps it nominally native to Marines who have learned how to read according to a standard protocol. It has a language all its own that can be dull. It's not meant to amuse, but instruct: Situation, Mission, Execution, Admin & Logistics and Command & Control.

Just fill in the blanks and make sure there are no holes; that it's all coordinated and does not run counter to itself. It needs to contain all contingencies, but leave lots of room for the individual commanders to operate and demonstrate their own style. I read every op order that had been promulgated since the Normandy Invasion. I visualized with Carl von Clausewitz exactitude my plan for the invasion of a hypothetical country by the Second Marine Aircraft

Wing and supporting elements. As well as the AV8A Harrier attack aircraft, the operation would include fighter, attack, transport, and helicopter support.

The operation was planned, and the order written, published, and delivered before the exercise began, which is rare, believe it or not. We conducted most of the coordination through message traffic that filled in the holes left blank on the op order. I had written in a special department to manage message traffic alone. Much that needed to be contained in the body of the order developed after we launched it. That's how flexible marines have taught themselves to be. The operation proceeded with few hitches and no fatalities, which to me was hugely successful. But I could not call myself a Lieutenant Colonel until "Operation Blue Axe" had been given a Hollywood spin.

The Marine Corps does very little without full movie documentation and archiving. The Corps has rarely gone into the field without a battalion of camera crews. When the after-action reports were all in, the blame liberally spread, credit amply given and Blue Axe was concluded, I had a trunk full of film and a script written for the movie.

I'd been in the field for ten days. I occupied a tin chair in the green camouflaged dome that housed the mobile command-and-control center whence Operation Blue Axe was coordinated. When I returned to the housing area after the operation expecting at least some lights to be on, I discovered the house was empty. Kim had left again. It could have been a 'help me through the night' episode. She never said; I didn't ask. But a week later, she asked if she could come back to Cherry Point.

They had given me temporary additional duty orders to Headquarters Marine Corps in D.C., where the Marine Corps Film Archive and I would create and edit the film. I thought this an ideal opportunity for Kim and me to take a working vacation and try to bring the marriage back on track. So, I told Kim to come home.

We packed the kids and moved to Washington, D.C. for a week while I went full on Martin Scorsese at the Marine Corps Film lab. If you're ever in D.C. to see the silent drill team or the sunset parade, go to the Marine Corps Film lab first. I'd have a clearance for X rated for gruesome, very explicit combat film footage. They gave me an even closer look at the war in which I thought I had taken part. I gained a much more profound appreciation for the troops I was supporting on the ground.

We enjoyed top hotel accommodations, played in the pool, let the kids swim and bake in the sun for an entire week. I had hoped this would keep us as a family afloat. All I had to do was stay at home or at least go to work and come home at lunch to watch "All My Children." Oh, my God, did you see the episode where Evelyn revealed her genuine feelings for Margo?

The movie, "Blue Axe," was not nominated for an academy award, but was received by the Wing Chief of Staff as if I had brought out his firstborn child from the delivery room. My final fitness report with the Wing stated I had exceeded the wishes and orders of the Commander. The Commander for all of that only watched half of the movie. He was interrupted by the very same Chief of Staff who told General Axtell that he had a call from the Assistant Commandant for Air. It was one of the few times I saw General George Axtell put down his cigar. He gave me a nod and a thumbs up. It felt at least equivalent to the thumbs up I got from Dark Tarnish on my first solo flight.

It was about this time that Hugh Montgomery, an ex-student of mine from the Advanced Training Command, told me that he had met a friend who wanted to interview me about my infamous tour in Atsugi. Hugh was a Major by now and attached to the Marine Aircraft Group in Beaufort. I had very little flight time that month and was in a billet where I could not encroach on the flight time of students. In order to log some flight time that would not rob any students of their time, I sniveled an airplane from Paul Sigmund's squadron for a weekend. Nobody else would be flying and I could plan a round robin navigation flight that landed in Beaufort for one night, and then I would get the airplane back to Cherry Point on Sunday night.

I landed in Beaufort, and Hubert introduced me to Pat Conroy. He had just finished his first book, "The Water is Wide," and was about to write about his life growing up in a Marine Corps family with a father who was a Marine Corps fighter pilot. He had heard about my exploits in Atsugi and wanted to interview me personally, along with some other fighter pilots, as research for his book. I gave him most of my material, withheld some, not sure of the statute of limitations on stupidity for a prospective Lieutenant Colonel. I also told him I had met his father, the Wing personal assignment officer in Da Nang during my last tour. He didn't want to hear what I thought of him.

I returned to Cherry Point and drove out to the housing area, suspecting that the place might be empty. My prescience was grimly rewarded. Kim had packed up the station wagon, all the children. This time, she was gone for good. I filed for divorce.

The provost marshal heard about the divorce and asked me if I wanted him to provide me with an affidavit of Kim's activities at the non-commissioned officers' club while I had been gone. I thanked him and said that I did not want to know anything about anything. It was time to move on. Kim needed to go her way; I needed to go mine. It was not long after this that a new assignment that was a Lieutenant Colonel billet pointed me in my new direction.

There are several fighter squadrons and several attack squadrons in the Marine Corps, but there were only two Special Weapons Training Units. One on the east coast at Cherry Point, the other at El Toro, California. They formed Marine Air Weapons Training Unit Atlantic from a requirement originally coming out of the Second World War that saw the need for special weapons delivery and handling in all tactical aircraft. They developed weapons and tactics training in both conventional and nuclear realms into curricula to address the enhancement and standardization of training. This was a great idea, and it would continue to develop.

MAWTULant was principally composed of a small complement of officers, particularly identified with their skills in weapons and tactics. Their larger talents provided the training necessary to implement these procedures. Strangely, this unit attracted iconoclastic types who were not ordinarily inclined to regulations or protocols. Or, sometimes to even wearing a uniform. This was looking like Captain Colin Ruthven revisited.

I was not sure if I was assigned as the officer in charge of MAWTULant, because of my expertise in tactics and weapons delivery or my capacity to convey the word to those who should have been wiser. It occurred to me a few months after they have given me the job that they had put me in charge of the asylum to bring the inmates into line.

Every officer was an instructor with a specialty that made most of them feel particularly unique. So special that the unit might not require their presence unless they were training a class, judging a competitive attack or weapons delivery exercise. It was the kind of squadron I would have fit into perfectly as a junior captain. It would only require my presence for those few hours when I would share the mysteries of my mind and how that applied to engaging with the enemy. Then I would be left at the mercy of my imagination, which is a very scary place.

The major problem was that the two senior officers, and there were only eight of us, wandered in and out of the unit area like bikers trolling for loose women. The only thing missing, and I was not about to mention it, were civilian clothes. My qualifications, as I had suspected, were that I had, at one time, been there and done what every one of these guys was doing. Everyone knew it and they saw the difference, the current version of Colin Ruthven. I was to do to them what should have been done to me years earlier. It took me awhile to get past that contradiction. I had no problem dealing with the hypocrisy. How do I ask of them what I manifestly could not do myself?

"That's why you got the job, Animal." Colonel Weaver laughed through a cloud of cigar smoke. He had been the Commanding Officer of the Air Control Squadron at Atsugi in 1961. "The Corps is loaded with cruel ironies. It's one charm that makes this outfit flexible and often amusing."

I got there on time every morning and I was there all day except if my duties at the unit required me to be some place else, like flying or inspecting tactical units. I set a standard I could never have followed when I was the loose cannon. There were about four junior officers who had been looking for an adult to show up. The greatest irony of my life was that I was the adult. The junior officers, the ones with the real brains, jacked up their game to the next level, and we made changes in the syllabus and the professional standard by which we behaved. And I waited for the inevitable papers to arrive.

A report finally crossed my desk first thing on a Monday morning, smoking with their scorched content. My two senior officers had been in an accident in Puerto Rico while they had been with a squadron grading a competitive weapons exercise. The inconvenient aspect of the accident is that it had nothing to do with flying or official duty. The two officers had commandeered a jeep while they were shitfaced. I gave myself a few minutes to remember exactly what that felt like and recalled with cringing revulsion the night Pennington and I had stolen the Group Commander's vehicle. The gods of all creatures rude and stupid had smiled on us that night. Bob Pennington and I had at least not driven the sedan over the side of a mountain, as my two officers had the jeep in Puerto Rico.

The pilots had to be jerked from the flight schedule until we completed the investigation. While that was happening, I required them to be in the unit area, professionally dressed, on a podium, or developing curricula.

A Marine Corps investigation of an accident, in the line of duty or not in the line of duty, is as protocol driven as an operations order and about as immune to loophole as the laws of gravity. It's simple and it can be lethal. With the two under investigation, it was swift and brutal. It didn't help their case that their previous fitness reports provided nothing in mitigation or extenuation. They were gone in six months and the unit thrived.

But one afternoon, as if to administer compensatory, evenly distributed retribution, I was visited with the saddest news I could have at one time imagined. It was during a competitive weapons delivery exercise. I was droning around in a tight circle above the bombing pattern, judging hits. We were flying out of the Marine Corps Air Station at Yuma. After thousands of hours in single place jet aircraft in every attitude and airspeed, I got airsick. I could have puked into my oxygen mask or into my helmet. The words of my primary flight instructor, Lieutenant Hart, came back to me as I circled the bombing range. "Puke into anything but your helmet. Never take your helmet off. You're gonna need it."

I did what Lieutenant Hart instructed me to do during my first flights in an SNJ. I removed my flight gloves and filled them with breakfast. I placed the gloves in my helmet bag, zipped it up and put it in the airplane bilge. I carried the bag back to the hangar and threw it in a dumpster. I wouldn't need the helmet bag or my helmet anymore.

Within a week, I turned in my wings. I'd worn it out. Not only did I no longer love to fly, it made me sick.

"What's happening, Julian?" His instructions were predictable.

"Follow what is clearly indicated, not how you wanted things to be or how you think they should be. Just do what's there, what's next, immediately in front of you. That's what Nature has been telling you to do." An obviously jarring event like this might be the only way I would respond to change and make the adjustment. He added, "Try to envision the unrehearsed life. Allow this to be nothing like you thought it would be. Let the moment reveal itself free of all your ideas of how anything should be. Shake off everything you think you know."

"But how am I to interpret this?" I went to the place in my body more than my head, where the dialogue between us took place. I could feel it more than hear what he would say. The communication had developed into a telepathic sense, a knowing.

"God will break your legs to get your attention." I had heard it through interior locution, but now I was experiencing the reality in my body and my psyche that I was no longer configured to fly airplanes. "Be alert to the new configuration," he had counseled. "We are constantly being transformed and newly realized, in a perpetual state of reconfiguration. Step away from the outer shell that has protected you from what does not fit. But when you emerge from the shell, walk away. Leave what's left to Nature. Nature knows best. She disposes kindly and efficiently about what has happened and directs our attention to what is taking place right now. Can you be the current version of who you are as in each moment when it is freshly revealed?"

My decision to cancel my flight orders had allowed me to examine honestly my genuine reasons for flying. I was in a staff billet that was robbing younger pilots of flight time. I was also retiring within a year, so I no longer needed to satisfy annual minimums. I was only flying to collect flight pay. This is the worst reason to fly. Central to my decision, was that what had once made me happy and gave meaning to my life now made me sick.

"It is very much like love, Colin. Love takes us where it wants us to go. She's always in charge and sometimes expresses herself in orders that are beyond our ethical and moral standards. But if love wants you to go someplace else, She will release you from that which you once held dear to that which She requires of you."

My God, what will be next?

My letter of intent to cancel my flight orders and to retire clarified that there were students just out of the training command who needed to fly and that staff officers were spending the budget allocations dedicated to training new pilots just to satisfy their minimums for flight pay purposes.

The letter was unpopular with some staff officers who continued to fly with the tactical squadrons while student pilots wasted their burgeoning years when they should have been developing new muscle memory in the cockpit.

I recalled with gratitude how generously I was treated as a 'nugget', cramming my logbook with flight time in the Fury and the Crusader. There were those incredible moments drinking at the Sweet Spot and dog fighting with Gil Henry over the skies of Hawaii. He in his Fury 3, me in my Fury 4. Debriefing over a drink on the other side of the island. These were precious moments that the new pilots should be enjoying, as did I in my early stages of development. What an abundance it fed me of that early milk that nourished the bones of every subsequent flight I was to fly.

I had indicated I would retire in less than a year. I was now dead weight. I was taking up someone else's airtime.

I needed to return to Memphis to deal with some of the legal aspects of our divorce. Kim and I also needed to clear on her reasons for leaving. I scored some space in a Hercules C 130 training flight to Memphis. Kim met me at the Millington Naval Air Station airfield.

She parked the station wagon in front of Base Operations. Kim sat motionless behind the steering wheel, looking straight ahead. As I approached the car, she slid over, showing that I should drive. She didn't look at me, still staring at some dead spot in the distance, like she was trying not to be there. I pulled out of operations, drove into the first vacant parking area, and stopped the car. I turned to talk to her. She was small, like a little girl. Kim was no longer the angry and nervous woman about to blow. She looked whipped.

"I think you should see these." I handed her a sheaf of affidavits from some of the Marines she had allegedly 'befriended' during my occasional absence. A major in the operations department, who drank at the staff non-commissioned officers' club, had asked them to describe Kim's activities at the club.

"Look, Kim, I don't need those. And I will not keep them, but I think you should at least see them. Dispose of them as you wish." The little girl didn't look at them. Kim knew what they were. She drew further away, pressed against the door, looking smaller still, holding the papers crumpled in her lap.

Kim had moved into an up-scale trailer park in a neighborhood between Millington and Memphis. I visited long enough to see the children. She'd sent her two older girls back to Pennsylvania to live with their father. It was just her and our two children in the trailer. They were safe and comfortable. She seemed "Globe and Anchor" happy at last. I left.

I took a rental car into the city to attend a meeting at Rainbow House and hopefully find Sheldon Elliott. I surrounded myself with drunks early into their recovery and sat silently enjoying the "sunlight of the spirit". After the meeting, I cornered Bert Whiting, a fellow traveler from my first days in Memphis in 1967.

"Have you seen Sheldon Elliott lately?" I asked cautiously.

I could not erase those last moments with Sheldon and the picture I had of the tragic runaway lovebirds, 'Stanley and Stella Kowalski.' I visualized him still bleeding from the head, paralyzed with love for his love captive and unable to emerge from his tortured bliss. Either that or he was drunk. Over and above this, I hoped he still somehow had a job and, further, I would have a job.

"He wants to be called 'Shelly' anymore," Bert chuckled cynically.

"What! Who is he, Johnny Carson, or something?" I could just imagine these new histrionics in Sheldon Elliott's life.

"He thinks he's some kind of celebrity. Won an award with some ad agency. He's become a circuit speaker too, for crise' sake." Bert had stopped chuckling. "Can't talk to the fucking guy."

This was good news; this was bad news. At least he was sober and still had a job, hopefully still had my job. Bad news because all a guy with an ego like that needed was celebrity. Any strokes to that kind of vanity would launch him supersonic beyond even a conversation, a humility overload. He would have absolutely forgotten about burying his broken head in his paramour's lap and sobbing like a wounded gibbon. He might never speak to an earth person again.

I scouted out The Sanderson Blake Advertising Agency the following day. It occupied the entire eighteenth floor of the Sterick Building downtown. The receptionist was behind a door and a glass wall, as if to repel anything unwholesome. She looked at me like I was a new strain of flesh-eating virus.

"I'm looking for Sheldon Elliott, please." I tried to sound as wholesome as possible.

"Do you have an appointment?" She had a second-grade schoolteacher tone like I'd just wet my pants. Jesus. An appointment! The last time I saw this guy I was delivering cold cheeseburgers to a secluded hideout in another time zone. His head was opened like a broken watermelon. If I had been morbidly curious, I probably could have seen his brain.

"No, I'm sorry. I don't. I'm a close friend and I thought I might surprise him." I sounded exactly like Mister Rogers at his warmest and most inviting. I was going to take off my outdoor shoes and put on my indoor shoes.

"Mister Elliott does not like surprises, sir." She grinned maliciously. I think I was about to be sent to the principal's office. "And he is very busy and requires that you make an appointment." She turned back to her nails and something else that was spilling out of her purse.

"Okay, then. Let me make an appointment." I pressed my face closer to the glass. My nose left its impression and my mouth some fog. I stepped back, gauging how much of a running start I needed to vault over the glass cage.

"Alright, let me see when we can fit you in." She appeared to be looking at some papers but kept clear of everything that might touch her newly painted nails.

"You don't understand, darling. I have traveled far, and I want to make an appointment to see Sheldon Elliott, like, right now. I would like to see him at this very moment. Can we make an appointment for right now?" I was doing a perfect Clint Eastwood menacing "Make my day" scowl.

"What's going on here, Verna?" Sheldon's ruddy face peeked around the corner of a hall. Then he spotted me. "Colin! My god, where did you come from? I heard you were in town."

I would have sworn he was speaking with an Edwardian accent. He looked down at a Rolex on his spindly wrist, shook his head, and said, "Can we get together later in the day, Colin?" He looked again. "Maybe 'round two-ish?"

"No, Sheldon, we can get together right now-ish. I'm here right, fuckin' now. 'Scuse me, dear." I glanced briefly at Audrey Hepburn. "I have come all the way from Vietnam and am about to disappear in the morning for parts even further away. I am not asking, I am telling you, that I am about to leap over little miss Candy Pants and choke your sorry ass to the floor if you don't very soon open a door and let me in."

"Go ahead, Verna, open the door. Jesus, Colin! Manners." He brought the rest of his body around the corner. He was four inches taller than usual, courtesy of a pair of surgical uplift snakeskin cowboy boots. The cuffs of his Armani suit were tucked into the tops. Candy Pants buzzed me in. I followed Sheldon into his new sanctum.

"Jesus, Sheldon, is that a zodiac medallion?" I followed him down a hall. His office was the size of a tennis court. He told me to sit down. Then he slowly and dramatically stationed himself with his back to me, looking out the window with his hands folded behind his back like General Patton. I sank deep into the largest chair of the stuffed leather suite, the kind of furniture that squeaks when you sit down. As I waited for our appointment to begin, I mentally pushed Sheldon out the window. I was hoping eighteen floors to the ground would kill him. Or, at least, open up his head again.

He spun around, nearly fell off his shoes and staggered to his desk, then pulled a cigarette from a pack and lit it with a strange, oversized gold lighter. He returned to the window and looked out at the Mississippi River as if he was thinking of buying it. "I've arrived, Colin."

Sheldon spun around. He nearly fell off his shoes again, steadied himself, leaving a sweaty handprint on the window; then he baby-stepped his way back to his desk. He sat behind a heap of paper and the little blue typewriter that had been clogged with his very own blood and hair the last time I'd seen him.

"Okay, Sheldon, I'm thrilled. Really, I'm genuinely happy for you and encouraged." I hoped I was not nudging too close to sarcasm while also asking him if I still had a job. "So, what does 'arrived' look like, Sheldon."

"Shelly, Colin. I prefer Shelly now. Please, Shelly." He took a long drag for emphasis. "Shelly. Kay?" he reasserted. I assented with a nod. "That's who I am in the biz' now." He wasn't kidding. This was not an ironic spoof. He didn't blink. He butted a cigarette from which he had only taken a single drag and lit another from a small blaze that jumped out of a miniature lighter modeled on a tiny little guy holding another tiny guy holding a tiny little trophy.

"Awards, Colin." He shook his head as if I was an idiot for not knowing anything about his fame. "Look over there," he crooned, pointing the non-Rolex arm toward a shelf. A thick gold bracelet and a woven leather band shook out of his sleeve. On the shelf were two statues, larger versions of the tiny little guy lighter. "Those are 'Addies' for my work on the Sealy Mattress account." I thought I detected a catch in his voice. His nose grew red, and one eye seemed to glisten.

I stood and walked to the shelf. "Can I touch one, Shelly?"

"No!" He stood quickly and shuffled to the shelf in a panic. "I'd prefer you didn't touch them." He stationed himself between me and the little statues. He shrank a bit and then worked his way back to the desk. Shelly had not quite learned how to walk in surgical uplift footwear. Either that or the cowboy boots were longer than his legs.

I returned to my chair, sat back; it squeaked. I took a deep breath, held it for the count of ten and then as quietly and calmly as I could summon, said, "Sheldon, 'scuse me, Shelly, I have traveled a great distance to see you and I will leave in five minutes." I stood up and walked to the door. "The last time I saw you I was under the impression that when I retired, I'd have a job, however menial and entry level, I don't care, but nonetheless a job to come to when I am no longer in the Marine Corps. I guess I need some assurance that it will be here when I get here. Else I can make other decisions." I was about to leave when he ran around from his desk and babbled.

"Oh, Christ, yeah, Colin. Oh shit, hell yeah. Of course. That's still a go. We're still on with that!" He was frantic. "By the time you retire I'll own this fucken dump and you'll be running the art department. Christ, sit down, please, please." He dragged me back to the chair, stroking my arm. "I'm sorry. I thought you'd just know. Y'know?"

I sat down, a bit embarrassed at my outburst and worse at his. "Okay, Shelly. Look, I've got to get going, but just needed to know we're solid on the job thing when I retire."

"It's in concrete, a contract, Colin. Again, I own this place. They love me. Shit, they'd change the name to Elliott and Ruthven Advertising if I asked 'em." He was standing in front of the window again, a brilliant Memphis light filtering through his bouffant bush of hair, his arms spread wide in the air. "You should hear the copy I'm writing. It's on print, radio and we're about to buy a butt load of TV time. We're in production, man. It's pure gold, Colin."

He turned to another stack of papers on his desk. "I nailed the Sealy Mattress account, and it's going to be huge." He riffled through the stack. "It's based on this character I created. I call him Philo Feely." He chuckled softly and beamed at me hopefully.

"Philo Feely?" I said, a bit incredulous. I tried not to sound too unimpressed.

"Yeah, he tests mattresses, you know, and falls asleep on them, almost too fast, before he can tell anyone how great they are. Sealy corporate just shit when they heard the concept and my pitch." He looked at me hopefully, as if I was supposed to be totally amazed and fainting from his brilliance. "The radio spots won all those awards and Sealy thinks I'm God." He fumbled with some more papers. "Or, at least Zeus."

"I guess I get it." I didn't want to sound too stupid, especially if he was going to lobby for my job. "What's the pitch line, or whatever they call it?"

"Yeah, exactly, the grabber. I knocked their socks off the first time they heard it. I invented the character voice, like a leprechaun with slumber music, sort of like muted Scheherazade. You know?".

"What's the grabber?"

"Dig this, Colin. 'Philo Feely, the Sealy mattress feeler.'" He stood beaming, waiting for me to fall into an ecstatic trance. He tried to look like a leprechaun in a Rolex and an Armani suit. "You should hear the music. Classic slumber sounds, sleep, you know. Get it? And did I say like, Scheherazade?"

"I like it, Sheldon." I stood to leave. "I really like it. I've got to get going, now." I was doing my 'be quiet, be calm–don't upset this guy–and I'll be out of here in a second' thing. It was like trying to calm a gunman who was holding you hostage. "I'll be in touch between now and the time I retire. Good luck,"

I turned to walk away, then turned back. "Really, good luck, Shelly. You and ... Philo Feely."

16

Retirement

With just a few months before I retired, the Second Marine Aircraft Wing could have hidden me some place, like on mess duty or the mail room. Instead, they wanted me to stay on at the Training Unit. MAWTULant was essentially running itself with a cadre of talented young instructors with top secret clearances. I was just breathing familiar life into the post until they brought in my replacement. In my mind I had retired, it required, but shortly, that the body would follow and take it all to Memphis.

They staffed Marine Air Wing Training Group Atlantic with the cream of all the disciplines: fighter pilots, attack, night all weather, nuclear, electronic warfare, and surveillance. Each of these had maintenance counterparts who taught the more exotic peculiarities of maintenance in these weapons systems.

The pilots spent most of their time in the classroom, teaching advanced tactics, air combat maneuvering, special delivery attack procedures, all the upper end demands of the several weapons systems in the Second Marine Aircraft Wing.

If they were checked out in the airplanes pertaining to their instruction, they would fly in training flights and grade in competitive exercises.

At this point in their readiness, I could leave the operations to the junior officers and concentrate on more personal matters.

I had almost completed my commercial artist correspondence course. I had a job waiting for me when I became a civilian again. There was no wife or children in the formula. Life suddenly seemed almost too uncomplicated. If I had been as suitably vigilant as Julian had cautioned me to be, I might have predicted that an event or person would materialize to fill the void. It was that calm before the tectonic plates shifted and the earth would no longer be what it had been.

I was in a dead sleep, the slumber of a life that had settled with itself. Reality is often revealed in dreams. My true state of being, behind the masquerade of my apparent peace, came to me as I slipped deeper into an innocent REM state. I dreamt that my legs were chained to the ground. I knew I had to arrive some place with great urgency, but I couldn't move and would miss a very important event. I didn't know what. Then, an earthly ringing insinuated itself into the dream state. I opened my eyes and looked around. Maybe the sound of ringing was a part of the dream. It was a phone.

The phone rang again and again.

I glanced at the bedside clock. It was just before five in the morning. I picked up the phone on the sixth ring and put it to my ear, only half aware of what I was doing.

"I'm here!" It said angrily. "What took you so long?"

"Who is this?" I sat up, attempting to compute. There was something very old and familiar in the voice.

"Come get me." It spoke again: harsh, rude, and getting more familiar with each waking moment.

"Oh, God!" I whispered hoarsely. Then I said, "Archie! Where the hell are you?" I realized I was standing at a very rigid attention beside the bed now. My father was calling from somewhere and telling me he was 'here!' I prayed that 'here' was not really 'here.'

"I'm in Washington, D.C. Come get me." The man had never said 'please' in his entire life. Then an amazing thing happened. Words came from my mouth that I had never spoken to this man.

"No!" I shouted. "Jesus, Archie. Washington is hours away even by plane. Please tell me you are not coming to visit me." Again, the amazing thing was that this was the first time I had ever said, "No" to my father, or even spoken to him with this tone. "Christ, Archie, the closest airport from Washington D.C is New Bern, North Carolina, virtually hours away. Goddam!" That first "No" had broken through a membrane. I could feel a flood of invective behind it, fresh blood entering weary veins. Thank God, he hung up before I made a meal of it.

The room filled with early morning silence, except for a dull dial tone. I could barely hear a Phantom in the distance whining to life. I lay back down, hoping that this was all part of that strange dream. I could have gone back to bed if sleep were remotely possible. I was fully awake with the worst memories and expectations. Nearly forty years of memories crowded out any inclination to relax.

I kept wondering all day if it had really happened. I waited until later in the morning, two time zones earlier, when she was bound to be awake, and called my mother. "Mom, he's here? Or nearly here. What's going on?" I could hear her exhaling a breath of smoke into the phone. "I haven't seen him or talked to him for ages and suddenly he's here with no warning?"

"I'm sorry, dear. I've just spoken to him. Your father is truly sorry he called you, embarrassed, I think. He found out from someone at the airport how far away you are. I guess he thought you were stationed there in Washington." We sat quietly in her mystic energy for a few seconds, then she added: "He won't be trying to see you now, Colin. So, don't worry. Your father will be flying back to Vancouver on the first airplane available."

I breathed for the first time since he had called. There was still this residual dread sense that hung with me through lunch, like that unpleasant taste first thing in the morning.

I had just completed giving a training lecture later that afternoon and was walking back to my office when I was suddenly stricken with a cold panic. The voice, not quite like Julian's, but similar, said quietly, "He's here." I knew in that moment that if I drove twenty miles up Highway 70 to New Bern, North Carolina, I would find my father waiting for me in the New Bern Airport.

I didn't rush, nor did I doubt Archie would be there. Ever since Julian had been with me, there was a natural 'knowing' about some contingencies that were about to alter the psychic scenery. And, true to form, as I turned into the parking area of the New Bern airport, I looked through the tall windows to the small waiting room and there it was: His form, the familiar profile of the man who had shaped a great part of how I had lived the first forty years of my life.

Archie Ruthven was handsome when he was young. The man who strode aggressively to meet me at the New Bern Airport was in his mid-sixties and was still good looking. Over six-foot tall, slender, dark hair with an impeccably groomed moustache, an arrogant profile, full lips and his most appealing feature, an aquiline nose that proclaimed a global sense of entitlement. He had been diagnosed with the current version of narcissistic personality disorder and wondered why everyone might think this was a problem.

"Look at this!" He was shaking the lapel of his suit jacket. "I spilled my drink." He frowned down at the fabric as if he might speak to it. "Actually, she spilled it on me." He looked around, trying to find the airline hostess who had evidently spilled, or more probably thrown, a drink on him. If something were going 'wrong,' and there was always something going 'wrong,' there had to be someone out there who was to blame. Archie required a constant nemesis. If he could not pull one from his thick roster of enemies, he would select one from the immediate vicinity, his very few friends, but more often the family. Mother was usually the soft but malleable target. It all just flew by her as if it were not there. Today, I would the most immediate candidate. He looked at me, shook his head and scowled.

"And she wouldn't get me another drink!" He looked around at his new surroundings and took off his jacket. "God's earth it's suffocating down here!" In his defense, it was July, and the humidity could pull moisture out of a rock. Archie was unaccustomed to the heat and humidity of the Carolinas. He would be hard pressed to find someone to blame for this. Mother would cheerfully take the hit for this one, too. Jean could suffer the blow of his ire untouched, insulated by a mysticism and intelligence that nothing could penetrate. Her innocence could stop any attack at the gate.

We found his luggage, a couple of bags, and walked to my Volkswagen bug. As he folded his huge and sufficient form into the passenger seat, he glared for a second to express his displeasure at the confined space. I turned on the air conditioning and was easing out of the parking lot when he handed me an envelope. I stopped the car and opened it.

"What's this?" Inside, there was a thick deck of twenty-five-dollar savings bonds. I looked at him with wonder, and a growing irritation, knowing what I was seeing.

"It's those bonds you send your mother every month. She gave them to me to pay for the trip. Cash them in." It was not a request, but a demand. Archie Ruthven had never asked a soul to do something. He would tell them. The guy just assumed it was a good idea because it was his idea. He looked at me as if to say, 'Why has this not happened yet?'

I had automatic payroll purchased them over the years so my mother could have some extra money. My father had all the money in our family. My mother saw nothing. She wore the same dress year in and year out, and now my old man was taking her money to pay for his junket. I was mad enough to get out of the car and hand roll a Volkswagen into the ditch. Then I realized that my mother had given him the money. It was what she wanted. I yielded. I stopped at a bank and cashed them in. They had my name on them, so they required my endorsement. It took a long time to sign each check. He had been sitting as close to the air conditioning unit as possible, flashing me glares that screamed for me to rush. When I was done, he grabbed the money as if I had taken it from him.

"What made you think I'd be here when you showed up?" I glanced at him as I drove him back to the base. "I could quite as easily have been on maneuvers and not been here. What would you've done?"

"Doesn't matter, I'm here. I need you to stop and get me some liquor." This was going to be interesting.

"How long do you intend to visit me, Archie?"

"How fast are you going?" He leaned over to look at the speedometer. "That in miles per hour or kilometers?"

"Miles per hour. The States have no intention of going metric very soon." I tried to pour some life into my comments, but it just wasn't working for me.

"That and a lot else is wrong down here," he advanced.

"Well, hell Archie, while you're down here, maybe you can straighten us out."

"You don't sound very glad to see me, Colin."

"Archie, probably for the first or maybe second time in my life, I'll be honest with you. I am not, in fact, glad to see you." I edited the comments that had been running through my head. I had writer's cramp from signing a hundred bonds and was still wanting to push the car into a ditch. "You are the last person in the world I want to see at this point in my life. There's a lot happening right now, and I do not need to add you to the equation."

As I turned into the base, the guard saluted the vehicle. Archie glanced at me as if I were a stranger that just entered the car. I turned into base housing. I continued. "I'm about to retire. I'm winding things up down here. I'll be moving to Memphis, to a new job. My wife has recently left me, and I'm going through some major transitions in my life. When I left Vancouver over twenty years ago, there was really nothing about the place I left that I needed to see ever again. What is it about you that should change my thinking about all of that?" I waved back at Joan Withers, one of my neighbors. She was cycling through the officer's housing area. Archie spun around and glared at her. She was wearing short shorts and a tank top. I pulled up in my driveway.

"What kind of way is that for anyone to speak to their father?" He looked back at Joan. "You know that girl? You see what she had on?"

"We're grown men, Archie. I don't think you realize that I've lived a life you could never have hoped to see, even in your dreams.

I'm going to talk to you like a man, not pretend that we are anything other than two men who have lived different lives and just happened to be here in the same place with nothing else between us but the time remaining before I drop you off at that airport. I hope you'll be well full of me, so you'll be glad to go back to where you belong. You have no business down here." I took a deep breath, wondering where all that had come from. "My God, the least you could have done was tell me you were coming."

His expression said, "Where's that liquor I ordered?" Why was I not responding to his needs before they were even known?

We stepped into the house. Archie lunged at the air-conditioning vent, took off his jacket and shirt, and draped his torso over the cold air. I put his bags in the extra room. I told him I was going to have to do some shopping now that I had a houseguest. I needed to buy him some Canadian Club, my choice if I were still drinking. He'd drink anything. What the hell! Why not "Crown Royal?" This is a special, although unwelcome, occasion that will hopefully never happen again. He's come a long way. Why not treat him like a sojourning Pilgrim?

"What do I do with this, Julian?" I walked out into the yard. Joan drove by on her bicycle again. She was another Beverly Weber. She'd been hovering around my place, wearing those short shorts on her bike ever since Kim had left. I drove slowly out of the housing area. Julian was always quick to respond.

"In the spiritual and physical realm, nothing happens by accident. There's always a previous cause, more often many, a train of several leading to this one event and likely others." He's here for a reason, something certainly beyond his limited understanding; and yours, I might add. He's burdened by a pathology that blocks his capacity to see clearly. A pathology operates independently of the host. He's along for the ride in an illness he will have until he transitions. Terrible handicap. It's sad, not bad."

I went through the main gate into the streets of Havelock. I was about to get out of the car when Julian added, "Your father has layers that insulate him from awareness. It will take him at least another lifetime. He would certainly not understand where he fit into this equation. He might be the last layer you have between yourself and awareness."

"Not in this lifetime, then?" I suggested.

"No, not in this lifetime. Be gentle with the man. But be alert to a new awareness he brings to you." A long pause offered more from Julian, "You might ask yourself during meditation if you might be one of your father's guides."

"I think I'm getting it, sir," I murmured.

"It will be difficult for you to know what you're supposed to see here." Julian continued. "Probably impossible, for the bias of those years that you qualify as 'difficult' living with the man. You speak to him with the voltage of that bias and not the power of understanding. Notice the vast difference in your paths. Because you are father and son does not make you related in the fundamental sense. It's but a physical relationship. What you will see is the vast difference that emerges out of the two lives who, after conception, have very little essentially in common. It's important that you acknowledge him in his difference and honor him in his own space, not the space he created when you were a child. Try to stop looking for that place where the two of you were related then, and you will see where you meet now."

He had gone through half the bottle later that night. He drank the "Crown Royal" as if it were a bottle of bad wine. We watched the news. The world was closing in on Richard Nixon. The tapes taken from his office revealed that 'The President had attempted to cover up activities that took place after the Watergate break-in, and he was using federal officials to deflect the investigation.'

"Think he's guilty, Colin?" It surprised me that Archie was asking my opinion about anything. He was famous for telling people what they believed. I also noticed that he had called me 'Colin.' Most of my life, he had referred to me as 'boy.'

"Oh, hell, yeah. That guy would do anything to win the election. He had it all nailed, but he let some nut cases loose into the Watergate Hotel to do whatever was necessary to win. And, like I said, he'd already won."

I watched my father drink. It wasn't doing anything for him. He was following a pattern he thought would get him back to a place that once worked. He was nodding without hearing.

I added, "Nixon could have stopped that war long ago, but if he had, he would have lost some election leverage. He had them postpone the cease fire until he could announce it just before the election." If I had not been rescued from the compulsion, I would have finished that bottle of Crown Royal and not allowed him to drink another drop. "No telling how many more died for him to win the election."

He ate a railway man's breakfast every day of his adult life: Two fried eggs, bacon, toast and tea. I made it as if he were a stranger who'd just entered my home. "What would you like to do today?" I asked.

"What do you do?" He replied. Years earlier, when I had been in Vancouver, he insisted on taking me with him to see 'A Day in the Life of Archie Ruthven. We went through the same ritual he had followed for years, since our family had arrived in Vancouver in 1940, when I was six years old. I wondered at the stress on a soul that would take itself through such repetition, a drudgery of sameness. If anything, or anyone, caused him to deviate, he would go into a rage and cancel the day.

"We'll go down to the Unit and we'll take it from there."

"Then what?" He lit a cigarette. I missed the smell of tobacco smoke. It reminded me again that Kim had left.

"We'll find something to do."

I parked in front of the Training Unit. A sign stood in front of the compound, Marine Air Wing Training Unit, Atlantic. Lieutenant Colonel Colin J. Ruthven Commanding. I noticed him glance, then look again at the sign. I could have sworn he rose in his seat and squinted as if he were seeing things.

"You can't go inside the Unit, Archie."

"Why is that?"

"This is a classified area, some of it top-secret. I can't bring a foreign national onto the property. You don't have the clearance. There are some Marines who aren't cleared to enter." I was waiting for him to scoff at the restriction and was a bit surprised by the silence. I looked at him getting out of the car; he had stopped halfway out of the door. He was looking at the sign again. I wasn't sure, but I thought I saw confusion, then a glint of light, or moisture, in the corner of one eye.

He got back in the car. I went inside the compound and explained to Major Wentworth, my second in command, what the situation was. He told me he had wanted to meet Archie. He and I went down the stone lined sidewalk to the car. I opened the door and said to my father. "There's someone here who would like to meet you."

"Colin, could we just go now?" He was silent. He didn't look at Major Wentworth.

I turned to Wentworth with an apologetic expression, shrugging. He responded with a nod that was loaded with understanding and a stroke of sympathy.

"Where do you want to go, Archie?"

He didn't respond.

"There's something else I could show you." I turned toward the flight line. I'd called Paul Sigmund earlier and asked if he could have a Phantom available for my father to see. When we arrived in the squadron area, Archie followed me reluctantly through the ready room. The place was alive like a college campus with junior pilots briefing, some of them on their way out to the flight line. There was really nothing classified about this Phantom cockpit. Paul had arranged for a bird in the maintenance hangar to be made available for us to look at.

I climbed up onto a maintenance stand and asked Archie to join me to look inside the cockpit. A young lieutenant was helping us. "Get in, sir." He beamed at my father and helped him step inside the cockpit. If I had suggested he get in, he would have refused.

The Phantom is a large airplane. Sitting in the pilot's seat, my father looked like a little boy with a moustache. He had his hands in his lap as if he were afraid to touch anything. Then he asked the question that would shrink the stubborn glacial distance that had frozen for years the space between us.

"Colin, do you mean you have to be cognizant of all this?" It was not a word Archie would have used. He was not a reader. My mother read vastly. Archie scanned small sections of the Vancouver Sun each day and got on with his life.

If he had encountered the word and looked up the dictionary definition, he evidently ignored the pronunciation. Archie pronounced the word Cognizant: "Cog neye zunt," accent on the second syllable. He spoke the syllable, 'neye' to rhyme with 'eye' scanning the cockpit intently, then looked up at me with nearly innocent eyes. His question hung empty in the air until the young lieutenant broke the silence, laughed and said loudly, "Oh, God, yes. Blindfolded for sure at night. You bet your ass, sir." "Then he laughed out loud. "You better not touch that thing, sir."

That afternoon I drove around Havelock, the little town just outside the main gate of Cherry Point. I took him out to Morehead City and onto the beach so he could say he had seen the Atlantic Ocean. Looking out at an eastern horizon, he said, "I think I might go home tomorrow if you could help me make arrangements."

"I have no energy for any more of this, Julian." I was alone at night in the backyard of the home I was leaving in three days. The packers had come. Everything, which was after all not much, was on its way to Memphis.

"It could mean you've both finished with the experience. Children hang on to parents too long, as do parents with their children.

There's a point where both need to separate and allow the other to live their lives. The longer either party hangs on, the more difficult it is, sometimes explosive, to separate. Try not to inject energy, or a projection, into what's not there." I had not allowed an experience to take shape, as it was by insinuating my idea into an event that had yet to unfold.

Julian continued. "Nature is very efficient and essentially practical. She will remove anything that no longer works with your current configuration. You are being constantly changed in the moment. If you insist on bringing what no longer fits into your scheme, then you'll lose the efficiency that Nature requires of the moment and the event for them to be compatible with the Truth. Modern man does the same thing with sentiment. There's enough grief and sadness to break every soul's heart in one lifetime, but the current world has made of grief an art form and exaggerates it compulsively. It manufactures more sadness than necessary. Sentimentality is a construct that insults the dignity of a genuine grief."

I called my mother to make sure Archie had returned safely to Vancouver. He had. She said that he had not told her much about the trip. He allowed he was disoriented by the sign over the Training Unit. "Something about your name and the word 'Commanding' and your rank. What is it, Lieutenant something?" I smiled at the pause while she exhaled some smoke from one of her famous homemade cigarettes.

"Colonel, Mother. Lieutenant Colonel." She was not impressed with rank of any kind, be it the Pope, Commandant or certainly, lieutenant colonel.

"Particularly, the airplane, dear. He was very disoriented. He couldn't fit all of that into the picture he has of you. He was confused, dear. Your father had nowhere to go with it."

That night, after I had spoken to my mother, I went outside. I had to get out of the house. I was leaving the following morning. There was nothing there. Kim and the children were gone. Strangely, I felt a comfortable distance from them. Not that I was miserable without them. I just knew they were better where they were than they were with me. Then a feeling arose that I had not expected.

I missed my father.

The thought had barely crossed my mind when an awareness followed that broke me in half. The man had come all the way to Cherry Point, North Carolina from the west coast of Canada because he wanted to be with me! He wanted to see me! And there was no way he could tell me that. Archie didn't have the language. He was a complicated person in his madness, but a very simple man who had made a living by putting things in order. My father had never read a single book. All he could do to show me he wanted to be with me was just show up. That's all he had, and he gave me everything that was in him. Some people, all they have of love to share, are to be inconveniently present.

My mother was intelligent, an autodidact. She had taught herself everything she knew. She read vastly and ruminated. Her life comprised taking care of a man who had no polish. Why would he need polish when he had Jean? He entirely depended on her and didn't know it.

I had never given Archie a chance. He was like an unpopular boy in high school who wanted to be in the gang, but I wouldn't let him. It crushed me to think about it.

Slowly, as if a knife was gradually methodically being driven into my abdomen, a sense of sorrow hit me, a magnitude larger than all the combined pain of resentment and disappointment I had ever felt for the man or my life. I sat up with the knife in me for the rest of the night. I did a slow unsleeping bleed.

As I sat with myriad memories, I saw light break against a wall. I went outside and listened to an early morning launch. I said goodbye to all of that and so much more.

I left Cherry Point, and the Marine Corps, both without regret. There was no sadness. That experience was over. I observed Julian's caution to avoid the temptation to add drama to any event. Neither was I to drag the past into the next moment. "Drama is a construct.

A drama addict must work to add what is not there to what is already sufficient." Years later, I would read the words from Hamlet, "Anything so overdone is for the purpose of the playing."

If ever Julian's words were apt, it was with ceremony. There was a retirement ceremony when a field grade officer retired from The Marine Corps. Most Marines who retire have put their lives into the experience and will want to acknowledge this achievement. When a Lieutenant Colonel retired, a parade is held with full band and pass in review. The celebrant standing on the reviewing platform with the Commanding General and any other field grade officers who were retiring. I had plenty of leave time on the books, so I left a month early to get a running start at civilian life. This would mean I would still receive a government check for a month while I was learning how to be a civilian. But it would also mean that I would miss my parade. I did not show up. There were enough other officers retiring. I would not be missed. I was definitely done with an amazing experience, much that I was not mature enough to enjoy while it was happening. I gave my uniforms away.

I had plenty of time to think as I drove the loaded Volkswagen two days to Memphis. Julian was with me the entire trip and remained silent. His presence was thick. I could have taken my hands off the wheel and the car would take us the rest of the way to Memphis.

I had just filled up my gas tank and pulled back onto the road West when I could sense Julian express something as if it were the last thing he would say for a while.

"Colin, how did you judge the experience you had with your father?"

"I'm afraid I didn't behave very well. Overall, I don't think it was very good."

"A caution, Colin. Western man recognizes events in his life as difficulties, rights and wrongs. They place a judgment on events according to their preferences and a vague floating standard. I invite you to discard this metric and realize that there are no polarities: no ups and downs, no rights and no wrongs. Everything cancels out in one long uninterrupted passage, the continuum of one lifetime. If one were to float at a thousand feet above transactions and look at the connection of these events, he would see that there are no isolated moments, no single points, but an uninterrupted continuum. He would see a straight line. Everything evens out into one thing. It's all One Big Thing doing one Big Thing, none of it lost."

I stepped into the elevator and punched the number eighteen. This is going to be the beginning of my new life, I mused. I hazarded a self-conscious glance in the full-length mirror at my civilian ensemble. I had hoped my slacks and open-collared shirt would not offend the dress protocol of The Sanderson Blake Advertising Agency. I wondered if my office also looked out onto the Mississippi River like Sheldon's. Should I own a Rolex and snakeskin boots?

There was a different receptionist. I could not imagine that her predecessor could have lasted long. The new woman was older, the very acme of professional courtesy. I hoped this was the fresh look of the agency I was about to join.

"Can I help you, sir?" She beamed through the glass partition, a gentle smile of apology as if it offended her that there was a barrier between us.

"Yes, I was wondering if Shelly is in." I stood on the verge of stepping through into the office spaces.

"Shelly?" she said, softly. Her head cocked curiously about ten degrees. Politely she said, "We have no Shelly here, sir. Does she go by any other name?" She almost laughed.

"He," I almost whispered. I felt the first stage of a sinking spell set in. "It's a he. Sheldon Elliott. Six months ago, he was here, hugely here." It was almost akin to the feeling I had during my last flight when an incipient puke crept over me.

"I'm new here. Let me try to help you. 'Mister Sanderson, there's a man here looking for a Sheldon Elliott.'" She was on an intercom phone. "Yes, he's here now, sir."

She invited me to take a seat, but I preferred to stand. I don't think I could have sat. I was examining the cracks on the parquet floor when I heard feet approaching.

"Trey Sanderson." I looked up to a towering gray-haired man in his seventies, reaching his hand to shake mine. "You looking for Philo Feeley?" he grinned.

"Afraid so." I knew he wasn't there, and I was pretty sure why. "My name's Colin Ruthven."

"I kind of figured. He left a note you might show up." He sat down beside me on a leather sofa. "How well do you know Sheldon?"

"Altogether too well, I'm afraid." I wondered if I could find that window through which I was going to shove Sheldon. "So, what happened, Mister Sanderson, if you are at liberty to share."

"Well, if you know him as well as you say, it will come as no surprise that he could not quite handle the level of notoriety and acclaim that comes with winning one account and two awards." He shook his head. "I've seen nothing quite like it. In a matter of months of but moderate success, it imploded, and he was seriously dead drunk. Philo lost us the Sealy account and about three others that were not even his. The man essentially bled out professionally and has disappeared. Mister Elliott owes us some considerable amount in advanced bonuses he believed were due to him for his work with Sealy."

"Philo Feeley, the Sealy feeler," I whispered.

"Quite so." We sat quietly for a few seconds, then he added. "If you see Philo soon, tell him that the act is forgiven, but the debt is not. If he shows himself in this office, or anywhere near The Sterick Building, I'll have him arrested."

"The act is forgiven, but the debt is not," I repeated, trying to compute. "Sounds Biblical."

"Yes." he said. "No less than God almighty would do in this case. He forgives all but assures that the instrument of the offense always experiences the consequences. It's one of the first laws of

Nature. In time, all will be reconciled." Julian channeling through yet another human face.

"Another sobriety success story," I muttered to myself.

"Excuse me?" he asked as he walked away.

"Nothing sir. Thanks. I will deliver your message."

Court Square was just a block away on Main Street. I sat on a bench and watched a small jazz group on the band stand entertain the noonday crowd. I was alone throwing peanuts to the squirrels. A homeless man sitting on a bench across from me might have wondered who I was talking to as I asked Julian, "How come I feel so good about this? I feel totally free, Julian."

"When you cancel out at zero, all options are available to you. You no longer feel the weight of irrelevant choices. There are no attachments to hold you. With nobody and nothing but yourself and your God, you can respond to any invitation. You are a free man."

Julian had never told me what to do. His observations were guidance. Back in 1968, when I was in Memphis, Reba had introduced me to the shaman, Isabel, who twice had ritually retrieved my soul and claimed to repair the tear in my psychic shield. The shaman's last words at the end of both readings were: "You weren't supposed to make it."

When I asked Reba about it, she said it was simple. I was supposed to die at birth with pneumonia. My mother must have loved me back to a life I was not supposed to live. But I would need additional help. It's like a child born with a veil over its face. It will require added help. If a soul requires that kind of exceptional company, he can expect to receive it. Julian had always been with me, sometimes speaking through Earthly entities like The Native Americans, Hastings, and Reba.

"Beth and Sarah, Colin," Julian had added. "If you had paid attention, you would have realized that everyone has been your guide. All your wives, your children, the beggar in the street. Margaret Campbell. Even Beverly Weber."

We sat quietly while the jazz group packed up their instruments and walked away. They became something else without their instruments, from how large the music had made them to something very ordinary and strangely smaller as they walked away.

After what seemed the rest of the afternoon, Julian spoke. "Colin, now what are you going to do?"

"Julian, I have no idea."

"The perfect place to begin, then."

Made in the USA
Columbia, SC
14 March 2023